AMERICAN CAPTAIN

AMERICAN CAPTAIN

by

EDISON MARSHALL

Farrar, Straus & Young

New York

To my steadfast friend,
Owen Robertson Cheatham,
A great builder in our times
On the solid rock of past times

BOOK ONE *The Innocent*

BOOK TWO *In Slavery*

BOOK THREE *Forging of Weapons*

BOOK FOUR *The Sword of Gold*

BOOK ONE

The Innocent

CHAPTER 1

Death of the *Eagle*

1

My NAME is Homer Whitman. I am a native of Bath, an ancient
port near the mouth of the Kennebec River in the District of Maine,
of the State of Massachusetts. My father, Captain Elija Whitman,
came of a family dwelling on and about the North New England
Coast for a hundred years and busied with ships. On the distaff side,
my blood was full as salty, for my mother was Ruth Luce of the whal-
ing Luces of Marthas Vineyard. A few of my ancestors and kinsmen
sailed their own vessels. Most, like my father, hired out to bottom-
owning merchants. Some were fisherfolk or coasters, but the main
were blue-water men, whether aft or before the mast.

I shall begin my chronicle on an April day in the year 1796, with my
sixteenth birthday well behind me. Although I had not yet come to
my full pounds and inches, I was unusually strong for my size. There
was nothing to mark my appearance from other down-East boys of
my age, except that some, whom I deemed the luckiest, had already
gone to sea and bore the bronze of wind and sun on their faces. Like
them all, I was blue-eyed. Indeed, I took it that blue was the standard
color of American eyes, having seen no other kind except on French
Canadians and Dons. I had the big nose with which so many down-
Easters sniff the wind, but perhaps there was more laughter in my
mouth than was common hereabouts, not that down-Easters are glum

by nature, but to make up for their wet lives, their humor is dry. My hair was rough, hard to curry, and the shade which our elders called dun, a kind of reddish brown. It was written in the stars that my body would bear several marks before my course was run, but so far I had none whereby a sheriff could nab me in a crowd.

Although the log begins on a day mentioned, I would lead you back to a June day of the preceding year, the saddest of my life so far. On a calm sea, under the mild early-summer sky, all of those most close to my heart sailed away—Pa on his quarter-deck, Mama by the rail, my two brothers, Silas and Jesse, before the mast. I could look for them back perhaps within six months, at least within a year.

"Pa, let Homer go," I heard Mama whisper to my father, just before I must go overside to an empty house, a desert town.

My heart stood still, and I would have heard a tear drop on the deck if any one of us five would let one fall.

"Ye know our plans and dreams for our last-born, him with the best gifts of us all," he answered. "How may they work out, unless he can read books as well as weather? He's learned all the master at Bath can teach him, and now he must study triangulation to help him with his charts."

She was still a long time. Then she said what I could never forget, speaking in little gasps.

"Besides—when I was young they taught me—when I was a little girl at Holmes Hole they told me true—not to put all my eggs. . . ."

The whisper faded out. I talked with them awhile, made my farewells, then went to shore. The *Eagle of Maine* made for the open sea. She was well named, I thought—one of the proudest and most seaworthy vessels ever to go down a New England ways. While she was gone, I would study hard. In six months, within a year at least, she would return.

That was in June, 1795. In mid-April of the following year a fishing smack, making in before the northeast wind, crossed her bows as she labored up from the south'ard, wearily tacking to gain a windward position off the river mouth. She had signaled all was well, meaning no door need be hung with black in all the town, and she would gain port soon the following morning. And it so happened, having finished my term at Dartmouth a fortnight previously, that I was in Bath, staying with a neighbor boy, when the news was brought.

That night I slept fitfully and dreamed strangely. The wind wailed about the house, shouting at times, still in the northeast, but it was only half a gale—my roommate, a knowing boy, reckoned it at thirty miles, and I, at thirty-five. It was a fair wind for following a south'ard or westward course on the open sea—no sailor could ask for better. On our narrow coasts masters had best take care, and their ships should be good sailers, but there was no cause for alarm.

I went to the window at least five times. The interval between seemed each as long as a December night; still I looked in vain for a glimmer in the east and listened sharply but, I swore, not anxiously, to the wind. The stars shone in vast array, jewel-bright and true. At last the tall clock in the hall donged four times. I rose and dressed; and why I did not keep my promise of wakening my friend, I could not have told. He had wanted to go with me to see the *Eagle of Maine* make her run. I needed to go alone.

The way was hardly ten miles by footpath. Since the tide was starting to make and the wind adverse, I left my little sailing dinghy at the Bath wharf and legged it. The morning broke fair as the night, the sky clear except for very high, swift-sailing wisps of cloud and the sun bright as in midsummer, but there was no warmth in the flat rays, for the wind blew it away. Still, I could not believe it as high as last night, in spite of waving boughs and threshing leaves. Admitting some anxiety unfit for a captain's son, my heart was light.

Not until coming in sight of Casco Bay did I get shed of wish-thinking. For all the bright sky and the dazzling water, this was a real northeaster. The land broke its full blast, but the whitecaps ran as far as I could see, a pretty sight for a picture painter, but not so fine for sailormen on a north'ard tack, yearning for the land. The waves that rolled toward Black Rock did not seem high, but they appeared to gather pace as they neared the barrier, then break in fury. The reefs beyond looked innocent in calm weather, but now had snowy crests.

All this I saw and counted over before stopping to gaze at a port-bound ship. Not that I need ever question who she was. Twin babes will sometimes be indistinguishable from each other, but never two ships since the first keel was laid. Although a good league distant, close under Seguin Island, I knew this vessel as well as my father's face.

She was a brig of one hundred and eighty tons and in the high respect of all who knew her, my mother's and brothers' pride, and my father's love and charge. She was the fullest expression of his being and manhood. He himself was her master in all that the word means; a firm, steady man, level-headed, no fancy sailor but sound, who played safe when he might and ran risks when he must to get his business done. He knew these treacherous waters, and also his ship and her powers. He had reckoned the strength of the wind and the power of the Labrador Current which, flowing southwest, abetted the northeaster. With all that in his mind, he had decided to press on home.

I could picture him on his quarter-deck, watchful, quiet, his orders few and terse. This was no emergency to him; it was only the day's work. The hands sensed his confidence as well as his care. My heart lifted with theirs in the joy of the home-coming.

People from the settlements began to gather to watch the ship come in. Among them was a black-bearded man to whom I touched my cap. He was Captain John Phillips, master and half-owner of the schooner *Vindictive*. He was above my father in learning and wealth, but they were long neighbors, mutual respecters, and, whenever their paths crossed, sharers of tots of rum and conferees in grave talk. Beside him stood Captain Andrew Starbuck, a whaler from Nantucket.

Captain Phillips acknowledged my salute and gave me one of his slow smiles.

"Why, Homer Whitman, I'm not surprised to see ye here, and 'tis a happy morning for ye, or I miss my guess."

" 'Twill be happier, sir, when she's passed Black Rock."

I wanted him to answer 'twas as good as done. I need have no concern—so my ears ached to hear—when his old friend Cap'n Whitman turned toward home. He did not answer at all, and instead looked at the vessel, less than a mile from us now, with Black Rock an equal distance on her larboard bow. A deep line came into sight between his grave gray eyes.

"Cap'n Starbuck, has the wind risen a bit?" he asked.

"Not that I notice, Cap'n Phillips," his companion answered.

Captain Phillips started to say something more, but kept a closed mouth. I looked long at the ship, then turned to him.

"If you please, Cap'n, why did you think the wind had risen?"

"Ye ask me fair, and I'll tell ye, for ye've right to know. I didn't think so. But I could be mistaken, and 'twas the most welcome explanation for something I see."

"What do you see, if ye'll kindly tell me."

4

"I don't doubt you see it yourself. The *Eagle's* not cutting water as she ought."

I had seen it, but denied it. As she came in on a windward tack, she kept making too much leeway. Her helm would be close up. Pa would be ordering her hauled closer still. Now he gave further orders. They were to shake out reefs of the two mainsails and another out of the spanker. We saw them fill.

Still she kept falling off. I had felt the cold wind biting my bones only a few minutes ago, but now my flesh grew numb. I dared not look into the two grave faces with such watchful eyes.

"I don't like the look of it, Cap'n Phillips, I tell ye." Captain Starbuck broke forth when long and aching minutes had dragged away.

"Nay, nor I."

Nay, nor I, either. The *Eagle of Maine* had got too far to leeward to the liking of anyone here. There was quite a crowd now, bigger than I had realized at first, it being silent and standing still. Mainly they were families and friends of various men of my father's crew. A few were merchants from the town.

A wild impulse came to me to raise a cry for help. If I did, the people would pretend not to hear me or turn their faces from my shame. The issue would be decided before they could run and launch boats; if my father, Captain Whitman, had decided to abandon ship before then, he would launch his own boats. Of this there was no chance—no hope would be a woman's way to put it—for captains cannot leave their vessels to be broken to pieces every time they hove into danger. He was committed to the trial. He had spread all the sail her shuddering masts could carry; now he must make his run or drift into the rocks. If the moment should come when he knew he would fail, it would be too late to save life.

"What makes her so slow to come up, Cap'n Phillips?" Captain Starbuck asked. "She was yare as any vessel out of Casco Bay save for three or four. What ails her, think ye?"

"I'll tell ye what I believe. She's up from warm water, and I fear her bottom's foul with barnacle. It can happen overnight, or so it seems. Sometimes a master won't notice her drag until he must tack for her life. Then she's too dull to cut water."

"If she can clear Black Rock, she'll make it in."

"Aye."

There fell a long silence which at last I must break.

"Ain't she about to clear it, Cap'n Phillips? It looks so to me."

5

"God forbid that she strike it!" There was a fervor in his voice I had never heard before.

Then a grievous weakness came upon me, so that I closed my eyes. When I opened them, only one deep breath later, the *Eagle of Maine* was swinging broadside to the wind.

A strange sound rose from the crowd, not loud, but eloquent of terror and despair. It was the most awful human cry I had ever heard. The ship lurched on a few lengths further, still clean-cut, vivid in cruelly brilliant sunshine, beautiful in the presence of death, then her larboard quarter struck the rock.

Every man forward of the mast was knocked down by the shock. We had seen them, small in the distance all this while—standing still a space, then moving quickly to obey the master's orders, then standing still again; they were men 'fore the mast, but every one was a man, as sure as God. My two brothers stood among them, but I had not picked them out even by guess; I knew surely, with such assurance that comes but rarely in a man's life, that all were my brothers. Suddenly all those by the bow lay prone upon the deck.

I saw them get up. Some leaped up, one hauled himself up. None of them doubted what would happen now; but their captain was shouting orders, and they would obey them to the last.

The ship broached to. Listing to larboard, she careened off the rock and drifted broadside with the seas into the breakers beyond. By now the mate had dropped all his sails. The helm had been put hard over, to try to bring her bow into the wind and give time to launch boats. But she lurched on, the crew on the doomed vessel and we watchers on the shore waiting in strange stillness for her to strike again.

We did not see the reef that gave her the mortal blow: we only saw her check and her men fall down. Still the invisible might of the wind and the rush of seas on her broadside flung her from reef to reef, almost on her beam-ends now, until some horn of rock gored and caught her fast, there to breathe her last. She had seemed to breathe when she had sailed forth on her brave adventures, so alive she was. In a few seconds more, she died.

She had not yet broken up and would not for an hour or more, so stoutly was she made. People watching from the beach could still make out reminders of her beautiful form. But most of her crew had been knocked or had crawled overside in the hope against hope of getting to shore alive—the final fight against the sea that was their right, now that their ship was lost and no boat could reach them.

Only four people still clung to the steeply listed deck, and it seemed to me they were trying to join hands. Then I wished there had been five, for the dead ship rolled on her side, and these, too, were gone.

3

The long watch was almost over. Every soul of the ship's company had been lost, and all her dead except three had been washed on shore or found in the surf. Of these three missing, only one was my very own—my brother Jesse, seventeen and the next youngest to me. He and two shipmates were still at sea in a way of thinking more strange than any dream; but they would have come in hours ago unless caught in the reefs, and now the falling wind was in the northwest, and the tide was going out.

In the last glimmer of the sun, Captain John Phillips came to a little place on the beach where I kept watch and vigil. I touched my cap to him and waited for him to speak. He was slow to begin, but when the words came forth, their tone was man-to-man and their burden plain.

"Can ye give me ear, Homer Whitman?"

"Aye, sir."

"Homer Whitman, the loneliest night I pray ye'll ever spend lies before ye, but I'd not want ye to feel that ye are all alone, because you're not. Of heaven's ministers I can say naught. 'Tis not my place or within my knowledge. But ye'll be thought upon in a hundred prayers, more like a thousand, that will rise up from the town tonight, and ye'll have a place in many a kind heart. And not only from those who know ye and your loved 'nes will feel for ye. Good folk everywhere who hear of your loss will be mindful of ye, and especially they that follow the sea. For mark ye, Homer Whitman, they are, in some way I cannot tell ye, your brethren. Aft or 'fore the mast, there's a bond amongst us all."

He paused, and I spoke.

"I thank you, Cap'n Phillips."

"Now I've a question to ask ye, the answer to which I must have before I can say more."

"Aye, aye, sir."

"Will this make ye hate the sea?"

"Nay, sir. How could it, when Pa followed it, and his pa before him, and my mother's father and brother?"

7

"I thought not. Love of it, for all its cruel ways, is in your blood and bone. Still, there's a question of fit time to say what I've in mind, whether now, or later. Most folk would have me wait till ye've watched and prayed over your dead and heard the reading from Holy Writ, and seen 'em returned to the ground. I reckon 'tis more fitting, for 'tis in the way of business, and yet more than business, if I judge aright."

"Cap'n, I'll ask you to speak now, whatever it is, if you'll oblige me."

"Then I will. I think it will be some comfort to ye, when ye need it sore. Ye've no home now, Homer Whitman, for an empty house is not a home, and ye have no kinfolk by blood closer than second cousins, now that your ma's brother was lost a-whaling. But I offer ye a home aboard my ship."

I could not speak, but Captain Phillips saw me nod my head. Instead of looking at my twisted face, he took his silver watch from his pocket and glanced at the dial.

"Ye can go aboard for biscuits and coffee as soon as ye come up to the town. There'll be plenty of neighbors to stay with your dead that little while, and they'd want ye to if they knew; for ye've gone all day without a bite in your stomach, and ye need strength of body to uphold the faith of your soul. Tomorrow night ye can sleep in the fo'c'sle. James Porter—ye know him as 'Giny Jim, the cook—will keep ye company, and the men of the shore watch too. There ye can live till we're ladened and set sail."

"But you mean, don't you, Cap'n, I can sail with you?"

"Blast my thick tongue! It was what I was trying to tell ye, Homer Whitman! Ye can make the *Vindictive* your home, at sea and in port, as long as ye serve her well and 'tis your desire. There'll be no business ye need stay for. My partner, Eli Morton, will look after it as faithful as his own. I'll sign ye as man 'fore the mast. Ye'll not be favored, for this is America, and we sail 'neath the Stars and Stripes, and every man has right to get ahead if he can make it, but ye'll receive your due in pay and promotion. And 'tis a snug ship as well as a tidy one, as ye know yourself. And I've got a friendship crew."

He fixed his eyes on mine.

"What say you, Homer Whitman?" he asked.

By that compulsion, my eyes cleared and the choke went out of my throat.

"I'll serve you and the ship as well as I'm able, Cap'n Phillips, and I thank you kindly."

8

"Then 'tis done. Now the dusk grows, and I'll leave ye. And may ye be of strong heart for the dark night ahead."

His hand lay briefly on my shoulder before he turned away. I wished that Pa and Mama and my older brother Silas—and Jesse too, whose manly form the sea had not yet given up—could see the fatherly gesture. If they could, wherever they were gone, they would be a little less bereaved over leaving me, having more reason to believe I would get along well.

CHAPTER 2

School of the Sea

1

WITH THE passing months, the returning seasons, that hope showed well founded. The outward signs of it were plain to see. An unusual strength of body, apparent during my boyhood, did not fail as I became a man, and was admired, and in no case resented, by my shipmates. Perhaps the right word for it was fortitude, as used by our well-schooled master, although my mates lumped me off as hardy.

At heavy heaving and other short bursts of exertion, I was little more than equal to Farmer Blood, who had come from Poultney in Vermont and had never seen salt water until past twenty-one. Rather, it was at long duty, especially under conditions which sailors called "miserable," that I showed up best. I was the safest man to be sent aloft in a howling gale. Although it dipped and swung me blind to make me giddy, battered and bludgeoned me to break my will, and wrenched and jerked me to exhaust my strength, still I clung there, watching my chance between blows to do the trick ordered, until I got it done. More than once the captain durst not send some other and turned white in the face at his burden, and I turned blue with dread; but pride helped lift me up. At last it seemed the winds knew me as I knew them.

There was no man aboard who could stand as much pounding by deck-sweeping seas. Sailors do most of their swimming in the scuppers, but when we lay in tropic harbors and wanted to cool off, I proved the swiftest swimmer and the deepest diver, although little brown boys going down for coppers made me look a booby. One offwatch sleep of four hours did me all day. Captain Phillips kept no

9

starvation ship, but when, after being long becalmed or blown off our course, we went on half-rations, I kept weight and strength better than any officer or man except small, wiry Enoch Sutler, whom we called "Sparrow" because he looked and ate like one.

I grew to one inch under six feet, slightly taller than Pa and my brothers, although outspanned by Will and George Greenough, both an even fathom long, and dwarfed by Storky Wilmot, as tall as George Washington and as lean and tough as a hickory sapling. Naked as a newborn jay, I tipped the beam at one hundred and sixty pounds, one pound over the average weight of our whole company—the thinly peopled District of Maine being famed for her full-sized men, having plenty of room to grow in. Sometimes I had backaches and legaches from heavy strain, but never a headache, a toothache, or a bellyache.

This up-growth would have been the same if my parents and brothers and the *Eagle of Maine* had lived and I had gone to sea aboard her in due course. I counted it good, but not wonderful, and it hardly crossed my mind from dawn till dark. But there were other consequences of my loss and my finding a home aboard the *Vindictive* that I could dimly sense, but could not put in words even if they had not seemed a sacred secret. One was my love of the ship. I knew then, and I know now, no other word than love. I could not really doubt that I loved her as much as her master did. Another upshot was my feeling of brotherhood with my shipmates. When I worked on the deck with them, I gave it no thought and the same when we frolicked in port, but sometimes when I wakened in the night watches and made out their forms and faces by the dimly burning lantern, I felt a swelling of my heart that seemed a sending from beyond, an augury of things to come, the inkling of some great predestination.

Captain Phillips had spoken of the *Vindictive* as a "friendship" ship. He meant that the men liked one another and got along together in a friendly fashion, whereby they signed on year after year. Such conditions cannot exist except under a wise, high-minded master, not found in every cabin. When the lash is law, when shipowners hire slave-driving captains and brutal mates, when the crew is recruited by crimps from boarding houses, the ships become jails of hate and fear. I came to see many vessels of this ilk. Most returned handsome profits to their owners, who dwelt in fine houses and sat in prominent pews on shore. Some were trig-looking, but had an evil smell. Beholding these and the filthy slavers we passed on every sea lane, I was all the more thankful.

Besides Captain Phillips, the mainstay of us all, our company consisted of Mr. Hedric, our first mate, Mr. Tyler, our second mate and gunner's mate as well, twelve hands, every one of whom could fire a piece, and 'Giny Jim, our cook. I could say with pride that every man was a picked man. We had very few replacements and no deserters. If a new man proved a troublemaker or a shirker, he did not stay long. We did not think our master's judgment was infallible, but every man knew its honesty, and that healed his heart of bitterness and set his mind at rest.

In my first two years of following the sea, we touched home port four times. At our first returning, Mr. Eli Morton, half-owner of the *Vindictive,* paid me $500, the remainder of my father's estate after the payment of his debts and some I had contracted in due care of my lost loved ones. I thought at first to buy a share in a ship new-building in the yard at Bath, truly a step upward in the world, but in the end I divided it equally among eight needy families who had lost sons or fathers or husbands on the *Eagle of Maine.* I had aimed to follow my father's wishes in this matter and to make a thank-offering for having found a new haven and home.

The heaviest gale we had ever weathered struck us off Cape Finisterre near the close of my second year aboard; and again I was shown the fatal power of the sea. Although we had heaved to, dragging a sea anchor, a green billow running atop the waves broke over our bow and came nigh to sinking us with one blow. We lurched up at last, but of six strong men nigh the mainmast, we counted only five. Our bosun, Thomas Childers, from our own neighborhood in Bath, once the boon-fellow of my brother Silas, had vanished without trace.

We had not even heard him cry out as the great sea swept him down—making light of him as of a loose spar. And forty hours more must pass before the captain could assemble us for prayers for Thomas Childers's soul. Fifty-four hours in all we fought or fled the storm, and no man of our company, master or mates or cook or common seaman, had dry clothes on his back, hot food in his belly, or sleep upon his eyelids. At the end, only one man had the strength to climb that mainmast and cut loose some fouled gear—and I was he.

When Captain Phillips had read from the Book and we had said our belated prayers, he paused a moment, then spoke in his usual voice.

"Thomas Childers was a good bosun, but he's gone, and now I'm under the necessity of choosing one of ye to take his place. I've pondered which of ye would fill it the best. I can't know for certain, but

11

in my judgment, it is one who came late amongst us, of less years and experience than many, yet fitted by natural gifts and assiduousness to duty to the highest position 'fore the mast.

"Homer Whitman, I appoint ye."

Thus that ill wind blew me good. I hated to think of it, for all that it was the way of life. Maybe the ancient saying was the wrong end to. It's a fair wind that does not blow ill to some one.

2

If I beheld the sea in his awful fury, I saw him also in his infinite majesty and glorious beauty. I was given glimpses of his mysteries, such as Saint Elmo's fire, leaping from mastheads and along our spars; waterspouts that tower like monstrous sea serpents, causing instant dissolution to any ship whose path they cross; house-high waves running without warning from the far horizon across calm, sunlit waters; mists haunted by the sounds of distant church bells, often with a pale, heavenly body, a duplicate of the sun, hanging near it with a glimmering train like a comet's.

But there was no greater wonder than the stars after a rain had washed the air and the wind had changed it. Besides the countless hosts that I could see, there were many millions so distant and dim that I could not distinguish them even as grains of silver dust, yet which somehow made their presence known unto my mind.

Once the fog held something more fearful than sundogs and ghostly voices and bells.

Early in the year 1800 we came once more by Finisterre, making for the Strait of Gibraltar. It was to be my first sight of the famous rock, for our captain had avoided Mediterranean waters during our hit-and-miss war with France. But although Napoleon had declared peace with United States, we must still tack from French sloops of war, our cargo being consigned to the military depot in the city of Syracuse, now under British rule.

We knew a better reason why we must pass the straits under convoy of British frigates—the Barbary pirates. A flock of them nested at Tangier, just across the passage, using these narrow waters for an ancient hunting ground. Beyond, the corsair fleets of Morocco, Algeria, Tunisia, and Tripoli raked the seas.

You would think that the great maritime nations of Christendom —England, France, and our own America, not least—would not put up with open piracy on one of the busiest and most important of the seven seas. You would suppose that Napoleon and Nelson would declare a truce while they razed the murderers' strongholds and sunk their blood-stained ships. Instead, all three of those nations sent annual tribute to the pirate kings, begging their promise not to kill us, buying their haughty consent that we might pass in peace.

My shipmates were outraged by it, and there was some wild talk in the fo'c'sle; but this quieted as we neared Tarifa; and we battened down our Yankee pride when a tall frigate, flying the Union Jack and bristling with guns, sailed up the Strait to meet us.

The officer who came aboard with a squad of bayoneteers treated us with surly suspicion. How did he know that our salt beef, pickled herring, and hides were not for smuggling into France? Could we prove that every man aboard was born on American soil? Our captain had a hard time keeping his temper with the high-handed dandy. We would have pitched into the whole passel at one wag of his beard.

As it turned out, he might as well have given him a blast or two of plain Yankee talk, of which our usually courteous captain had a firm grasp. We had hardly started through the Strait in the frigate's wake when a dense fog settled in, concealing us from friend or foe alike. It had come out of the Atlantic on a light breeze, blinding our eyes, chilling our bones, and darkening our spirits. The captain had us take in sail until we could barely keep steerage-way, then we crept along by chart.

Then Andrew Folger, sharp-eared as a school of weakfish, cocked his head as I had seen him do before.

"What is it?" I asked, instinctively low-voiced.

"I think it's a ship to windward."

"Then the frigate must have fallen behind us. I'd better tell captain to sing out. I wouldn't want her bearing down on us in this cursed smother." For we had been warned against ringing our bell in these pirate-rank waters.

"Wait a minute." Andrew climbed the shrouds of the foremast, listened a moment, then swung down. "I could hear voices—and they weren't speaking English."

"What did it sound like?"

"Like nothing I ever heard. Some fellow was cursing and he kept saying, 'Allah——'"

"Report to the captain that there's a Moslem vessel close on our stern."

I gave him the duty to free my hands for duty elsewhere. It was only to secure some stays that occasionally slapped against the block.

13

The captain's orders came forward to me, passed from mouth to mouth.

"No man make a sound."

Meanwhile he had put the helm to larboard, to take us off the pirate's course. All of us could hear her now—her reis bawling orders in what I surmised was Arabic, her rigging making far more noise in this light breeze than any Christian ship except a Dago. She came up no more than two cables' length on our starboard stern. Carrying a little more sail, she would pass us in a matter of minutes, in point-blank range. We knew her ilk—the same that had captured and looted the *Salem Queen* only last year, killed some of her crew, and held the rest for ransom. Suddenly I must do something, hit or miss.

I sped to the break of the quarter-deck and saluted Captain Phillips.

"Cap'n, may I speak a plan o' action?"

"Aye, if ye make it short."

"We'll be looking for her sharp, and I think we'll raise her outline in the fog. If you give her a broadside at her waterline, we'll disable her sure, and likely sink her."

A glow came in his eyes that soon died away.

"Nay, I'll fall away a bit more and let her pass in peace. She may have prisoners aboard, and we'd drown 'em with the rest. And she may be a Turkish frigate on honest business."

I saw instantly that he was right, but nothing in his words or manner made me ashamed. I felt my fealty to him glowing through me, a force in my life I could not yet measure. I saluted and returned to my post.

Long moments passed. The sounds from the pirate ship reduced to a murmur, for we were no longer in her wind; we sailed in a silence as strange as it was chill. Enoch Sutler, whom we called Sparrow, signaled down to us from the masthead where he perched. We gazed hard. The fog glided by in tattered sheets and twisted skeins. It is the most cursed of all the elements by sailormen, but no man complained of its blinding, or uttered a sound.

Then the cold smoke thinned a little for no more than a second. Through it we saw the outline of a ship more ghostly than those a marooned man comes to see in visions from his lonely lookout on a desert isle. There was only one solid spot. That it showed black and real while all the rest was shadowlike was the fog's trick or the devil's jest.

It was the form of a man floating in the fog. The clouds rolled above him and around him and below him; there seemed no connection between him and the ship. His head was oddly bowed and his neck was long and he leaned a little forward and his toes were pointed down.

There was a connection, though; it was merely invisible in the softly blowing mists. It was a rope, for no sailor would use our word "line" for a strand of woven hemp put to such use; and the form was of a man hanged to the yardarm. Whether he was a captive or a crewman, Christian or heathen, we never knew.

3

In the next year, the *Vindictive* scurried about as though the ocean had the itch and we were his hand. Having passed my twentieth birthday, I got so close on twenty-one that I let it go at that, a notable number pleasant in my ears.

A ship at sea is a good place to study human nature. Men's strengths and weaknesses show plain, and while bound together to fight the sea, their separate identities stand forth. Of human generosity, fortitude, and especially bravery, I had seen an abundance. There was sin to be found at every waterfront—often to enjoy, occasionally to repent—and it seemed natural as breathing. It was in the knowledge of evil that I remained an ignoramus. Our fellowship under Captain Phillips had held it at bay.

What I had learned heretofore of ships and sailing was being expanded and better ordered and more deeply entrenched. As for learning navigation, I could not have picked a better school than the *Vindictive*. Captain Phillips was an old octant man, still awkward with Captain Campbell's sextant that came into general use about the time of our war with King George. Mate Hedric could shoot the sun as straight as old Chief Baldpate of the Kennebec, with his ceremonial arrow at a time of drouth; and with not much more consequence, since he was too thick-headed to chart a course. Our second mate, Mr. Tyler, was an excellent navigator, but when he went off watch, more and more of the figuring fell to me. The schooling I had had at Hanover no doubt proved useful to me, though I would have been hard put to it to say how; and my desire to please Captain Phillips and to get on drove me to study the science in my spare time. So by the spring of 1801 I was as fit for second mate's papers as most who held the post.

In all truth, the second mate of a 200-ton schooner is no great

15

shakes. This last sounds like a Vermont expression, and since the Green Mountains grow folk of lively imagination, I wonder now if "great sheiks," pronounced the same, and of the same comic grandeur as "high Mogul," was not the original meaning. The sailors put it best by the saying that a second mate must still get his hands in the tar bucket. The fact remained that he was an officer, quartered aft the mast, and a long step up from a bosun. Even so, I could not take it now if it required my leaving the *Vindictive*.

This was my secret. I could not stand the thought of parting with her yet; as I had stood on the beach that late afternoon before Captain Phillips had spoken to me, I had drunk a cup of loneliness that I wished never to taste again. Time might heal the wound—time is the gentleman, say the wise Chinese—or when we brought the vessel home for an overhaul, I might find me a blue-water sailor's daughter, comely and shapely, who would banish the blue devils forevermore.

My best quick chance lay in Mr. Tyler getting a ship of his own. He was of quarter-deck size, and being considered for the captaincy of a sloop being built at Mr. Derby's yards in Salem. In March, when we touched at Lisbon, bound again for the Mediterranean, the harbor master brought him letters, the contents of which he had not divulged. He was patently cheerful over their reading, and our master somewhat glum.

We were fetching a cargo of Nantucket whale oil consigned to an English merchant in Naples. Again an English frigate undertook to convoy us and some other merchantmen through the Strait—and on this occasion she did not lose us in the fog. Moreover, her manner was more polite. Yankee clippers turned privateer had shown their mettle once more in our huggermugger war with France, and one of these days even England might need our help. It was true that Napoleon talked of peace, but the sailors said his treaties were only fit for Josephine's commode. Also, the Barbary seahawks, rifer than ever and more bold, pulled the whiskers of the British lion unless he gave them meat.

We raised no lateen sail on our voyage up and along the instep of the boot. When we had discharged, we took our empty bottom into the harbor of Marsala. Here we would lade the pale sweet wine of the same name, to fetch to Copenhagen.

Marsala lay on a low spit on the west coast of Sicily. We liked the look of her as we ran in, and I think of this and the whole scene as kind of a prelude of some events to come. Prelude means usually an introductory strain of music. There was a kind of music on the deck that morning, expressed not so much in sound as in men's harmony with one another and their surroundings. The sun was bright, the weather warm, and every face was cheerful at the prospect of going to shore, seeing new sights, eating spaghetti with grated goat cheese washed down with sweet wine, and larking somewhat when the evening lamps were lighted. Every one of us felt in close bond with the rest. We were happy in the strength of our body.

We were making toward our intended anchorage under close sail. Captain Phillips stood on his quarter-deck on the weather side; four hands waited about the 400-pound anchor on the fo'c'sle head; and its 4-inch cable was bighted to run out.

It must be that our master, too, was daydreaming of the port and good ground beneath his feet, because we had run in farther than he had at first intended. I saw him start, glance at the shore, then bawl his order.

"Heave your iron."

The urgency in his voice was transmitted to the minds and muscles of the four sailors. They made haste to lift the big hook, two grasping the flukes and two the stocks. "O-heave-O," they chanted in quick rhythm; but their grunt as they let go was cut from our hearing by a sharp cry. George Greenough, a fine six-footer from Falmouth, had got out of balance in the heavy heaving, so that one of the stocks had rammed under his belt and caught in his clothes. As the black shape plunged down, it looked like some sea beast that had snatched human prey from our deck and was bearing it to its weedy lair.

A thrill of horror passed through me the same as every soul aboard. In the ensuing instant there was no sound on the deck, and only one man left his place. George Greenough's brother Will, one of the steadiest men in our company, was thrown off another kind of balance by the sight. With his arms shooting out before him and his hands meeting to cleave water, he sprang to the rail. But before he reached there, our master had drawn his breath. Forth it came in a clear command.

"Will Greenough, hold your post."

I sensed a slight pause as his mind worked. Meanwhile I had raised my head and stood squarely with my eyes fixed on his. This was to attract his attention and make him remember what he knew about me germane to the present pass. Instantly he responded.

"Bosun Whitman, if you think you might help him, go down."

I had deemed the chance fair, and perhaps good. The depth here was three and a half fathoms—I had looked at the charts before we ran in—and the bottom well-packed silt. In respect to the warm weather, I was already barefoot. Before Captain Phillips could complete his orders to Mate Hedric, I had shed my shirt and kicked out of my breeches. Then I ran aft to the point where the running cable slid hissing into the water and dived in.

In one gasp I had filled my lungs with air. Aye, they were brimming with it as casks with water, when men must abandon ship in mid-ocean. Grabbing the cable, I climbed down it hand under hand, my feet kicking to give me every possible jot of speed. But the slanting course seemed heartbreakingly slow. George had not buoyed up and was pinned down by the ponderous shackle. Perhaps it had wounded him to death. If not, how soon would it lurch forward over him?

I could be sure that the same horror lay on Captain Phillips. Every sailor finds out at last the power of a ship's headway—how she lunges on, making mock of wind or tide, despite dropped sails and hard-set helm. Now he must stop her before the cable could run out and come taut. Otherwise the anchor would be dragged a distance, its great flukes plowing the harbor bottom, and tearing to pieces any soft thing in its way.

But the terrible prospect soon faded from my mind. All other fear passed with it, driven off by a kind of elation I was never to understand or which folk can hardly believe. Truly, it was like that which rises to the brain from drinking wine. I fought the sea and the danger with devilish joy. Worse yet, I had not the least feeling of pity for George Greenough, dead or insensible or mangled or struggling feebly. Getting him out alive would be only a token of victory, proof of my own powers.

My ears throbbed, my head swam, my heart thumped my side. It seemed that many minutes had passed since my plunge; actually it was little more than one minute, for I was still holding my breath. And now I made out through the milky waters a weird shape that I knew was the anchor. Half under it, I saw a dark form.

At that instant my breath gave out. It was suck air or take in water, so I let myself buoy up fast as in a children's swing. My lungs filled with a sobbing sound, then I fought the hardest battle of my life so far—whether to go down again, or to give up.

The fresh air had sobered me instantly, and gone was my fool's glory, and I was afraid the soon-lurching anchor would catch me too. Surely George Greenough had died in all this while. I could not believe what my best mind tried to tell me—that he had been under less than five minutes, and perhaps no more than three. I might have known it, could I reason that far, by the still-slack cable. Perhaps by some counting deep within my brain, I did know it.

It was a hard fight, but short. I could not keep this place in the slow tidal current, and any life left in George was ebbing fast. I never knew what moved me, but I turned over like a striking fish and went down head first. Most likely I was still obeying Captain Phillips.

I found the anchor in the deep dusk. Laying hold of it, I turned it on its side. This task required great strength, although the iron had lost part of its weight in the heavy water; then my heart fainted to see George's form still hanging from its stock. God help me, I feared the iron knob had entered his body. A numbing terror gripped me now, for I knew, I know not how, that the captain had paid out all his cable with his ship still lurching on.

An instant later I received the warning. Although the length that I could see remained slack, I felt a stir of water close by, maybe a hissing, creaking sound. Lying belly down close to the bottom, kicking backward to keep down, I laid hold of the captive. My frantic hands could not loose his belt, but my tugging forced the stock's end from beneath it, and he was free.

I had barely caught him by one arm when the slack cable sprang taut. It was as though life were in it, the life of a sea snake wakened from his sleep, and the iron, too, looked like a living thing as it lurched forward. One of the flukes struck me just below the knee. Although floating free, I was not spared a cruel blow, racking me with pain and knocking out of me the little air remaining in my lungs. It seemed too that I heard a faint crack, such a sound as I had never heard before.

When I tried to kick backward with that leg, it floated out from me like a frond of seaweed. But now I held George Greenough's wrist in a firm grip as I thrust strongly against the bottom with my sound leg.

The anchor was lurching forward again. Just in time to avoid its clutch, I and my silent companion wafted upward. In brief seconds we had gained the surface and the blinding light of day; and I took a great gulp of air. Stroking lightly with one arm and one leg, I drew him along side, his head on my shoulder; and for the first time since I saw him heaving on the iron, I looked into his face.

It was ghastly pale where it was not blue, and his eyes were wide open and staring, but a boat made toward us now—the long oars flashing in the sun and the stem cleaving the gentle ripple—and the thrilling inkling came to me that he could be brought back from the darkness to life and light.

I lay on the sunny deck where my mates had gently spread me. Others of our company, the most knowing and experienced in the task, went to work on George Greenough. First they rolled him, with hanging-out tongue, over a barrel, and the men cheered at the amount of sea water he was ridden of. Then, while one of his nostrils was pressed shut, air was shot into the other through the stem of a bellows. He could take only a little at first because of the congestion in his lungs, but thus began a wonderful process, no less than causing artificial breathing in the apparent dead. Alternately pressing the air out of him and giving him more, his rough-and-ready doctors were at last rewarded by a faint gasp rising of itself from his pale lips. By their keeping at it, he was soon thrown into a paroxysm of violent coughing and retching; and then the welkin rang with the boys' shouts, for they knew that he was saved.

With George coughing and spewing, but able at last to swallow a tot of rum, my good fishing for him had proven the greatest triumph of my days. In my pride in it, I had almost forgotten my own hurt. Presently a stab of pain, as from a knife blade stuck deep into my calf, made me remember it well enough. Then my spirits took a great fall, for at last I confronted the scurvy fact that George Greenough would return to duty long before I did. He would be clambering to the tops and taking his turn to hand reef and steer while I sat flat-bottomed on the deck, my leg broom-stiff before me, splicing rope or —an even duller shipboard task—shredding oakum.

George was carried to the fo'c'sle to have his harrowed spirit balmed with sleep. Captain Phillips, Mate Hedric, and three or four would-be doctors among the crew gathered around me to look at my helpless leg. The master himself undertook its examination. No doubt he tried to be gentle, but his main forte was being thorough, and I must bite my tongue to keep from howling.

" 'Tis done, and I fear 'twas far from pleasant," he told me at last, in his old-fashioned speech.

"Nay, sir, it wasn't."

"I'd 've given ye a gill of grog, to dull your sensibilities, but 'twas needful that ye feel and indicate pain, to disclose to me your condition."

"What is it, sir, if you'll kindly tell me?"

"The shinbone, called the tibia, is surely broke. I can't be sure of the smaller legbone, known as the fibula, but I think 'tis whole. Moreover, I believe the break to be clean and not compound, which should expedite its healing."

"I'm glad to hear it, Cap'n."

"Mate Hedric, what would you recommend to be done?"

"Why, if 'twas mine, I'd rather have Owens here put his hand at setting it, than leave it to some Sicilian sawbones, always singing and wine-bibbling, or a Frenchman either."

Ezra Owens had joined our company soon after we had lost Tom Childers off Finisterre, and except for 'Giny Jim, he was the only man aboard not a New England Yankee. About forty, somewhat windy, and a Philadelphian besides, he would fit the part of ship's lawyer; instead he aspired to physic. However, I had never seen him perform any medical feats beyond giving pills for a binding, sumac to stop a flux, removing slivers, and curing gurry sores.

"I reckon we'd best not have any journeyman doctors setting the bosun's bones," the captain replied. "And since we can't get him to an American leech, the next best would be a British, who when he means 'leg,' can say 'leg,' and not 'jamby.'"

"I'm of the same mind, Cap'n."

"Then why not run him down to Malta, where there's an English naval hospital, and doctors most as good as we'd find in Boston? The bone was broke helping a shipmate beyond call o' duty, and if my charterers revile me for doing what I deem fit, to hell and damnation with 'em."

It was not lightly or on small occasion that Captain Phillips cursed. It seemed to me that those Boston merchants must look about the rooms they were sitting in, wondering what had shaked the walls.

Captain Phillips turned to me and spoke in his usual manner. "We'll land you there, then lade our cargo of Marsala wine to fetch to Copenhagen. By the time we get back here—say nine weeks—your leg will be fit to stand on, though not as good as new. We'll pick you up as we come by for duty aft the mast."

The last three words were spoken by him so calmly, and heard by me so fervently, that my head reeled. Perhaps his tongue had slipped, when he had meant to say, "'fore the mast."

"Sir, I'm not sure I understood you," I replied as steadfastly as I could, while the men gaped.

"'Tis no wonder, since I'd given you no hint of it before. In truth, I'd meant to wait till Mr. Tyler went his way. But some good news to raise your spirits while we're away will surely help the healing, so I'll tell you now. In short, Mr. Tyler's returning to Salem as soon as I can

21

spare him, to be master of Mr. Derby's two-masted sloop a-building in his yard, and I mean to appoint you to his berth as second mate."

There was only one thing I had breath to say. Happily it was the best and proper thing.

"Aye, aye, sir."

"Ye should know that I'm sole owner of the vessel, having bought Eli Morton's share when we last came up home, so my choice is final. But ye've a hard duty ahead of ye, to equal Mr. Tyler, and I'll expect you to come to it, and so will all hands."

"Sir, may I speak free?"

"Every man has the right to speak free on this ship until he speaks unfit for a man, for we sail 'neath the flag of freedom."

"It's that difference between us and foreign ships that makes me ask this favor." I had sat up, my broken leg stiff in front of me, but it was not its throbbing pain that wet my face with sweat. "You know how British officers look down on men 'fore the mast. I'm not used to it, and it would go hard with me. So if you could see your way to brevet me second mate before you leave me in Malta, I'd be better treated by all who deal with me."

"Now that's to be thought of, and if 'tis a little irregular, since when have Americans bowed down to regulations? By God I'll do it."

I had been weakened more than I knew by my ordeal underwater, for now my chest heaved and I must bow my face in my hands. For a little space I feared I had shamed myself before all hands, but it was not so.

Until I could master myself again, they looked away, talking to one another of other matters.

CHAPTER 3

The Visitor

1

Malta was known as the Crossroads of the Sea. I reckoned it a good name, since it lay almost an equal distance from Gibraltar to Alexandria, and you could not sail from any western Mediterranean port to any eastern without passing its door. It was the rock that had stood between Turkish fleets and the Christian coasts. In olden days, before America was discovered, it was the Crossroads of the World.

Only a little larger than Marthas Vineyard, but almost in cannon shot of the pirate strongholds of Tunis and Tripoli, it caused many a turbaned reis to tug his beard.

We came into Valletta, called the New Capital, on the northeast side of the island. At a distance it looked like a multi-colored rock, all its buildings being yellow, red, or orange-colored stone. When we anchored in the roads, under the guns of St. Elmo, lighters came rushing to us in the shape of gondolas, manned by medium-size, agile, somewhat handsome men, fairer-skinned than the Sicilians and more soberly dressed. These were the genuine Maltese. The captain told us they descended from Phoenicians settling here three thousand years ago, and their language, although sounding like Arabic, was incomprehensible to any other people in the world. Many of the lighter-men spoke Italian, and now the island had come under British rule, no few were learning English.

Much of the hill above the harbor being too steep for roads, long flights of steps served the townfolk, and most of the freight went up on donkeyback. For the nonce, I myself was a piece of freight. Although our carpenter had fixed braces of board to hold my leg steady, I must be lightered in and toted pickaback to the nearest *carrozza*—a carriage so small that I almost, not quite, had to stretch my leg on the horse's rump—then drawn by a roundabout course to the hospital. Even so, the dignities of my new rank were properly preserved.

Before making the trip I had bought part of Mate Tyler's wardrobe. Although not quite as tall, he weighed almost the same, so the clothes fitted me well enough; and since he was a neat and sparing man, they were nearly as good as new. Better yet, they were of a quality befitting a junior officer of a little trader, respectable but not in the least rich; in fact they would hardly be in keeping with his captaincy. Yet when the jollies guarding the hospital gate saw scales on the shoulders of my broadcloth coat—these were distant, poor relations of epaulets—and anchors embroidered with gilt thread on my sleeves, they gave me a routine salute.

The hospital occupied one of the lodges of the Knights of Malta, who had ruled the island until the French conquest three years before. My mates who had brought me here stood about a moment, their arms dangling, then with glum faces and blunt farewells, took themselves off. Three hours later, a snuff-taking dandy with a train of flunkeys condescended to glance at my leg, pinch it, wipe his hands on a towel, and call in a small, pale-colored, soft-spoken Maltese addressed as Doctor Korda. When I had looked well into his face, marking his quiet, quick, sure ways, I was glad my case had not been worth the bigwig's attention.

"'E knows a bloke's bones as I knew the spars of a hooker," an old seadog told me. He had learned his art as an orderly at the great hospital of Saint John. Before laying hand on me, he gave me a tot of rum and a pill of opium; after that, with my leg battened down till I could not wiggle a toe, I could curse or complain as the notion struck me without him pausing an instant or modifying his treatment in the least jot. Actually I did neither, for the honor of the *Vindictive* in sight of other patients from great ships o' the line. And once my silence stopped his small, strong hands and caused him to look at me, smile, and wipe some cold drops from my face.

After this there was nothing to do but wait for the bone to knit. I could progress from bed to chair, from chair to crutches, at last from crutches to a little walking, favoring the leg like a lame mule. Meanwhile my acquaintance ripened with the plain kind of Englishmen. Once the ice was broke betwixt us, I found them more like us Yankees than I could hardly have believed.

The greatest difference between us, and which puzzled me the most, was the way they bowed down to great folk. A common American envies and greatly admires the rich and famous, and he may feel awkward and uneasy in their presence, but he would take a beating if not a hanging before he would call them his "betters." But I found them manly in their other dealings—brave, tenacious, more honest, I thought, than most Yankees, less inclined to boast, patriotic, and jealous of their freedom.

The humble could come up by industry and thrift, an earnest young chaplain assured me. I told him that the shortest route to the reward would be by way of America. Many of my fellow patients harbored the same thought, for they could not hear enough of our fields and forests, where the poorest farm boy could go a-hunting; of the lakes and rivers free to fish in; of the vast, fertile lands over the mountains where every comer bold enough could carve out a farm. But the thing to which they listened with bated breath was our doctrine of equality. Seeing that we had rich and poor, intelligent and stupid, honored and dishonored, I could not explain it to them. But I could tell them this: no man was lord of another by birthright, and none need bow his head or bend his knee against his will.

When talk and tales ran short, I took to reading. It so happened that I had read very little for pleasure. Except for the Bible, most of the books available in Bath had been sober tomes—collections of sermons or state papers, the theological works of Jonathan Edwards, and essays so dull that *Pilgrim's Progress* seemed lurid by comparison. Now I got my nose in a battered copy of *Robinson Crusoe* lying about, and the covers snapped shut upon it like an angry clam.

Later my clerical friend lent me a heavy tome, containing ten of Shakespeare's plays, warning me that many of the words had disappeared from the language. Actually, I found very few unused by old settler families in Maine; and when he and I compared notes, the astonishing fact came forth that Maine speech was more like Shakespeare's than the king's English of the day. The truth was, he said, that the latter had a German flavor, caught from the Hanover kings, so that *ass* was pronounced with a soft *a*, *ant* almost rhymed with *taunt*, and *either* sounded as though it were *eyether*. Hereafter, I would not feel so countrified when I heard rich Boston shipowners talking like Londoners.

Now eight weeks had passed, and I longed to return to duty—hard work, happy leisure, good fellowship, and day-by-day adventure of life at sea. Stiff and still weak, my leg limbered and stoutened with every day of use, and you would have thought it was Doctor Korda's leg instead of mine, such pride he took in its mending. I could begin to look for the *Vindictive* in another week or so, but not to expect her for a good month. The reason was, hard to heavy gales still swept the northwest coast of Europe, the effect of the late spring. These were reported to the Navy bigwigs by pinnace from Gibraltar, the news sifting down to the lowest jack-tar in quarantine.

I began taking in the sights of Valletta, such as the great palace of the Knights and the Cathedral of Saint John. Perhaps my favorite resort was the fish dock on the West Harbor. From here the gay-sailed smacks set forth with a priest's blessing and a long-furred, dark gray cat, of a kind peculiar to Malta, fetched along for good luck; and here they returned, with the cat on the masthead if they had made a good catch. But no gray malkin saved from disaster some of the tall ships from the west.

Two Yankee vessels that had passed the Straits had failed to come to port, their fates unknown. One limped into Genoa after a two-hour stand and fight with a Moroccan gunboat. Another, a Medford brig, struck her colors under the guns of a Tripoli frigate, was brought in shame to his rockbound den, and her crew enslaved. Indeed, the Pasha of Tripoli was the bloodiest pirate of the whole evil passel. The rumor had spread far, with much to support it, that he had become dissatisfied with the $83,000 annual blackmail America paid him, and had sent new demands through our consul there to our President. God knows that "blackmail" is an ugly word, but I liked it better than the right word, which was "tribute."

If the people at home had known the shame, they would have ridden John Adams on a rail. Maybe he could not help himself, but with a new president in the new mansion in our new capital and new hope in the air all over our broad land, with our flag flying undaunted from a thousand mainmasts, unbowed before the tricolor and the Jack, I took it we would not demean ourselves again before a heathen pirate. It was said he wanted fifty 24-pound cannon as part of his blood price; but if we did not speak our answer out of their black mouths, I did not know my nation.

Having stoutened my leg by walks in the country, now I ranged the whole island for pleasure's sake. I admired the intensely cultivated fields behind walls of stone, the olive and orange groves, and the clean warm villages full of church bells and laughter. Often I followed the shore, to gaze out at the cobalt water or to look down from some rugged cliff to the white line of the surf.

2

In one of my rambles along the northwest shore, I marked a school of large fishes feeding in the shallow water of a small inlet. I soon made them out to be bass, running from twenty to sixty pounds, silvery colored with bluish backs; they were feeding on small crabs. On the following morning I went crabbing, then with a bucketful for bait and a hand line twenty fathoms long with hooks and sinkers, I went a-fishing. The big school of bass had vanished, but hopeful that they would return, I fixed a crab on the hook, whirled the lead, and cast it some fifteen fathoms. Then I sat down on the warm sand, under the balmy sky, to wait a bite, to daydream, and to enjoy my outing.

It happened that this reach of beach ran longer and straighter than any hereabouts. No houses were in sight, and I shared it only with little sandpipers, flying and settling and piping along the water's edge—the hindmost ever the first to take off again. Since the breeze blew offshore, the cobalt blue of the sea stood almost unruffled; and all I could see of it was forsaken, too, except for gulls so far out that they were only visible when the sunlight glinted their snowy wings, and once in a while a small flock of pelicans, flying parallel to the coast on business that brooked no delay. The whole effect was of solitude deeper and more touching than any I had felt since I came to Malta.

That solitude was not broken, only oddly changed, when I made out a dot of life moving slowly along the beach a good mile off. It was a human being, walking—or rather wandering—in my direction, his gait unusually slow for the brisk, businesslike Maltese. He stopped now and again, and at one point he turned and began to retrace his steps. I felt pleased when again he stopped, hesitated, and came on.

Sitting as still as the old sand-sunk snag beside me, I did not think he had discovered my presence. When ten minutes had passed, his raiment began to puzzle me a great deal. The low-crowned, narrow-brimmed hat and the full skirt suggested a priest, but the latter was too short and the waist too narrow to fill the bill. On the other hand, the Maltese women invariably wore the *faldetta*, which is a black headdress extended into a cloak.

Suddenly I knew the person was female with a youthful step. Sometimes women working in the fields pinned up their dresses just below the knee, but she had more likely done so to cross the runnels of the making tide. Her tan skirt and tight-fitting jacket looked foreign to the island; still she might be a fisherman's daughter, going to meet her father's smack at some cove up the beach and carrying something fairly large, brown, and glossy in her hand. If she had time to loaf along the way, I thought I might persuade her to stay awhile with me.

I rose slowly to my feet so she could see me. Drawing in my line, I rebaited and cast again, to show her I was here on honest business. To my joy she kept her course, and with quickening step. This last puzzled me more than any other incident so far. It was one of those little things that go against one's positive expectations. A child might hurry to look at me and at what I might be doing, but girls of courting age should be more circumspect.

Only when she drew within fifty paces and I had bowed my head and touched my cap in salutation, did I surmise the strangeness of the adventure. The girl was not a Maltese. I did not think she belonged to any Mediterranean nation. Although she went barefoot and bare-legged to her knees, she was a far cry from a fisherman's daughter. She wore a beautifully fitted buff riding habit, pinned up for her comfort, and carried glossy riding boots in her hand.

She stopped about forty feet away and regarded me with frank curiosity. I expected to speak first, but she beat me.

"Are you catching any fish?" she asked, in a cheerful, rather friendly, completely assured voice.

"Not yet. The tide's still a little low for them to start biting."

She cocked her head a little in puzzlement or surprise. I did what I had learned to do in situations I did not wholly grasp—waited in silence.

"What is your shire? Your accent is—I was going to say York or Lancashire, but it isn't quite like either. I'm not sure I ever heard it before."

"I'm a native of Bath," I told her with a straight face.

"Wiltshire? I don't believe you. I mean, you must have left there before you learned to talk. I know Wiltshire from one end to the other."

"I lived there all my life, just up the bay from Portland."

"Portland is in Dorsetshire. You're a liar—and no English sailor would dare lie to me—and that means you're not English. I know what you are. I was a fool not to tell it right away. You're a Yankee."

"I am, but I didn't lie to you about Bath, or Portland either. I came from the District of Maine, in Massachusetts."

"Massachusetts! The hotbed of rebellion! Well, what are you doing here?"

"Fishing."

"Stop being impudent. You're a sailor, aren't you?"

"Yes, ma'am."

"Haven't sailors in America any manners?"

I did not answer at once. It came to me that this girl was not naturally as high-handed as she showed. Her eyes had brightened, and I believed she was pleased to come on a young Yankee so unexpectedly, and her baiting me was a kind of game, to see what I would do. With that to go on, I could perceive her more clearly than before.

There was no getting out of it—she was an aristocrat. I had seen only a few in my life, since America was settled almost altogether by yeomanry with a sprinkling of gentry, and we were too young a nation to have developed many. The delicate molding of her hands and face gave me the clue, and her easy manner, complete composure, even her high skirt and bare feet which she had forgotten, clinched the matter in my mind. Indeed, she might be one of a high order, since she felt no need of putting on airs or minding Mrs. Grundy. Most likely she was rich. Her riding habit and boots looked expensive, her little hat was beaver, and a dark red stone, probably a ruby, burned in the clasp at her throat.

Still, I did not feel dismissed from her by this. Almost all except great folk know the feeling of dismissal—maybe these know it, too, although it cannot happen to them so often as to the poor—when we are brought to the attention of people who have everything. It is not that they are out of our reach. They simply do not want anything we can give them, and that brings a bleakness upon our souls. I felt a strong fellow humanity with the girl, and something more that did not seem to make sense. It was a desire to please her and make her laugh and be happy, not to gain her esteem, but for her own sake.

As I stood there, drinking her in, I knew there was something touching about her, which no amount of wealth or position or beauty could gainsay. But beauty is never something to drive people off. It always draws them in. There could be cold perfection in a face that would wither a bunch of posies, but that is not beauty. Real beauty makes every nonevil person feel warm-hearted and generous and happy along with being a little sorrowful. Unless they can have it for themselves, evil people hate it to the bottom of their hearts.

3

The girl's clean lines gave a trimness to her figure and a vividness to her face. They curved boldly or subtly, with no straight line on her, unless it was her nose; and on second look, it had a little upward tilt. Barefoot girls almost never look tall. She did so, for she was a good five and a half feet and slimly made; but that slimness never suggested fragility or dimmed her femininity. Bosom and butt are the badge: in her case neither was large, but both were prominent enough to take a sailor's eye and breath, trim, and, as is proper to young girls with spirit, rode somewhat high.

Her hair and rather heavy eyebrows appeared dusky black, and her skin might be called dusky too, as compared to the fair skins of England and New England. Actually it was only what we call a deep brunette, but it looked darker than her light gray eyes and set them off. The sea lights upon them in contrast with their thickets of sable lashes gave them a jewel-like brilliance my gaze could not resist.

Over her small, prominent, finely worked and fitted facial bone, the flesh was spare, taut, and given to high lights. Her mouth was unevenly shaped—the upper-lip thin, the lower full, and the curved line at one corner was deeper than at the other. I did not know what had attracted my eyes to this minor oddity until I perceived it as a clue to her identity. Perhaps it was a flaw in her beauty. If so, I did not want it changed. Perhaps it only caused her mouth to appear wistful and childlike, denying that she had everything and no use for me.

I had not yet seen her smile, but wished I could.

"Won't you sit down and go back to your fishing?" she asked. "I'd like to watch you the little while before I must go."

"I reckon I haven't stopped fishing. I just haven't paid it any mind." This last was a Maine expression.

I sat down at my old place by the old snag, and she dropped on the sand beside me.

"My name is Sophia," she told me. "What's yours?"

This was deeper water than it seemed but, aroused and alert, I almost instantly saw through it. My last name did not matter, but hers did. I might have already heard it and its placing of her would prevent any easy communion between us. She wanted our meeting to be pleasant and interesting and uncomplicated; she might meet me a good halfway in that. But when we had parted, it would be over with.

"Homer," I answered.

"*Homer?*" she echoed in agreeable surprise. "How would you like to be named Ulysses?" She was watching me closely.

"It would suit me all right. I liked him a lot better than Achilles."

"Then you *have* read Homer! How wonderful!"

"Of course I read the poet I was named after!"

"Well—forgive me—but I was under the impression that most Americans can't read, and if they can, they read only the Bible and their account books and that terrible traitor and mob-inciter—maybe I'm mistaken about him, too—Thomas Paine."

"I think, ma'am, that you are."

"Don't get stuffy, Homer. Tell me about him later. Now I've got a surprise for you. The poet Homer visited this very island, possibly this very beach."

"I didn't know that."

"I'm sure of it. Do you remember that Ulysses fell under the spell of the witch Calypso on an island? That island has since been identified as Malta. So doesn't it stand to reason that Homer came here to get the proper background? In fact, I've positive evidence of it, but it's secret."

"I know what it is. You saw him with your own eyes three thousand years ago. You're the witch Calypso."

Her smile broke then, not a very brilliant one or beautiful either, yet wonderful to see. I could not have explained this very well. It broke slowly and was one-sided and twisted her mouth out of shape—not a smile that an artist would try to paint unless he was very great, then no one could forget the picture. I felt she did not smile much in front of folk—that kind of smiling was hard for her. But she smiled a great deal when she was alone at little things that amused and delighted her.

"Good for you, Homer!" she cried. "Only a London beau would say that, giving himself airs; but even they are more fun than the rough-and-ready fox hunters. I *like* Americans."

"Good for you, Sophia."

She was just a little startled, but remembered and smiled more.

"And you didn't miss it as far as you think—about Calypso. I've been here only six months, but at least she and I know the same secret. I might even tell you someday. How long have you been here?"

"Nearly three months."

"You said you are a sailor, no doubt 'fore the mast. But in America where people can get ahead——"

"I'm a second mate." I did not tell her my honors were brevet only.

"Oh, that's fine!"

"Why did you assume I was 'fore the mast? I have been until very lately."

"Well, the only ship officers I know are Royal Navy. The younger they are, the more swagger—but some of the old captains are plain as you are. What are you doing in Malta?"

"Resting my leg after breaking it in an accident at sea."

"Will you tell me about it?"

"Not now, if you please. Did you say you were from Wiltshire?"

"No, I didn't. I said I knew Wiltshire. I was raised in Cornwall. My mother was Cornish—she was dark Cornish as I am—and I lived at her old home while Papa was at sea."

"Well, I've been to Cornwall. We put in at Boscastle when running Napoleon's blockade—and had a heavy haul getting in."

As I spoke, her expression was changing in a wonderful way. The color rose in it until her cheeks were a dark quince and her mouth was a dark red.

"Did you hear the ghost bells?" she asked.

31

"No, but a passel of us went inland——"

"Wait just a minute. What does 'passel' mean?"

"We use it to mean a bunch of us."

"Go on. If you went to Bodmin moor——"

"That's where we did go. We went to see the stone monuments. They were more strange than the ghost bells. The whole moor was strange."

"Tell me about it."

"It's a great green and gray and brown waste. The only houses are stone huts where shepherds live. There are no roads but sheep paths and grass-grown ruts. I didn't see many trees, but there are great masses of granite that look like shapes of things——"

I stopped, because I knew from her eyes that she knew all this far better than I.

"Please go on," she said. "Like the shapes of what?"

"Of nothing you could recognize—something outside the world; they suggest mystery and sorrow."

"How did you come to have such clear eyes, Homer? What did you hear?"

"Nothing but the wind—I reckon it never stops blowing—and curlews shrieking and gulls crying and once in a while the bray of a marsh donkey way out on the moor."

"Did you see Brown Willie?"

"How could we miss it? We would have climbed it if we'd had time."

"I've climbed it a score of times."

Those few words painted a picture for me of Sophia on the moors, her dusky hair blowing in the wind. It caused me to look at her again. She was long-legged and of light build and light on her feet, so she could walk far and fast when the way was long, or run with an old shepherd dog till his tongue hung out. This was so out of keeping with my ideas of a daughter of nobility that I reviewed the evidence. No, I had not been misled. She was of ancient lineage and proud name. But her mouth was not proud and cold, one that could not speak to me in a common language. I could not keep my eyes off of it. Her strained and crooked smile, at once joyful and forlorn, had made us intimates.

Then there came an exciting interruption. The line coiled about my wrist, with one loop in my hand, tightened so violently as to jerk my arm straight and me half off my seat. I caught it with the other hand and sprang to my feet. There was a great splashing and tugging as the fish's run was checked and some excited squealing from my beautiful companion. Since I must not hoist him in lest the hook pull out—or give him any slack with which to throw it—he gave me a busy time for a minute or two, paying out and taking in line. When he tired, I worked him into the surf, then slid him onto the sand.

He was a beautiful blue-backed sea bass weighing at least twenty pounds.

"Oh, how wonderful!" Sophia cried.

"Would you like to catch one?"

"I'd adore to—to show Papa. He laughs at me when I tell him about the salmon I used to catch in the moor rivers—he thinks I made it up."

"If a school's come in to feed, the biting might be right lively. I'll cast for you——"

"No, I can do that."

When I had baited the hook and coiled the line at her feet, she whirled the lead and made a sixty-foot cast. Evidently she was a handy girl as well as a healthy one. However, the hook fouled the lead just before it plunged, and she had to haul in.

I reached to untangle the gear, but she showed eager as a child to do everything herself, so I sat down at my ease. Looping the end of the line about her waist to free her hands, she soon had it clear. Her second cast was clean and apparently the bait fell just in front of a fish's nose. The line began to run out. With a shriek she seized it with both hands, but it ran through them, no doubt burning the skin. The thought flashed through me that she had hooked a shark, so swift and powerful was the run, so I rose quickly to give her a hand if she needed it, or if it came to that—such things had happened at beach-fishing—cut the rope.

By now the last coil had jerked straight and, being caught off balance, she was being tugged toward the surf, her legs flying to save her a fall. But I was quite sure now that she had hooked nothing more formidable than an oversize bass, and watched her in great joy. As soon as she could apply her strength, she began to break his run. When she had splashed into shallow water, she stopped and held fast.

But the fish had not yet confessed her his master. He fought with fury, causing the line that held him yet to flay her waist and burn her hands. I had no idea of helping her, for my own satisfaction as much as hers, but I waded out to stand beside her. Of course I watched her instead of the fish. I had seen few sights as thrilling as this slender young girl, her skirt flying like a dancer's, careless of

33

showing her shapely legs, her jacket so tight that her saucy breasts bid fair to break through the cloth, her hands gripped on the rigid line that ripped in great arcs through the water, her face quince-red from excitement, and her eyes ablaze. She did not squeal or shriek, for she had no breath to spare. And I, too, was short of it from wanting her to win.

My fear of the hook tearing out proved groundless, but he was trying hard to throw it, and once the fish leaped clear of the water, shaking himself and shining, splendid and immense. Soon Sophia began to force him in. Whenever he yielded line, she took and held it, her face dripping with sweat and splashings, and its bound-and-determined look gave me great joy. Before long she hauled him into the low surf where he flopped and threshed in a final frenzy, then to the water's edge. There he lay, all blue and silver, a wild, new-found sixty-pound inmate of the ocean, brought up from the dark depths to shine in the shallows at our feet.

But he was not yet in hand. A ridge of sand prevented Sophia from sliding him up the beach. Then my eyes bulged to see the hook hanging, all but torn loose and its barb exposed, at the corner of his mouth. One flop could easily dislodge the point; then instantly he would feel the thrill of freedom and surge back to sea.

·"Be careful," I told her.

She nodded, and carefully shortened her line to about a yard. Then she waited for the next high wave—the seventh, as it is called, although truly such waves do not come at any regular sequence. It rolled lightly in and lifted the fish to the top of the ridge of sand. At the same instant she drew him gently over. Then I must holler, for a second later she had him by the gill, dragging him clean up the beach.

4

Before she looked twice at her prize, she turned her eyes on me. They were snapping with excitement and triumph, and for a few seconds I thought she might give me a prize, long to remember, lovely to keep. But if she had an impulse to do so, she repressed it. Perhaps the gulf between her station and mine was too wide for her to make the brief crossing, regardless of any passing closeness between her and me. Quite possibly the interdiction was bred in her bone.

In due course I had bent a 3-ply line on the fish's gills and secured him to the snag in shallow water. Meanwhile I had reached a stage of happiness, the exact like of which I had never known, and as nearly perfect as some of the cloudless happiness of my childhood. There was no enchantment about it: it was down to earth as Sophia's bare toes; it rose from the combination of hers and my victory, the bright sun, the warm sand, the noble arch of the sky over us and the dark blue sea beside us, and being with her instead of away from her, both of us alive. Whether she experienced anything like its equal, I did not know. I only knew that her face shone like a child's.

"Let me see your hands," I told her with a doctorlike firmness.

She held them out to me, the beautifully molded hands of the high-born. On taking them, I found them more strong and more adroit than I had guessed at first, and not as badly burned as I feared. Still, they could use a little unguent that I carried in my haversack for anointing my leg when it stiffened on long walks. I took a long time for its application, so pleasant their touch against mine.

"I'll carry your fish home for you when the time comes," I told her.

"I'm afraid it's come already." A quite real shadow crept across her face.

"But I'd love to show him to Papa," she went on when I kept silent. "I think it will knock him over—just once. But you'll have to tell him I caught him, or he won't believe I didn't buy him from some trawler."

"All right."

"He'll believe you and treat you politely. He's far from a fool. Dick may pretend he doesn't believe you, but he'll be green with jealousy."

"Dick?"

"My half brother."

Her expression changed, and I saw something in her eyes I could hardly believe.

"You hate him, don't you?"

"I dare say I do. I don't like the idea of it, but can't seem to stop. Papa admires him much more than he does me, so part of it may be jealousy."

She did not expect a reply. I was thinking how many things I had found out about her without knowing her name or gaining any real insight into her nature. It was like one of those old-fashioned books with metal covers, closed by lock and key.

"My brother is a bastard," she went on. "I'm not just calling him a name. He's a real one. But his mother was a lady."

35

I nodded.

"You've never hated anyone, have you?"

"I've never had any reason to. We've a friendship crew on the *Vindictive.*"

She looked startled. "That sounds more like a man-of-war than a merchantman."

"I reckon it does. The word's come to mean 'vengeful.' But Cap'n says it came from *vindicate* and should mean 'ready to defend her honor and deal retribution to her enemies.'"

"I doubt if there's much difference. Homer, we live three miles from here, just outside of Notabile, and that's seven miles from Valletta. Won't the fish be a big load?"

"I could carry him thirty miles—after I've had my lunch. And I've got enough for us both."

"You have!" She spoke incredulously and looked delighted at so slight a matter.

"Look here." I brought out the good bread of the country, with plenty of tasty crust, cheese made from goat's milk, small sweet oranges for which Malta was famous, and a flask of the pale, delicious wine of Marsala. Moreover, I had thought to bring a napkin for the spread, not from any daintiness, but because I was used to a tidy home at sea and objected to sand in my victuals.

"Homer, you've shown United States of America in a new light," she told me, greatly elated.

We ate bread and cheese, sucked oranges, and took turns at the bottle. "Old Farmer George in his castle never fared better," she remarked, rubbing her stomach.

"Isn't that a little disrespectful to His Majesty?" I asked.

"I think he likes to be called Farmer George. Anyway, Papa doesn't consider any Hanover his equal." At once she was contrite. "I shouldn't have said that. It isn't true either—exactly. As the king, he's Papa's liege lord. Papa himself would never dream of calling him anything but the king. And I've got to go home now."

I fixed a wooden buffer on my shoulder so I could sling the two fish on my back. They were cold and slimy, but no great load; and Sophia's incredulous glances at her catch, out of eyes childishly proud, made the task pleasant. The whole household would feast tonight, she said, and her father would gorge on the "hump"—the oily piece behind the head that I had told her was the most choice in any high-backed fish. I wondered how big her "household" was, but decided not to ask.

She soon fell quiet, and I was not inclined to disturb her thoughts. Meanwhile we walked hand in hand, and although I expected her soon to become ill-at-ease with this slight intimacy, she made no move to break it off, and indeed seemed happy in it. Her small hand relaxed more and more in my big one, and she did not mind the sweat.

We came to the mouth of a creek in a distant view of a fishing village. A little farther on was a grove of carob trees, their greenery so dark that on cloudy days it looked black. Here she slipped her hand out of mine, stopped, and faced me. She had come to some sort of decision, and there was no doubting her earnestness in it.

"I left my horse in that village," she told me slowly, her eyes on mine. "So leave me here and give my fish to some people who'll make good use of it."

I believe I kept my countenance, and when I spoke, my voice gave nothing away. But what I said seemed to have no meat.

"Then you don't want to show it to your father?"

"I want to, but I won't."

"You don't want him to see me? Isn't that it?"

"I don't want Dick to see you either."

"You're not ashamed of being with me. That doesn't fit in with you. So there must be a better reason."

"If there is, you'll have to find it for yourself."

"It's none of my business, I reckon, but I'll ask you something that is my business. Will you meet me again on the beach?"

"Yes."

"Tomorrow?"

"If you want me to."

"Where we met today or where we turned off?"

"Where we turned off."

"I want to a mighty lot. And I'm sorry about the fish."

"I am, too. And you did find the reason why I can't take him. If Papa knew we had been together on the beach—and his eyes are terribly sharp—he wouldn't forbid me going there again, but it would turn out that I wouldn't go. So good-by until tomorrow——"

"There's just one thing more," I said.

I took her in my arms and held her close and kissed her beautiful warm mouth again and again. Since we stood in the dense shade of the carob trees, there was little likelihood of being seen. A far greater danger, plain as day, I could only disregard. My ship could never come in unless I spread her canvas and sailed close to the rocks.

Sophia did not resist or answer. When I let her go, her face deeply flushed, she turned without a word and walked away. I gazed after her, hoping she would look back and wave her hand, but she only grew small again, impersonal, unrecognizable, a moving dot of life.

CHAPTER 4

Cave of a Witch

1

IN THE end I lugged both fish to the hospital, where they caused great stir. Having told of catching them on a beach far from our meeting place, I could only hope that some finny beauties were biting there, for many of the walking patients and several of the staff planned to set forth at dawn. The two lunkers furnished a feast both in the wardrooms and the common tables.

That night I did a little fishing of another sort in talk with Chaplain Blain. Although the low cunning attributed to Yankees had not come out in me yet, by mentioning Captain Ball, governor of the island, I led him on to name other bigwigs in and about. It turned out that there was only one other. He was Captain Sir Godwine Tarlton, in command of all navy installations. And the chaplain's eyes glassed as he spoke his name.

" 'Sir' means that he's a knight?" I asked.

"Yes."

"But that's not as high as a lord."

"According to precedence, no. A new-made baron sits above Sir Godwine, but it would make him very uncomfortable. I don't mean Sir Godwine—I mean the baron. The old marquisate in North Ireland was lost. Again and again his ancestors have been offered peerages, only to decline. All they'll accept is knighthoods, a different thing entirely."

"Excuse me. I'm not well versed on English nobility and gentry. Why would he accept a knighthood when a knight is below a lord?"

"A knighthood is not hereditary and has little to do with family. In feudal times, knighthoods were often won in battle; it was a personal honor, not a family one. Sir Godwine accepted a knighthood for service against the Colonies; but it's the names Godwine and Tarlton, not the *sir*—more than that the man himself—that chills the backbone of impostors and upstarts. But of course you don't understand that. No American could."

"I find it mighty interesting."

"He was the only gentleman of England who refused to meet Beau Brummell, who's hand-in-glove with the Prince of Wales. Dukes bow and scrape to him, but Sir Godwine said he did not accept the acquaintance of clerks' sons and shopkeepers' grandsons. It made the prince furious, but what could he do? Sir Godwine has plenty of money. He didn't want any honors that the prince could pay him."

"I'd like to see him. Does he lodge in Valletta?"

"No, in one of the old palaces near Notabile—with his young daughter and his natural son. But his official headquarters are here. And if you see a small man, dandyish in dress, with a cocked hat and powdered hair and always carrying a stick instead of wearing a sword—that's one of the marks of the Tarlton family—you needn't look much farther."

"Will his natural son be able to take his place in society?" I was getting warm now, in the words of the old game.

"I doubt if he'll encounter any difficulty. It's pretty well known that his mother was a countess. The daughter is almost a beauty, I hear, although a bit odd-looking."

"But if she's an heiress——"

"She's not, according to the talk. The Tarlton money goes to Dick. Still, she won't be a drug on the market. There are too many young officers, of good name and prospects, loose on these seas. I hear of one in particular."

I did not ask his name. Maybe I was afraid of showing too much interest. Perhaps I did not want to know.

2

Despite temptation to put on my best clothes, I went to the rendezvous dressed the same as yesterday—a linen shirt with a fly collar and rolled-up sleeves, kersey trousers slashed off at the knee, and brogue slippers unhurt by wet. At first I was inclined to walk fast, but on thinking this might not be good for my leg, as well as lowering to my self-esteem, I took an easy pace. My haversack contained a flask of Tokay wine instead of Marsala, imported from Hungary and of deeper color and more heady, but hardly more dear.

By the time I arrived, I had convinced myself that Sophia would not come. I took out my silver watch and looked at it. It had been found in my father's pocket, strapped to his belt, and I had thought I could never bear the sight of it until I remembered what a friend it had been to him, serving him almost as well as an Earnshaw chronometer serves a great ship o' the line; then I had felt ashamed of my weakness, had it cleaned and oiled, and kept it by me constantly. Even in gales at sea I had worn it in a bag of oilskin lashed to my pocket. Gazing now into its candid face, as cheerful to instruct a man of the hour of his hanging as a child in the long time ere she must go to bed, I came to a sober conclusion.

I was not going to count time in my affairs with Sophia. I had nothing important to do with it even if I saved it, so I would give the day to her. If she made no use of it, it was still hers. If she never knew of the gift, I would still be glad I had made it. There were plenty of rocks to sit on, sand to doze in, sea to look out upon, sky to gaze into, birds to watch, wool to gather, castles in Spain to build. I was still aglow with the wisdom of the resolve when a little warm hand slipped into mine. From some unseen station behind the rocks, Sophia had stolen upon me, noiseless as an Indian. A thrill of happiness filled my body and being.

She was dressed more gaily than yesterday. Presently I recognized her costume as that worn by Sicilian peasant women, whose husbands and fathers leased vineyards in and about Notabile, and whom I had seen tending vines. She wore her hair in two black braids. In her hand was an almost empty oilskin bag of the expensive kind used by English naval officers to protect precious belongings from salt water.

"Homer, did you bring any lunch?" she asked before I could quit grinning.

"Of course."

"Will you be hungry for it in an hour? Bad news first—I can stay only two hours. I brought something nice to go with it."

I nodded.

"Now here's something much more important. Can you swim? Papa says lots of sailors can't swim."

"I could swim from here to . . ." But I stopped, deciding not to brag.

"Oh, good. I can swim a little—I learned on the moor pools, with an old nurse who could swim like a salmon. We're not going swimming, but we have to go in deep water to get where we're going. And we must start at once."

She led me to the end of the stretch of beach, then up and on rugged cliffs. When we had kept the high ground for about a half a mile, she took me down what looked like a goat path into a cove, surrounded by crags and cliffs except for a cleft, clean-cut, blue with the light of sea and sky, appearing more narrow than it was, but still not forty fathoms broad, by which a ship might enter. The water lay as still as in one of our little lakes in the hollows of the Maine hills in deep summer. Since the cove opened to the south, sheltered from the prevailing northeast winds, I thought it would rarely roughen enough to rock a fishing smack. It was a deeper blue than the darkest sapphire, except on the shoals, where it appeared emerald green.

Part of the cliffs rose almost sheer; some of the multi-colored crags overhung the water, shutting out the sun, so the effect was of wild grandeur. I had seen many coves somewhat like it on Malta's rock-bound coasts, but had missed this one somehow, the most impressive of all.

A rough path, part of which appeared hewn out of the rock, encircled the basin. We followed this until a steep crag barred our way.

"We've got to swim for it now," Sophia told me, flushed and sweating from the exercise and lovely with happiness. "When we're ready, the most proper way would be for me to leave you here, go alone, and then call you."

"Don't leave me."

"What have you under your breeches?"

She perceived the odd sound of this as soon as it came forth, but she gave no sign of embarrassment and trusted me to make courteous reply.

"Nothing but me."

"Do you mind getting them wet?"

"Not in the least."

"Well, I brought an old pair of our groom's breeches for you to put on when you get there. Take off your shirt and brogues and put them in my bag, also the lunch, and your valuables. Leave your haversack here. I've got to strip down to my shift and slashed-off pantalettes. My aunt in Bodmin wouldn't think that very modest, but I think it's all right. When we've got everything we need in the bag, we can ferry it over on a board. Even if it falls off, it won't sink with the air in it, or let in any water. There are plenty of boards around here—I see one close by the path."

I saw it also and two more. They were hand-hewn, four feet long and two feet wide—very handy for the purpose. Obviously more than one swimmer had employed them to convey small articles and bundles across a water gap.

"Then we'll get ready," she went on. At once she went half out of sight in a cleft in the rock.

I caught only one clear glimpse of her before she slipped into the water, and it would take not a gentleman, only a clod, not to catch his breath. Suspended by a band on each side, her shift was cut below the round of her shoulders and across the swell of her breasts. No doubt it was the kind she wore at balls to permit a low-cut bodice, often the strings tucked away not to mar her partner's view of her glossy shoulders; but she could have worn a more modest kind on today's adventure. The white cloth enhanced the dark glow of her flesh. As she laved, she did not shrink from the crystal clarity of the water. Indeed no crystal I had ever seen had its illuminating quality; it emphasized every tint of color and grace of movement. I made haste to put in her oilskin bag my shirt, silver watch, flint-and-tinder which no sailor respectful of the elements ever goes without, and my packet of lunch; then clamped it watertight and balanced it on my board. The latter was easy to steer with one hand, and I needed only my feet for paddling, so when I came up to her, I took her hand.

A little way around the side of the crag, she stopped and tread water.

"You see the dark shadow on the limestone beginning about three feet down?" she asked.

"Of course."

"It's the mouth of a cave, but its floor rises steeply, and within fifteen feet comes up above water. All the rest of the cave is dry as a barn."

Such are the vagaries of the human mind that I thought of the beaver houses on the ponds at home, whose entrances are likewise water-sealed, but whose interiors are snug and warm.

"It's easy to go in empty handed," Sophia went on. "Do you think you'll have trouble taking in the bag?"

"I don't think so."

"Then I'll lead the way."

She dived, kicked once, and disappeared. Close in her wake, I carried down the bag and swam head first into the arched aperture in the rock. The sudden loss of the brilliant Mediterranean sunlight all but blinded me, but I had entered no realm of total darkness, and after a stroke or two I became aware of diffused light and then the ghostly form of Sophia emerging from the water above me. It

42

shoaled swiftly with plenty of headroom. I waded out of a luminous pool, about twenty feet in diameter, lying in the lower end of a dim chamber in the rock. Entering had been no feat at all. Anyone who could hold his breath for a few seconds could do so with ease.

I had already guessed that the gap in the limestone had once been the outlet of an underground watercourse. Except that this lay some feet below sea level, the cave was no doubt similar to numerous others in the rock-bound coasts I knew. However, it was very strangely lighted, partly by starlike fissures high aloft, but mainly by the luminous waters over the cavern mouth. These cast a glimmer into the cave as soft as candlelight and no stronger than that poured down from a rounding moon, yet having a fairy quality such as imaginative people associate with fata morgana and will-o'-the-wisp.

"I know now the secret you share with Calypso," I told my beautiful companion.

"I thought you'd guess it when I brought you here. Of course this is her cave. Where else could she have held Ulysses in enchantment for seven years?"

She was more beautiful than ever—my Calypso—in the dim, blue-tinted luminance; and my pulse leaped at our utter solitude. Still my wonder at her bringing me here lived on. I did not find a cheap explanation of a kind dear to riffraff. Whatever she gave me would be Beauty's gift to a chosen one; whatever she yielded to me, it would be my fair winning in her sight. At present she held me her companion in a happy adventure.

3

"Did you come on it by accident?" I asked.

"I might have. If I had seen this cove, I would have been tempted to go swimming. Actually, an old Maltese gardener who had fought against the French told me where it was."

She opened the bag, took out her peasant's dress and a dry shift, and disappeared in the darkness beyond. In her absence I donned her groom's breeches and my shirt. In a few minutes she called to ask me to light a candle she had brought. The small, clean-cut blue-and-yellow flame burned punily close to the entrance in the water-screened sunlight, but further on it made a brave showing, so thick the dark grew. Near where Sophia waited for me, it showed me the charred sticks of a cooking fire, a copper pot, and a pile of clean-looking sheepskins.

"A hermit's retreat?" I suggested.

"It probably has been, now and again. Its last use that I know of was during the French occupation a year ago. The Maltese people revolted and sent to Lord Nelson for help. We couldn't land troops there at first, but we managed to smuggle in gun powder and guns to the revolutionists. The powder was in watertight canisters, and one of the main caches was in this cave."

"Then a good many people know about it."

"Very few, I believe. Those that do know it keep the secret in case they revolt against us and need it again. No one goes swimming in the cove, and the few fishing smacks that come in don't find the opening."

As she spoke my light fell on some carvings on a near-by wall. They were in low relief and clear enough to recognize. They showed the figure of a man with a high cap, a square-cut beard, and a long robe offering a bowl to a slender woman with narrow waist, shapely breasts and hips, and a long skirt with several circular bands. Fish swam about her feet, and a crescent moon hung over head. Below was an inscription in some strange-looking language.

"What do you think it is?" Sophia asked.

"I'd guess a king offering wine to a goddess."

"That's a good guess. I copied some of the letters and compared them with those in one of Papa's books on ancient history. They were a little like Hebrew letters and more like Assyrian. I think they're Phoenician. If so, the cave's old enough to be Calypso's."

"Is she a sea goddess? She's followed by fish——"

"I think she might be Astarte herself. One book said that fish were sacred to Astarte. If so, this cave, opening under the sea, might have been used as her temple. Come and sit by the entrance."

For our comfort I brought an armful of the sheepskins. Our happiness slowly increased, why we could not tell. When I opened my packet of lunch, the food's delicious taste was out of all proportion to its plainness. Sophia's "surprise" was a big piece of fruitcake marvelously spiced, and it proved of perfect affinity to the golden wine. Wine and cake were necessary adjuncts to all important ceremonies and celebrations, Sophia told me, and had been so this thousand years.

"What shall we celebrate today?" I asked.

"My coming here—if you will."

"You know I do that."

"You don't know that I barely made it. Papa asked me to do some-

44

thing else. I got out of it only with a lie. I don't know when I can come again——"

I did not answer except to draw her into my arms. For a long, blissful moment she let me kiss her lips, then her breathing quickened, her mouth moved against mine half in protest, half, it seemed, in waking hunger, and breaking the lock of my arms, she sat up.

"We can't do that," she told me.

"You'll have to tell me why, because I don't know."

"I thought we could. When I left you yesterday, I intended to let you make love to me today—as far as was safe. I wanted you to treat me as you would treat an American girl you were paying court to. But no part of it is safe. I should have known it."

"Why do you seek safety? If you insist on that, you can never go anywhere or do anything."

"Then I'll put it another way. I've got to keep the way open to go somewhere else—in a very short time—and do something else. I wanted a day of freedom before I did so. Another day I should say— I had never felt as free as yesterday—perhaps not even when I was alone on Bodmin moor. But wanting that doesn't mean I don't want the other—what's in store for me. I do. I'm sure of it. But just once I wanted to do something that Papa didn't decide for me to do —that I wanted to do and he, if he knew it, would not permit. And when you're gone—after you've sailed away on the *Vindictive*—I'm going to tell him."

"Why not tell him tonight?"

Her eyes searched mine in amazement, then she gave a rueful smile.

"You say that because you don't know him."

"I know his name and how he looks. I didn't ask anyone—just a little conversation about the bigwigs on the island brought it forth. I know that he refused to meet Beau Brummell. I know he carries a stick instead of a sword—as though he didn't need a sword. You see, that gives me a kind of picture."

Her eyes had rounded as she spoke. "A very good picture. And you still——"

"Yes, because if you tell him, I'll have a better chance of seeing you, not just once more—twice more at the most—but as many times as you like. If he found it out himself—as he surely will on such a thickly populated island, and you so prominent and so beautiful— he'd have the advantage. If you tell him tonight, you'll have the advantage."

45

"Do you suppose a man so haut that he refused to meet Beau Brummell would let me receive attentions from an American second mate who rose from the tar bucket?"

"I don't know. I wouldn't think it would be as easy to forbid you to as you might think. I heard he commanded a sloop-of-war when he was twenty-four. If he's that clever——"

"He's more than clever." Sophia had interrupted me with a strange eagerness. "Many officers have told me he's the most brilliant tactician in the Royal Navy."

"Then I don't think he'd forbid you to receive me."

"I wonder. He's always surprising me. Let me tell you the rest. He had a great love affair before he met Mama. The lady was the estranged wife of an aging nobleman, and they lived together in Italy for two years. After that she broke off with Papa—I don't know why—and he insisted on taking Dick. So I always believed that my mother—beautiful and highborn though she was—was his second choice. I have the strangest feeling that she believed it too, the little while she lived.

"Papa had taken her to London; after her death I lived with my grandmother in Cornwall," Sophia went on. "I saw Papa hardly once a year. He would put his ship into Plymouth and come up to old Celtburrow—that was the name of my mother's home—in a great coach. He was a small man, always magnificently dressed and powdered. He terrified the coachmen and—you won't believe this—made the horses tremble and sweat. He walked about—I was going to say like an eagle, but eagles don't walk gracefully—more like a phoenix just come out of the ashes. But he told me I needn't be afraid of him —I was his daughter, one of his very blood, and look what he had brought me—always a wonderful gift, and one that I had yearned for without letting anyone know. When I was old enough, he would take me to his house in London and choose a beautiful young nobleman for me to marry."

She paused. "Did he?" I asked.

"It amounted to that. The war kept him at sea until he got shore duty here, then he sent for me. The man he chose for me to marry is not quite a nobleman—he's a younger brother of a new baron—but he looks like the statue of Hermes come to life."

"Do you love him?"

"Harvey? I would if I'd picked him myself—or he had picked me."

"It's a curious thing, I reckon—but I wasn't asking about him. I was asking whether you love Sir Godwine Tarlton? I take it that's who he is to you, more than your pa."

"It *is* a curious thing. And how do you hit upon truths like that? No, I don't think I love my father. If not, it's because he doesn't love me. I wanted him to, for Sir Godwine Tarlton to—nothing on earth could be so flattering—but I think he never loved anyone but Isabel, Countess of Harkness, and maybe his son by her, and the *Our Eliza*, his first ship."

"It's human for a captain to love his first ship."

"Papa's love was more than human."

"Did he name her after the Countess Isabel? Both are forms of Elizabeth."

"No, he commanded *Our Eliza* in '81 and lived with Isabel between '82 and '83." She paused, glancing away. "I forgot something. There's another woman in his life now."

The thought came to me that Sophia had forgotten on purpose.

"A girl, I should say. She's hardly older than I. I believe she's a great beauty, although without name or wealth. She came from the Isle of Jersey. Papa found her two years ago at Brighton. I—I believe he's married her."

"Don't you know?"

"He hasn't told me so. But I heard she's lately gone to Celtburrow, my mother's old home."

There was a look in her eyes that made me change the subject. "Did you promise Harvey you'd marry him?" I asked.

"No, but Papa promised I would, which comes to the same thing."

I looked at my watch. "Your two hours are up."

"Did you think I meant that?"

"I don't know. You said it."

"I did mean it, but I'm not going to keep it. You said you'd been lonely. I've been awfully lonely, too. If you want me to go back into your arms——"

I held them out to her and she lay in my lap, her breast against mine. Her mouth was close and enough of my kisses took away its strange crook and touching strain, so that it could smile as quickly and wholly as a child's. It came to meet with mine, and for a while we asked no bliss greater than their making free. But there rose within us a hunger that these lovely passages could not satisfy. It had been waiting long in both of us, and there was nothing here to cry it down. There was only silence and solitude, the sense of being hidden from the world—safe from its dangers, free of its rules, sealed

47

off by the very sea. The water in the pool at our feet, just now brimful of the hot June sunlight, gave off a gentle warmth. Its strange lights shone on our faces, gracing them in each other's sight and filling our eyes with guilty yearnings.

Her dress was a peasant girl's dress, which must not be invulnerable when the swain of her choice beckons her away from the other harvesters into a warm bower. No one knows better than she how easily its lacings and buttons and clasps may be circumvented by trembling, awkward hands—unless it was her mother who fashioned it and her grandmother who watched and her great-grandmother of failing mind, who has not forgot the spring-sowing, the sunlight on the fields, and their deep meanings. My hands found their way to her virgin breasts. They made love to them with unstudied art, whereby she gave me unstinted countless kisses, and her arms crept and clasped around my neck.

I broke the silence with a murmur strange-sounding in the whist.

"I love you, Sophia. Will you marry me?"

She drew a long, deeply troubled breath.

"I love you, Homer, and I wish I would!"

"Do you mean, you wish you *could?*"

"No, for I could if I would. Don't speak of it now, or I'll have to go home."

"Do you understand that if you stay here, I must do the same as though you'd promised?"

She hesitated, then brought her lips close to my ear and whispered one breathless word.

"Yes."

The spell that love casts on youth and maiden grew deeper and more rapturous. Yet it did not quite eclipse a sense of guilt that returned again and again to me, bequeathed to me by my Puritan ancestors, a shame of the flesh that is always an anomaly in nature and often base. Sophia had no such shame. She was eighteen, free, and falling in love with me. I wanted to marry her, to have her beauty always, and I had no fear that I could not make her happy once her old ties were broken; and instinct told me that I would not succeed unless we became interbound so firmly that some older chains fell off.

One moment I had brought her breasts into the strange sea lights and half-bared her glimmering thighs, and she was whispering to me of love. The next, she raised her head as though listening, then gazed wide-eyed into my face, and very slowly, reluctantly, I thought, drew back.

"I fooled myself, Homer, and tried to fool you," she said quietly, after her hands had busied. "This isn't Calypso's cave. I wanted to believe it, to make untrue—to take out of the world—anything we did. Instead it's a limestone cavern that happens to run down under water, and not even secure against surprise."

"It's a beautiful place," I told her.

"Oh, do you believe that?"

"Don't doubt your eyes, Sophia, or yourself. Will you meet me here tomorrow?"

"No."

"The next day?"

"Not here. Perhaps on the beach."

"No, on the cliffs above the cove. The view's good there." I meant I could keep better watch.

"I'll come if I can. The day after tomorrow, early in the morning."

"Will you tell your father I'm in love with you?"

"I might tell him that. But how could I ever tell him—I'm in love with you?"

"Remember what you said? You could if you would. I can, and if you give me leave, I will."

"And I'll tell you now—still playing Calypso and Ulysses—that you'd be safer in the cave of the Cyclops."

She smiled to tell me she was only joking in some trenchant way and came once more into my arms. But she wanted only to feel my warmth and strength; and as though in augury of long farewell, there were tears in her eyes.

4

My dreams were troubled on the night following Sophia's and my visit to the cave, and I was glad to get shed of them when, coming wide awake, I heard seven bells, denoting half past three. I would buy my breakfast from a street vender, I thought—they always had bread and goat's milk and fried fish, a combination pleasing to my innards—then return to the cavern. I wanted to look again at the carving on the wall and search the upper chambers for other mementos of long ago.

I had brought a piece of oilskin to keep dry a couple of candles and my flint-and-tinder. At the last minute I put in some bread and fried fish left from my breakfast, not with the intention of a long stay, but half-unthinkingly in the way of habit. Sailors are not nearly as thriftless as the adage makes them out. At least this is true of those who live long and win authority, for mariners are subject to sudden and deadly attack in various forms. More than any other guild's, "secure" is a sailor's word. I lashed the oilskin tight enough to stand a brief ducking. My other cargo for the short voyage was a flask of water on a strap over my shoulder and a stout ten-fathom line I might use in climbing.

When first coming up from the luminous pool, I must stop and daydream, then doggedly I went ahead with my plans. The flickering glimmer of one of my candles guided me past the carving into a short passage Sophia and I had not entered yesterday, and into a chamber so lofty my light would not glim its ceiling. Although not a hundred paces from the entrance, I had left behind the last dim sifting of daylight or sea light, and no slightest rift appeared in the blackness overhead. The wall that I examined was deeply pitted, as in many limestone caves. These black gaps in the faintly sparkling stone and my own shadow endlessly changing shape and pouncing whenever I moved my hand began to excite my imagination. Although reason told me there was nothing to fear, my sense of separation from everyone became sharp, my nerves tightened, and I found myself on guard.

Holding the candle high, I looked in vain for any carving in the stone. Then the glimmer showed me a tiny object whose surface was either wet or smooth enough to refract light. I picked it up, and to my stupefaction, it was the seed of a date. Still sticky, it could not have been cast here more than a few hours before.

I was looking at it, my skin prickling, when the furthest dying glimmer of my candle disclosed something else foreign to the scene. I would not have believed that its beam could cast so far—a good thirty feet—and there seemed a gap of darkness between the aura and a wan glint further up the cavern wall. I saw it out of the side of my eye which, as all sailors know, will sometimes detect a distant beacon light invisible to a straight glance. And because I was already on high guard, in which every instinct of survival was awake and moving, I did not turn my head or give any sign that I had discovered it.

I knew to start with that it was a high light on metal, and almost instantly surmised that the latter was the steel barrel of a pistol.

I gave my candle a quick jerk to whisk out the flame. The act was as natural and unthinking as a scared rabbit's dive into cover. My body, too, moved swiftly to get out from under the gun's aim if it blazed in the dark—I think with a deep crouch and twist that brought me about six feet from my former position. A second passed in silence. My enemy kept his head and held his fire. At first I could hardly doubt that he was Sophia's lover, father, or brother, or their hired bully. Evidence to the contrary put my mind in turmoil. The date seed on the floor; the ambush being laid—if it were that—in a back chamber of the cave which Sophia and I or I alone would not necessarily visit; the high improbability of any of these three men resorting to crime to stop a love affair that had barely started. . . . Then the heat and confusion passed out of my head, and I was almost certain I had surprised the hiding place of a fugitive whom I did not know, or who knew not me, from Adam. He could be a smuggler with contraband. Quite possibly he was waiting for darkness for his chance to fly the island.

The belligerence went out of me as soon as I became persuaded he was not seeking my life, and I began creeping along the wall toward the cavern entrance. If I walked carefully, my bare feet would make no more noise than the wings of a bat. I intended to make a run for it as soon as I neared the pool, dive in, and swim to the shore of the cove. Except by carefully wrapping his gun in oilskin, he could not cross the water gap with dry powder.

The thought struck me then that he, too, might be stealing his way toward the entrance along the opposite wall. Rather than let me go to call the provost, he might make another ambush behind the dim glimmer and try to shoot me as I made for the pool. The possibility fetched me up short. I wanted no lead whistling by my ears as I beat an inglorious retreat, much less coming nearer home. Meanwhile, the thick darkness and the silence that I kept remained an almost certain shield. It was true that we might run into each other—a one-in-a-hundredth chance that yet chilled my backbone —but if so, I reckoned I could get hand on him before he could fire, then need have little doubt of holding my own.

I crept on again, intending to draw into distant view of the twilit chamber ahead, then wait my chance. My right hand, drawn lightly along the wall, encountered the Phoenician sculpture: now I knew exactly where I was, not far from a sharp turn in the passage, here about thirty feet wide. A second later my foot touched a limestone fragment—big enough to be called a boulder—that I had noticed the day before. If my adversary should trip against it, he might fall down.

That was too much to hope for, but the wish was born in my brain to set a trap for him, and without conscious volition, almost without my consent, it set to work to devise one.

I had the means looped over my shoulder—ten fathoms of stout line. In a moment I had lifted the boulder enough to slip one end under it, fastened it with a knot on top the boulder, and ran the line out across the corridor. It was a long chance that I could find an anchor on the other side that would hold the line taut about shin height, and in my brief search I found only bare, unbroken walls. Then the heart-stopping fact dawned on me that I needed none, provided I had good New England nerve. Where was a better bight than my own strong hands?

Seeking the best lair in the limited space, I found in a few seconds' groping a part of the wall leaning sharply inward, with room for me to crouch at its base. The fellow would certainly draw his hand along the wall to keep his course: to make round the bulge he must swing out into the passage. If he touched the taut line without tripping over it, I still could ram him in good mughouse style in the region of the knees.

I could see all this in my head. And I had no more than crouched down, the line bighted about both of my hands but easy to shuck, when there came to me the sure inkling of my foe's approach.

Always the cavern had a dank smell that sailors call fresh. I was too used to it to notice it, but I noticed its eclipse by a musky smell. Meanwhile the silence became less deep—for I could not swear to hearing any sound. It was like an awareness of light that cannot consciously be seen—an experience known to every sailor. But as my ears pricked up like a dog's, listening with concentration so intense that it hurt my brain, I detected what seemed a succession of faint sighs. The movements of the person making toward me along the wall remained inaudible, but I heard him breathe.

I knew then he was somewhat short of breath, whether from exertion or excitement, or his bellows would have worked as noiselessly as my own.

He reached the bulge in the rock, stopped, stood still a long second as though baffled, then began to grope his way around it. His step was not carefully guarded, for his leg hit the rope hard. As he stumbled, I drove at him. As my shoulder with my weight behind it struck him in the thigh, he raised a despairing cry.

I would never forget how it rang through the silent cavern.

"*Bismillah!*"

I did not know then what it meant. Many tides would ebb and flow before I discovered it was the good Mohammedan's entreaty for the mercy of God. I only knew that the outcome of the adventure was showing far from my expectations.

As the man fell, he dropped his pistol, and I heard it clatter on the stone. With one sweep of my arm I slid it far out of his reach. Fearing he might seize a knife, I clamped his arms, only to find his struggles so feeble that they seemed spasmodic. In a few seconds these, too, ceased, and he lay in silent surrender that seemed to be not servile, but in some way proud.

Thinking it might be a trick, I drew his arms behind him and lashed his wrists, although half ashamed to do so when I observed their thinness. His smell was now as strong as any clean human smell in my remembrance—plainly he smoked heavily, drank not at all, ate highly scented food, and anointed himself with perfumed oils. Eager to see his face, I withdrew a few feet, got my spare candle from my pocket, and lighted it with my flint and tinder.

The flickering luminance steadied. It showed a pale-brown bearded man of about fifty—gray hairs glimmered among the black—wearing a high black felt cap that had somehow stayed on his head and disheveled but richly colored garments. That was my first quick view. The second view brought out that he was quite noble-looking in an alien way—his nose high, arched, and delicately molded, his eyes black and handsome, the skin of his face tight over strong, symmetrical bone. In that survey, I identified his brocaded jacket and coat and silk ankle-long pantaloons as Turkish or something like it. All had been recently wet and had lost much of their fine appearance in the drying. No scimitar or dagger hung from his broad belt, and it became hard to believe that he bore any other arms.

Although somewhat frail-looking for the post, still he might be captain of a Barbary pirate. I hoped so, if it became my fate to deliver him to the provost; actually, after looking at him—thinking of his years and my easy victory—I hoped for a happier outcome. With that in mind, I retrieved the pistol. One glance at the pan showed that it was not primed. Plainly, he had intended to use it only as a bugbear threat.

Somewhat stunned by his heavy fall, he was slow in perceiving me as an individual instead of an inimical force. When he did, he exclaimed hoarsely.

"*Anglais!*"

Before I could answer, he drew a sharp breath and spoke as carefully as possible. "Ing-lish."

"No, American," I answered.

The word meant nothing to him. "'Meerican," he echoed dully. "Yankee."

"Yan-ki?" He tried to sit up and presently succeeded. "You—speak —Ing-lish?"

"Yes, yes."

"I speak—Ing-lish—little."

"What are you? A Barbary reis?"

"No, no. I—Arab. My nom Suliman, Sheik el—of—Beni Kabir. My house at Baeed Oasis, raise horses on desert. I go Ing-land one time, for sell horse. One time I meet Ing-land man in Gibraltar, talk sell many horse for lancers, but no trade. My—king?—he Yussuf Pasha of Tripoli, but I no reis, no pirate. Just now I come by Alexandria on Tripoli warship with Ahmed Reis. Ing-lish frigate stop us, capiton see we same ship Ahmed Reis take away from Ing-lish two, three years. He take us to Valletta, provost maybe hang us all, place us in prison. Provost no believe I stud-horse man, say I pirate like Ahmed Reis. But I hide fine poniard with ruby hilt. I give to interpreter-man if he help me. He get me out, hide me last night this place, tonight Tripoli sponger boat come get me. I speak truth before Allah. I too old, too proud, to go felon's prison. If you make send me there, I beg you kill me."

He spoke haltingly, still short of breath. I thought over what he had said, glancing now and then at his drawn face. It was hard to believe that his spindly legs clothed in silk pantaloons had ever straddled a horse.

"What do you think of Eclipse?" I asked.

This was a shot in the dark if ever was. Although Eclipse had eaten his last oats about ten years before, the sailors still talked about him and held up all other horses in invidious comparison. Yet as I made the test, I knew it was unfair. Even if Suliman did breed horses in his benighted country, he wouldn't have heard. . . .

In that gloomy candlelight, the brown, bony face shown forth.

"Allah! Allah! He was descend of Darley, three, four generations. My father's father bred Darley—so Ing-lish call him—we call him Sultan. Eclipse was greater than Sultan. Ah, that is so!"

That fixed it as far as I was concerned.

"I reckon I'll let you go."

"Dakkil-ak ya Shaykhe!" But I did not know what he was saying.
"Are you hungry?"

"No, malik. Interpreter-man gave me some dates last night."

I thought this might be only pride, for he looked pinched enough, so I brought out my hunk of bread and piece of fried fish. After cutting his rope, I used half the edibles in making him a sandwich, which I handed to him.

"Eat, O Sheik," I told him.

He took a small bite and then a big one. Seeing him munch away, I fixed myself a sandwich to keep him company. I had hardly tasted it when I thought of something.

"O Sheik, the fried fish contains salt."

"Ah!"

"So we have broken bread together and eaten salt."

"By Allah, it is true."

"Doesn't it mean that we have become brothers?"

"More than that, Yan-ki mariner," he answered, choosing his words with care. "We be father and son."

CHAPTER 5

The Gentle Knight

1

MY STAY with Suliman, Sheik el Beni Kabir, was not long. If the English chased him here, I could do nothing to help him and I did not want to see him fall into their hands. If any of his shipmates or his rescuer had sudden business with him, my presence would complicate it, if not ruin it. So I shook hands with him in Yankee fashion—he touched his forehead and his heart in a stately gesture —then I took off through the water gate to the shore.

Wanting to share everything with Sophia, I could hardly wait to tell her of the adventure. But long before the day's end, I perceived that I must not. My best hopes hung on our revisiting the cavern and succumbing to its strange charms. If she thought of it as a hiding place for fugitives, it would spoil her play. For me the game was in deadly earnest.

I returned to the cove soon after sunrise, stripped to my breeches, and began a cautious scouting of the cave. Just inside the entrance, lying on a white silk kerchief carefully spread on one of the ferrying boards, I found a curious little memento of Suliman's visit. It was a plait of black horsehair, about ten inches long and an inch wide, each end of which was bent on a brass ring. I had told him I intended to return early this morning to continue my explorations and could not doubt that he meant it for me to keep as a souvenir. Handy enough for securing a pocketknife or a watch or some personal belonging, now it served to free my imagination for a long, pleasant leap. I believed it was from the mane of a great and famous horse. Perhaps he was Darley, whom Suliman called Sultan, forebear of Eclipse.

The money-worthless but meaningful gift convinced me beyond any doubt that Suliman had gone. Still, I searched the cave carefully and thoroughly, this time with the penetrating light of an oil torch. I found no one or anything more of interest; even the happy ghosts of yesterday would not walk, and the rock was cold, and my shadow lonely looking against the wall.

What did all that matter, when, having come out into the sunshine, wrung out my wet breeches and dressed, I caught sight of Sophia light-footed as a young nanny on the clifftop?

She made her way toward me slowly, as though half-inclined to turn back. A level rock about twenty feet above me gave her a good view of the water and a comfortable seat. Finding one beside her, I noticed that she wore a long-sleeved, high-necked, dark blue dress fit for an English governess and a blue bonnet over hair drawn back and fastened in a big roll on the nape of her neck. Still she could not look anything but beautiful, vital, and, in this setting at least, adventurous.

"I came in a *carrozza*, as a young lady ought—as far as the village," she told me.

"I came on shank's mare," I answered.

"We say we go on the marrowbone stage or by Walker's gig. I mean they're folk sayings—I wouldn't say them any more than I'd say 'bloody.' Well, I do say 'bloody' sometimes—it's so patently low that it's all right, but I never say the worse one—the adverb used as an adjective. And do you think I'd as much as mention its existence to any Englishman? I'd be strangled first."

"My being an American——"

"Changes everything. But Papa would not be as shocked at either one—provided I'd pronounce it like a Cockney—as he would at my saying I came by Walker's gig. Do you understand that?"

I shook my head.

"He'd think it was common, and he demands that I be absolutely apart from, and untouched by, commonness. Poor people who had no horses invented the expression—it still has a folksy sound Papa couldn't stand. You see, common people don't say or do vulgar things—things are vulgar because common people say or do them. I know what you're thinking. High and low have to do a lot of the same things, but the great aristocrats get around this, somehow."

"That looks as though a lot of it is put on."

"No more than any cult is put on. Listen. As late as a quarter of a century ago there were lords in England who went to their chambers and changed their clothes if a common man touched them. Their feeling of being sullied was perfectly real."

"It makes me awful mad."

"You'd better know it, though, so you'll leave me alone."

"Leave you alone sounds like——"

"I am saying it just right. That's what you'll do. You'll go away—and leave me—alone."

"If I do, it will be because you've sent me."

"No, because your ship will have come in."

"Do you want to get close to me now?"

"Yes."

My arms had been aching to hold her, but I had hardly hoped she was in the same boat. Now she did not try to hide the hunger of her mouth seeking mine, and she was neither ashamed nor afraid of her passion. It was a lovely flame that swept through us both, its like unknown to me before these meetings, as it was to her. I need never doubt it was her maiden passion. The wonder was that I had been its waker; only I, Homer Whitman, a seaman late before the mast, had received these gifts.

It was a long time before her first yearnings were satisfied, then I would not let her go. At last she drew away so she could speak.

"Homer, what were you doing in the cave before I came?" she asked.

"Making sure that everything was all right for us to go in. Are you ready?"

"No, we can't go there any more. I'm afraid of being caught."

I marked the last word and was made thoughtful by it.

"I know how that sounds," she went on. "Maybe I should have said disturbed or—better yet—interrupted. But I mean caught. You see, I didn't tell Papa after all. I intended to—but I couldn't. And if we should get to the same point we did before—and he should happen to visit us at that moment—well, as you say, he'd have the advantage."

"You don't imagine he'd follow you——"

"It would be awfully infra dig. It would seem so, that is, until he did it; then his poise would be so perfect, his manner so flawless, his little smile so—but no one can describe that smile—that only you and I would be ashamed."

"If you'll promise to marry me——"

"Don't mention that now. We'll talk it over later."

"I have to tell you that anybody looking for you—especially with a spyglass—could be watching us this minute——"

"That wouldn't be quite so bad. We're not hiding. It would be just bad enough. And who's afraid of spyglasses? From long range, they don't show too much. From a half-mile we'd still look a hundred yards away."

"Not with a twelve-power glass."

"He could tell we were sparking, but not distinguish the details. And that sounds pretty wanton, doesn't it?"

"No." It only reflected a reckless frankness.

"Anyway I don't see any lookouts that near."

Lying in my arms, she was gazing over my shoulder. Suddenly she leaned back and fixed her eyes on mine.

"Homer?"

"Yes?"

"Are you truly brave?"

"I don't know. I hope so."

"Then will you hold me this way until I move to get up? When I do, rise politely and give me your hand? We're going to have a visitor. Will you keep from showing any embarrassment—or any shame or fear?"

"Of course. You should have more faith in me. Is it your father?"

"No. I might have known he wouldn't come. He sent Harvey, the man I'm intending to marry."

"I love you, Sophia. I want you to marry me."

"I don't think it's possible. Now hold me close."

Sophia did not look again over my shoulder, and I was careful not to turn my head. A minute or more passed in silence. Since the emissary had not called Sophia's name, it seemed certain that he hoped to take us by surprise; and happiness welled through me that thus the advantage lay with us after all. His approach from that direction would not have been visible as much as a furlong away, so he was surely close upon us now, and soon I believed that he had stopped on the path above and behind us hardly twenty paces off. I bent my head and gave Sophia a passionate kiss.

Then his voice rose, not loud, simulating surprise and lofty nonchalance, but roughened by emotion. This last was partly jealous fury, partly malicious triumph at what he thought was our predicament.

"Oh, there you are."

But he had pulled his trigger without even a flash in the pan. He had expected to give us a great shock—he himself had braced against its recoil to his own nerves as might a gunner bringing match to touchhole—but his words died away in silence. I did not stir. Sophia raised her head, as though in moderate curiosity, until she could look over my shoulder, then spoke in a tone of friendly, cheerful surprise.

"Harvey! What are you doing here?"

"I came to bring you a message from Sir Godwine. It was a pity to interrupt such a pretty scene——"

"I'm sure you wouldn't have unless the message was important." Sophia sat up and made to rise: I sprang to my feet and gave her my hand. The new event had a different mood and meaning. Sophia's brave defense of me and her own independence would thrill me when I grew old, but this simple issue had begun to be obscured by some sort of personal duel between Harvey and her. She was too well in command of the situation for my best hopes. High color ringed her cheekbones, and her eyes glimmered as she began to bait him in games and for gains not of my sharing.

"I want to introduce you two gentlemen, and you'll have to excuse me for not knowing which of you to ask for permission," she said gaily, yet with a touch of histrionics. "Harvey, your 'honorable' is a courtesy title and doesn't count, but does a sublieutenant in the Royal Navy outrank a second officer of an American merchantman? Anyway, Harvey, this is Homer Whitman, from Massachusetts. Homer—Harvey Alford, my father's aide."

I bowed properly; he gave a curt nod. But I did not blame him, considering his anger and jealousy. That Sophia was not in love with him was a sure thing. Either a real presentiment or a wild surmise told me she might never be, with great passion. Certainly he took her too much for granted. That was more than a Sunday obstacle to get over on Monday, because it reflected deep conceit. But I

59

warned myself against wish-thinking. Conceit is no proof of weakness and often a sign of strength. The character that she took lightly might have a tough core.

Quite possibly his studied elegance of dress had been copied from Sir Godwine Tarlton. I was greatly impressed by it at the same time that I perceived, very deep and faint, a feeling of advantage. His figure was too fine to need careful adorning: taller than me by two inches, he had big shoulders tapering to a narrow waist and hips with long, clean-cut legs. Most tall, flat-muscled men with extremely handsome faces are occasionally called Greek gods. She knew, if I did not, that the comparison here was better-warranted than usual. His hair was truly golden and had an attractive wave. His head set proudly on the tomcat neck seen in Greek and Roman statuary and no doubt doted upon by sensuous women. The lack of a deep indentation between the eyes gave his nose a Greek sweep, and the eyes were deeply set, deeply blue. Just now he had been taken aback—a good seafaring phrase—but doubtless his mien was somewhat godlike in smooth sailing.

"May I give my message now?" he asked stiffly.

"If you please."

"Sir Godwine wants you to come home at once. Captain Ball is having tiffin with him, and he wants you to grace the table."

The word *tiffin* had a trivial sound. The whole message seemed unequal to the occasion. But the high color dimmed in Sophia's face, and I thought her games were through.

"In case you don't know," she said to me, "*tiffin* means 'lunch.' The word's become fashionable lately in military circles—I think Lord Cornwallis brought it back from India." Then to Harvey: "Is that all?"

"Not quite. Sir Godwine was reluctant to break into your engagement—perhaps I should say rendezvous——"

"Assignation?" Sophia proposed.

"I dislike the word as applied to a lady."

"How did Papa know where to send you?"

"How should I know? I assumed you'd told him."

"Well, I didn't. I sneaked off, as you damn well know."

"That's not my affair. To continue—Sir Godwine regretted interrupting it, and wishes to make amends by inviting Mr. Whitman to dinner tonight."

And now he need only look into Sophia's face to feel his hurts balmed and his losses recouped. It had turned white, and her eyes were big and dark, and a strained smile drew her mouth. He loved her, he thought, but she needed a lesson badly, and Sir Godwine was the one to give it to her. Master of the situation now, he turned to me and spoke formally.

"Sir, I've been instructed to convey to you that invitation. Since the company will be small and you no doubt travel light, full-dress is not obligatory. Eight o'clock is the hour set. Sir Godwine Tarlton requests that you answer at once, so I may bring him word how many covers to have laid."

He stopped. A second before I had had no notion what to say. Now the answer came easy enough. I need only speak truth.

"I've not had the honor of meeting Sir Godwine. I can accept only if his daughter will add her invitation to his."

I turned and looked her in the face. You could hardly believe how wonderfully it changed.

"Homer, I want you to come," she said.

"Then I'll be pleased to come."

2

Sophia and Harvey took up the goat path while I slung my haversack. When I looked again at them, they were walking side by side on the crest of the cliff—a fine-looking couple, surely, their tallness and easy stride taking the eye.

Before going to my quarters, I visited the Valletta waterfront, and my eyes could not help leaping from ship to ship throughout the teeming harbor, in search of one I could recognize two miles at sea in one flash of lightning, and whose every spar I knew. She had not come in. No news of her had reached me by the pinnaces from Gibraltar. What did I want of her anyway, for she would not loiter here—a night's shore leave for the land-sick crew likely her only detainment—and I needed more time than that to settle my affairs.

To answer truly, I wanted her Yankee deck beneath my feet before they took me through the door of Sir Godwine's palace. The essence of the New England oak would stouten my knees. I wished to see the faces that I need never search for hidden malice or veiled mockery. I needed their rough hands clasping mine or whacking my back. If I could have all that, I could settle my affairs before daybreak.

The clothes I had bought from Mate Tyler needed only laying out and putting on. By virtue of New England thrift and the habits learned on a tidy ship, I had kept them spotless and well-brushed, and their silver buttons bright. At no great outlay I bought a new stock and a linen shirt with lace cuffs. When I had dressed, I would not be ashamed to sit down at the table with Captain Phillips, Captain Starbuck, or Captain John Paul Jones if he were still alive; and that settled it. In due course I rode in a *carrozza* to Notabile, through a gate in a high wall guarded by sentries, and up to the arched door under stone towers. I found the iron knocker in the gloom and an ancient liveried servant admitted me to a dim hall.

"Your name and titles, please, Your Honor," he murmured in my ear.

"Homer Whitman, second officer of the United States ship *Vindictive*."

He tottered forward and repeated the words to a burly fellow standing near a wide, high, intricately carved door. He too wore wig and livery, but these could not conceal a positive personality. Seeing better now, I knew the cut of his jib. Unless he was an old man-of-war's man, probably a petty officer handy with the lash, I missed my guess. He opened the door wide and called in a queer mixture of salty and Cockney.

"'Omer Wittman, second orcifer of the Unity States *Indicative*."

I felt grateful for my small interior smile. It lightened my load a little as I walked into the room. I could call it a room—in fact I did not know what else to call it—although it must have been the main chamber of an ancient palace of the Knights of Malta. White marble lined the high walls, the floor and domed ceiling were mosaics of animals and birds and trees in rich color, the chimney piece was rose-colored marble with blue veins, reaching to the ceiling. Above the pillared mantle, griffins as big as wolves supported a huge sculptured square, surrounded by nymphs standing or lying down, and bearing heraldic devices. The doors were intricately carved black wood fastened with chains, the windows had many small leaded panes. The chairs were massively carved, not as cold-looking as the room, but too thronelike for comfort. The tables and cabinets had beautiful inlay of ivory and shell. A chandelier of a hundred candles, each in a crystal holder, gave forth clear but not brilliant light.

At first I got only an impression of all this, to grasp in detail later. Seen far more sharply, briefly arresting my attention, was the central feature of the splendid room—a stately teakwood table bearing a glass case that contained the most perfectly wrought ship model I had ever seen. It was about four feet long and in exact proportions, and its building must have taken a year's labor by a superb artisan. It was a sloop of war with all her canvas spread.

The main search of my mind was toward the four people seated at the far end of the room. One of them I knew well. She had not changed by being in this setting or by wearing a low-cut silvery dress and a necklace of pearls and a pearl wreath in her hair. She looked straight at me and smiled a smile I loved. One other I had seen before—Harvey Alford, Captain Sir Godwine's aide. He wore a brocaded waistcoat, pearl-buttoned coat, breeches of dark red plush, blue hose, and decorated slippers.

Another man near Harvey's and my own age I had not seen before, although I never doubted he was Dick Tarlton, Sir Godwine's bastard son. I had time only to notice the perfect proportions of his small form and his somewhat careless dress and catch a glimpse of his intense, dark face when I became busied with Sir Godwine himself. He had sat in the biggest chair and was the first of the four people to gain his feet. He came toward me, walking a little like an eagle, more—as Sophia had told me—like a phoenix. I could recognize him by that and by his dandyism and his walking stick; still, if I had seen him on the street, I would have felt confused. Sophia had said her father was forty-four. This man looked thirty-four or twenty-four, whichever figure you had heard. There was no age anywhere on him. His skin was perfectly smooth, his small hands white and elegant as any young lady's, his movements as young as Sophia's.

"Why, Sophia, 'tis the young American you've made so thick with, damn me if it ain't," he exclaimed, the hearty words spoken in a queerly rattling voice. "Mr. Whitman, I'm Godwine Tarlton, your happy host." With that he gave me a graceful bow.

"Pleased to meet you, sir," I answered in Maine parlance, bowing in return as my ma had taught me.

"And the same to you, Mate, and welcome to Lepanto Palace."

"It has a famous name, Sir Godwine."

"Why, blast me, have you heard of that set-to?" he asked in evident surprise as Sophia held her breath. "But wait a bit before you tell me. I'm keeping you from greeting the pretty lass. By God, I'd give her a kiss while about it if I were in your boots. 'Twon't be the first one, or you can blow me down."

As I came toward her, she raised her face and breast. Neither of us stinted the caress or prolonged it either, and my arms were about her the while. I looked up to find Dick's black eyes fixed on my face, his lips curled in a small gray smile as close to evil as any human expression I could remember.

"'Twas a good job!" Sir Godwine cried. "Now to finish the formalities—you've met my aide, Lieutenant the Honorable Harvey Alford"—he paused while we bowed to each other—"but not my son, Dick."

"Your humble servant," Dick mouthed with a fine bow.

"Sophia spoke of you, sir," I answered, not knowing what else to say.

"Did she indeed! My half sister—on the right side of the blanket, you understand—rarely honors me so. But perhaps an American doesn't know that expression."

"Yes, I do."

"So all you have to do now, Dick, is recite, 'Thou, Nature, art my goddess'!" Sophia said quietly.

"Perhaps you're acquainted with that, too," Dick suggested, his lips smiling, but his eyes cold and intent.

"I read it only recently. It was in one of Shakespeare's plays, which I've made acquaintance with only since coming to Malta. I believe it was the bastard's speech in King Lear——"

As I spoke, I was comparing the two small-sized men standing on either side of me. Dick's countenance was sallow; Sir Godwine's very fair. But the latter was much more delicate, its bones finer molded, the nose more than Roman, so high its bridge.

"Why, sink me, he's right again," he cried. "Now all of you sit, for I've years on my back, and they call for an easy chair." Then when he had appointed us our places: "Young Whitman, how did you hear of the battle of Lepanto?"

"Our cap'n told us when we came by the Strait of Messina."

"Now, dash it all, who do you mean by 'us'? You and the other mate while you sat at table?"

Perhaps it was his rattling voice that seemed to lend undue emphasis to the question; yet I thought I saw tension in his posture, and his eyes gleamed.

"No, sir, the whole crew. It was on Sunday after prayers. He told how the Christian fleet assembled at Messina and set sail, and the reasons for the battle, and its outcome. I guess he spoke an hour."

"Is it the custom of Yankee skippers to be schoolmasters for a pack of lubbers? How did the cap'n know of it himself? Why, damn me, it was fought two centuries before John Paul Jones fired his first broadside at his king's ship." But Sir Godwine did not speak emphatically now. His voice had dropped very low, the rattle had gone out of it, and its tone was soft.

"Captain Phillips is the most learned man I ever knew."

"I'm glad to hear it. The Yankees that I knew could do better with account books than with history books."

"They do pretty well with ships, Sir Godwine, and with guns."

I couldn't have kept from saying it short of a broken jaw, but I said it as quietly as I could.

"Damned if you don't speak truth, and you're a man of spirit!" He turned to the others. "'Twas the answer I deserved, and he gave it to me. They do well with ships and with guns, says he, and who can gainsay that? Not me, by God! Homer—I'll call you that, by right of my years—I found it out myself. The hardest fight in my life was with a Yank. 'Twas my first ship and my first fight——"

"And your first victory," Harvey broke in.

"Never mind about that. It cost me dear enough. And 'tis no wonder the Yankee people have got ahead, with good shipping and good shooting, and with their noses in history books as well as account books, and in that respect, we should be proud that they're English stock."

He turned and looked at Harvey. "Isn't that so?" he asked.

"You never said a truer word, Sir Godwine!" Harvey answered crisply.

His eyes moved to the hot black eyes of his son.

"How about it, Dick?"

"Aye, aye, sir."

"I needn't put it to you, Sophia, my love. You've already made it plain how you admire Americans."

"Yes, and I wish you'd change the subject." To my surprise, she had little color and her eyes looked haunted.

"Why, 'tis one of the leading subjects of the world, or you can sink me. Homer, I'd like to meet your Captain Phillips, and for the time being let it go at that. And there's that blasted Millen."

The burly butler stood in a different door than before, announcing dinner. No one moved or spoke until Sir Godwine got gravely to his feet, and I could not help but marvel how all eyes, including mine, were fixed on him. All of us waited on his words by some unknown compulsion.

"I'll lead the way with my blasted stick," he pronounced. "Homer, if you'll follow with Sophia, Harvey and Dick will fetch up the rear."

The stick was a fine Malacca that he sometimes toyed with or whipped about, but never leaned on. I noticed now that he walked like an Indian, his feet in a straight line, and at a slow pace; still, that could not explain the effect of regalness that everyone felt. I could imagine him on the quarter-deck of a great English man-of-war. The wintry rattle in his voice would terrify every man aboard. The officers reporting to him would turn pale.

Why? I wished to heaven I knew. I could pick him up and heave him to his death against the stone wall—*if I would*. No one ever would, no matter what he did.

Sophia slipped her hand under my arm. Her ear was close; the others were out of easy hearing.

"Sophia, I'm going to ask his consent to marry you."

"You'd better get mine first." She giggled at that, a childish giggle that comforted my heart.

"Then I'll ask his consent to pay court to you."

"He won't grant it. He'll give you the nicest refusal you ever heard. So why expose yourself——"

"He doesn't think I'll do it. He's invited me here to give me the chance, but he's sure I won't take it. Tell me you're with me in it. Say you love me."

"I love you, Homer—and want you to pay court to me—but it's not any use."

We were walking through a dimly lighted hall. It led to an immense dining room with another wall-high fireplace, walls of plaster marvelously worked, and a frescoed ceiling whose central figures were a goddess of some sort with a pitcher in her hand, a bearded Greek with a short sword, and a crouching leopard. The table in the candle-light surpassed all my imaginings. I had not known that even kings and queens sat down to such boards—the covers of lace showing the rosewood and satinwood beneath, the shimmering crystal of glasses of many shapes and kinds, the white antique silver, and the ivory-colored china.

"I've never seen anything like this before," I remarked to Sir Godwine.

Watching his face so closely—as we all must—it seemed that he did not like my saying that, that it was not on his program. I could not even guess why it was not. In the brief silence, Harvey spoke.

"Not even in Boston?"

The words were addressed to me, but his eyes moved instantly to Sir Godwine's.

66

"He hasn't mentioned Boston, Harvey," Sophia said clearly. "Why do you?"

"By God, you're right, Sophia! If he has, you can stove me. Homer, to tell you the truth, it's a rare Yankee who doesn't mention Boston with his first glass, and 'tis come to be a bit of jest. You see, we've a Boston of our own. The name came from Botulph—Saint Botulph in Saxon times; six hundred years ago 'twas a great port next to London, while only two hundred years ago Massachusetts was a wilderness. So we've got to stop and think what Boston the Yankees mean."

"Sir, I wouldn't think it would take much thought, with our Boston three times as big already."

"You can lay to that, by heaven!"

"Anyway, there's nothing like this there. What does the picture on the ceiling represent?"

Not that I doubted that the figures were of Ulysses and the witch Calypso. That would be fitting decoration for a Maltese palace. I had been about to say so, with the idea of scoring again, when a kind of prudence taught in New England warned me not to go too fast.

"Answer him, Harvey."

"I dare say it's Oenone of Mount Ida, Paris's wife, trying to stop him from skipping off with Helen."

"Right!" And Sir Godwine looked at me more pleasantly than before.

"How did the palace come to be named Lepanto, if you'll kindly tell me?"

"I will, with pleasure. There was an ancient edifice here under Sicilian rule—the room we just left is part of it. That goes back to the late eleven hundreds, and maybe longer. The Knights of Saint John acquired the island in 1530—by 1565 they were fighting for their lives against the Turk. They turned him back, and six years later Don John, with the Knights' help, destroyed his fleet. An English Knight of Saint John, Sir Oliver Starkey, took a lively part, and shortly after, he rebuilt and enlarged the old structure, naming it for the sea fight. So I felt happy to be quartered here, in the home of a countryman of no short spell ago."

As he talked, something giving the effect of beauty came into his face. I heard Sophia, beside me, catch her breath. I noticed, too, that the bluff salty speech he usually employed quite disappeared, as did the wintry rattle from his voice.

He had glanced at Millen as he began. This seadog butler and the footmen, too, froze in their places. As he finished, he gave him a slight nod; and at once the work of serving the dinner went forward. There were at least a dozen dishes of fish, meat, and game—prawns, scallops, eels, roast, quail, and venison pastry—and, it seemed to me, a different wine to go with every one. Before long I took thought of the parade of glasses before me, each kept brimming full. The beverages had delicate taste and fragrance; sailors would swear they were weak as water, but I was not in a mughouse now surrounded by my friends—I had more to lose than a thin wallet slipped out of my pocket by a kittling barmaid—so I had best take care. Thereafter I drank only one pouring of any one wine, by one means or another foiling the diligent footman at my elbow. Thus I fell far behind Sir Godwine and his sallow-skinned son, but ran about even with Harvey, whom I reckoned no more than my match in hardness of head.

Instead of easier, I figured the trial would be harder when all the glasses were whisked away except tall narrow ones for champagne and short barrel-shaped ones for brandy. When the pale-gold sparkling wine glimmered in the candlelight, Sir Godwine rose.

"Homer, you're not called upon to drink the toast I'm about to propose—unless you care to. It's to an old man not popular in your native land." He lifted his glass and his tone changed. "To the king!"

I stood and drained my glass with the rest. We had hardly sat down, the goblets brimming once more, when I rose again.

"No one here is called upon to drink the toast I propose," I told the company. "To the President of the United States."

"Wait just a moment." Sir Godwine was gazing at me with a thoughtful expression. "Perhaps some of this company doesn't realize that the President is no longer Mr. Adams of Boston but Mr. Jefferson of Virginia. I understand he's of gentle birth."

"If you please, that doesn't enter into the toast."

"Well-spoke, by God! Let a man stand up for his own—I like to see it. I'll drink to the President's good health. I'll even add a bit—may he lead the American people in the way they should go. All of us on our feet. . . ."

But Sophia had no need of the command. She was already up beside me, standing by me, her pearl wreath setting off the dusk of her hair, the glimmering necklace in contrast with the dark glow of her face and the gray luster of her eyes. She turned to me as she drank with a smile touching and beautiful, as though in pledge and pride and profound communion between us alone.

When we sat again, Sophia slipped her hand into mine.

"I'm going to leave the room as soon as we've had dessert," she told me in a low voice. "You must stay until Papa walks out—or is carried out."

"I see no sign of the latter."

"It doesn't happen very often. Now listen closely. He's got something to tell you—something he thinks important. I don't know what it is—something about America that will involve you. Whatever it is, play it as you have the rest."

"How soon can I see you again?"

"Maybe tonight in the salon. If not, come in a carriage about seven tomorrow night. There's a carnival near Rabat that we can watch."

"Have you a passport?"

"Of course——"

"Will you keep it with you? We might want to go further than Rabat—maybe across to Gozo, or even to Syracuse, where there's an American consul."

"Elope?"

"Yes."

"I'll have it with me, but—change the subject."

"Can't you stay to hear what your father has to say?"

"I wish I could."

"Can I say, 'Sir, Sophia said you had some news for me'?"

"Why not? Of course you can. This isn't exactly a love feast, and remember, an American goes after what he wants."

For the moment Sir Godwine was in earnest conversation with Harvey. Before I could break into it, Dick rose.

"I've a toast to offer, too," he said, his face darkly flushed. "To one who is with us no more, but whose gallant spirit inspires us yet. *Our Eliza.*"

There followed a brief period of intense silence and complete stillness. It was charged with suspense I could share but not understand. Sophia stiffened in her chair. I caught a fleeting expression on Sir Godwine's face that was perhaps beautiful, perhaps sublime, but whose effect on me was frightening, although I could not possibly have told why. His love for his first ship was more than human, Sophia had told me. Perhaps his look was godlike.

"I don't know that we should do this, Dick, at this time," he replied after a thoughtful purse of his lips and in calm, level tones.

"Remember that at *Our Eliza's* first and greatest triumph—twenty years ago next Christmas Day—a fine American ship and crew went to the bottom. Still, our American guest knows that it was war—and I can assure him both vessels did themselves proud!"

He rose slowly. "Yes, we'll drink to the soul of *Our Eliza!* May she sail the seas of the hereafter as gallantly as she sailed our sea!"

I stood with the rest. I thought of offering a toast to the Yankee vessel who had engaged her and met defeat and death, only to decide against it. Afterward, Sir Godwine sat in reverie, the champagne in his glass casting a pale golden gleam on his white hand. When he emerged from it, I spoke.

"Sir Godwine, Sophia said you had news of America for me."

"Why, so I have! The minx had no business telling you until I gave her leave—but young ladies make their own rules, it seems, and feel free to break all others. But the tail of the cat is out of the bag, so I'll bring forth the body. The long and short of it is, your country's gone to war."

I answered with great care.

"With France—or again with England?"

Not that I harbored any real doubt. Most long-headed Americans believed that another war with England was in the stars. I could understand better now the talk and events of tonight's dinner—my feeling of something in the air, of emotions held in tight rein, and of words carefully chosen. The enmity and danger I had felt seemed of a different character than my affair with Sophia should create. All this was explainable by our two countries being at war.

But Sir Godwine had been struck speechless, as by great surprise.

"Sink me, but you're a cool one!" he broke forth at last. "With France, or again with England, say you, not turning a hair. Harvey, here's a Yankee as bluff as they come!"

"Bluff?" Dick asked quietly.

"I mean plain-spoken. No, sir, Homer, 'tis with neither one. On the fourteenth of May last, the Pasha of Tripoli cut down the flagstaff of the American consulate and declared war. Your consul there, by name of Cathcart, set out for home. My advices are there's no doubt the Yankees will meet the challenge—that they committed themselves to it when they refused the Pasha's demands—and will send a naval squadron to these waters to protect their shipping. If it ain't already on the way, 'twill soon be."

"Sir, I'm not surprised. I've heard talk of the Pasha's insolence and our exhausted patience for a good while."

"Then why didn't you guess Tripoli straight off?"

"You said, sir, we were at war. We wouldn't call it war, to be teaching a pirate king to stay clear of a Yankee ship."

He stared at me as might a sleepwalker. I thought that his bellyful of wine had finally washed up upon his brain. But he recovered with a little tremor and turned to Dick.

"Did you hear that?"

"Yes, sir."

"Harvey, you'd better listen to it, too, for our future's sake. Maybe all Europe had better stop their fooling and take notice. Homer, my lad, you'll have to forgive me for my old-fashioned ways. It seems just yesterday that what you call 'United States' were some English colonies, ruled by royal governors, a region where our yeomanry could buy cheap land. They rebelled against the king—France took their side—and we bitched the business right and left. Still, I can hardly believe you've got ahead this fast. After all, the king of Tripoli, pirate nest though it be, is still a king. But there's the new century, the New World. And Homer, you're as fine a representative as I'd want to meet. By heaven, I'm glad you came tonight! You were just the man to set me straight. A real, life-size, full-blooded young Yankee——"

He stopped, because Sophia had stood up. Truly she seemed to spring up, and her eyes were haunted and her mouth was drawn.

"Yes, daughter," he said in an indulgent tone.

"We've finished dessert, and with your permission, I'll withdraw."

"I fear I've bored you by reciting what you already know."

"You never bore anyone, but may I go?"

"Yes—yes—you may."

He rose and gave her a stately bow. We others were on our feet, but she would not look at Harvey and Dick, and it seemed she could not look at me. When Millen had bowed her through the door, he, too, went out.

"Now we can settle down to a good old-fashioned sailor's brandy bout," Sir Godwine remarked, "unless the company has other notions."

"I need a bit of air," Dick said. "Will you come with me, Harvey?"

"If Sir Godwine and Mr. Whitman can do the honors alone," Harvey answered, his tongue a little thick. Then with a sly wink at Dick, they went out together.

I did not care about that. I had more important business on my mind.

"Sir Godwine, I'd like a glass of brandy, but mainly I wish to make a request."

"Then come into my cubby. I've brandy there, and 'baccy and pipes, too, if you've a taste that way."

We climbed steep stone steps where it seemed likely his drinks would hit him. I did not believe it, though, and was not really surprised when he ran up them like a boy. He led me into an eight-sided room that might once have been the top of a battlement, now walled in and furnished like the captain's cabin on a man-of-war. The chairs, chests, and charting table were of massively carved teakwood; the broad-based cone-shaped decanters, of heavy graven crystal, would not tip over in a heavy sea; a drunken man could fall down without knocking anything down, so well secured was all gear. I admired especially a telescope, two feet long and light as a spyglass, with magnifying power of some fifty diameters. I wondered if it had been used on Sophia and me.

"I'd hazard that your request concerns my daughter," Sir Godwine remarked in a pleasant tone when we were comfortably seated.

"Aye, sir, it does. I wish your permission to pay court to her."

"Now that's a different thing than asking her hand in marriage, yet it could come to the same thing. Suppose I granted your request and then you and she should take a notion to marry, could I refuse you, when I'd given you a clear field? Still, it's a proper request, when you're of a different nationality and station."

"I'm ignorant, sir, in matters of station. But I wish to court Sophia at her home, and in the open, without your forbiddance."

"I'll instruct you somewhat. In practice, only young men whom we call eligible pay court to an English girl of Sophia's station—being her escort at balls, riding with her, and such as that. They'll not ask her father's consent to pay her such attentions, but if one of 'em shows unfit, he'll get the chuck; and should she get thick with one, so it looks serious, her father will either let it go on or try to stop it. If he lets it go on, the young feller need have little fear of being refused when he seeks his consent to marriage."

"Aye, sir."

"I take it Sophia wants your attentions, or you wouldn't pay 'em."

"Aye, sir."

"Has she promised to marry you if I'd let her, or even if I wouldn't?"

I did not feel obliged to answer that question, but I did so, thinking it would be in my favor.

"No, sir."

"Wouldn't I be doing wrong to you both to consent to your courting her, when I could never consent to your marrying her? And the reason why—to put it in a nutshell—both of you would rue the day."

"Sir, I dispute what you say last. I think our chance of happiness would be first rate."

"You'd intend to take her to America?"

"Aye, sir."

"Out of all you've seen tonight, to a little house in some American seaport? For mark you, she has the merest pittance of her own."

"To Bath, on the Kennebec River, where I was born. It would be a small house to start with, but get better as I get on. As for what I saw tonight, Sophia wouldn't miss it as might most young ladies, if I judge aright. In America even the poor sit down to tables laden with meat and game, and as an officer of a good ship, on my way to be a captain, I'd not count myself poor."

"Would you count yourself rich on ten—fifteen—maybe twenty pounds a month?"

"Ten pounds is close to fifty dollars. I'd make thirty dollars to start with, plus my rations. Still I'd be in middle circumstances; and in place of luxury, Sophia could have adventure."

It seemed to me that he blanched a little as from sharp pain; and as he reached for his glass of brandy, he knocked it over. I offered him my cotton kerchief to wipe it up, but instead he used his own, heavy silk with a lace frill, on which a coat of arms had been embroidered. As he mopped, he smiled. It was such a smile as I never knew, making mock of God it seemed to me, and the sweat came out on me in cold beads, for at last I had seen evil.

"I'll go back to my original question," he said softly. "If I let you pay court to her, when on no account would I consent to your marrying her, wouldn't I do you wrong?"

"Nay, sir. You'd do wrong to refuse me, when there's no mark against me, and her knowing the truth about me, and still wanting my attentions."

"Then I'd do wrong to myself. I'd be flying in the face of what's best for her, according to my greater experience and knowledge. Still, it would go hard with me to shut my doors to you, for the reasons you gave, and you a ship's officer of a nation with whom the king made peace. And it would go harder yet to lock her in room, she being of marriageable age and proud."

"Then what do you say, Sir Godwine?"

73

"Will you give me your promise to take her or leave her when the *Vindictive* sets sail from Malta?"

"I'll sail with my ship when she leaves here, if that's what you mean, whether or not Sophia will go with me."

"I'll not forbid you—although it's against my wishes and advice—to pay court to her the short time you're here."

While I sat dumb, hardly able to believe my ears, he filled his glass and drained it. The respite allowed me to catch my breath.

"I thank you kindly."

"You've no news of the vessel, I dare say?"

"No, sir."

"Captain Ball gave me some today. Our frigates convoyed her through the Strait two weeks ago. Some days past she was at Palermo, unloading Danish butter, and was due to sail on last night's tide. If this weather holds, she ought to make it in sometime tomorrow."

Battening down my heart, I looked into Sir Godwine's face confronting mine. There should be a gleam of mirth, however sardonic, in his pale eyes. I could even expect a trace of a smile, triumphant but human, such as a winner should give a loser in fellowship's sake. But the blue around the diamond-bright black points was like blue sky in December, and his mouth was slightly pursed, showing the perfect molding of his lips, as his thoughts flew far.

He had dismissed me from his attention. He had not denied my existence—he would not bother to tell the lie—but he had become oblivious to it. But I had another night in Malta. I remembered with a rush of joy, a sense of power, and I would not be surprised to hear from him again.

CHAPTER 6

The Ship Comes In

1

THE HIGHEST hill overlooking the northwest coast was the hill I climbed. In midmorning I had gained its crest; since the day was clear and fine, I could gaze halfway or thereabouts across the Malta Channel. Besides fishing smacks under lateen or square sail, ketches, and suchlike craft, I marked a Yankee brigantine, an English frigate, a Barbary brig whose heavy bow spelled pirate as sure as a skimming

74

fin spelled shark, and three sloops in a flock making straight east, too far away for me to know their nation.

Amid all this shipping, a white speck on the northwest horizon need not excite me. I thought it a brighter white than any skysails I had seen, but that was a trick of the sun. As all her tops rose into view, they were still too distant to show peculiarities of rigging. Still, I would bet a dollar she was my own ship, and not a dime that she was some other. Maybe she came up with a little different motion than other ships. Perhaps I merely felt it in my bones.

I waited a half hour longer. Her hull hung still below the horizon, but my head was free of doubt. It was no trick to walk down to Valletta in time to see her make her harbor run, or to catch a ride on the first lighter scampering out to meet her. She had hardly finished her first swing upon her cable when I had cleared her rail.

An officer now, as my shipmates kept in mind, I received no banging about, but there was no sea rule against Captain Phillips pumping my arm and turning red in the face with pleasure; or Mate Hedric from jesting broadly about my shore adventures; or the sailors from giving me hearty handshakes and big grins and simple words of welcome to stow in my heart. 'Giny Jim came out of the galley with his black face alight. He had laded a coop of fowls, he said, and tonight there'd be fried chicken for all hands. I did not see Mate Tyler, but no other face was missing from the ring, so all was well with the *Vindictive*. I had been ashamed to worry about her, it seeming a breach of troth with so stout and brave a ship, but I must have done so regardless, to have such a load off my mind.

"Mr. Tyler left us at Lisbon, catching a ride to Boston on the *Rainbow*," Captain Phillips told me. "Mr. Hedric and I spelled each other this little way, and 'twas like old times."

He looked somewhat heavy-eyed, I thought, but his sleep would not be easy for a good while yet, or I missed my guess.

"Sir, did you hear the news from America?"

"I heard rumors of trouble with Tripoli, and the true report of our consul there taking ship for home."

I repeated what Sir Godwine had told me. Straightway Captain Phillips beckoned Mr. Hedric and me into his cabin. After a tot of rum together and a brief palaver, it did not take him long to lay a course.

"I reckon this will be a job for our Regular Navy," he remarked. "Tripoli has no merchant fleet, only pirates decked and armed for battle. 'Twould be folly and worse for us to hunt 'em until we can refit in a Yankee yard—far more weight, more stanchions to support it, and holds turned into magazines and quarters for four times our number. If we're needed, we'll do it, and you can lay to that. But tomorrow we'll sail with an empty bottom for Naples and lade wine, hemp, silk, and olives for New York. We'd have run up and got it before hoving in here if 'twould save time, but the small gain in distance would be lost by contrary winds." This last was to inform me that he had not wasted our charterer's money to relieve my homesickness.

"Aye, aye, sir."

"When we're home, I'll see what's to be done to serve our country."

That settled it. Mr. Hedric went on deck to appoint his shipwatch and give shore leave to the rest. I asked Captain Phillips's permission to broach another matter. He looked at me closely and offered me a chair.

"Cap'n, I've proposed marriage to Miss Sophia Tarlton, the daughter of Captain Sir Godwine Tarlton of the Royal Navy."

"Do tell!" It was not often that Captain Phillips employed this ancient New England expression of surprise. Then, feeling that he owed me an explanation, "I should say, Mr. Whitman, that I'd heard of him more than most English officers of his rank. 'Twas natural enough, since we served our respective countries in the late war. We were both young captains, and 'twas his ship, *Our Eliza*, that engaged and sank the brand-new *Saratoga*, commanded by my boyhood friend, Cap'n Ezra Fairbank. It went hard with me, for Cap'n Fairbank and every soul aboard was lost."

"Then I reckon there's not much hope for my petition——"

"What is it? Do you think 'twould prejudice me against Cap'n Tarlton's daughter? Why, I've naught but respect for Cap'n Tarlton himself. He had heavier guns, but the *Saratoga* wouldn't strike her colors. And he did yeoman service against Napoleon in the Battle of the Nile."

"Sophia will accept or decline tonight. I'd like permission to bring her aboard, to see what a Yankee ship is like, and to have her to myself without much interruption. There will be only the shipwatch, and they'll give me a wide berth. If she accepts, I'll ask you to marry us tomorrow morning, and to let her come home with me."

"Well, I see little wrong with either thing. Marriage is a mighty serious matter, but you're a serious man. Ye can bring her aboard, and since ye're not trifling with her, ye can entertain her in your cabin if ye both see fit. As for taking her to America, we've had ladies

aboard before—my own wife before I lost her and Mr. Hedric's wife—
and the men were pleased, and 'twas good for their manners and
language. But I doubt if I've right to marry ye here in the harbor.
'Twould be best for the knot to be tied on the open sea."

"We won't be there till some time tomorrow."

"How old is the young lady, Mr. Whitman?"

"Just past eighteen."

"Then she has the right to marry by her own choice under English
common law. Now let me give ye a word of advice."

"I'd welcome it, Cap'n, 'cause I'm sorely troubled."

"Bring her here, and if ye can, get her promise. If she will, take
her tonight to the Baptist mission, and ask the minister to marry ye.
I don't doubt he'll do it. 'Twould be his duty, which Baptists believe
in no end, and anyway, 'twould rejoice him to jar an English Navy
captain, who no doubt belongs to the Church of England. But if he
won't, consider well whether ye should elope with her aboard our
ship. I'd relish it, I confess—although his hands were lascars and conditions unfavorable, I was never persuaded Captain Tarlton did his
utmost to save life from the *Saratoga*. He could never get Captain
Ball to give us chase—'twould make him a laughingstock of the whole
Royal Navy—and I could marry ye as soon as we gain the high seas.
But 'tain't as though you're running from Bath to Boston. And sever-
ance of that sort—with no chance to ask and give forgiveness—might
cut 'em both a wound that would never heal."

I did not worry about this last. It would hold true to all other fathers and daughters I had known, but my mind refused to apply it
to the small, stick-swinging knight and beautiful Sophia. I thought to
tell Captain Phillips that they did not love each other, but I had
nothing to back it except Sophia's remark, and it would sound ill in
his ears.

I wished he could perceive how desperate the matter was. He
could not because I could not tell him—I knew, but not why. I had
no proof to offer of brooding evil, not even plausible evidence. How
could I say I was frightened to the marrow of my bones?

2

Before setting forth in a *carrozza* for Lepanto Palace, I took a few
stitches in time. One was to provide for a pleasant supper to be served
Sophia and me in my cramped cabin. Another was to engage a shore
gig, actually a two-man gondola, with a lateen sail, whose owner I

77

had come to know, to wait my call. The most important was to pay a visit to the Baptist mission for a brief conversation with its head, a balding, square-jawed, ruddy-skinned Welshman known as Preacher Morgan. If we came to his abode about midnight, would he marry Sophia and me?

After he had questioned me briefly and sensibly, I left in high spirits and ranged the waterfront in search of a shipmate. The first I encountered could not be beat—Farmer Blood from Poultney—and his plain red face lighted wonderfully when he knew my need of him. On my drive to Notabile my spirits never tumbled, and I trimmed my tackle better than before. It was only to engage a closed *carrozza* in the way of an anchor to windward.

We had hardly driven through the gate of Lepanto Palace when I saw a postern door open narrowly and Sophia emerge. She walked lightly to the courtyard as I sprang out to meet her, and in a few seconds we were under way. But I had caught a glimpse of someone at a window.

"I didn't think you'd come," Sophia said as soon as we were out of sight of Lepanto Palace.

"What could stop me?"

"That dinner last night. It would stop anyone but a fool. And isn't your ship in? Papa told me this morning that you were expecting her today."

"She's in, and I think she'll sail tomorrow."

"Then why did you come? You could have gotten a pretty Maltese girl for your last night on the island. I'll only bring you bad luck——" Still, she could not keep her eyes from shining.

"I'll show you in a few minutes what kind of luck it is. Now I need your help giving directions to the driver."

Well versed in French, Sophia could follow the Italian patois known to most Maltese. Without much trouble she informed our Jehu that he was to let us out at the carnival, take his stand with other carriages until shortly before midnight, then return to Valletta by a roundabout route. If in the meantime anyone asked for us, he was to say only that he was waiting our return. For this I would pay him two shillings extra, but if he disobeyed orders, I would report him to Ernesto, king of the carriage drivers and a name to conjure with.

"What will we be doing in the meantime?" Sophia asked me, big-eyed.

"I've arranged for another carriage to be waiting out of sight of the crowds. As soon as we can slip off, we'll make for Valletta."

"What then?"

"We'll take a shore gig out to my ship."

"And then sail away?" Sophia laughed raucously.

"Did you bring your passport?"

She sobered instantly. "Yes, but you said you wouldn't sail at least until tomorrow."

"We won't weigh anchor tonight. I intend to bring you home before dawn. Is that all right?"

"Yes, provided someone doesn't come for me before then. I've danced all night more than once. No one will kill me—no one will even hit me. Tomorrow night——"

"It may be tomorrow night you won't leave me at all."

"Has my passport anything to do with that?"

"Yes, and I'll tell you later."

"Homer, it's incredible. The whole thing is. Yet when you're with me, I believe it. You plan something—and it comes true."

"I've got to ask you something. Is your father going to look for us soon, or late, or not at all?"

"If at all, it will be late. His present intention is to indulge my whims. He thinks I know what side my bread is buttered on, and if he doesn't bear down too hard, I'll obey his wishes. If he kept me at home tonight, I might run off and marry you. He couldn't conceive of it himself, but I believe Dick told him so. Harvey will be furious but he won't do anything—he's under Papa's thumb. And none of them believe that I'll do anything very serious."

We were drawing close to the carnival. Fiddles shrilled, drums beat, clowns shouted, and crowds laughed.

"Sophia, do you think he'll guess I've taken you to my ship?"

She mused a moment, then shook her head.

"I believe it's the last place he'd look. You see, there's a certain pattern to his thinking—if I look far enough, it always fits. No English captain would let one of his crew bring a girl aboard. Not even an American would be crude enough to invite a young English gentlewoman on to his dirty hooker. If he did, of course she wouldn't come."

While hooker could mean a two-masted Dutchman as clean as a whistle, usually it meant an old, disreputable trader swarming with rats and roaches. All hands but Captain Phillips applied it affectionately, along with "The Old Bitch," to our trig lady, but never in his hearing or before outsiders. I had not foreseen that Sophia knew the

79

word, though I should be sensible to her wide vocabulary by this time.

When the driver let us out at the carnival, we were hard put to it to leave the happy scene. There was an Italian troupe of jugglers and acrobats, monkeys and dancing bears, a merry-go-round that Sophia called a carousel, and peep and puppet shows. But great urgencies confronted us. Sophia faced them as squarely as I did; and her straits were worse than mine because she must make the desperate decision. But even if we could have spared an hour from our night of trial, the presence of some English man-of-war's men with pretty, vital-looking Maltese girls hurried us off. Quite possibly they knew Sophia by sight. Anyhow, they quieted her laughter.

When we were out of sound of the merrymaking, she took note of the closed carriage, better sprung and more luxurious than the other, and the spanking team that took the highroad at a good eight miles an hour.

"Homer, isn't the hiring of two carriages, and a boat, and I don't know what else, rather expensive?"

"I had sixty dollars when I hit Malta. I've still got almost ten."

"That's a lot to spend out of six guineas'—thirty dollars—pay."

"I rather thought Sir Godwine wouldn't tell you that."

"Why not?"

"Wouldn't 'pittance' do well enough? I guess I thought that giving exact figures would be beneath his dignity."

"Nothing is. That's a strange thing to say. He feels so high he can do anything. Anyway, aristocracy is rooted in money somewhere along the line—cut the root, and it dies."

"I told him that instead of luxury, I could give you adventure."

"He told me you said that—and he didn't smile over it. He even acted quite impressed by it. In that he was very clever."

"That's too subtle for me."

"Did he tell you that I have a little money from my mother? I can draw it all after I'm twenty-one, and it might be enough to buy a small ship. It yields fifty pounds a year."

"I'd think that would buy a fine sloop. And until then, we could live well and keep a hired girl."

I began to tell her about America—little things that English travelers would hardly notice. I described our clambakes and lobster-boilings on the beach, to which every youth and maiden in the town could come and be welcome; husking-bees and cider-pressings and apple-butter making, with kisses for prizes; excursions to the snowy woods when word went forth of sap a-running; quilting parties in the winter and barn dances in the fall and kissing games at Christmas. In Charleston and Richmond people asked who your grandpa was, and the question was beginning to be put in Boston, but if you did not want to answer, you only had to move a ways west, where no one cared and life was even livelier than on the seacoast. I tried to make her understand the bigness of the land—room for nine Englands in the part already settled, while over the mountains it ran on and on, forest and prairie, deep black soil, corn land and pasture to come, and cities and towns to be, clear to the Father of Waters.

But I could not tell her how it felt to be an American—the inwardness of it. Very rarely a sharp feeling, hardly ever thought upon, yet it was with all of us, all the time. It made us different from every other people in the world. It worked upon our minds and changed our souls.

She listened almost in silence. Her hand in mine sometimes opened and closed. Once she stopped me with a kiss. Once she wiped away tears.

3

So we came into Valletta, and got out of the carriage not far off the Strad Reale; then we made our way down the half-mile staircase to the harbor. A short and breezy sail brought us alongside the *Vindictive;* and since she was no great ship o' the line, Sophia needed no Jacob's-ladder to gain her deck. I handed her up; Storky Wilmot's long lean arms reached down. After the light hoist, he touched his cap to her and vanished in the fo'c'sle.

"She's not as big as I thought," Sophia said, looking fore and aft.

"No, you can pitch a stone from knightheads to taffrail."

"She's very low to the water."

"Yes, the Yankee traders have low freeboard, which makes her get wet decks when the green seas roll, but helps her spank along in fair weather."

Sophia looked up. "She's quite tall."

"That she is. Foreigners say that Yankees carry too much sail."

"Does 'foreigners' include the English?"

"I reckon it does—until they come to live in America."

I showed her all parts of the ship that were fitting for her to visit, and told her the use and meaning of the gear. Lastly, I led her to my cabin and lighted the lantern bracketed to the wall.

She saw a room about six feet by five, containing a bunker cot with my chest pushed underneath, a bench, a washbasin hung on a nail, and a draw bucket. The dead light gave plenty of air on cool nights like this, and in tropic heat I could open the hatch. I could stand erect, although Storky Wilmot would have to bend his head. The room smelled clean, and there were no bugs in the bed, roaches in the boards, or rats in the walls.

"Is this all?" Sophia asked with round eyes.

"Yes, but it's as big as the cap'n's cabin on a ketch."

"I must say it's snug."

"I must say it isn't Lepanto Palace or the mansion—your mother's old home—Celtburrow—in Cornwall."

"The bed's wide enough for two."

"Plenty wide for you and me."

"Could two people cross the ocean in this little cabin?"

"I know of nothing to stop us but your will. We'd be on deck most of the time. We'd mess with cap'n and Mr. Hedric."

"To America?"

"Where else?"

The time had come to tell her about the Baptist mission and how we could go there any time tonight. It was a far cry from any scene of marriage she might have dreamed—as different from that as this cubby from the captain's cabin on a great ship of the line. Yet if people did not want to be married in a strange and empty church, and their own homes were out of reach and no friend's home was open to them, they were glad to come to the small, cheaply furnished parlor with its tiny organ, and the plain-faced, plainly dressed minister who officiated there. If we went there, I would have a witness whom the minister would believe, and our passports would show our age and, to any sensible man's satisfaction, our eligibility for marriage.

"You want to take me there tonight?" Sophia asked in low tones, her eyes on mine.

"Yes."

"Hold me a little while and don't kiss me, and I'll try to decide."

I sat on the bed with Sophia in my arms. Her mouth lay against my throat, so that her breathing seemed part of mine. Her eyes closed, and I thought she dropped to sleep. I kept vigil over her, careful not to waken her, although I did not keep the letter of her injunction. In a short while she woke with a start.

"I thought you'd gone," she said.

"No. Can I kiss you now?"

"Wait a moment. I want you to think of something. I met you only five days ago counting today. You count them up and see. Isn't that too soon for you to expect me to make a decision changing my whole life? Suppose when your ship is ready to sail, I've almost decided to go with you but need a little more time. Will you give it to me?"

"I wish I could, but I can't."

"Together we—or you alone—could go to America on another ship. You could get a berth, or I'd pay the way. Our way—or your way."

"I must stick to my ship."

"Is it because you promised Papa so? You wouldn't have to keep a promise he got you to make through trickery."

"I wouldn't think he would have told you."

"He didn't. He didn't tell me the other either—about your pay. The truth is, he hasn't mentioned you since you left. I made it up."

"Then how did you know?"

"I sneaked up the stairs when he took you to what he calls his cabin, and listened at the latch."

"Will you tell me why you did?"

"Yes, I was afraid you might take him and kill him."

"That wouldn't seem very likely, would it?"

"You Yankees went to war with your own king when he wouldn't give you what you thought were your rights. You killed the soldiers sent to put down your rebellion. Why wouldn't you kill Sir Godwine Tarlton, far more kingly than plain old George—indeed as kingly as the cruel kings of the Middle Ages—when he wouldn't give you what you thought were your rights?"

"Did you want me to kill him?"

Her eyes shot wide open. "No. . . . No. I'm not even sure I want him dead. But go on and answer me. If I can't decide tonight, will you stay a few days more?"

"I can stay only until my ship leaves."

"Then I must decide tonight?"

"It's come to that."

"If I go with you, what will I leave that I love?"

"You know, I don't."

"I love my old nurse, Melissa. Papa wouldn't let her come here. I could come to love Harvey, because he's in the same boat with me, but not passionately and wildly as I love you. I love pearls out of the sea. Those I wear are his, and I couldn't take them. I love beautiful

83

clothes. I love old pictures and statuary and wonderful things of all kinds."

She paused. "A few rich merchants in Boston have some, but not many," I told her. "There are almost none in Bath."

"Sometimes great men come to dinner. Lord Nelson came once. They stop at Malta, and Papa entertains them. In London, married to Harvey, I would meet many prominent men—soldiers, statesmen, poets, and actors. Whom would I meet in America?"

"Well, a few like Cap'n Phillips. There are great leaders in our cities, but mighty few come to Bath."

"That's all right. People must pay for what they get. If you need me as much as I need you, I'd never be sorry I went."

"I reckon I need you a whole lot more."

"Haven't you plenty of others?"

"The ship and the men, and that's all."

She leaned out in my arms and searched my face. Her eyes looked depthless in the lanternlight.

"Where are your parents and your brothers and sisters? You haven't mentioned them—I thought you had had trouble with them —or maybe were ashamed of them."

"I had no sister. I haven't mentioned the others because I couldn't —my throat filled every time I started to, I don't know why. I can give you the main fact. My two brothers and my parents went down with my father's ship, the *Eagle of Maine*."

"The *Eagle—of Maine . . .*"

"It was a good name. It fitted her."

"How long ago?" She spoke quickly now.

"Five years."

"You were younger than I am now."

"Yes."

"Where were you when it happened?"

"On the beach watching."

Her hand came up and caught mine. "Tell me about it! Will you? Confide in me, Homer—no one ever has. I'll bear it with you, whatever it is. It's a terrible thing—I can see it in your face—and I think it will set me free."

I did not understand all that she meant, but I began to tell her of the wreck. Sophia saw the sparkling bay and the ship making too much leeway. She heard Captain Phillips and Captain Starbuck talking in low tones and watched their faces. I must not hide from her the sight of the ship striking and her men falling down and then

84

her last hurtling from reef to reef until one of them gored her and held her fast. At last only four people clung to the steeply listed deck, and it seemed to me they were trying to join hands. Then another sea smote her, and they, too, were gone.

I felt Sophia's tears on my cheeks and tasted their salt in my mouth. Then the wreck of the *Eagle of Maine* withdrew gently into the past; it could not happen again because it had already happened; it belonged to a chapter that had closed. Sophia and I were back in my little cabin in the warm, still night, facing the days unborn.

"I love you, Homer."

"I love you, Sophia."

"I want to be with you always, and you to be with me."

"Then let's have it so."

"I want to go with you to the mission parlor, but I'm afraid."

"There's nothing to be afraid of."

"Nothing that I can tell you or even explain to myself. If only I were yours already and we were far at sea——"

My heart began to bound.

"If you were mine already—if we belonged to each past all doubt so no one could separate us—would you still be afraid?"

She lay still a minute, then shook her head.

"Will you, Sophia?"

"It's so with many lovers who go to the priest," she whispered, her lips moving eagerly against my ear. "Why can't it be with us?"

"Afterward you'll go with me to the little parlor and—stand up with me?"

I had almost shrunk from the expression used by so many plain folk in America, but as it came forth, I saw how fitting and strong it was.

"If my gift to you means enough. Will it count any less than if we'd waited? You see, I have waited until now—waited for you."

"I've waited for you, too."

"What do you mean by that?"

"Just what you mean."

"Is that true? I see by your face it is."

"I guess it's not true. I didn't want any of the harbor girls."

"That makes it true enough. I wouldn't have minded—but I'm so glad."

She rose up out of my arms and turned the lantern low. In the pale glimmer that remained, she took the pins from her dusky hair and shook it down about her shoulders. Her preparations for her bridal adventure went unhurriedly forward, but I could not keep my own hands from flying. Before long, the tresses were more beautiful than before, their dark waves set off by a dim and secret luster of naked flesh. I became aware of beauty in its realness, beyond fancy's reach. All men who have loved woman know a like moment of revelation, of breathless unbelief, and those who have not loved woman cannot know it, because their eyes are dim.

"Be gentle with me, Homer," she told me as we lay side by side.

Passion came upon me as a gale upon a ship, gathering and rushing, so strong that it seemed an exterior force rather than one expression of my own strength, but when I remembered it was no more or less than that, that I was its master and it could not master me, her trembling ceased and the fear went out of her eyes. Then the storm within me shook me no more. Sometimes I had dreamed of sailing wide, still waters of infinite depth, and I half-remembered that dream, and instead of tumult I knew mystery and bliss.

She was giving me her beauty in mysterious ways. Bliss came upon us both, rising and growing until it seemed to pass all bounds, but it was not an unworldly dream from which we would wake; it was real as the lantern's glimmer. Like a long wave rolling under the moon it broke at last.

In that ecstasy and its warm and lovely aftermath, I could not doubt that we were joined forever.

CHAPTER 7

Far Voyage

1

A SENSE of triumph over evil stars stayed with us. As we dressed for a short journey of great consequence, we must pause and kiss and laugh; and in the bravado of our elation we were tempted to dally with time, for who could harm us now? So we asked each other by our gaiety or quiet joy; but perhaps we did not ask ourselves, from being not quite as brave as we wished to be. Although the midnight bells had not yet rung, our movements became increasingly brisk. We did not wait even to eat the supper Jim had prepared, but promised to do justice to it as soon as we had run an errand.

Truly I had no deep fear of Sophia's father or brother or suitor making us trouble. Somehow it did not fit into the picture. The tenuous shadows cast across my mind seemed to be fear of fate. Sophia appeared to be spared even this. Darkly flushed, she poured two glasses of wine, kissed the rim of one, and handed it to me. "To us in America."

I signaled with a lantern for our shore gig. It took so long to come that we fell silent and felt a little chill. But its sail filled with the crackle that sailors love to hear; the boatmen need not break out their oars; one dark hull after another dropped behind us as we skipped up the bay. When we had gained the dank wharf, Sophia slipped her arm into mine and we strode out. The inshore wind helped fly us up the steps, so soon we gained the byway on the hillside where the Baptist mission perched. It had been founded close to the waterfront, handy to sailors and longshoremen and their ilk.

From the wine shop at the corner, Farmer Blood had kept watch for me. Now he joined us quickly, and my heart glowed over his plain face and powerful, solid form. A lamp glimmered dimly in a window of the mission; when I had knocked on the door, there was only a brief wait, then it opened, disclosing an old Maltese woman in a black cloak with a candle in her hand.

"Ah!" she breathed at sight of us, her worn face lighting with a smile. "Coom tees way."

She led us to the little parlor of our destination where the lamp burned low. Turning up its wick, she said something in broken English, nodding and smiling, and withdrew. I followed Sophia's gaze to the window fronting the street and now clearly lighted.

"Please draw that curtain, Homer," she said.

I did so, then could not help but watch Sophia's struggles with her fears. They were rising now; they had prevailed over her elation, and she could not even simulate it now; the beautiful dark glow was gone from her face, and her eyes moved quickly. I thought she was trying to hold her fears at bay by fixing her attention on her surroundings. She looked at the plain, cheap, but solid furniture and the clean floor with its Brussels carpet, and she smiled a little tender smile over the small organ. Then she fixed her eyes with a curious intensity on a picture that I had barely noticed and forgotten.

It was a colored print of a portrait of George III, and apparently a very popular picture, since I had seen the same several times in English customhouses and the like. Its accent was on regalness, not humanity. The large features of the Hanover had been idealized to look like those of a Roman emperor; the eyes had a haughty stare; the shoulders were draped in ermine. With that dreadfully strained smile I had thought never to see again, she turned her back on it. I took the opportunity to ask for her passport. Although standing close together, it seemed that we three stood one by one as Preacher Morgan came into the room.

The big, balding man was smiling and self-assured. If he had stuffed the tail of his nightshirt into his trousers and hid the rest under his waistcoat, clerical coat, and stock, it was no one's business but his own. He greeted me warmly, then turned expectantly to Sophia. When I introduced her, he did not bow—clergymen should bow only to God—but shook hands with her cordially.

"Your hand is cold, my dear," he said, "but they say that is the sign of a warm heart."

When I had introduced Farmer Blood, he asked to see any papers verifying Sophia's and my eligibility to marry. He took these under the lamp to study through spectacles; I turned to find Sophia staring again at the king's picture, her eyes wide and black in her pallid face.

"What is it, Sophia?" I asked.

"Can't you tell him to please take it down and hang it somewhere else?"

"Of course I can't. It's his king."

The thought came to me that I might get rid of it by some subterfuge, but instantly I dismissed it.

"I can't stand to have him looking on——"

"That's just nerves, Sophia. It doesn't go with my gallant girl——"

"I'm not gallant. *Our Eliza* was gallant and so is the *Vindictive*, and all the ships are gallant, but I'm a coward——"

The minister's sonorous voice broke in.

"These are quite satisfactory. They establish beyond any doubt that you two are unmarried and of age to marry by your own will. Mr. Blood, I take you for an honest man. Will you take oath that this man and this woman who've come to me to be joined in matrimony are not close kindred?"

"Sir, I know all about Mate Whitman's family, and they're not kin at all."

"Then you two may take your places in the center of the room.

88

I'm sure my wife is about ready by now, and I shall summon her."

Opening an inner door, he called "Dear?" At once a pleasant-faced woman of middle size and age, neatly but plainly dressed, came in and kissed Sophia on the cheek. She sat down at the stool, thumped with her hands and pumped vigorously with her feet, and out came "Drink to Me Only with Thine Eyes." Except for a few squeaks in the first bar, it was a melodious and pleasing rendition of the ancient love song, in my mind the most noble ever composed. I took Sophia firmly by the hand and drew her beside me. The minister stepped in front of us with his open book. When the music died away, he began an ancient ceremony.

"Dearly beloved, we are gathered together. . . ."

Sophia's eyes fixed on his face. Her cold hand opened and shut in mine. I heard what he said only in my outer ear—a prayer—a moralism—soon the famed injunctive.

"If anyone knows . . . let him speak now . . . forever hold his peace."

As the words came forth, Sophia put her head on one side as though listening to some very distant voice. I saw a change in her countenance, but I did not know yet what it meant; her eyes grew narrow and wildly bright. Then as Preacher Morgan paused, waiting a polite second as though for someone to burst in the door, Sophia herself spoke.

"There's no use of him asking that," she said to me.

"Be still."

"No, because I'm not going through with it. I'm backing out."

I said something, but it made no sense. "You shouldn't treat me so."

"I know it. I'm just as sorry as I can be. There's no use of my trying to explain——"

I turned to the minister. "Excuse us a moment, please." Then I took Sophia's hand and led her to the window.

"What are you going to say to me?" she asked, such dread and shame in her face that I could hardly bear to fix my eyes upon it.

"I was going to say it might be a kind of hysteria. I want you to steady yourself and consider everything. You're not a slave. You're a free human being. If you love me——"

"Loving you only makes it worse."

"You know what's between us——"

"There's a joke that answers that. It was popular last year in Bath —our Bath, not yours—all the toffs told it. A countess went there for the season and spent the night with a handsome coachman. Later he wanted to call on her in London. She sent him word that sexual intercourse and social intercourse were two different things."

This was not Sophia, or else she had put on a mask. Her face was drawn with mockery, but not of me—she would not look at me. Suddenly I knew it was mockery of herself.

She became grave, as though looking into a mirror. "Now watch this," she told me. "Have you ever seen this before?"

One corner of her lip curled up.

"I know what you mean, but it isn't like that at all."

"I dare say no one else can do it. It's completely unique. Now go back to your ship, will you? I don't ask you to forgive me—I know that's impossible—but maybe you can forget me. Do it if you can, I beg you. I don't want you ever to think of me again. I want to hide from you—my very existence. Every time I imagine you thinking of me, I'll want to die. I love you, Homer, I'll always love you. I want to be your wife more than anything in the world, but it's against orders. Do you believe me?"

"Yes, I believe you."

"Now will you get me out of your sight?"

"I'm going to put you in a carriage and take you to someone you know——"

"All right. And don't wait any more. . . ."

I spoke to Preacher Morgan and, beside myself over my loss, offered him a fee. He refused it gravely; in a moment we were in the street. Up the street from the wine shop where Farmer had waited for me, stood another of a better sort: from one of the tables under the balcony, a small man rose and came toward us. I knew he was not Sir Godwine by the way he walked. As he came under the street light, I recognized him as Dick Tarlton. He gave me a brief bow, then spoke to Sophia.

"You didn't stay very long."

"No, I didn't."

"Papa laid me a bet you wouldn't go through with it, and I dare say he won."

"Yes, he did."

"Well, I'm out ten pounds, and if you were any kind of a sport, you'd come down with half——"

"I certainly shan't. You should've learned your lesson by now."

"You may wonder what I'm doing here. Old Poison, Mrs. Dawson, found out you'd taken your passport. This looked pretty serious to me, so I searched for you at the carnival and then dashed out to the *Zealous*, where Papa was dining with Captain Hood. He was a bit irked by my disturbing him and said you'd probably gone either to the mission or out to your friend's ship. I could look for you here—after he'd finished his brandy he'd go there—anyhow he wanted to pay respects to the Yankee skipper—and if he found you, he'd escort you home. I soon found out that the wedding party had gone in, so I sat down to wait. It wasn't to let you stew in your own juice—I wanted to win that bet. But I didn't have much hopes I would—and I was right."

"Yes, you were right. It's all very logical. Now what?"

But logical was one thing it was not, nor was it truthful. I smelled lies as strong as the taint of a slaver upwind. Sophia was caught in a cobweb of lies, evil and strange, but I could not set her free.

"I've got a carriage and we can go home," Dick said.

"What about Papa?"

"He's either at Mr. Whitman's ship, or on the way there—or has left there. Mr. Whitman, if you see him, kindly tell him we've both gone home."

I nodded my head.

"Then let's start at once," Sophia pleaded. "Good night, Homer, and a happy voyage." Her eyes were dry and burning.

I could not look at her or speak.

"You're a victim of circumstances, Mr. Whitman," Dick said. "Damned rotten luck, I tell you."

"Good night to you too, Farmer," Sophia said. "Thank you for wanting to help us. Homer, what I told you the last thing was true. And I'll always be glad you took me to your ship."

I nodded and had a hard job raising my head. When I did, she and Dick were walking off. One shadow after another obscured them until, thick and dark, the night lay over them.

I still stood under the street light, but the night was in my heart.

2

When a shore gig brought Farmer and me out to the *Vindictive*, a very fine craft, bearing a pennant and manned by blue-jackets, lay beside her. As we swung aboard, we came full upon a small man with beautifully carved features and powdered hair, carrying a stick. Behind him, looming over him and around him, stood Captain Phillips. Plainly the noble knight was just leaving.

91

"Why, bless me, if it ain't young Whitman," Sir Godwine burst out at sight of me. "I was hoping you'd come aboard before I must end my pleasant visit with your cap'n."

Meanwhile Farmer saluted and withdrew. Sir Godwine spoke on in an anxious tone. "How have things gone with you?"

"Not well, sir."

"Is that so? Then I take it your hopes of winning Sophia have failed."

"Aye, sir."

"I thought they would. 'Twas one reason I regretted your harboring 'em. It was partly her fault for leading you on."

"No, sir, I wooed her with all my might and main."

"Yet she encouraged you, as I know right well. To tell you the truth, she doesn't know her own mind, and like many young girls, she's prey to her whims." He turned to Captain Phillips. "One day she wants this, the next day that."

Captain Phillips nodded, but did not speak.

" 'Tis my fault, too, that she's caused you pain," the knight went on. "You see, she's a dutiful girl at heart, and perhaps I sway her more than a father's right, more than I wish, for she must live her own life in the end. I'm used to command. Cap'n Phillips knows what I mean. I've a commanding way about me that I can't leave on the quarter-deck where it belongs. I never told her to refuse you, and that's my word on it. But she knew I disapproved you two making a match—for reasons that I told you—and it moved her in the end."

"Something moved her, sir," I said.

"I believe it's for the best." He turned again to Captain Phillips. "When will you sail, Cap'n? I'd hoped to send you a few flagons of my ancient Spanish brandy."

"They'd be welcome, Sir Godwine, if there's time. I've got to clear with the harbor master, and I reckon 'twill be about noon."

"Where are you bound? I'd be carrying out Cap'n Ball's wishes if I'd tell you the safest lanes."

"For Naples, and I'd thought to go through the Strait of Messina."

"Between Scylla and Charybdis? For no doubt you know, being a knowledgeable man, that these were the classical names for the rocks and whirlpools."

"Yes, sir, I did know it."

Sir Godwine's expression changed slightly. "They were a rightful source of terror in those days," he went on. "Their ships were such bad sailers. But the current's strong this time of year, and you'd not like to meet a Barbary frigate in those narrow waters, and we've none of ours about to chase 'em off. Although it's the longer sail by at least a day and more likely two, you'd do well to take the safe route by way of Marsala."

"Have you frigates on that side, Cap'n Tarlton?" For Captain Phillips had forgotten his guest's title.

"We're keeping a close watch for Frenchies from Cape Bon clear to the Aegadian Isles. Good night, Captain Phillips, Mr. Whitman, and the profitable voyage you deserve."

With that, he went overside. Cap'n Phillips wished for a piper to do him the proper honors. I was too stunned to want anything, even to take him and kill him as Sophia had said. I felt dimly that one of us should do it before too late—Captain Phillips or I, not Sophia or I —but that made no sense in my own mind and it faded away.

"Mr. Whitman, ye'd best turn in and rest that leg," the captain told me. "Ye've used it hard today."

"Aye, sir, I will, and thank you."

Presently I found myself in bed, only to worry about my clothes. When I got out to see about them, I found I had put them away with the usual care. It seemed that Sophia's wraith came to me, not to remind me of ecstasies so short time past, but able to come because of them—because for a while we had been one flesh and spirit, and the bond had not yet dissolved; and her business here was to bid me remember some other event and incident of the past few days, things heard and seen of great import yet, but they meandered through my mind without connection, and soon gave way to confused dreams.

I slept as heavily as though soaked with drink. In the morning I asked Captain Phillips's permission to adjust our compasses, an exacting task that took my full attention. When we weighed about noon, I had the watch, my long-awaited first command dear to my dreams; and after the captain had taken us out of the harbor, as was his custom, he went to his cabin and left the deck to me.

The keeping of a northwest course in a northeast wind took lively enough sailing to occupy my mind and to hold the hands' attention. They were a cheerful lot this afternoon, glad to have me back, pleasurably anticipating the cool sweet wine and the warm sweet girls of Naples; but when one of them fixed his eyes upon my face, his own was inclined to fall; which was proof to me that I did not look aright. I did not know how to remedy it, but would do so as soon as possible. Meanwhile I blessed the ship and every soul aboard.

So time passed until at sunrise of the third day we raised the

Aegadian Isles on the west coast of Sicily. These were the scene of one of the great naval battles of the world, Captain Phillips told us—the Roman admiral Catullus's victory over the Carthaginians, ending the First Punic War. Having sailed wide of the eastern capes with the wind in the northeast, we would round Marettimo, the outermost island, now it had shifted north: I was as sure of that as though I could look into Captain Phillips's head. From thence we must take a north'ard tack into the Tyrrhenian Sea.

Marettimo was rugged and thinly peopled. The morning being fine and bright, the men off watch lined the starboard rail to see what they could see. We were about to clear her—the view beyond her northern end was opening—when Enoch Sutler, whose small, hard body was always eaten up with curiosity, made a wondering remark.

"Where are all them Dago smacks that was out here fishing the last time we passed this way?"

"I reckon the fish have pulled out for some other bank," Sam Hopkins answered.

A few seconds thereafter someone raised a cry. We need not look at the cryer and ask the cause: all of us saw it plain. Out from the headland, a small, fast frigate with lateen sails scudded before the wind. Because of her speed and the swiftly widening vista, she came instantly, it seemed, into full view. In the same instant, we knew her purpose. Before we could check our way, we would be broadside to her.

She did not wait till then for her first salvo from her bow guns. These were heavy guns that she had bought with the blackmail and ransom money paid by England, France, and United States; and the black-bearded crews manned them well, used to training them on little merchantmen for loot and the glory of Allah. She did not aim to sink us. There would be no profit in that. She aimed to disable us so we would strike our colors to save life.

Men do not cry out in agony of soul, no matter how sudden and extreme. If, as Mussulmen relate, Mohammed revels in Paradise to hear a Christian wail, none had tickled his ears yet. In an awful silence we saw our foremast shot away, the jibs fall, the main topmast broken off and fouled, and the jiggers down. The shock stopped every man in his tracks, arrested every sound. Then, for one instant, our hearts stilled in our throats and our ears gaped in travail to hear Captain Phillips's command.

If it were, "Mr. Hedric, strike our colors," we would have seen the sense of it, for why throw away life to save breaking hearts? Instead his deep voice brought other tidings to us. It rang over the deck.

"Helmsman, hard her over and fall away. Mr. Hedric, clear the fallen gear from the bow guns, and blanket your magazines and fill your fire buckets. Mr. Whitman, man your starboard guns, but wait till she's nigh broadside on us and make every shot count. Men, stand by your flag and your ship."

3

I saw the flush on the faces around me and felt the same fire in my heart; then we were occupied, speaking little, at our various tasks. The pirate saw we could not fly or maneuver, so she was in no haste to give us a broadside or to run down and grapple on us, for either action would expose her to costly fire. I could now undertake one small, delicate, but fateful operation. It pertained to the captain's orders to make every shot count. The pirate's lateen rigging of short masts and long yards would be hard to cut down with our little sal-vos, and we could not hope to sink her except by a lucky ball to her magazines or many broadsides at her waterline, almost too much to hope of any providence as long as we were disabled and she was not. But while we were yet fully manned—while the pirate, hoping for a free victory and bettering her position every moment, still held back her shattering broadside, there was one great counting possible to one well-sped ball.

"Strike your colors or we'll sink you," a renegade Englishman or Yankee, common enough on the Barbary pirates, shouted down the wind.

But I, the gunner's mate of the *Vindictive*, made other reply. At our best bow gun, a long, carefully cast nine-pounder, stood Andrew Folger. He had not only the keenest ears aboard, but the sharpest and truest eyes, and no hand I knew was steadier than his. My next best gunners, Storky Wilmot and Edward Piper, waited by our star-board battery with matches in their hands. Our vessel's bow swung into the wind as we fell away; the pirate's stern came into clearer view.

"When you've got your aim, fire."

Andrew was the first to bring match to touchhole; a few seconds later the midship-guns roared out. A piece of wood flew over the pirate's quarter-deck at the first report, but not until after the second did we have the answer we craved—a high-pitched howl from someone, I guessed the helmsman—thin and strange upon the wind, and then a yell of fury from the crew. No doubt the pirate would not answer her helm. It might be a rudder chain had been cut, but far more likely her rudder posts had been shot away. She could not play with us like a wolf with a hamstrung stag. Until she fixed a jury rudder, she could not run us down and grapple us.

She could sink us soon with repeated salvos, but we would be at the bottom, of not much profit to the Pasha of Tripoli. In the meanwhile, long or short, we could fight, harming her all we could until the fight was over.

So it came to pass that both ships fell away before the wind, keeping a distance of half of a sea mile. But the pirate was not nearly as lame as we; her guns were being trained on us as we tried to come up on her beam; two balls screamed through our mainsail and shrouds, narrowly missing the mast, before our starboard battery could again be brought to bear upon our foe. The gunners fired on the instant. At least one of our nine-pounders struck her close to the waterline and another carried away a davit from her main deck. Some bearded heathens soon would be busy below, shoring up wadded timbers over the hole in her hull, and one of her boats was kindling wood; but we had only borrowed a little time, and she had not begun to teach us our lesson.

Her bow guns blazed again. We waited for a whining shriek that did not rise. Instead there was a terrible swishing sound, then many hard thuds, almost but not quite simultaneous, with the effect of a swift tattoo. Some spars fell and shrouds were cut, and that was the only harm done our rigging. But Jeremiah Wilson, who had climbed our mainmast to cut away the broken topmast, lay on the deck with a yawning hole in his breast, and Storky Wilmot's head no longer had human aspect.

"Grape!" someone cried.

We had no grapeshot. All our shot were solid balls. Our guns had been shotted to fight off enemy vessels, to sink them if they would not let us pass, not to kill crewmen.

Near the break of the quarter-deck Farmer Blood said something to Charley Jervis. Lightning played on Charley's face, and he turned and repeated it to Edward Piper, who had picked up the match dropped from Storky's hand. When Edward passed it on to Will Greenough, I was near enough to hear it, but the thunder of our bow guns drowned it out. But when Will called it to Andrew Folger, I heard it plain.

"Fight on till Cap'n's gone!"

In a second or two more, every man of us had it in his heart. Thus a sending unto Farmer Blood's soul, or an impulse rising in it and sounding forth upon his lips, became our watch cry. It was not a sailor's saying. Sailors would think of us as fighting as long as our captain bade us, and stopping at his command. But Farmer came from the Green Mountains, and he saw what we had not yet seen. The murderous fire would go on. It would be Farmer Blood's turn next to fall, or some shipmate of his that he loved in his manly way, or Mate Hedric's or mine, but might Captain Phillips be spared to be among the very last! Until he fell we would fight at his command, but we would also fight by our wills, by the injunctions of our souls. Captain Phillips would know that dual motive. He need not bear the burden alone; he would not bid us stop against his own will, his own soul's injunction, in the hope of saving life. We were Americans, believing all men were created equal. While we fought on under his high command, we would put it to proof.

He sent men to the hold to bring up sheet iron we were using as ballast, with which to make flimsy shelters for the guncrews. These could not stop the cast-iron hailstones, but they might turn fragments of metal and splinters of wood flying in their wake and prolong a few lives. Before they could return, the pirate raked our decks again with the lethal grape. George Greenough, who less than three months ago had gone down to the gate of death only to be hauled up by my right arm, went back to stay. Edward Piper, one of my best gunners, had a ball through his belly, but it mercifully broke some lock of his life, probably his spinal cord, for he fell down dead. And then Mate Hedric, whom no one knew had been hit, reeled to the mast, clutched it with both hands, then spoke in a tone of command.

"Blast the dirty black legs—blast 'em—blast 'em."

Only then we saw the crimson torrent pouring from his trouser leg. As someone sprang to his help, he shook his head and quietly lay down. When I glanced again at him, the swab of death had been drawn across his face.

But meanwhile we had fired two salvos, and one of our balls had hit cleanly one of the pirate's guns, for we heard it blow up, and saw the flying metal shining in the sun, and it stood to reason we had wiped out its crew.

Now the pirate's rigging was thick with spotters and spies, showing black as buzzards on a death-watch tree. No doubt they knew

97

our loss—five out of our company of sixteen—for again they held fire, as the English-speaking traitor bellowed through a megaphone. The sound came thin but clear.

"Strike your damned Stars and Stripes, or we'll kill every man."

Our answer was a blast from four guns, fired one after another as our ship swung clumsily. Two balls hit the pirate close to the water-line, hampering her awhile, and giving more time for our rescue if an English frigate were running to our help. Sir Godwine Tarlton had told our captain there were several in these waters. We had seen none at Marsala, but it was not unlikely that one lay in the harbor at Trapani, fifteen miles away, almost in sound of our guns beating back against the north wind: anyway her scouts might bring her news of the battle. I did not believe it. I could not, but did not ask why not, lest an unspeakable horror should numb my brain. The fact remained that Captain Phillips believed it, and it had been one of the props to his heart when he had ordered battle. No doubt he, too, shared the crew's most fond, wild, but poorest-grounded hope that one lucky shot would strike the pirate's magazine and blow her to pieces.

Her crew were putting out a spar, fast to the rope. When they had done the same on her larboard, she would have a jury rudder whereby slowly and clumsily she could get the wind on her beam and run down on us. Meanwhile she would not dally with us any more. She had forsaken the hope of making slaves of many of us, to sell or hold for ransom. All the guns she could train blazed in a broken salvo, and each had been shotted with grape. The deadly hail swept our decks in swishing flurries, in such rapid succession we could not see who fell.

But soon we saw how many more lay on the deck and how few remained. Will Greenough went to join his brother, George, a ball in the lungs serving to end their brief separation that I thought neither could bear. The wonderful eyes of Andrew Folger, the sharpest I had ever seen in a human head, were instantly turned to still, dark jelly by a three-cornered fragment of casing striking him full on the forehead. Washington Peabody, our youngest and most gay, son of a prosperous shipowner in Boston, reeled to the rail and pitched over. And like a tower shattered down the man most brotherly to me of any man aboard, a man who loved me and whom I loved. I looked at his plain face and rugged form. He turned his eyes upon me and spoke once more.

"Good-by, Homer. Better luck next time."

"Good-by, Farmer Blood."

Then up spoke Sparrow, Enoch Sutler, in the piercing treble that he employed in his greatest moments.

"Fight on till Cap'n's gone!"

That would not be long. At the next burst of grape, I saw Captain Phillips clutch his belly and sink down.

I sprang to the quarter-deck and crouched beside him to hear any last command. His greatness was in his face, stamped on my soul, when he raised his head and spoke.

"Mr. Whitman, I'm wounded unto death. Bring one of the crew to bear witness to my last words, and both of ye lie beneath the gunnels while I give 'em ye, and order all left alive to protect themselves the best they can."

I called the order and summoned Ezra Owens, who had longed to be a doctor, the oldest man before the mast. He was gray in the face, but steady and in perfect mind.

"I've a dreadful question to put to ye, Mr. Whitman, but I'll require the truest answer ye can make."

"Aye, sir."

"Has it crossed your mind that the captain who advised me to take this course might have betrayed us?"

"It's been deep within my mind, but I've not confessed it until now."

"If ye live, and if ye can, establish the truth of it. If it be true, which God forbid, do all ye can that lawful punishment may be visited upon him."

"Aye, aye, sir."

"Now mark me well. The reason I engaged a ship so greatly stronger was I could not bear for the *Vindictive* to fall into her hands, and be made a pirate, and prey upon American vessels and other Christian ships while we wore chains. But maybe I shouldn't have done it. I'll not know until I stand before the judgment seat of God."

"Right or wrong, we bless you for it, Cap'n," Ezra Owens said when I could not speak.

Then our talk was briefly arrested. In the belief that all our men were dead or had fled the battle and our guns silenced, the pirate captain had ordered his longboat launched. Into it had dropped thirty or so of his turbaned crew, who now were making toward us. They did not know that our signal gun, a short four-pounder light as a carronade, was shotted and primed.

Enoch Sutler wormed across the deck with a lighted match in his hand, Sam Hopkins and Charley Jervis crept from their cubbies to join him, and then 'Giny Jim, who had swabbed out guns and passed powder and shot throughout the battle, crawled along the scupper and lent them his strong black hands. Prone under the gunnels, they somehow moved the carriage and depressed the muzzle. When the pirate's longboat had approached within two cables' lengths, Enoch found his aim and brought his match to touchhole.

No cannon shot ever sped more true. The boat heaved up from the water as though struck by the flukes of a whale and broke into countless pieces. Now there were only black dots, strangely like a flock of ducks, to mark the spot, and these swiftly scattered or disappeared.

There came a passing glint into Captain Phillips's eyes. Ezra Owens flushed and nodded to himself, as though a job were finished, some great account closed.

"Mr. Whitman, I'll leave ye the ship—to be her captain and her owner, for she's mine to dispose of as I see fit—and with her I leave ye a cruel decision to make. I can't make it for ye, for if I did what my heart prompts, 'twould not be fair to ye few remaining because I'm nigh to death and have naught to lose. It's whether to blow her up, so she can die in honor and not be sullied by falling into pirates' hands. By using a long fuse, ye few who are left can swim clear—ye good swimmers can help the poor ones—but I fear the pirates will not give you even a slave's chance, but take a cruel revenge."

Before I could answer, grapeshot burst three times over the deck. Two of the four gunners—big 'Giny Jim and little Enoch Sutler—continued to make for their cubbies. The other two, Sam Hopkins and Charley Jervis, stopped and lay still. A dark red puddle under them became a swiftly spreading pool.

"We'll sink her and swim clear, Cap'n Phillips," I told him in the stillness.

"I count it for the good of God and man. Now I'll go off watch and to sleep."

We left him on his quarter-deck, for that was where he belonged when the ship went down, as his soul would bid us if it could speak. The four of us who remained alive made our way to our magazine. Swift moments later we had bent six feet of fuse to a fifty-pound cask of powder, lighted its end, and crept back to the deck. I wished we could use a longer fuse and hide the cask, so that the ship would be swarming with rats when fire and powder met, but there was no surety they would not find the set and foil our last great stroke. Dropping overside, we joined hands.

When we had swum a cable's length from the ship, we slowed our pace and kept a close watch behind us. So it came to pass we saw the first red burst of the explosion. The beautiful ship seemed bathed in crimson flame a good second before the thunder reached our ears, and by then the billowing smoke concealed her dissolution. What I thought was her wheel rocketed into the air, stopped, then fell with increasing speed. The smoke drifted away. Nothing was left but scattered flotsam a-rock on the gentle waves.

"I'll tell you a good game," said Ezra Owens. "Let's all get a load of air and dive as deep as we can before we take in water. The man who drowns shallowest is a lousy lubber."

"No, I'll play every chance for life and want all of you with me."

"We've taken a good toll of the dirty dogs. We've better than played even when you count heads. Why let 'em sell us into slavery to live and die at their mercy—all who're left of the *Vindictive's* company, us four Americans?"

For a few seconds, my heart yearning for death, I almost yielded. Then Enoch Sutler—Sparrow—the smallest man of our great company, spoke strangely.

"Who'd remember her name?"

"I spent ten years in prison, and this'll be longer and harder," Ezra Owens went on, not understanding what Enoch had said. "We sailed 'neath the flag of freedom, so let's go free."

"Stay with us, Ezra, to the last," I said.

"I'm sorry I can't oblige you."

Jerking free from Jim's hand, he dived under the waves and instantly disappeared.

We three remaining looked toward the pirate. A boat manned by a score of Mussulmen was making toward us.

BOOK TWO

In Slavery

CHAPTER 8

The Crucible

1

WE THREE survivors of the *Vindictive's* company had lost too much too suddenly to feel any great concern over what remained. We looked at the approaching boat with vague fear and dulled interest. The savage shouts of its rowers rang hollow in our ears and we stared blankly at dark bearded faces and fantastic raiment and belts stuffed with pistols and knives. The officer standing in the bow, of more gorgeous dress than the others, brandished a scimitar as though intending to hack us to death in the water, but my heart kept its slow, cold beat.

Yet by coming aware of the lethargy, I could try to emerge from it. It was necessary that I make a hard try—instinct told me that—because our stunned condition greatly increased our danger. I heard myself giving an order in low tones.

"Obey their commands. Don't either of you show any defiance. If they tell you to kiss their dirty feet, do it. It won't hurt us, and remember, it's for our mates."

Enoch gave a little nod. Jim turned wide eyes into mine. "Our mates is all gone," he said. "What do you mean, please, suh?"

I racked my brain to answer. "Their murderers must get their just deserts."

It sounded flat and queer, but Jim's stroke changed a little, as though from a different set of his brawny shoulders.

As the boat came nigh, the crew's shouting died down and the officer's gestures became less ferocious. Apparently they were overcome with curiosity. After being searched for weapons, we were allowed to sit on a center thwart.

A few minutes later we were climbing a Jacob's-ladder to the pirate's upper deck. Some of the Tripolitans drew knives as the officer led us through the swarm; others scowled and made faces; most of them watched quietly. When we came to the break of the quarterdeck, one of the crew thrust us roughly into line. A richly dressed man, whose scimitar hilt sparkled with jewels, was standing by the lee rail watching the boat being hoisted aboard; when the job was done, he turned to look at us. By now my heavy eyes had come wide awake, and I saw him sharply.

He was a renegade from the West, several of whom had become reis under the Barbary kings. I guessed at once that the English threats shouted down to us during the battle had come from his bearded lips, spoken in his native tongue. He was about forty, tall, well-formed, of feature indicative of aristocratic lineage; and although he might be an Englishman, from the cut of his jib I judged him an American. If so, he was no better than Simon Gurty. If he did not prance and howl about the stakes where his countrymen burned, the sneer on his sharky mouth and the snaky brilliance of his eyes denied human mercy and betokened wickedness as great as Simon Gurty's and evil perhaps more deep.

"Stand at attention," he ordered.

Sparrow and I were already at it, but knife points jabbing our backs brought them straighter still. Jim clapped his long arms to his sides and stood with feet apart.

"Are any of you officers? Address me as Murad Reis."

"I am, Murad Reis," I said.

"What is your name and rank?"

"Captain Whitman, in command of the *Vindictive* when we abandoned ship."

"Do you dare lie to me, you Yankee swine? I saw the cap'n through my glass. He was a black-bearded man."

"Sir, Captain Phillips appointed me captain of the vessel just before he died."

"You're quick to assume the honors—in that like the rest. But I take it you're telling the truth, so you may follow me to my cabin." He called an order in the Arabic tongue to our guards, and at once vanished down the companionway.

I was brought to gaudily furnished quarters and given a seat on a chest. With some histrionics, Murad Reis half reclined on an ottoman, smoking a water pipe lighted by a Negro servant.

"Have you been long enough in these seas to have heard of me?" he asked lazily.

"I heard English sailors speak of you when at the hospital in Valletta," I answered. At least I had heard his name mentioned not long ago.

"And of my brother, Hamed Reis?"

"Nay, sir."

"Did they speak of my nationality before I embraced Islam?"

"They thought you were English born, but I think you were born and raised in America."

"'Tis a fact I curse to hell. However, I praise Allah for letting me see the light in time. The long and short of it is that my brother and I, both from Baltimore and not subscribing to the proposition of equality with peasants, were Loyalists in the late war. For this our manor house was robbed and burned, our plantation laid waste, and we forced to flee from the mob. We managed to get through to the English lines and finally on an English ship where we gave 'em some of their own medicine. After the war we wanted nothing more of an English king who'd make peace with traitors, or nothing more of the traitors themselves except to harry 'em whenever we came upon 'em. My brother found his heart's desire serving the Sultan of Morocco. I found mine under Pasha Yussuf. *La illaha ill' Allah!*"

There was a small Turkish quarter in Valletta and the latter cry was not uncommonly raised along the waterfront. It was the watchword of Mohammedans everywhere, and seemed to mean, "There is no God but God."

"I told you this much so you won't think it a piece of good luck that the reis into whose hands you've fallen was American born," Murad Reis went on.

"I won't think so, sir."

"In fact, any good luck you've ever had has run out."

"I'm resigned to being a prisoner of the Pasha of Tripoli."

Murad Reis removed the stem of the pipe from his mouth, threw back his head, and bayed with laughter. I had never heard such a laugh out of an American throat. Plainly he had learned it since he had turned pirate.

"You are, are you!" he cried when he had wiped his eyes. "You a New England Yankee and as dull-witted as that?"

"I don't understand you, sir."

"It's true that my Pasha has declared war on your Yankee Doodle. Many a Yankee captain will be ransomed or sold into slavery when your president prostrates himself before my Pasha's throne. But you and your two hearties won't be among the number."

His eyes glistened with mirth as he waited my answer.

"What is our status then, if you'll kindly tell me?"

"Gladly. You are three dead men."

"We didn't know it."

"You may take a long time to find it out, but in the end—if you breathe that long—you'll see what I mean. In resisting capture by my Pasha's frigate *Ayesha,* the *Vindictive* sank with all hands. No doubt the *Vindictive* caught fire, which reached her magazines and caused her blowing to hell. It's not the first time that a Yankee vessel, presuming to do battle with her betters, went down with no soul saved. In fact, I was present at a similar event in the late war."

Murad Reis, was the ship you mean the new Saratoga, *commanded by Captain Fairbank and sunk by* Our Eliza *under Captain Godwine Tarlton? The latter's crew were mainly lascars, Captain Phillips said. Were two of his officers young Loyalists fighting their own countrymen and now reis of pirate kings? My blood runs cold.*

But I did not speak, and under Murad's searching glance, my face stayed still.

"Your blowing up the *Vindictive* to keep her out of my hands will never be known to living man except myself," he went on, the evil mirth gone from his face and his tone low and earnest. "You'd naturally ask how I could pull the wool over the eyes of my crew, and what would be the good. Let me tell you. I have the only glass on board. There's method in my madness—I have my own ways of doing things —and before long I'll be the Reis Effendi, which means the admiral of my Pasha's fleet. When I saw four men come overside from that bloody, empty deck, I suspected you'd set fuse to powder. It was just what Yankee dogs would do, God damn their souls to hell!"

At the last his voice did not change in the least, but the pupils of his eyes spread and almost filled the pale-gray iris.

"As you swam out, I called to my crew that the ship had caught fire—you were quitting her like rats—I could see it with my glass close to the deck, under the fallen foremast—it must be a pot of Greek fire turned over, for it burned without smoke. Couldn't the lubbers see it in the scupper vents? So when she blew, not one of 'em guessed the truth."

What was the truth of the Saratoga's *sinking, Murad Reis? It was not what was given out, if I believe the intimations of my soul. Did Our Eliza's captain have the only glass—or the only witnesses of standing—in his white hands? What great cause was served?*

"What had I to gain?" Murad Reis asked, languidly blowing smoke. "Since you're a dead man, I'll tell you. My rascals fight for loot—each man his appointed share. He'll risk his life for it, but if there's no booty to be got, he'd rather lie in the sun. We'll have many fights with Yankees in the next year, and we don't want the word to go out that they'll sink their own ships rather than strike their colors, for that's madness worse than a dervish's, and Mohammedans hold madmen in holy terror. The *Vindictive* fought us to hell as it was, if 'twill comfort your soul. What have we got to show for it but a leaking ship—we'll have to turn back to Tripoli with our cruise barely begun —forty-two men lost in trade for your thirteen, and a prize of three breathing corpses!"

"That's the exact number, sir. You kept a good count."

" 'Twasn't easy, with so much running back and forth, but I thought it about right. You other three are no longer Whitman, Jones, Smith, however you've signed on. What's your given name?"

"Homer, sir."

He looked a little startled. "Slur it a little, and that's Omar in Arabic. But I don't think it will be any use to you. We'll call the black by the number fourteen—fifteen for the little cockerel, sixteen for you. You'll be put ashore, and before we sail again, I'll tell my crew you were set upon by street gangs—Yanks are hated in Tripoli almost as bad as in London—and stoned to death. But that won't happen. You're going out on the desert to disappear. Now what's that in your pocket, fastened to your belt by a black thong?"

"It's my silver watch, wrapped in oilskin."

"Does it keep good time?"

"It loses only a minute in twenty-four hours."

"Hand it over, for you'll not need to count minutes where you're going—you'll not even need a calendar to count years, perhaps thirty of 'em, before your bones are dry instead of wet." He paused, relishing some secret meaning that was meant to make me quail, but my face was turning into stone, and he talked on. "I'll keep the turnip as a souvenir."

"May I keep the thong?" I asked. "It's only horsehair with brass ends, and I've a sentimental attachment to it."

"Certainly, and I trust 'twill be a comfort to you, for I'm a man of sentiment myself."

It would not be my only comfort. Another was my youth, whereby I need not count years as a spendthrift counts a last handful of coins in his purse. And as I careened into darkness, I found strange solace in the limitless range and sweep of human fate. Fate that had brought me to this pass could bring me to any other within the bourn of man.

2

The effort made to conceal the arrival of three American prisoners at Tripoli boded us no good. Irons were welded on us before we left the ship—mine the heaviest in the armory; but I did not complain at that, because thus the chains running from wrists to ankles were extra long, giving me full leg and arm room. Turkish rags of dress concealed our white skins. Then we were brought on one of the *Ayesha's* boats to a deserted wharf far from the busy docks we had seen from the ship, and bundled into a kind of goblin dress, with eye and nose holes, used by women in extreme purdah when forced to go abroad. Hustled into a donkey cart, we jolted over cobblestones, then along a shingled beach. Half-suffocated, we were hauled out at last and put on baggage camels. When dawn broke, we were on a desert of pale brown sand, limitless in every direction except north. That way we could see the distant sheen of the Mediterranean coast, the green of the oasis, and a cluster of white specks marking the town.

Thus began a two-day journey toward some high rugged hills that our Tripolitan camel tenders called the Jebel. Long before we arrived, we knew the first agonies of thirst—our ration of water was hardly half our guards', and our bodies were not yet innured to the burning sands and sky—and the sharp pain and soul shock of the lash laid across our backs. We came at last to a small but green oasis at the foot of a bleak wadi. There were several wells, a large grove of date palms native to the desert, and sick coconut palms imported from the steamy coasts; and in the shade stood one imposing house with a tiled roof and several huts of baked mud roofed with split palm trunks under packed earth. Here, we were to learn, dwelt the quarry master, Sidi el Akir, and the foremen and guards. Up the hill in the glaring sunlight rose a palisade of tree trunks, each topped by a wooden spike hardened in fire. This structure, about a hundred feet square, was the life-long home of about a hundred quarry slaves, their number now increased by three.

These were work hours, so the gate was open and the pen seemed deserted. An off-duty guard who had seen the approach of our little caravan spoke to our captain, made entries in a leather-bound book, and led Sparrow, Jim, and me around one end of the stockade, where an iron hook, about six feet long, jutted out from the wall. He pointed to it, and snarling like a dog, told us something in Arabic. When we were brought inside, I saw a gaunt form of a man lying on a black cloth. It was naked except for a few rags; the pale color and scant beard of the face turned toward the burning-glass sky suggested that he was an Arab. The enclosure contained nothing else but a hole dug in the sand for a latrine, a water trough made from a hollowed tree trunk, a much larger wash trough that could be emptied into a sluice under the wall, and about a hundred rolls of cloth scattered a few feet apart, no doubt similar to the woolen robe, called aba, that comprised the Arab's bed.

Such robes were tossed to us three newcomers. Also, since we had not tasted food since the night before, we were given a handful of dates and allowed to drink from the trough. The guard now walked to the still form by the wall, gazed at it fixedly, and then bent to touch its eyelid. At once he turned, snapping his fingers, and beckoned to Jim and me. We came, our chains rattling.

"*Muerto*," he said—quite companionably for one so exalted—pointing at the form. Then he told us in sign language what we could do.

It was only to drag the corpse about a cable's length up the hill and leave him there. I thought to pretend to misunderstand and heave it on my shoulder—in respect to the human being it once lodged—but the danger of plague and some half-glimpsed necessity of living long caused me to do precisely what my lord commanded—to take hold of one bare foot while Jim gripped the other and drag the body to the appointed place. As we came near, a flock of hideous vultures hopped along the ground and took to heavy flight. They had feasted richly only a few days before, we thought from the signs. Now their table was spread again.

"Ye reckon we did wrong not to play Ezra Owens's game 'at day we went overside?" Jim asked me, his eyes wheeling slowly to mine.

"We did more right than we knew," I answered.

By now the sun of molten brass had pitched and set; with the failing light the arid air turned chill, and the gathering dusk gave out metallic sounds in cadence. As they loudened slowly, I recognized them as the heavy rattle of many chains of men walking in step. Peering through a crack in the palisade, I saw bobbing torches. The rhythmic noise frightened me more than any experience of my slavery so far— I did not know why—and vibrated the bones of my head before the gate opened and the long file of dust-encrusted human forms trudged through.

All were naked except for loincloths, proof that none were Mohammedans. As they washed in squads of eight, the torchlight glistened on a rapidly increasing number of ebony black or dark brown skins. These were not all Africans: a few with long hair and bearded faces I took to be Indians, quite possibly lascars captured at sea. Several more were pale brown or brunette Levantines of various sorts, Armenians, Cilicians, and Maltese; and at least six were either Circassians or Western Europeans. But only one of the latter—a powerfully built man with reddish hair, big features, and a devil-may-care expression, quite possibly a black-sheep member of a respectable Irish family—gave me a second glance.

After the washing, two Negroes gave each man a palm leaf on which was scooped black beans and several flaps of unleavened bread. The men ate rapidly, licked the palm leaves, and threw them into the latrine. Then all but a few immediately spread their woolen abas and lay down.

The man who had noticed me sauntered to my place and crouched on the sand beside me.

"I'm an Irish gentleman known here as Kerry," he told me in the warm and winning voice of his kind. "Who are you?"

"I'm known here as Sittash."

"That means sixteen, and evidently you've learned a lesson or two already, and mean to get along the best you can."

"Yes, sir, I do."

"I'm glad of that, and I'll tell you why. My teammate, a Salib—they're Christian Semites—began to break up a few days ago; this morning they couldn't whip him to his feet, and since he's not in sight, I assume he's been dragged to the Hill of Mercy to feed the birdies. Well, it stands to reason you'll be put in his place. The little larrikin who came with you hasn't long enough reach to cleave stone with me, and the black will probably get a shade lighter duty, for our job foreman is a black Mohammedan from the Sudan who favors his own color. A teammate who can't face the facts could make me a great deal of trouble—slow down my output, get me a lot of whippings along with his own. I'd arrange for a bad accident to happen to a man like that."

"It's a fair warning, and I'll return everything you said."

"Good for you. Now let me guess how you came to fall into the Pasha's tender hands. You're a Yank, and the hostilities that we heard were threatened have begun."

"That's a good guess."

"But it doesn't explain you and the other Yank and a Negro without rings in his ears or nose being sent to this extremely exclusive club."

"I didn't know why it was."

"I think that's a lie, but you've your own reasons for telling it, and I'll not gainsay you. Now I'll give you a free English translation of this club's Arabic name—the Sepulcher of Wet Bones. Pretty ugly, isn't it? But wet means only not yet dry. Very imaginative people, the Arabs. Your being sent here means you're never to be offered for ransom or for sale or associate with any prisoner who will live to tell the tale."

"What tale?"

"The one you might tell him—the one you may tell me."

"Is there always one?"

"In every case where the prisoner is something more than the dullest workhorse. This quarry belongs to the Pasha. It is well run and reasonably profitable, but your services here could be done by a Nubian Negro worth, in the great slave markets of Constantinople, about a hundred dinars. You would bring five hundred to become an attendant on some Central Asian sultan or artisan, or clerk for a merchant or manufacturer. Did you invade the harem of some noble Tripolitan? Did you cause a reis to lose face?"

"Our ship's company did. I'll tell you later. You say this quarry is well run. I don't see how that could be true if the slaves are worked or whipped or starved to death in a few years."

"We're not. We labor from sunrise to sunset—that's the Mohammedan law—which means from ten to fourteen hours, depending on the season. Going back and forth takes two hours more out of the day. We're given enough to eat to keep us lean but strong. We're whipped for any idleness or the slightest offense, but rarely more than twenty strokes, after which shock sets in and the man is not up to mark the following day. By the way, you get twenty every month whether you earn 'em or not. That's a matter of principle with our quarry master, Sidi el Akir. He thinks it keeps us out of temptation— maybe it does. He, too, is a Tripolitan—use the generic term Moor—

as opposed to an Arab. I suppose you know they all speak Arabic."

"Yes."

"A sound man can last twenty years or more. The climate is quite healthful when you've become adapted to it. By turning into animals —not nearly as difficult as you think—men have lived and labored here for thirty, even forty years. Those who don't, go mad and are very soon destroyed."

"You said, too, the quarry was profitable. How could it be, if they have to transport marble on camelback for seventy miles——"

"You're a cool 'n. I wonder what the story is. The marble here is known as Carthage onyx, highly translucent, of very rich browns and yellows. It's in high demand all over the Orient for temples and palaces and is costly as alabaster, but the bed is not large and devil-ishly hard to work. We get it out in thin slabs with drills and wedges, and it's sent in five-hundred-pound loads by baggage camels. The men who want to live long—not necessarily the more intelligent— wear a cloth over their mouths and noses. It's hot and uncomfortable, but it stops most of the fine dust. Those who don't use it wear out fast. I can foretell you'll wear it."

"Yes."

"Now I've got a question to ask you. I'll explain its importance later. Are you a boozer?"

"I like a drink——"

"That isn't what I meant. Does booze count more with you than self-respect—life, women, everything?"

His voice changed, and his hands shook.

"Not one of those things, let alone all."

"It does with me. Indirectly, that's why I'm here. After a terrific bout in Lisbon, I found myself on a Dago ship without a passport. I jumped her in Tripoli, got some fig wine, and knocked down the *Chiah* in the palace *kiffer*—he's the direct representative of the Pasha and next to the Reis Effendi in rank. It's a wonder I wasn't hung alive on an iron hook. To avoid trouble for everybody, I was quietly shipped out here."

I nodded, waiting for the business.

"Every Friday—that's tomorrow—the Mohammedan Sabbath, we're issued a pint of palm toddy made from those wretched coconut trees. The quarry master believes that it 'thins our blood' and winks his eye at the fifteen or so per cent of alcohol. One pint gives about twenty minutes' glow. But I've a little jug hidden away, and if two people will give me their ration—and there is one left who does—I've enough for one night's drunk. It doesn't faze me the next day—not an old guzzler like me—and it gives me something to live for."

"The man who died today gave you his portion?"

"Sold it to me, rather."

"What will you give me for mine?"

"Good advice. Oriental sayings—in perfect Arabic—to please the foreman. I was once considered a rising Orientalist at Dublin University. I can be useful to you, Sittash, if you're my friend."

"I agree for the time being."

"Thank you. I can't thank you enough. If I could go to bed drunk every night—not soaked, not crazy, just gentlemanly drunk—I'd be happy as a king."

"Do you mean it?"

A deeply moving dignity came into his face.

"Why not? I'm a good workman—I get almost no disciplinary whippings—that one good dusting every month makes me remember public school and cleanses my soul. I've no fault to find with the hard labor and the simple food, for what would I be doing if I weren't here? One prolonged bout after another, ending in red spiders and white mice—jail sometimes, always disgrace, shaming every one who loves me. Now they believe me dead. I am dead in a sense more true than you know, most of us are—this is the Sepulcher of Wet Bones; I have all the advantages of being dead, yet I labor and eat and sleep —the last two the reward of the first—and when I can lay hand on the wherewithal, I can still get drunk."

"I see." But my eyes darkened, as though in prelude of death.

"What have you got to live for, Sittash?"

"A commemoration."

"That means an observance—or an action—in someone's memory."

"I'll let it go at that."

"Good night, Sittash."

"Good night, Kerry."

I lay down on my aba and went to sleep and began to dream. Before the stars began to pale, I was wakened by the beat of a kettle-drum. The day had begun. The first day of how many? It would be unmanly to count in tens. . . . My common sense denied I could count in hundreds. . . . What remained but thousands?

The first thousand days had gone by.

As Murad Reis had told me, I needed no watch to tell the hours, no calendar to count the days. The procedures of the prison served as my sun dial, and in my dreams I heard shipbells thin and far away. My first thought in the morning was the sum of my days as a slave, yesterday's figure plus one more; and there was no use of cutting notches in a log or adding a pebble to a pile, since I never came even close to confusing the number.

The most marked change in me was a reshaping of my body that at first alarmed me. Although my one hundred and sixty pounds had been all brawn and bone, I gradually lost weight until Kerry guessed me at no more than one hundred and thirty-five. My flat muscles became longer and thinner, my legs and arms lost their look of power, and my torso was so gaunt that my shoulders appeared ungainly broad. But I came to believe at last that the transformation was the almost miraculous fulfillment of my needs. Kerry and I were invariably given the heaviest and hardest labor of the gang—I could credit no reason other than the quarry master's spite against imperious England and hence all English-speaking people—and since my teammate was not quite equal to it, I must be more than equal to save us both from nightly beatings by the guards.

Little Enoch Sutler, whom his shipmates knew best as Sparrow, and whose name in the prison was Kamstash, remained as dauntless of spirit and as true a man as ever walked the deck of the *Vindictive*. But if his fortunes seemed better than mine in the eyes of our fellow slaves, I greatly feared they were worse. Because of his small size, he had been put in the finishing gang, whose task was to smooth and then polish with pulverized lava the thin blocks of granite hewn from the bed. In spite of constant wetting of the abrasive, some of it was breathed in along with other dust too fine to be caught by a face cloth. According to prison lore, the finishers lived better and died sooner than any other gang. Like all the rest, Sparrow developed a cough and bloodshot eyes.

In the depths of Sparrow's mind I was still Mate Whitman—even Cap'n Whitman, now that Cap'n Phillips had been gone so long. If I had bade him do so, he would have asked for harder but healthier labor; but I could not do so against his own will. He greatly feared that the foreman, irked by what he might deem ingratitude for mercy given, would put him at some task beyond his strength and lay him open to the torment of the kurbash. It was quite possible; and since Captain Phillips had appointed the duty, to me alone, I had no right to ask him to live longer than he desired.

Of us three survivors, the lot of 'Giny Jim was the happiest. Long before they could communicate with words, he had made friends with a tar-black Nubian named Zimil, a former slave who had been permitted to embrace Islam and had since become second-in-charge of the palm groves. Zimil had managed to have Jim put to work there, with plenty of dates and coconuts to eat and the delicious milk to drink. Since he could not climb trees in our heavy irons, he got shed of all except light ankle rings. Although he still slept in the stockade, the two were inseparable in daylight hours, and could soon talk an astonishing mixture of Arabic and English.

Sparrow and I profited indirectly from the friendship, since Jim never missed an opportunity to give us dates and coconut meat. Of equal importance to me, almost every night he was able to bring into the stockade a wooden flask containing a quart of palm toddy, one of the strongest fermented drinks, nearly the match of the fortified wines of Spain. This he slipped into my hands; I in turn sold it to Kerry, but at a higher price than a little advice and a few Arabian sayings. Thereby I slowly obtained possession and use of a wonderful tool.

It was no less than the Arabic language in its pure and classic form. If Kerry's teaching while we labored was assiduous, that night he got pleasantly drunk; but if he slacked the task, he remained unpleasantly sober. It demanded strong application of mind on his part as well as on mine, patience, and much use of dusty throats, but when he found that I stood firm—and drunkards can hardly believe that of anyone—he usually earned his tipple.

All this while we three had listened in hidden and desperate hope for news from Tripoli. None was good until December, 1803, when Kerry heard a vague rumor of a large American frigate and a heavy-gunned schooner blockading the pirate stronghold.

On Christmas Eve, a brutal guard named Caidu summoned Kerry and me for what I feared was a whipping. Instead of leading us to the post, he let us squat by the watch fire while he seated himself grandly on a bench. At once he began to speak rapidly in Arabic, which I had barely started to learn.

When he paused, Kerry turned to me.

"The gentleman begins by reminding us that since tonight begins a great Christian feast, he is going to give you some news of great interest to all Yankees. And you'd better brace yourself against something pretty rocky."

Caidu spoke again to considerable length. I did not glance into his malicious face, but I could not keep from watching Kerry's.

"Sittash, have you Americans a fine frigate named—as near as I can catch it—the Fee-deff?"

"Yes, the *Philadelphia*."

"Well, the bastards have captured it."

"I don't believe it."

"He seems pretty damned cocksure. Thirty-two guns——"

"That's right."

"About three hundred officers and men——"

"They could guess that——"

"Don't fool yourself, Sittash. They've got her, I'll bet five quid. America's a little nation and far from here. Well, how about us splitting what your friend brought tonight? It's Christmas Eve, and we'll toast to the old brig yet."

"Thanks, but he brought the same to me and to the little fellow. We'll celebrate Christmas as merrily as we can."

I would hear more of the *Philadelphia*, I thought—Caidu would not miss letting me know how she had been given a Moslem name, the flag of Tripoli flown from her mainmast, and sent forth with a swarthy crew to capture Yankee traders. But he remained queerly silent, and it was in February, that 'Giny Jim—entered in the book as Oribatash—finished her story.

"It come out better dan we 'spected," he said, "but don't you tell nobody but Sparrow, 'cause Zimil, he got it from de quarry mas', and if it gets out, he'll s'picion Zimil tol' me, and hell would be to pay."

"I won't even tell Kerry."

"The *Philadelphia* was lyin' in Tripoli harbor, guarded by de guns of de forts. But some o' our boys sneak in at night in a ketch and set her afire, so de pirates couldn't use her 'gainst us, and she burn to de waterline, praise God!"

He fell silent then, and in his eyes was a vision. I saw it too—a smaller but no less gallant ship for a second bathed in flame. . . .

The American war with Tripoli—which I was once too proud to call a war—was waged fitfully for a year and a half more. Although there were no decisive battles, the Pasha had lost at least one frigate and several gunboats and had reduced his blood-price for his American prisoners by more than two-thirds. When he surrendered at last, how many would be returned? Would the Yankee admirals be content with the *Philadelphia* men, or would they scour the remote slave pens for countrymen captured in unrecorded piracies and spirited away?

Sometimes I visioned marchers across the desert, flying a bright flag, playing "Yankee Doodle," coming to burn our stockade to the ground and hanging any whipper who had ever laid lash to a Yankee back or kurbash to the sole of a Yankee foot. It was at least a fair hope. And until it had been fulfilled or failed, I could not run desperate risks with Sparrow's, Jim's and my own life in an attempt to escape.

In the blaze of summer, four years and four days after I had met a dark-haired girl roaming the beach of Malta, the hope failed. Sparrow was the first to bring me word. He had had it from an English-speaking marble buyer who had paused in his survey to watch him polish the beautifully marked onyxlike stone.

"We assembled a great big naval force in front of the town," Sparrow told me. "The *muley* tol' me—and he was right polite and nice—we had six frigates, four or five brigs and schooners, a dozen or more gunboats, and a sloop of war. The Pasha seen he couldn't do nothing against a force like that, and besides another American, a General named Eaton, led a army of Moors and Arabs and some Greeks and a few of our boys from about Alexander clean to Derna— six hundred miles it was—and captured Derna. He was going to put Hamet Pasha on Yussuf's throne to make peace with us. So Yussuf seen he'd better not fight us no more, so he let the *Philadelphy* men go for sixty thousand dollars and signed a peace treaty to leave our ships be."

Sparrow paused, a strange expression on his small, peaked face.

"Is that all?" I asked.

"Aye, sir—'cept our ships went home."

"They wouldn't if they'd known we were here."

"You can lay to that, Cap'n."

"Our boys who were with General Eaton—I reckon they went home, too."

"Yes, and I wonder if we can call 'em our boys any more, us so lost and forgotten for so long."

He coughed hard, and tears rolled out of his bloodshot eyes. He wiped them furiously away with the back of his hand.

"They are our boys as long as we live," I said. "They've lost us, but we haven't lost them. Hang on with your teeth and fingernails and everything you can, as though you were in the tops of the Old

Bitch in a full-reef gale. As soon as the time's ripe—and it may not be very long—we'll leg it. It's a better hope than I've ever told you."

"Then don't tell me now. If they got wind I knew anything, they could make me cough it up. I couldn't stand no real long whippings any more."

"You can stand anything you have to, Enoch Sutler. You're one of *Vindictive's* men. But we've talked too long, and I'll bring you the good word later."

He nodded and quickly turned away. I waited to speak to 'Giny Jim. To carry messages or tokens from any prisoner or slave was an offense against the Pasha punishable by a hundred blows of the kurbash, while the sender thereof must die on the iron hook, yet Jim might know some camel driver or baggage wallah whom he would dare ask to run the dreadful risk for such reward as we might sometime, somehow, pay. If he consented, it would be more likely for friendship's sake alone. *Sahabti*—the Arabic address of friend—has great meaning throughout Islam. Poor people everywhere set more store on friendship than do the rich.

There came upon me a sense of urgency, akin to panic, that dizzied my brain. That way lay death.

CHAPTER 9

Token of Hope

1

'GINY JIM recalled a Negro camel wallah named Giafar who passed this way three or four times a year and with whom he had drunk many horns of palm toddy. When Giafar had admired an ostrich skin Jim owned, its beautiful plumes stained with blood, that Jim had got when a mortally wounded cock strayed close to the oasis, Jim gave it to him to take to his wives and children somewhere on the hot side of Ghaira. Now that Jim could talk a bastard Arabic taught him by Zimil, they had greatly enjoyed each other's company at their far-apart meetings.

"Is Giafar slave or free?" I asked.

"He free."

"Does that mean he can go with any caravan captain who employs him?"

"He does 'at already. He like what we call a tramp in 'Giny. And he so good wif camels he no trouble gettin' a job."

"If you asked him to, would he carry a message for me clear to the Baeed Oasis?"

Jim's brow became furrowed with deep thought, then he made his answer in the argot that the *Vindictive* men had known and loved well.

"I reckon when he got around to it, he mo' o' less will."

But nine months fled—and fleeing from me was what they seemed to do, vanishing like the duration of a dream in the deep of night, dropping out of my life with only a hole left where they had been—before Giafar's kismet bore him this way again. Day in and day out during this while, I had noticed no change in Sparrow. But on the day Jim told me that this watch was over at last—at best only a fragment of the time required for one chance to succeed or fail—I recalled how Sparrow had looked on the day that it began, my gaze probing back nine months to behold his face, and compared it with the way he looked now. Then I knew he had changed for the worse, and unless the slow deterioration was arrested before long, he would not be with me at journey's end.

"Did you tell Giafar what I want of him?"

"Nay, suh, but I tol' him you wanted to speak to him."

"Would the chance be better if you told him, or I did?"

"I don't know, Cap'n, but you's the right one."

I did not gainsay that. I should have known it beforehand.

"I'll take him to de quarry high sun tomorrow to watch de marble bein' cut. You make out like you gotta pump ship, and since de boss man neva let you do it on de bed, you walk to de little gully. We'll be on de knoll and start down. I'll stop lak I speak to you, and you look at me when you talk, but he'll know it's for him. Nobody can hear you if you talk quiet. Whatever you got for him, you lay on dat big white boulder. He'll pick it up after you start back to do wo'k."

During the long wait Jim and I had discussed a dozen different ways of effecting a brief meeting between Giafar and me, but since most of them had depended on careful timing, this was the simplest and the soundest yet proposed.

"Tomorrow morning, while you're taking him to the quarry—not tonight, because his tongue might become loosened by palm toddy —ask him if he has ever heard of Sheik el Beni Kabir, a horse breeder of the Baeed Oasis in the Libyan desert."

"I sho will."

The night passed, not quite like other nights, the sun rose with a somewhat different aspect, I ate and trudged to work aware of more color and changing lights than on other mornings. When the sun rose high, the two black men came to the quarry. Jim was often seen there, to bring a message between bosses or to borrow tools; and visitors from the caravans were not an unusual sight, so the guards did not glance at them twice. When they were on the knoll, I signaled to the foreman in our custom; as usual when he was in a good humor, he nodded and did not appear to watch me as I made for the little gully. At that moment the two visitors started down the knoll. As they came nigh me, Jim stopped and spoke to me.

"Giafar knows him. He's helped drive his horses to de Big River. Speak quick."

"In Allah's name, will you strive to take to Suliman, Sheik el Beni Kabir, a little horsehair band I'll leave on the rock, and tell him it is from his son in the Sepulcher of Wet Bones?" I asked in the Arabic tongue, facing Jim but my eyes turned to meet Giafar's.

"By Allah, I will."

I leaned a moment against the rock as though to wipe off sweat, then started back to my post. The guards did not look at me, nor did I see any sharpening of their idle gaze fixed on the two Negroes. Presently they walked on. All that day I watched fellow prisoners go to the gully on the common errand, but none stopped and stared at the rock, and I could believe that the hank of horsehair with brass ends was on its way.

How long a way? My heart that had beat staunchly with no support but hope and resolution, sank like a stoved boat.

2

Hours, days, phases of the moon, whole moons, and seasons fled by and away almost, it seemed, as if compressed into one drab, dimly remembered yesterday. In my waking life I strove to protect Sparrow and Jim. That striving required no magnanimity, no self-sacrifice; they were all who were left of my shipmates, and it seemed I needed them more than they needed me—that the ship that I must bring into port could not sail without them. In my dreams I felt no great concern for Jim—he moved silently and gracefully through them, climbing trees but never falling, surmounting every difficulty, evading every peril—but I fought endlessly and terribly for Sparrow. Now in that gray world of dreams I had another charge. It was the token-bearer Giafar, journeying through illimitable deserts toward a great dun pasture somewhere beyond the last oasis, where ran the mares and stallions of Suliman, Sheik el Beni Kabir.

There came the day that Giafar had been gone a year. Just short of six years ago, I had become a slave. My most vivid life was in dreams—therein I knew conflict, victory and defeat, ships, seas, and storms, and sometimes the ecstasy of love realized in the flesh but with some paramour whose face I saw mistily and never recognized. If I had dared reveal my mastery of Arabic—it remained a last shot in my locker for what sudden and secret use I could not foresee—I could have established a stronger human bond and even a kind of companionship with my fellow slaves; as it was, I listened without speaking, always on the outskirts of some dreary cluster of half-entities, and my only confidants were Jim, Sparrow, and Kerry.

Of the rich stock of Kerry's mind, I still made use. If, during our day's labor, he had the energy and patience to give me my fill of instruction, his fee was enough palm toddy to get mildly drunk. If he sulked or gibed or ranted, he must confront the night cold and ghastly sober. Often he complained that he had taught me all he knew, but by delving a little deeper I uncovered another layer of learning, or broke into a storehouse he had forgotten, or found a hidden vein.

So I myself could wait a great deal longer without taking harm. If after two years, or three, or five, I must at last abandon hope of an answer to my message, there were other chances, however hopeless they seemed now, that a desperate and cunning man might take. But on the first dark of July 1, 1807, as our dust-smeared file neared the open door of the stockade, I went dizzy and must brace my knees against falling when the guard Ibrim stopped us, spoke to the attendant guard, and then approached Kerry and me.

"You two Christian dogs step out of file," he told Kerry in Arabic.

"We are your protected, effendi," Kerry replied.

"Ker-ree, foul Giour though you are, you know our tongue," Ibrim declared when the file had trudged on.

"Aye, O Caputan."

"Then speak what I bid you unto the Yanki called Sittash, in the tongue you two employ, adding nothing and leaving nothing out."

"Allah bear witness!"

"When Suliman ibn Ali, Sheik el Beni Kabir, was on Malta many years ago, he had business with a Yanki with dun hair and blue eyes, whose given name sounded not unlike that of Omar ibn Al-Khattab, faithful servant of the Prophet whom may Allah bless."

"Bless him, O Allah!"

"The business being uncompleted, the great Sheik spoke of him to the Yankis treating with our Pasha, who told him this man had been lost at sea. But it came to Suliman in a dream that it was not so, and it became his kismet to search for him more diligently, whereby he heard from the Reis Effendi of a Yanki of his description becoming our Pasha's slave and sent hither. Therefore in his journey from the capital to Kufurustan, he has come seven marches out of his way to see if he is the one. Ask this Yanki his given name."

Kerry turned to me. "It may be death and it may be luck. You'll have to decide for yourself."

"Homer," I answered, slurring it so that it sounded almost exactly like the Arabic pronunciation of Omar.

"There is no majesty or might save in Allah!" Ibrim proclaimed. "Ker-ree, tell the Yanki Omar to come with me to the Well of Fatima's Tears by which the great Sheik has pitched his tent, and there he may speak to him in a tongue that they both know."

My chains jangled in the dark. The dull red of a distant fire swiftly turned bright gold. We came to a large and luxurious pavilion. Ibrim spoke to a wild-looking Arab sentinel who vanished within. At once the door curtain was again drawn back and Suliman emerged, followed by an unbridled, unsaddled horse. The sentinel held high a thornwood torch that threw a garish light.

I recognized him instantly. I could hardly believe he had changed so little in this long time. He was more richly dressed, his beard slightly more gray, a linen turban had replaced the high wool cap, but his slight form and bony face were the perfect reality of a long-dimmed image. But there was more than this to read in his countenance and unconscious actions. In them I somehow saw myself, as though I were looking in a mirror.

He gazed at me first in disbelief, then in sore trouble. As the beautiful sable-brown mare nudged him for pettings, he spoke in an undertone to Ibrim.

"Is this Omar known as Sittash?"

"Yea, O Sheik. Isn't he the one?"

"It comes to me that he's the one, but he's greatly changed."

"Men change greatly in the Sepulcher of Wet Bones, or they die."

"Allah have mercy!" He turned and addressed me in a gentle voice. "Do you speak Arabic?" he asked in that tongue.

"In secret only," I answered in English.

"I will try—I forget—most all. Speak truth, by the bread and salt. I make speak to Reis Effendi. He put you with trust to me. If I take you to my oasis, work on stud farm—must you—you must swear before your God not to escape. So?"

There it was, this soon, as solid and tall as a mountain. But there might be a pass. . . .

"In my great need I must speak."

"Speak, my son."

"Will you take two more?"

"Nay, I cannot."

"One more?"

"Nay, nay. Not once in Yussuf's reign did man come forth from Sepulcher of Wet Bones. It be Yussuf's pride. If Reis Effendi need not my tribe against Egyptians, he would not let one go. And when I die, you must go back."

"You can't take me unless I swear?"

"No, my son."

"Tell the guard I must speak to the other Yankees about the business you had with me—say I've forgotten some point of it. Say you want me to return in an hour."

Suliman did so. Ibrim marched me back to the stockade, but long before I arrived, it had come to me to speak only to 'Giny Jim, and there was not much need of that. I did not want Sparrow to see my face by torchlight.

Jim was still at the date racks with his friend Zimil. We stood together in the warm dark, Ibrim in easy sound of our voices. I told him quickly how it was.

"You know I can git along all right," he said when I was through.

"Yes, I know that."

"Dis here is what you've got to figga. Whiles you can't break no oath to him who stood by you, maybe you can make friends among 'em sheiks, and send letters by the drivers, and such as that. Maybe you can git 'em to help git Sparrow and me out. You might even git a letter to the President of U. S. A. Wouldn't 'at help Sparrow more'n stayin' here wif him?"

"Where would Sparrow be, by the time help came—if it ever comes?"

"If you order me to, Cap'n, I'll answer 'at true."

"It's my order."

"His bones would be dry up yonder on de hill."

123

"You can lay to that."

"Worse 'n 'at, when his time come to die, you wouldn't be wif him. I'd be wif him, if I could, but I can't put courage in his heart like you kin, so when Old Man come for him, he could look Him in de face. Wifout you, he'd die 'fraid and shamed, not brave and proud."

"So you see what that means, James Porter." I called him by his real name without thinking.

"Aye, suh, I see plain."

I turned away, and still in Ibrim's care, trudged back to Suliman's pavilion. The sable-brown mare, excluded now from her master's tent and lying like a dog outside its door, heard the distant rattle of my chains and sprang up. "Is it he, Kobah?" Suliman called in Arabic to his pet. "Ah, my ears bring the sorrow-laden sound."

He came forth, and in the torchlight his face looked drawn.

"You—not—stay—the hour," he said in careful English.

"Nay, sir, I didn't."

"I fear your answer, but give it me."

"I can't go with you now, O Sheik."

"How soon can you go, if ever?"

"When I've lost one of my last two shipmates."

"How you give me word? My caravans can pass, only short out of way between Tripoli and Gjaria, summer and winter."

"Did you notice the rook's nest in the big acacia tree above the wadi as you came down to the oasis?"

He turned and spoke quickly in some dialect of the desert to the wild-looking Bedouin torch-bearer. The man nodded and salaamed.

"Hamyd marked it."

"It's been here as long as we have. If it's missing, I can go with you."

"Then, Omar, I bid you farewell."

He touched his hand to his forehead and his heart, tears flowing down his brown cheeks. In spite of my rattling chains, I made the same noble gesture, but my eyes stayed dry and burning from having lost the power to weep.

3

It seemed to me that in the few weeks following Suliman's departure, Sparrow's slow decline was arrested, if not changed to barely perceptible improvement. The thought of losing him was intolerable, and, hating the prospect of ever profiting by his death, I felt a renewed surge of energy and hope. These quarries had been worked by slaves for more than fifty years. In all that time, not one had made good his escape; some had been killed in the attempt and others who had fled into the desert had been brought back to be hung on the iron hook on the stockade wall. This did not mean that escape was impossible. Indeed, the complete conviction that it was, held by the guards and almost all the prisoners, was itself a loop in its walls.

Irons could be chiseled off. Food and water could be stored in limited amounts by favored slaves like Jim; camels might be stolen. The great chain I knew not how to break was the immense stretches of desert between us and any refuge. Flight through Tripoli to the sea was unthinkable without the prearranged help of friends or a bag of gold. The other coastal towns in conceivable reach were too small and far-scattered to be of use to us unless we could disguise successfully as natives, an almost impossible feat to aliens unsteeped in the country's language, lore, and ways. Westward lay the interminable sands of the Algerian Sahara. Southward stretched the empty wastes of the Fezzan and the Tibbu, a thousand miles of thirst before we might find shelter among the savage Negro tribes of the equatorial wilderness. Eastward the Libyan Desert, breached here and there by oasis, was a camel journey of forty days to the greenery of the Nile.

Our best, if not our only, hope lay in some fellow prisoner with friends in the country. Jim constantly searched for such a person—his guileless ways, easy address, black skin, and even corrupt Arabic were touchstones in gaining the confidences of the terror-stricken captives out of the Bush. Thus far he had found none to begin to fill our needs; but I pinned some little hope on a newcomer to the pen, a bold-looking, hard-bitten Englishman of my own age who did not admit to speaking Arabic, but whose manner breathed a long stay in North Africa. He might have many resources fitting him for an ally.

"You're a rum-looking cove," he told me at first sight.

He had a light, tough build, sandy-red hair, blue-green eyes, bold features, and a sardonic expression. I had no trouble finding out his odd name—Holgar Blackburn—or that he had run away from a workhouse in Devon at the age of fourteen. His family had been wiped out, not by the sea, but by a smallpox epidemic. Having only distant kinfolk whom he loved no more than they loved him, he had never again set foot on English soil.

"If you'd go back, you might find you are heir to a fortune," I said—a strangely ritualized joke around the prison.

"All they had for me there, they've given me already, and I've got it with me." He showed me an X mark burned deep on the back of his hand.

I had not noticed the mark. I think he had kept his hand turned palm up. It would be a serious handicap to a runaway.

"What caused it?" I asked politely.

"A barrel-stamping iron in the hands of the master. I had raided his larder and made off with a meat pie. He heated the iron and did the job to his satisfaction. I got off easy—I could have been hanged for breaking and entering—and that's quite a satisfaction."

At our next meeting he told me that he had sailed on a French ship that was captured by Moroccan pirates. Sold into slavery in Tripoli, he had taken the eye of an effendi and elevated to the Pasha's corps of Mamelukes, mainly blond Greeks and Thracians. But after winning a rare prize—permission to embrace Islam—he had suddenly made a break for freedom with ten thousand pesos of the corps' funds.

"If I had gone through the ceremony beforehand—circumcision and declaration of faith—I would have been counted a recanter and hung on the iron hook," he told me, grinning strangely. "As it was, I was sent to pass my declining years in the Sepulcher of Wet Bones."

"You've got a lot of years to decline."

"I'm of yeoman stock and country bred—from a little rented farm near Tavistock by the Cornish border. . . ." His voice died away and he peered sharply into my face. "That hit home, didn't it?"

"It hadn't ought to've. I've only been in Cornwall once, to my remembrance. I went with some friends into the country. I remember a big house called Celtburrow. We saw the moor——"

"Celtburrow was the seat of the Linden family, 'most as old as Adam. They've about gone to seed, but there was a beautiful woman whom I saw when I was a little boy. A little girl, her granddaughter, lived with her. The child's father was a naval officer and a great blood. I was caught stealing flowers—but all that makes a lot of difference to a bloody abandoned bastard in the Sepulcher of Wet Bones."

"That's right," I said with a small inward smile. "How did you come by the name of Holgar?"

"It's a variation of Orgar, Earl of Devon in the tenth century, who founded our great Abbey of St. Mary and St. Rumon. When you go to Tavistock, don't fail to see it."

"I won't. What were you saying about being country bred——"

"I was answering you about my living a long time. I'm tough enough of meat and bone, but I've got a fatal weakness. I'm unable to resist impulses if they're very strong. Some are criminal, and although you won't believe it, some are quite decent, and the latter can be as dangerous as the former. It's brought me this near to death at age twenty-eight, and will finish the business soon."

I could not help but believe him.

The same month that brought my hope of Holgar's help to a quick death, saw a dark shadow fall on a great hope. Sparrow wakened in the night with an attack of coughing that brought forth blood.

I heard the spasm, so prolonged and violent that I rose and went to him, although fearful of shaming him in the men's sight. He grinned at me in the torchlight and tried to hide the telltale flow. I pretended not to see it and slipped him a little bhang, another of Jim's provisions, to put him back to sleep.

"Thanks, Cap'n," he told me. "I'll dream I'm back on the Old Bitch." But I dreamed I stood on a lonely beach, watching the *Eagle of Maine* lurch broadside to the seas before she struck the rock.

Thereafter Sparrow broke up like a gale-racked ship on reefs. Both were a continuous, remorseless action, and although one took weeks and months and the other only hours, time meant little here, and they had something of the same shocking effect upon the mind. I had never known a better man than he—in the sense that sailors would use the expression, a most true and real sense. His small body and brain, reflecting his bright spirit, had been compact of all the male virtues—strength limited but fully appliable, quickness, economy of motion, wonderful resilience, coolness in times of stress, courage without rashness, loyalty to his own. The last three of these, qualities of the spirit more than flesh, would stay by him to his last breath, but the others melted away.

Late one summer afternoon a sudden gush of blood flooded the slab of marble under his hands. Thrice the long lash of Caidu's ox whip curled about his wasted form before a savage roar from the quarries made him leave his helpless prey to scourge the bare backs of the shouting, howling madmen in the pit. I was struck only once, partly because I stood still and silent and perhaps because Caidu was afraid; and the reason I did not join in the tumult was the clearly perceived reality that however I might share my fellow slaves' yearning for death, I must concede it nothing.

That night I laid Sparrow's aba in a corner of the stockade far from the watch lanterns. When I brought him some bhang to chew, he gave my arm a little tug, to let me know he had something to tell me. The drug must have eased his rasped throat, because his words came forth in a feeble voice without pain or strain or attacks of coughing. I could not make out his face in the heavy dusk, but I thought his eyes were burning.

"Cap'n, I've only a few days more," he said.

I thought to answer with false cheer that he had lots of life in him yet, and that men worse off than him had gotten well; but I remembered we were shipmates and I was his captain now, and I would not treat him so.

"I know it."

"I'll hate to leave you and Jim, me so lucky, lying and sleeping and never having to wake up in this world no more, the work done and the whipping done, while you and him must stand the misery and then the duty."

"Why do you put it that way?"

"'Cause that's what it is. I've known it from the first. When Ezra Owens and me was bending the fuse on the powder cask like you'd told us, he whispered to me the orders Cap'n Phillips gave you. To find out if that English lord betrayed us to the pirates and bring judgment on him."

"He said to bring him to lawful punishment."

"Thank God he didn't lay it on me. I could run him down and shoot him, but what good would that do, for he'd only be dead as I'll be dead 'fore the moon's full again? I don't want to think about it no more. It lays a dreadful burden on my mind. Now, Cap'n, I got three favors to ask of ye, two of 'em to do if ye can see your way, and one ye must do, for my soul's sake."

"Speak out, Enoch Sutler."

"One of 'em is for you yourself, if they'll let ye, and nobody helping you but Jim, to carry me up to the hill where them ugly birds is waiting."

"I'll do it if I can."

"If you live long enough, and have the means, I want you to go to Newburyport, where I was born, and inquire for Bessie Sutler, who's my baby sister, and for Calesta Peck, who is my aunt. You needn't bother about my parents, for my ma's dead and my pa went off and left us. But if you find Bessie and my Aunt Calesta, tell 'em I didn't do no great wrong, such as murder and treason and suchlike, and that I loved 'em to the last."

"I'll tend to that if I live long enough. Those two are easy, but I'm afraid the third one will be hard."

"'Twill be hard, but you can do it if you're the man I've took you for since first I knowed you. These next few days is going to be bad. They'll put that old whip on me plenty before they find out it ain't no use, and 'twill be hard for you to watch. So tell Jim to stay clear away, and you give me your promise, before God in heaven, and for the sake o' all the boys who're gone, you won't raise your hand."

"That's a heavy haul," I answered, hardly knowing what I was saying.

"Aye, but ye got to make it, for you're the cap'n, and everything 'pends on you. Let me hear you say it, or you'll do me mighty bad wrong."

"Enoch Sutler, I swear before God, and for the sake of our lost shipmates, that no matter what they do to you, I won't raise my hand against them."

Sparrow heaved a long sigh.

"You don't know how that comforts me, Cap'n Whitman. It's my part in the big duty—the part assigned to me by Almighty God—to protect you in this danger so you can live and carry out the rest. No matter how much you hear me holler—or maybe even beg 'em to let me be—you'll know it's just the flesh that's weak, and I'm standin' by the ship like Cap'n Phillips ordered us, and I'll die proud."

CHAPTER 10

Stout Dogs

1

Sparrow proved a true prophet. The next few days were bad. On the morning following my pledge-giving, he had difficulty getting to his feet, then staggered and fell. Only after three cuts by Caidu's whip did he rise, his face and his naked back both stained with blood, and join the file. Because Caidu had had the night watch, Ibrim and another guarded the quarry gangs; and by the mercy of Allah, they pretended not to see Sparrow's faltering hands and nodding head over the blocks.

On the second and third mornings, Sparrow rose and ate and took his place with the rest, but on the fourth, the cruel lash cracked six times against his shuddering form before he could lurch up; and meanwhile the men stood mute with dull, bestial faces, their chains hanging loose and silent. The fifth morning was one that every prisoner would remember as long as his mind lived, no matter how inured he was to violence and horror.

The ordeal began when Sparrow did not waken at the drum. Caidu kicked him once in the side, then gave him three brutal lashes with all his strength. Sparrow's body jerked at each one and short grunts came forth from his bloodstained lips, but he did not appear to waken. As Caidu turned away, I did not even dare hope he had left him to die in peace. As we ate and then formed our ranks, I was not the only man gray and glassy-eyed with ineffable dread. Now the gate was thrown open and Ibrim and his fellow guard took their places at the head and the foot of the file. Ibrim already carried an ox whip, and Caidu passed the bloodied one into the rear guard's hands. We knew what would happen now; we had seen the signs. He was not satisfied, monster that he was—the uproar the men had raised a few days before still stung him—and he took down the kurbash from its nail in the stockade wall.

It was a pliant cane made of rhinoceros hide, amber-colored and somewhat translucent and rather pretty in the eyes of those who did not know its use. It had a cutting edge for inflicting ineffaceable stripes and a blunt side for dealing extreme pain. Caidu turned it in his hand so that the blunt side was outermost. As he walked slowly toward Sparrow, a man behind me vomited on the ground.

Caidu sat down beside Sparrow and, clutching his ankle, raised his foot backward and up to expose the sole and instep. At the first blow another man retched, and as one after another fell in measured pace, hard as a carpenter's hammer driving a nail, the sickness ran up and down the file as might some instantaneous contagion. At first there was no sound other than the sobbing and retching of the vomiters and the dull thuds of the kurbash; but in a little while I heard a more terrible sound. Sparrow had roused up from his merciful trance and was uttering a shapeless yell at every blow.

Kerry's hand closed about my wrist, shaking but strong. I did not need its restraint; something stronger than either muscle or iron had me in its grip, and I watched steadfastly without sound or movement. Not so a man nearer to Sparrow, Kerry, and me than any other in the double file. He stood three ranks ahead of me and nearest to the torture. His name was Holgar Blackburn, and sometimes he had impulses that he could not disobey.

Like us all, Holgar wore chains between the shackles on his wrists and ankles. Yet I had never seen a man move so fast as Holgar moved in the three strides he took. His feet rose high and his arms rose and fell with them as in some grotesque, long-practiced dance, and thereby his chains remained taut enough not to rattle, but not too taut to impede his movements. The cry of warning from the watching guards broke forth too late. Caidu's back was to us, and his attempt to spring to his feet was far too late. After his third stride, Holgar kicked high with his right leg, at the same time taking a doubled length of the slackened chain in his savage grasp. The weapon was less than a foot long, but we knew well its weight, and Caidu had time to turn his head and anticipate the might of the blow in the instant ere it fell.

It was the last instant of Caidu's life. With that furious gigantic blow, the chain broke through his skull to the eyeline. We saw him topple back under a crimson geyser; and now there was no sound—the slaves watching with the stares of madmen—for Holgar was not quite done.

Alternately kicking high and bending low to keep his grip on the chain, he moved quickly to Sparrow's fore.

"Forgive me, little Yank, but it's for the best," he said.

"Hit hard, and Jesus bless you."

Again the chain fell, a tempered blow, but hard enough. Sparrow's taut body grew limp as a child's in slumber.

2

There followed a little pause. It was caused by the sudden arrest of the violent movements of Holgar's body; it was deliberate and in some way ceremonial. It put a period to the preceding action; it ushered Sparrow out. We waited in silence and immobility for what would follow.

Holgar wiped his mouth with the back of his hand and turned glittering eyes and a half-grin on Kerry.

"I say, Tipperary?"

"Kerry, not Tipperary," my workmate answered.

"I can speak Arabic as well as you can, but I want to talk to the big Yank before I go up the spout, so tell 'em you need him to help interpret something of great importance to Yussuf Pasha."

"Right."

"Now tell Ibrim that I'll submit to arrest. I could break some bones and maybe kill one or two, but I haven't the inclination."

"Ibrim Effendi!" Kerry intoned in Arabic.

"Ah!"

"I cannot understand the mutineer very well, for his accents differ from mine, even as the accents of Somaliland differ from those of Oman. Although I believe he said that he would surrender, I entreat that I may ask Omar known as Sittash, who knows that dialect, if I heard aright."

It was flawless, classical Arabic punctuated by Kerry's right forefinger in the palm of his left hand. His quick-thinking amazed me no more than his histrionics in the wake of horror and in presence of the blood-drenched dead. Nothing could be more Irish and at the same time better calculated to impress the Arab guards and gain our point.

"You have my leave to speak to Omar known as Sittash."

"If you've got anything to tell Holgar, you'd better blab it now," he said to me. "I'm doubtful if you'll have another chance."

"Holgar, I'll get you the pure resin of the hemp if I possibly can," I answered, looking at Kerry. "If I live and am able, I'll pay your debts and honor your memory and pray for your soul. Kerry, bring in about his important message for the Pasha."

Kerry responded instantly in Arabic.

"Ibrim Effendi, my workmate understood the Englishman well. He will surrender to you and he has secret tidings to tell you of great moment to Yussuf Pasha."

"They will have to be short," Ibrim answered grimly.

At that moment a panting guard appeared in the open door, followed in the next few seconds by our foreman and Jim's friend Zimil and several husbandmen of the plantation. There was a curious lack of excitement; they only stopped and stared. Last to come was the quarry master, Sidi el Akir, in the company of his gray-bearded scribe. Tremblingly, Ibrim told him what had happened.

The master acted quickly. Kerry, Holgar under guard, and I were led out the gate, followed by the free men. The gate was shut and its log dropped behind us, penning in the file of slaves; and we heard them howl as we tramped around to the western side of the building. Well they knew the business to be done there. An iron hook six feet long jutted out from the wall, eight feet above the ground. The guards had shown it to me when I first came to the Sepulcher seven years before; because our march to the quarry and back was by way of the eastern side of the stockade, I had not laid eyes on it since.

We stopped, and the master spoke.

"Which of you is Omar known as Sittash?" he asked.

Fearful that I would speak, Kerry pointed to me.

"Bid Omar speak to the slayer of Caidu and discover what are his tidings of concern to my Pasha, if indeed they are not a dog's trick to delay his doom. These Omar may recite to you to convey to me in Arabic."

Kerry looked at me, but spoke to Holgar.

"This must sound good, or they'll take it out on us. How about a big meteorite you could have found when skipping from Misda to Nulat with the paymaster's chest? Meteorites are greatly venerated by these Moslems. The Black Stone of the K'uba is one."

"Holgar, would there be any use to ask Sidi to reprieve you, while you lead a party to the meteorite?" I asked in English. "At least you'd have a chance to cut your throat——"

"For the love of God, don't do it. That's what they're expecting me to ask, then my eyes and ears and tongue would go before they hang me."

I would have known that, too, if my mind had not failed me.

"The prisoner will now give important tidings to Omar known as Sittash," Kerry told the Sidi in Arabic.

"I wanted to put you on to something, Yank," Holgar went on. "At first I decided against it—why torment you with it when old brother vulture would soon be on your bones? But you've survived and I think you alone, of all the gangs, may live to go free——"

"Make a few gestures as though describing a scene——"

"I heard all kinds of rumors when I was with the Mamelukes. The renegade pirate skipper who attacked your ship and his brother, called Hamed in Morocco, were American Tories who served as officers under Captain Tarlton in the American War. Tarlton was in Malta when your ship put out from there. He's my countryman and I hope to hell there was no connection——"

I could not bear for him to stand there, facing death by torture, using his last breath to tell me what I already knew or could find out.

"I'll attend to it, Holgar, without fail."

"Righto."

"The master's getting impatient. You've got one more turn to speak, so be ready to tell me what I can do to pay part of my debt."

Then I described to Kerry an imaginary scene near the foot of a wadi, the biggest Holgar had crossed on his third day's run from Misda. The hills looked so-and-so. The tamarisk thickets grew here and yon. The stone lay in a little crypt fashioned by afrites. . . . Touching hands to forehead with a rattle of chains, Kerry repeated all this, with various embellishments, to Sidi el Akir. The Sidi could not conceal his excitement; but at the end of the recital, he smiled haughtily into his grizzled beard.

"Have Omar known as Sittash ask the mutineer what reward he expects for this guidance to a lost stone from heaven?" he commanded.

"This is the last round, I think," Kerry told me.

"Holgar, you said there was something I could do for you if I live and go free. What is it?"

"You've got to take another name to go after what you want," Holgar answered. "Why not take mine? I'd be proud to have you wear it. Make a good showing for me in Tavistock."

"I'll take it and keep it and live up to it until I can go home."

I turned to Kerry, tried to speak, and could only shake my head. There was something upon me that had come from afar, and the fresh dawn air was sharp in my nostrils, and it seemed I went a little distance into death. Kerry turned white, then spoke with great resource.

"I understand what Holgar said then, O Sidi el Akir. He will ask no reward or no mercy, for he is a Frank of a great clan, brave as a dervish of Jahad. Why he has told us of the stone I know not, for it comes to me it will never be found, but it may be the spirit of the very Omar, whose name is akin to his, spoke through his lips."

"If he had asked for mercy, he would have received none," the Sidi answered. "He would be flayed, blinded, his tongue cut off, his eardrums broken, then thrown so that the hook would pierce his belly, and all day tomorrow he would dangle there, the cup of death brought close to his lips, but ever snatched away. But since he did not ask, this mercy shall I grant him. He will be thrown for the hook to pierce his chest, whereby the cup of death shall be brought speedily to his lips, and he shall empty it without respite. More, his body will not hang there until it falls, a shame and torment to the men within the walls, but it shall be taken down and dragged to the hill where the birds of death will quickly strip its bones."

"That will be a great mercy, O Sidi, if your men can throw straight."

"That's the hell of it," Holgar said under his breath.

"If they do not throw straight, and he is caught by the belly, it be the will of Allah. Now speak what I have spoken to Omar known as

Sittash, who, it comes to me, may be of the same clan as Holgar, for truly their names have something the same sound, and he may tell the condemned one, for the comfort of his soul."

When it was repeated to me, Kerry blue-lipped and gasping, I still could not speak. Then Holgar spoke.

"Ask if they'll let you do it, Big Yank."

"What?"

"The stroke of grace. I gave it to Little Yank. Those bully boys of Sidi's are edgy and will bitch it sure. They'd take my legs and arms and heave, but you can do it with a good grip on my ankles. You're strong as a lion—and you ought to see one jump over a six-foot *boma* with a man in his jaws. Your chains are longer than mine and will give you room enough. Great God, if you only could——"

Sidi spoke imperiously. "Bid the mutineer lie flat on his back."

"Both of you heard that," Kerry said. "You know what it means."

Holgar started to lie down. I had started to say to him, "If they'll let me, I will." Then, in one instant of recognition of my bond with him, I turned and touched my forehead and spoke to the Sidi the Arabic sentence that every prisoner knew.

"Your slave obeys your command."

As Holgar lay belly down, his head raised up and his gaze met mine, and I had never seen such human need in a brave man's eyes, or in any face such prayer that a cup might pass. I seized him by the shackles on his ankles, and as he stiffened to help me, heaved him off the ground. Whirling, I raised him higher and swung him faster, and now the Sidi was shouting orders that I need not hear because there was thunder in my ears to drown them out, and now lightning flashed before my eyes. Some of his followers sprang forward, but stopped outside the orbit of the human wheel, lest it strike them and break their bones, or a flying chain smash their skulls.

All these and the master, too, fell silent. Faster it sped until, at its fourth revolving, my arms and Holgar's body made one rigid projection level with the ground. By now I saw how high his chest must rise above my head in order to strike true; and with a great wrenching sweep, I swung him upward and backward.

My chains were long enough. The strength of my shoulders and loins stood the inhuman strain of stopping him in mid-air. My back bent, my arms lowered with great power, and hammerlike over my right shoulder, Holgar swept forward and down. Suddenly there was no more weight in my hands, and there was still no sound.

I raised my eyes. The point of the hook had passed cleanly through

Holgar's deep chest, and he dangled limply as a sparrow impaled on a thorn by a murderous shrike. His head bowed like a sleeper's, but his wide-open eyes were dark.

Sidi gazed and stroked his beard and was the first to speak.

"Behold a wonder!" he cried to his followers. "This dog of a Christian died with only a pinprick's flow of blood and without one wail."

"He was a stout dog, O Sidi, fit to unleash on the Day of Jahad, had it been his kismet," Ibrim replied. "So it comes to me that Allah showed him mercy."

"What of this Yanki wolfhound? He, too, is no lamb in strength. It is my belief he played a fox's trick, knowing well I would not order him to hang the meat alone."

"But truly he hung it well!"

"It comes to me that the two dogs were in close bond, out of the same pack if not the same litter, and if so, he has been punished more than by fifty blows of the kurbash. The rest I will leave to Allah, who alone gives meat and what is meet to men and dogs."

3

Between dusk and dark, when he would not be seen or himself missed from any head count, 'Giny Jim climbed the acacia tree above the oasis and tore down the abandoned rook's nest, a landmark old when our earliest comer went down to the Sepulcher.

As our files tramped at daybreak past the place, the scantily leafed tree stood naked and empty against the paling eastern sky. No man raised his shackled hand or his voice above a mutter, but in a few seconds the void was known to all. Many breathed hard. They believed they had seen a sign of ominous import. The guards cracked their whips.

"How could it fall?" my leader murmured in Arabic. "No gale blew last night."

"It rotted out at last, as we will," Kerry replied.

Kerry said nothing more until we were on the bed, then spoke in an evasive manner I was awake to long ago.

"Bloody queer, after all, that rook's nest falling down."

"So?"

"They're made of sticks and earth. If used long enough, the earth turns into a kind of plaster from the droppings, and you've got to break 'em up and pull 'em down. Well, I think that one was pulled down."

"What for?"

"A signal. There couldn't be any other reason. But if a great horse-breeding sheik could get you out—not free, of course—abandon hope ye who enter here—and at last you were free to go——" Kerry stopped, his face gray.

"Go on, Kerry," I said.

"If you couldn't take Sparrow, you certainly can't take Jim—or me."

I knew I must not let him build in vain.

"No, I can't, but if such a thing would happen, it would be a long time off."

"Time as it passes in the Sepulcher—one day as long as a year—a year like one day."

We did not mention the matter again for about four months. I did not invite it into my mind, for the uncertainty was more harrowing than the hope was comforting; indeed, I tried to keep it out, since it caused my thoughts to move in the same futile orbit they had completed a hundred times. I had been warned that any circular path worn deeply in the mind led to madness. Almost all of us had to fight madness or drift into it; those that went too mad to work were beaten with the kurbash until they recovered their sanity or died. I had counted the chances in my favor—confronted those opposed—and could only wait.

At the end of four months, one of Suliman's caravans came out of the north, the second since his visit here, rested a day in the oasis, and departed into the blue. I had seen a robed figure beside the road close to the acacia tree as we trudged to the quarry at daybreak, but he did not give me a sign or, as far as I knew, a glance. Kerry mentioned the caravan, his eyes sunk in his head, then the subject was dropped for half a year more.

Then, on May 19, 1809—with eight years of slavery almost through—a wheel of fortune set turning in a sea-bound cave in Malta came full circle.

As we marched in from the quarry, thornwood fires glimmered on the camp ground, and we heard the ugly bubbling cries of many camels and the shouts of their drivers. We had hardly gained the stockade when Ibrim summoned me from the rank, and Kerry rattled his chain—the slaves' way of wishing good luck—as I was led away. With hardly a word he took me to the house of the quarry master set among date palms which none of the quarry gangs had ever come nigh. Its walls were marble, of quality not quite fine enough to be worth exporting, yet beautiful, and so were the pillars and floor of its portico. It was not meet that I should enter the master's *gulphor* or that any guest of his should descend to the courtyard to talk to me. So Ibrim brought me into the *kiffer*, an entrance hall.

In only a moment Suliman came through a screened archway. I saw no change in his countenance, unless its pale brown skin was slightly more taut over its fine bone; but he had dressed more richly than before, in robes of Kashmir and a large turban with a brocaded sash and a diamond plume. In his broad belt the hilts of three daggers sparkled with red and green jewels. Behind him stood the master, his Moorish dress as gaudy as that Murad Reis had worn on the day I first wore chains.

Suliman touched hand to heart and forehead. I did the same, my chains jangling harshly. Suliman's eyes filled with tears, but there was no danger of my weeping. I had lost the power to do so—for tears are often a sign of manly power—just as I had forgotten how to laugh.

"You—can—go?" Suliman asked.

"Yes, O Sheik."

"You must make vow to me and Sidi el Akir, Allah and Christian God to witness. For long as you stay by me—all while you in my charge—you escape not. You not try escape. You be true to me and to vow. When I die, must you return to prison. No, you will not run off, but come here back without try escape. So say the Reis Effendi in name of Yussuf Pasha. Not till you back here come, and irons put on you, is bond between us broke. You understand?"

"Yes, sir."

"Reis Effendi say, 'What is vow to Christian dog but barking at the moon?' I say you, I, break bread, eat salt, and I, Sheik el Beni Kabir, give bond for your bond to me. Do you swear before Allah, before God, without two face, to keep promise, keep faith?"

"I do."

Suliman spoke gravely to his host.

"Sidi el Akir, the Giour Omar known as Sittash has made the required vow, and I, Suliman, Sheik el Beni Kabir, warrant his keeping of his given word even as one of the Faithful."

"So be it. One day more shall he labor at the quarry with his fellows, and when he returns in the darkness, Ali the smith will cut away his chains, leaving only the bands on his ankles; and he may pass that night among your camel drivers, and when you start forth

in the dawn, he may go with you, not to return until you have
drunk the cup of death."

4

A moment later I was under the young stars, sniffing the dry, cool,
aromatic desert air. When the gate had been opened for me, Kerry
gave me a quick glance in the glimmer of the watch light, then
looked away.

"You needn't tell me," he said. "I can see it in your face."

When I went to my accustomed place, Kerry and Jim crouched
beside me, and for a while—without knowing why—we did not
mention tomorrow's business, and spoke of happenings of long ago.

"Will you leave at daybreak?" Kerry asked me abruptly.

"Not till the next day. I'm to work tomorrow as usual."

"It won't be as usual. Still—if you don't mind—I'm glad we'll be
teammates one more day. What does one day count? Well, children
know it can count a great deal—I remember that—and I dare say the
very old know it, too."

"I'm glad of it, too, Kerry. After that, you and Jim keep in close
touch. Jim, you're to bring him the toddy that you brought me. Don't
fail him any more than you failed me. He needs it to keep going and
to keep strong for the day we'll break out and go free." For somewhere along the line I had learned to speak clearly and well.

"Aye, aye, Cap'n," Jim answered.

"Do you think you'll come back someday?" Kerry asked incredulously.

"When Suliman dies, I'll be sent back." I told them about my bargain.

"He may live for twenty years—lucky dog that you are! Forgive
me, man."

"That's all right. Each of us has got to think of himself in proper
measure. For the next few years, my chief business is living. I'm
going to make up for the lost years as far as I can. But all the time I'm
going to be battening down against the day that Suliman dies. Remember, there's no chance for any of us to go free without outside
help or a pile of money to bribe with. I'll try to get one or the other—
lay plans—make preparations. And if the hope becomes bright
enough while Suliman's still alive, I'll ask him to send me back here."

"It would have to be pretty damned bright," Kerry said. "To come
back to this tomb from out in the open air——"

"I wouldn't have the nerve to do it unless it's almost a sure thing. At least not until I've stowed away a lot of living. I reckon it gets down to this. Your chances of escape are no worse for my being gone, and in the long run, somewhat better."

"That's all we can ask and more." Kerry turned quickly away.

My next day's labor would have been like all the others except for Kerry's attempt to make it memorable. I had learned to labor rapidly with great exactitude while listening to him, largely oblivious of heavy exertion, long hours, baking heat, or piercing cold. My body had stayed equal to it, and I had not let it torment my mind. Today we had a delicate layer of marble to cleave and lift out while Kerry recited to me tales and ballads of ancient Ireland—of great heroes who fought in chariots with packs of war dogs running before, maidens beautiful past dreaming, cattle-stealing, great loyalty and terrible revenge, fairies, witch children, and banshees—lore that he loved above all other. His low voice became vibrant with emotion, and I was afraid his brilliant eyes would attract the guard's attention.

Late in the afternoon the team just below us in the bed filled two oversize wheelbarrows with shards preparatory to dumping them into a ravine about two hundred paces above the quarry. The path was rough and largely uphill, so the chore was one of the most dreaded of the day, coming at its close when the men were near exhaustion. The teams took it in order, and today it had fallen to one of the weakest in the gang—a frail-looking Jew on his way to the Hill with bloody urine, and a broken-spirited West African Negro.

"I can't watch any whipping today," Kerry said. "Let's offer to take their turn."

"Good."

When Kerry caught Ibrim's eye, he touched his hands to his forehead in entreaty.

"You have my leave to speak," Ibrim said in Arabic.

"Effendi, Omar known as Sittash is grateful unto Allah—although he calls Him by another name—for the friendship of the great Sheik Suliman, and hence he wishes to do a deed of friendship toward a sickly fellow, which is to take Ishmael's appointed task of dumping the shards. If you will give him your consent, I ask to relieve Na'od of the same duty."

"There's no harm in that." This was a frequently used form of assent to a petition.

Kerry chose the heavier barrow and led the way. When he came to the steep part of the hill, he took it in one rush, and he never broke the thread of a tale he was telling me—of a great warrior Chuchullin and his phantom chariot. As we came to the ravine, he pushed on further than our usual dumping place, to the top of its steepest wall. Then, setting the barrow down, he walked quickly to the brink.

He turned to me, his face still, and spoke.

"Please stay where you are a moment."

I nodded and stopped.

"That's the end of the story of Chuchullin. You see, he was a ghost even then. The witches raised him out of the grave for that his ride. And it's the end of my story, too."

"I hope you'll reconsider."

"Why should I? I made up my mind last night, and all day I've been happy over it. Today I've told you the stories I hold most dear —the only way I could honor our farewell. Jim would bring me the drinks as you told him, but I know a deeper draft than that, and sweeter to a man in my boots."

"I wouldn't want to feel that my going away caused you to do it."

"Your coming here prevented me from doing it. I was about ready when you came—I lasted eight years more. Will you tell me good-by—and wish me good luck?"

"Yes, and I wish you'd shake hands with me."

"I trust you not to jerk me back."

"I'll keep it."

He gave me his hand. I shook it, and then could do nothing but step back.

"You see it's a clean pitch," Kerry went on. "I'll hardly know what hit me. And back home in Kerry County—beside a peat fire in a smoky old house—a woman old before her time will hear a banshee scream."

"I have to tell you something."

"All right."

"Ibrim's coming on the run."

"Thanks. Good God, I thank you. Make good use of all that lore. You're my prize pupil—my friend—my only heir. Here I go!"

"Good-by, Kerry."

He smiled again, and forgotten tears flowed down his cheeks once more. Then he sprang out far, his chains rattling fiercely, and hurtled down.

CHAPTER 11

The Horseman

1

I BEGAN to live again the moment that Suliman's caravan passed out of sight of the Sepulcher, with no one running after us to summon me back. Asleep or awake, in the tents or far afield, feasting or famishing, lolling in the pools of the oasis or licking damp *zeirs* on the desert, at work or play, under chill stars or the molten sun, I lived without respite for so many days of joy that I hardly dared ask for more, yet day after day—a genie's treasure dropped jewel by jewel into my horn—I still lived on.

No labor appointed me was too heavy for my liking. No hardship, even the dreadful khamsin—the blast off hell's furnace with its pall of dust and sand—could harden my heart against the gift of life. My companions, the Beni Kabir, of smaller build than me, had been strengthened and toughened by their deserts to a degree almost unimaginable by civilized people—their only equals being other nomads roaming wastelands as harsh as theirs and the desert wolves—but I, too, had been hard-schooled. To their amazement, they need not favor me even on our first journey together if the trial was of physical endurance only. They must teach me the lore of survival in a deadly land—I was a child when it came to riding and shooting and other prowess that they prized—and at first sight of my lank body, ungainly-looking with its wide shoulders, immense, almost fleshless chest, and long, gaunt limbs, ill-hidden mirth ran up and down the line, and many jests of an indirect sharp-pointed sort made the Bedouins bark with laughter. But before the end of that month-long journey, they sang a different tune.

To the unredeemed, it would have been a dreadful trek. We crossed ever-shifting sands, climbing interminable dunes or else sand hills flat-topped by the wind. Whole deserts were hard-baked clay so thick with stones that the camels suffered, and the worst was sunbaked mud, almost snow white, that shot arrows of fiery pain into our brains. Our way wound far to touch at every oasis within fair reach. Sometimes we rested at desert wells, drinking foul or bitter water, and when they failed, the camels screamed and gnashed their teeth in vain. In stretches of total desert, we must carry water for several days, and if used too soon, to do without or die. When the moon gave us enough light, we set forth at sundown and traveled until morning; then lay in such shadow as we could find or make through the pitiless white-hot days. But I had left my chains at the Sepulcher of Wet Bones, and no long-haired, wild-eyed son of the Thirst, with gazelle's feet and camel's belly and lion's heart, need ever pass me his water jug or lend me his hand.

Only Suliman, no longer young and weakened by capture and torture by robber Bedouins ten years before, and the caravan captain, Mirsuk Effendi, did not share the labor of the camps. I became a baggage wallah, a hewer of wood and a drawer of water and a toter thereof, an uprooter of *asla* bushes for fuel where no thorn trees grew—it took a strong grip and a sudden jerk, at which feat I promptly had no peer—a tent raiser and a subduer of refractory camels. Before long I meant to be a rider, a hunter, and if the need came, a warrior second to none.

The Beni Kabir were essentially Bedouins—a nomadic race of Semites whose history was lost in myth—but a good half of the tribe grew dates, groundnuts, grain, lentils, and indigo in well-watered gardens of the Baeed Oasis. In the village stood Suliman's palace, an ancient, many-arched edifice of cool stone and sun-baked brick, bare of all furniture except divans and weapons hung on the walls. But his wild-eyed men and their leopard-lithe women followed their flocks and herds on the far-flung steppes, where many a sun-baked hillside furnished camel fodder and the wadis grew herbage fit for fat-tailed sheep. Much of this domain was a series of depressions, too arid to be called oases, but sending forth scanty but strong grass in the wake of far-scattered showers. Here Suliman and his nephew Zaal, with their retainers and slaves, raised horses of the ancient Arabian breed.

I became a helper to Timor, pale-skinned, hawk-eyed, and eagle-beaked, who corralled and broke to bit and saddle stallions, beautiful geldings, and a few half-wild mares. It was Timor who taught me to ride. Although I was a slave, Timor knew I had broken bread and eaten salt with Suliman, hence the teaching was of no makeshift sort, for I must not shame him in attendance on him before his fellow sheiks. Daily for six months I must ride bareback, with no bridle and only one halter rope to guide and control my mount. This taught me balance and harmony with the mare's gaits and, most important of all, a kind of fellowship with her more than a master-servant relationship—as though she lent me her back for the pleasure of my company and our runs together on this great dun pasture of my dreams made only sport.

Many mares were hand-raised. Those that showed great promise drank camel's milk and were coddled with bread flaps. Almost all became gentle as shepherd bitches, partly because of the care and caresses lavished on them from the day they were foaled, partly a matter of breeding. The Arab had no use for a vicious horse, whether stallion or mare, and when one showed the signs—the rolling eye, the backdrawn lips, the head swung in a scythelike motion—his life was short and unproductive. The stallions that got many fillies and few colts came to honor, but the Bedouins barred them from their tents and largely from their hearts, and composed no verses in their praise such as every sheik and water boy sang to the melting-eyed mares. They almost never rode them in sport or war.

A well-bred, well-trained mare became incredibly loyal to her master. The Bedouin had ceased to marvel at her refusing to leave him wounded on the desert, waterless or in the dread khamsin. And it was no myth that she would fight for him to the death against desert wolves, whether four-legged or two.

Timor praised my progress in riding—for a *farengi* (foreigner) I did quite well. Actually, I was doing better than well, as he well knew; and it would have surprised me if I weren't. I was a hard-taught rider of the horse-of-tree. I had learned to grip with my knees and my thighs, to resist sudden jerks, and to keep my balance under difficulties. My weight was light, yet I had powerful hands and forearms. A man who had come up out of the Sepulcher of Wet Bones need not be afraid of horses or of painful falls. Now that my chains had fallen, I loved to fly—and there is no such soaring motion in reach of man as the full run, neck and tail arched, of an Arabian horse.

I wished to please Suliman and to gain *izzat* in his tribe. Both would make for fuller living and for higher hope of the future. I did not intend to stop with being a good horseman. I proposed to be among the very best of the Bedouins, who are among the best equestrians in the world. If I stayed whole and long enough among them, I would succeed.

That was a far cry. Meanwhile, there were days crammed with living and nights—such nights as we need not be abroad—of light, dimly blissful, refreshing sleep. The lot of slaves is almost never hard among the Bedouins. Suliman did not favor me above other of the slaves who had striven and starved beside him, except in one particular. Once with every change of the moon he summoned me to his great pavilion, usually at midnight, to receive me as a kinsman and give me sirupy green tea and a well-bubbling water pipe. We talked in English on such large and eternal topics as the excellence of women and of horses; the splendor of heroes and the glory of war and the joys of hunting; of black-maned lions that killed in one terrible, silent rush; of leopards that slew colts and sometimes mares in the ambushes of the night; of hawks and hounds; and of those two obsessions of all undegenerate Arabs, the beauty of poetry and of the stars.

But he never spoke to me of Allah or his prophet Mohammed. Even if we had both desired that I embrace Islam, I could not do so because slavery was my kismet as long as I stayed in Suliman's charge, and no Mohammedan may keep a slave of his own faith.

Suliman occupied his palace in Baeed Oasis for about one week in each of the four seasons. Most of the year he "followed the grass" with us, the life that he most loved. His pavilion was about sixty by thirty feet, with removable curtains of black felt. About half of this space comprised the *mukaad*—a rug-strewn hall where he ate, smoked, conferred with his captains, and entertained male guests. The rest was given over to cooking and what little other housekeeping nomads considered necessary, and to the *haremlik*, the curtained-off quarters of the women of his household.

At present Suliman had no wives. His last, the daughter of a minor emir of Hejaz whom he had married late, had died at the birth of his only son four years before my coming. Two crones, relations of the lad's mother, cared for him; and the other occupant was a young Nubian slave girl, a Coptic Christian, sable-brown, with clean-cut features and form. Her children by him would be born free—so far there had been no loosening of her robe to rejoice the tribe—but even if she bore Suliman a son, he would not take her to wife, and for a peculiar reason. In case of his death before his son Selim reached sixteen, his ranking widow would become the boy's guardian and have far more power over the tribe than would be easily credible in more settled and civilized Islamic lands—especially since Suliman's nephew Zaal loved the fleshpots of the cities and would not live the life of a Bedouin. For this office and influence Zara was fitted neither by hereditary place, education, nor intelligence. Thus the elders would be left free to direct the boy until he came of age.

A few other maliks—close kinsmen of the sheik—pitched tents in our longer stays; the rest slept under canopies only in the blast of the midday sun. These were hastily raised, often no more than a felt curtain hung on a thornbush. The wives and daughters of my companions did the same, unveiled, often bare-bosomed, with little thought of purdah; sometimes at night we must erect shields against wind-blown sand, but we almost never shut out the lovely starlight or the enchanting glimmer of the moon. Our other living customs seemed sybaritic compared with those of the prison, yet settlers on the American frontier, who can carry their goods in one wagon, would have considered us savages.

Our staple food was camel cheese well-crusted and rank, dried dates, and beans and bread flaps cooked over a fire of camel dung, thornwood, or thornbush. Our favorite drink was fermented camel milk, instead of the mare's milk beloved by the Tartar—all the milk in our mares' bags must go to their frail-legged babes. The Bedouin was no stickler for strict Mohammedan dietary laws—our greyhounds often caught rabbits, or we rode them down and clubbed them; any kind of bird's egg in any stage of development was a welcome dish; and if gophers, owls, and even jerboas found a way into the pot, what I did not know did not hurt me. Often we shot gazelles, and we never hankered very long for boiled mutton.

When Suliman feasted guests, we slaves were given our turn at the leavings. These would be on a six-foot metal platter, carried on camelback, still laden with a hollow ring of rice filled with fat meat and liver wallowing in gravy. Like any sheik, we dipped in our right hands, rolled rice-and-meat balls deftly in our fingers, let drain the surplus juices, and conveyed them to our mouths. Occasionally the dish was a whole camel colt boiled in milk. When no other meat was in reach, we slaughtered aged or unpopular baggage camels. But we would not dream of eating the beautiful white riding camels with sweet breaths, and it would have been a kind of cannibalism to devour a worn-out horse. Our single greatest treat was wild honey of spicy flavor, the same with which Canaan flowed.

Occasionally in the dead of night—for I must never go naked before a Mussulman—I swam in the pools or canals of the oasis. Out on the desert I never dreamed of using precious water to wash with, depending on sweat to keep my pores clean and open and rubbing off surplus dirt with sand. Although unwashed, these Bedouins could not be called an unclean people. They would not tolerate filth of any sort, and the parched lands were their habitat along with the gazelle, the ostrich, and the desert fox. The life they lived was as clean as theirs.

I would have gladly lived it all my days if my body and soul were free.

By Mohammedan law, a slave could not own property of any kind, and the clothes on his back and the tobacco in his pouch belonged to his master. Actually, most slaves had personal effects, and some accumulated valuables. Barter went on among us, and buying and selling—with Indian pice and annas, Spanish pesos, and Maria Theresa dollars—was not uncommon.

I had not stayed long in Suliman's charge before making the beginning of a hoard. Whenever Timor smoked or ate hashish and the drug took hold of him, he would give me a share, which I only pretended to consume, and instead saved to sell or trade for something useful to me. He taught me how to snare pigeons, sand grouse, and bustards at the water holes, which I exchanged with my fowl-hungry mates for cloth or worked leather; and thus I evolved a stratagem that in the course of time put several pieces of gold into my pouch. It was the catching of saker falcons, greatly prized throughout Islam. It required burying myself in sand except for my head and one arm, which I concealed under bush. In my hand was a small net on a stick; in easy reach was a live pigeon tied fast to a piece of thornwood. The bird's fluttering attracted the towering hunter; when he stooped for the kill, I covered him with the net.

By the close of my second year among the Beni Kabir, I had bought from a wandering mullah paper, pen, and inkhorn, and had five Maria Theresa dollars with which to bribe an Egypt-bound camel driver touching at our oasis. The letter I entrusted to him, to be passed secretly to any Christian in Western dress, was addressed to the President of the United States. It stated that an American, Homer Whitman, a native of Bath in the District of Maine in Massachusetts, and known in Africa as Omar or Sittash, was a slave in the care of the Beni Kabir about the Baeed Oasis; and at the death of the sheik, he would be returned to the Jebel quarries of Yussuf Pasha. I did not feel that my sending it broke faith with Suliman. It was not an attempt to escape; if American authorities tried to help me they would do so, of course, through the Tripolitan government. But it took far more courage than sending the horsehair token to Suliman, simply because my plight was not as immediately desperate. If the letter were intercepted, the camel driver would be cruelly punished and I would pass my last hours on the iron hook.

My fears proved as vain as my hopes. I did not hear of the letter then or in the future: in the words of another Omar, the tentmaker, his verse and epigrams known by heart to many Beni Kabir, the matter passed away like snow on the face of the desert. Meanwhile, I undertook a less momentous but exciting venture, that might win me *izzat* with Suliman and my wild companions.

The Stone of Kismet had been cast in the Pool of Life when the world was made, causing ripples throughout eternity. But the real starting-point understood by us mortals, occurred four years before my arrival and was of no great mark. During a journey from Derna to Alexandria, Lilla, the riding mare of Zaal, Suliman's nephew, one of the Beni Kabir's most beautiful and swift mares, came in heat. There was no reason to think any stallions ranged in five days' journey of that sun-blasted shore, so Zaal did not order a special guard and had been content to put hobbles on her forefeet. In the midnight amid blown sand, a stallion came up the wind, covered her, and was trying to make off with her when the hostlers heard the uproar and drove him away with rifle fire.

In due course she was delivered of a colt straightway named El Shermoot (The Bastard). A large colt that had brought great pain and danger to his mother, he fell immediately into ill repute with the hostlers, and perhaps that had something to do with his subsequent career of crime. Gawky and odd-looking, he had an oversize head with a Roman nose and dark gray dapples with soot black rims—such color as was never seen on a pure-bred Arab and, in the men's eyes, ugly and of ill omen. Only his luxurious black mane and tail recalled his beloved dam; from his knees to his big feet— and well-bred Arabs have small feet—he was likewise black.

In three years he stood sixteen hands, weighed a good twelve hundred, and was a raw-boned bastard if the Bedouins ever saw one. His big, block-shaped head with its hook nose was ugly as a baggage camel's, and he carried it low instead of lifted, as does a queenly Arab. He had a very long neck, powerful sloping shoulders to take the shock of his down plunge, great depth of chest and hence lots of heart, and the most awe-inspiring quarters that these Bedouins had ever seen. By now he kept to the most distant flank of the herds, but after his first capture of a mare—and generally our mares were not attracted to immature stallions—they could see him at close range simply by chasing his bride. At middle distance he

148

would circle between the rider and his beloved, pawing, snorting, and trumpeting. If the pursuer drew close, El Shermoot would charge him in screaming fury. Whether or not he would press home the attack remained an open question. When a small Bedouin on his delicate-looking fifteen-hand-high mare saw the dappled monster bearing down on him, he beat a swift retreat.

In the next three years he stole several mares and successfully resisted all our efforts to recover them. Some, with Shaitan in their hearts, followed him from pure sluttishness, my companions maintained, but some were plainly seduced by whirlwind courtship, his bravery and fleetness, the scent of the wild upon him, and even his ugliness, which is known to appeal sometimes to the most delicate females. Their foals grew up in outlawry, of no use to Allah or man, stealing precious grass out of our children's—for the tender-eyed mares amounted to that, in the Bedouins' sight—mouths.

Still Suliman would not consent to our shooting El Shermoot. Our sheik was born and raised on one of the most ruthless of the seven deserts, yet was gentle and chivalrous to a noble degree. When a horse had to be destroyed because of sickness or broken bones, he would get out his silver-mounted rifle, load it with great care, and then hand it to the executioner with these words that every one of us knew by heart.

"Are you going to bungle it? If you are, I'll do it."

Invariably the answer was: "If I bungle it, O Sheik, I entreat that the next bullet may be mine!"

The hard job was never bungled. As Suliman walked quickly away, the bullet was placed with greater care than in the breast of an arch foe in a blood feud.

For other reasons than humanitarian, I rejoiced that the liberty-loving ungainly brute was spared. And when he came five and I thirty-one, I found a special justification for his survival.

I stood concealed on a rocky hillock, less than a quarter of a mile downwind from El Shermoot's herd. The season had been severe, so he had driven off all his barren mares and well-grown foals, retaining only gravid mares and those giving suck, by no means exceptional behavior by a stallion in hard times, but proving to me that his ferocity toward us was not viciousness but the instinct of protection for his charges worthy a desert king. As I watched, a mare acting as sentinel was remiss in her duty. She failed to see a cheetah—the long-legged hound-shaped hunting leopard—stalking a young foal.

If I called or shot or moved, I would attract the attention of the herd, giving the cat a better chance to do her deviltry. Still, I thought she had been rash to approach this near El Shermoot, and I became sure of it when he caught sight of her between the thorn clumps. Whirling, he charged her, uttering short, sharp neighs of fury in rapid succession, a far-carrying and truly terrifying sound.

The prowler took off, gathering speed at every bound, until she reached her top pace. This, the desert men believed, was the swiftest gait of any earthly creature without wings. Zaal had told me that an Indian prince had timed his pet cheetah's dash from the instant that he was slipped until he overtook a fleeing buck at 18 seconds for 430 yards. Yet in the covering of about that distance, I thought that the stallion might overtake the marauder. Perhaps he could have done so in a longer race—the hunting leopards are short-winded—but the cat dashed into brushwood and disappeared.

I lost no time in seeking admission to Suliman's presence to report the incident.

"O Sheik, it comes to me that the stallion that stole upon Zaal Malik's camp six years ago and covered his mare Lilla was no common cob, but a great runner and jumper of good lineage."

"I've been long of the same opinion, but how did you arrive at it?"

"When I was in the Sepulcher of Wet Bones, I heard of how General Eaton, from my native land, led a force from Alexandria to Derna in the hope of casting Yussuf Pasha from his throne and putting there Hamet Pasha. It was said that he set forth on a gray stallion, bought in England, and a gift from Hamet, but on his arrival in Derna his mount was a white camel. Perhaps the stallion had escaped and strayed away."

"Verily it was so. The gray stallion that the Yanki sirdar lost was none other than Ottoman, whose pedigree began with the Byerly Turk, and one of the greatest 'chasers of our times. The dapples of his skin were ringed with black, and he had black points."

"That's almost certain evidence, O Sheik."

"Furthermore, one of Zaal Malik's slaves caught sight of the raider as he thundered about in the dust storm, trying to take away into his deserts the hobbled mare Lilla. He gave him as dark gray with black points."

I told Suliman of the race I had seen today. There came a faint flush under the parchmentlike skin on his cheekbones, and he watched me closely.

"O Sheik, of all our horses, there's only one who can race with Ottoman's bastard son, the mare Farishti, full sister of Kobah."

"That I believe."

"Farishti will pine for a mate on the next moon, and if you give me leave, I'll take her to El Shermoot; and if she drops a filly, it may be her like will have never been seen on the Seven Deserts."

"She would not be pure-bred, but—by Allah, she would fly like an afrite. And what family is so old and noble that it will not benefit from a little bastardry? Omar, how could you bring Farishti to El Shermoot without putting yourself in great danger?"

"I'll speak of it to Timor, O Sheik, and we'll devise a plan."

"You have my leave, but only if you carry your rifle, and, if your danger waxes great, shoot to kill."

El Shermoot remained in easy distance, perhaps because the mares divorced from his herd had returned to our bivouacs. Timor gave me good advice and fixed me a twenty-fathom line, one end of which I looped around Farishti's head for a halter. Riding her bareback, I encircled The Bastard's band until I was straight upwind, then cantered straight toward him. When we were still a mile away, he gave forth the prolonged, deep-pitched neigh that all horsemen know.

But he was soon aware of me, too. Instead of rushing in, he continued to circle between us and his mares. Often his lusty trumpetings changed to staccato blasts of rage, not ineptly transcribed as "Ahah!" in the Book of Job. He was moving toward me now, with mingled pugnacity and fear. When he was still two furlongs distant, I came near a pile of rocks that would give some protection if I must face a lethal charge. I slid off Farishti's back and ran, the rope uncoiling in my hand. Taking a bight around the rock, I crouched down behind it, my rifle primed and cocked.

El Shermoot saw the movement and broke into a furious run. Still I did not believe I would have to shoot. A motionless figure seems to become almost invisible to animals—I had learned to take advantage of this fact when hunting gazelles—and often allays their belligerency. Besides, the counter-attraction was a force as elemental and mysterious, akin to that which makes a tree root shatter a stone wall.

Timor's foretelling came true—El Shermoot forgot or scorned my existence. This scene of the dynamics of procreation was one I would never forget, never cease to hold in mystery and awe. The dun desert stretched afar, the sun blazed down, before my eyes these two—the great gray steed, fit to lead a battle or found a breed honored by equestrian brotherhoods all over the world, and the gentle, sable-brown mare of small and beautiful contour—joined flesh to make new life.

Their chorused scream of agony and ecstasy woke the sleeping desert, and they shone in the sunlight with ineffable vividness. I could not begin to grasp the significance of the event, for it was cosmic and eternal, but when the storm had passed and the stallion tried to drive his mate into the herd that he led and protected, surely I witnessed lowly kinship with human love.

These were my moments of greatest danger. If I made the slightest motion, quite possibly he would come and tower and strike with his terrible front hooves. As it was, the rope that held Farishti, bighted about the rock and in my hands, had no clear meaning to him, and my scent, long in his nostrils, had become cold or without power to arouse his rage. Meanwhile his mares were drawing further off, calling with high-pitched neighs. He began running in ever larger circles between them and his tethered bride. When a great sweep had taken him nearly a quarter of a mile, I freed the rope, coiled it as I ran, and sprang on Farishti's back. Lashing her with its end and kicking her in the side, I headed her toward the bivouacs fast as she could go.

This was no mean pace. She had feet that she picked up cleanly, and an arched neck and tail, and the desert wind whistled past my ears. Looking over my shoulder, I saw El Shermoot coming full tilt. A whole mile he chased us, but our lead was too great for him to overtake in this distance, and at last he must return to his wards.

3

My mullah Timor and my fellow hostlers were delighted with the match, and many bets were laid and speculations made as to its outcome. My companions held the Old Testament belief that whatever took the sire's eye at the instant of conception would mark the offspring; and since I could make no capital out of a pile of rocks, a rope, the sun-baked desert, and the blazing sky, I told them of beholding a vision of countless horses marching in file from one horizon to another, stallions of valor and mares of matchless beauty, the posterity of El Shermoot and Farishti's for a thousand and one years; and perhaps the same vision was given to El Shermoot and would thus come true.

The months flew by. There came a night that all our horsemen ringed about a thorn-log fire with their women crouched at the flickering rim of shadows. Farishti had been in labor more than six hours. In the early part she had alternately stood or laid down; now she lay grunting, panting, and moaning, and unless she could be delivered of her foal in a short time, she would never rise again. Suliman crouched beside her, stroking her muzzle, letting her hear his voice. Three of our best veterinarians—and truly they deserved the title better than many alumni of Lyons—worked with cool, steady, but desperate diligence to save life.

At every labor of the brave mare, the colt's shoulder or hip blocked passage. All spoke of him now as the colt—his size settling the question. In my great desire, I had been among the last to abandon hope of a filly, and now my dispute with kismet when his finger wrote so plain had frightened me, for my mind had become deeply inured to Arab superstition.

Actually, the danger grew greater every minute. The doctors had fixed halter ropes to the colt's forefeet, but all they could do was keep them taut, so that when Farishti's labor thrust him outward a little further, the retraction of her muscles would not draw him back again. There was no sound now but the crackle of the fire, Farishti's pantings, and the low voices of Suliman and his helpers. The rest seemed hardly to breathe.

One of the doctors, the graybeard Ali ibn Ahmad, rose, touched his hands to his forehead, and spoke to Suliman.

"O Sheik, it comes to me that we cannot save the colt, and unless we slay him and take him forth piecemeal, we cannot save Farishti."

"Would that be a surety of saving Farishti, Ali ibn Ahmad?"

"Nay, but I count it the best hope."

Suliman pondered a moment, stroking his beard. Then he turned to Ali ibn Ahmad, the eldest of the three doctors, and asked for a lump of musk from the medicine box. While Ali held Farishti's mouth open, he forced it down her throat. After waiting a few minutes for the stimulant to take hold, he began to coax the mare to her feet. Perhaps he believed that her dead weight in her prone position prevented the full extension of her womb. More likely he wanted to make the utmost appeal to her spirit. It caught the imagination of the Beni Kabir and arrested every movement.

"At her next pain, pull hard," he told the holders of the ropes.

As Farishti laid her muzzle in his hands, we heard his low but insistent "*Jhai—jhai!*" Jerkily and feebly at first, but with growing strength, she got her feet under her and heaved. Once her foreknees buckled, but she tried again, and with a surge of her quarters—whose

153

beautifully rounded muscle structure is the driving force of the great runners—she lurched to her feet. The exertion instantly brought on a heavy labor pain. The ropes tightened ruthlessly, heightening her agony and causing her to bear down with all her strength. Farishti gave forth a long-drawn scream, humanlike, awful to hear, that carried me back to the terrible outcries from the Sepulcher of Wet Bones. But as it died away, we saw the whole form of the colt emerge and drop into Ali ibn Ahmad's waiting arms.

Seconds later the dam and her foal lay side by side. We saw Farishti raise her head to put her muzzle in Suliman's hands—that was all the proof we needed of her well-being—and the faces of the doctors soon assured us that the colt had taken no hurt. Wet and dust-smeared though he was, I soon had a good enough idea of his appearance.

He was dark gray in color, the dapples being ringed with black. His mane and tail were jet, and so, too, his legs from the knees down. His head was too large even for such a big colt, and if he would not grow up raw-boned, I missed my guess. But not until he raised his head for his first clear look at the world was my final suspicion confirmed. The hook of his nose would do credit to a high-born Hebrew elder.

As we waited for the next development, we watchers were too elated to do more than hold hands and hug one another and beam into one another's faces. It came when, about thirty minutes after birth, the colt tried his legs. We feared to cheer lest we frighten him, but we watched in greatest joy. Without one tumble he rose on the spindly stems, wobbled, got his balance, and took four precarious steps nearer Farishti's teats before he sprawled.

"The time has come to name the newborn one," Suliman announced solemnly, after Ishmael ibn Abdul, our tribal bard, and a markedly handsome youth, had composed a song in honor of mother and son.

The elders nodded wisely.

"It comes to me that the slave Omar should have a say in the matter," Suliman went on. "Omar, have you thought upon a suitable name?"

"Nay, O Sheik." For it was honor enough to be asked, and I must not press it in the hearing of my mates.

"When I first met you, before you went into slavery, you were a rider even then—of a horse-of-tree. You told me her name, and it was a stirring one—though I have forgotten it. Think you it will be good fortune, or ill, if the colt were named after your good ship?"

Deeply stirred, I could not at once reply. That did not count against me—the sheik thought I was giving due thought to the question.

"Good fortune, O Sheik," I said, when my breath came back. "And the name of the ship was *'The Vindictive,'* which in Arabic—as near as I may come to it—is El Stedoro."

"Allah bear witness it is a good name, one of great meaning to us Bedouin. So shall he be known among us and, if Allah wills, far beyond our deserts, for truly he has the makings of a great steed, and even now I would not sell him for a hundred gold dinars. Furthermore, I will entrust him to your care. See that he does not grow up an outlaw like his sire, at the same time making sure you do not break his spirit. You shall put the first halter on his great head, the first saddle on his stout back. When the time comes to train him as a hunter and jumper——"

But Suliman stopped, white and short of breath. We had forgotten the late hour and the strain he had been under; and while the others remembered these things now, I thought of so much more.

"If Allah spares my life that long, you shall do those things," Suliman went on, his eyes sunk in his head.

There were visions before my eyes.

"Yea, yea, O Sheik," I answered.

I had been waiting my chance to ask permission to trap El Shermoot at a water hole, in a steep-walled wadi, let him go hungry until I could half-tame him with food, then ride him until he acknowledged me his master and have him for my use. But I could not afford the venture. It would take thought and effort for which my pleasure and such *izzat* as I could win would not recompense me. My usual tasks plus the care of El Stedoro would keep me busy enough; the life in the camps and the field was good enough. What extra time I had must be put to a greater use. That much I knew. What I did not know was which way to turn.

CHAPTER 12

Signs and Wonders

1

IF COMING event cast its shadow before, the only one who saw it was Timor, my mullah.

When El Stedoro was a yearling, we had followed the grass to the extreme southeastern border of our hereditary domain. At a water hole, Timor set traps for far-flying pigeons; and in the crop of one he found pearl millet, not grown west of the oases of Central Egypt, south of Baeed Oasis, or east of the lands of the *muleth themin*—the Veiled People—the lordly Tuareg. It was unthinkable that a bird could cross such expanses in a matter of hours, but she could have robbed a caravan on a rarely-used road some sixty miles southward.

"A great caravan," Timor remarked thoughtfully, stroking his beard.

"It may be so, but how can you know?"

"From whence would a small caravan start, and where would it go? There is nothing but desolation, with a few water holes in the wadis, from the Oasis of Kawar eastward to the Nile. The Tuareg had traveled a whole moon when they came to Kawar. Would they have set out those many miles with fifty camels? Nay, there be five hundred, and the sheik and his sons and his women and their riding beasts subsist not on bread flaps and camel cheese and thorn! A trifle among good things, they carry enough pearl millet to waste it on the ground!"

"*Bismillah!*" I cried. This was to invoke the mercy of Allah on the wasteful rich and the needful poor.

"They are passing even now within a stone's throw."

"Nay, the toss of a stone—by an afrite tall as a mountain. We can almost see their dust!"

"Truly they are in two, at most three days' journey. And why should the lordly Tuareg come to these wastelands accursed of Allah? Listen, my son, to what I unfold. The Beni Tuareg are not Unbelievers, but they have strange ways. The men mask their faces instead of the women as with us."

As for my face, I kept it straight, although one of the most amusing of the Bedouin's illusions was that their women wore veils. Actually I had seen them worn only on one or two ceremonial occasions.

"Also, the women sway more power in the councils and over their husbands than is meet," Timor went on. "Still, it must be admitted that they are most beautiful."

I had heard all this before and a great deal more. The tall, light-skinned Tuareg, although nominally Mohammedans, were the scandal of all Islam. They ate what they pleased, prayed when they liked, venerated the Cross—perhaps from some early contact with Christianity—and, most impious of all, allowed their women as much freedom as they enjoyed themselves. The bold-faced Bedouin girls were models of modesty compared to the tall daughters of the Tuareg, who sang and danced and recited poetry in open assembly, took the leading part in courting, and uncovered their breasts. Descent was traced through the distaff as in matriarchies. Wives were treated with real chivalry.

"About five years ago the Emir of the Kel Innek—that is one of the greatest and richest of the Tuareg clans—fell under the spell of a marabou from Yemen, and since then you would think him a whirling dervish for piety," Timor went on. "And it comes to me that he has now set out for Mecca on holy pilgrimage."

It was good enough guessing, I thought, but far from a surety. If indeed an emir of the Masked Men was on pilgrimage to Mecca, I wished that I could fall in with him on his return journey. If excessive piety had not dehumanized him, I could be confident of arousing his interest in a Yankee slave, and quite possibly make an arrangement of shining hope. He was not subject to the Pasha of Tripoli, and the Tuareg held sway beyond Ghat, only four hundred miles from the Sepulcher of Wet Bones. When my time came to break out, some of his riding camels might be waiting. . . .

But kismet had written otherwise.

In the middle of the night following Timor's finding of the millet, I was brought up out of my dreams by being gently shaken. I wakened to hear Timor murmuring "Omar," and to see his finely wrinkled ascetic face by the rays of the moon. Plainly he had just come in from riding herd.

"Saddle and come with me," he told me in low tones.

At once he set about filling extra water jugs and fastening them to his croup. Finally he saddled and haltered one of the spare mares—there were always a number in camp, either lying underfoot with the greyhounds or having to be pushed out of our way—and with her

157

bridle, tied her to my saddle strings. Stuffing some balls of camel cheese into his bags, he mounted a fresh mare and led me onto the silvered desert.

"None but Allah knows what may come over the desert," he remarked when we were riding up the steep slope above the wadi.

"Yea, verily," I responded, as he would wish.

"There may be an afrite, tall as a mountain, or there may be only a whirlwind, and there may be a caravan of the dead that lost its way and died and must wander for a thousand and one years, or there may be a great emir with his thousand horsemen, or a hermit following a dream. Truly there are no bounds to its wonders. But tonight a thing comes over the desert I have never seen."

The back of my neck prickled fiercely, but I did not speak.

"It may bring evil, and it may bring good. Only Allah knows. Certain signs given to me were favorable, such as a jumping of my left eye and a jerboa bounding to the right across my path. As I came in to waken you, I saw the sheik's female slave coming from the well with a brimming water jar—in daylight a good omen, but at this midnight hour a foreshadowing of great portence, whether for woe or weal. Yet I kept my resolve to waken you, and to let you ride foremost on a path we will presently come on, if such is your will, so thereby the good or evil fortune waiting at the path's end will mainly fall on you."

"I am your protected, O Mullah!"

"Nay, but you have learned to ride under my teaching. Mark, now, that I am no longer young and have no sons. If great fortune came, I would not know what to do with it, and I am hardly worth evil fortune's trouble. Also, your lot is a most strange and terrible one, for when the cup of death is brought unto our sheik, you must go again into living death. Tonight I saw what may be a lucky chance. At least it comes about from no common happening on our desert. It is all I have to give you and it is yours to play or to pass by."

"Whatever it is, I won't pass it by."

"Then hear me now, while our horses labor up the hill, for when we gain its crest we must ride fast. There I found the hoofprints of a horse going straight north. They had been made since sundown, for before then there was light wind that would have effaced them with blown sand. The horse had not veered in his course for rough ground or smooth, and once had crushed through a thicket of tamarisk that he could have avoided by swerving no more than twenty strides."

"If he were blind, he wouldn't keep a straight course. He would go mad and run into the rocks and die. It must be his rider is blind."

"No, for the horse can turn right or left enough to avoid a single rock or bush. That I saw. I think the horse is still in his right mind, although his rider may be dead. I think he wears a thing that I had never seen, but which I heard of long ago—which certain tribes on the far deserts use when one of their number is sent into banishment forever. It is two rods of wood or iron fixed under the edge of the saddle on both sides and running forward to the rings on each end of the bit. Thereby the horse cannot turn his head to right or left except for such play as the rods might give. The banished one is set in the saddle with his hands tied, and the horse headed in the direction the tribe wishes him to go. Sometimes he is seen and stopped before he runs over a cliff or into a cul-de-sac, but on deserts such as these, usually not."

"Can't we go faster?"

"Is that my good teaching, or has all I've taught you run out of your head when you need it most? If we wind our horses on this climb, how may they run when the race is to the swift?"

"Your pardon, O Mullah!"

"Aye. And in the tamarisk thicket, I found this." He took a small bundle from under his burnoose and put it in my hand. It was a tattered scarf of heavy Kashmir, richly embroidered.

Neither of us spoke again till we gained the height. At once we slipped into the easy, seemingly effortless canter of the trained, true-bred Arab, the gait we call "the wind off the hills of Hejaz." It was the pace that would take us farthest fastest between now and dawn.

2

Timor led until we came to that strange straight line of footprints, then turned out to let me pass. My first comfort was, the horse that had come up out of the south into our domains was walking, not running, and at a steady pace. I saw no footprint out of line to show reeling and staggering. Of equal importance, his northward course had brought him onto the gently rolling Plain of Jerdaz, with low bush scattered here and there, but no rocks and no deep-cut wadis for thirty or more miles. The bare ground showed clean tracks about two inches deep. It was of yellow clay that blasted a man's eyes at midday, and its fantastic mirages were the wonder of our tribe, but now it lay cool and luminous, silent and empty; and now my soul became serene—open to any wonder—and my mind worked better.

"If the rider is a Tuareg, why isn't he on a camel?" I called back to Timor. These pale-colored nomads of the Sahara were cameleers second to none, and rarely seen on horseback.

"Their emirs keep a few fine horses for show," Timor answered. A little later a patch of clay damp from underground springs showed the prints perfectly sharp.

"I've never seen a horse shod like that one," I told my companion. "I think the shoes are silver or gold."

Thereafter we rode in silence for about two hours, cantering or trotting fast. The horse we were tracking was not quite as steady as at first. I pulled up for a quick glance at an unfavorable sign about a thicket of asla bushes. The horse had tangled his feet in the growth and fallen—plain proof he was close to exhaustion—and had staggered badly before he had gained good foothold. Yet this evidence raised a thrilling question in my mind. Would he have risen at all except by the strong will of his rider?

I did not waste breath putting it to Timor. Anyway, our wasteland horses know the necessity of marching on—knew that immobility on the desert spells death—and the dauntless beast might have won the fight alone. He had fetched up heading in a slightly different direction, so now his course was more to the west. That way lay rougher ground and, not far off, rocky gullies.

I made a calculation for the twentieth time. If the tracks we had intercepted had been made after sundown, the horse could have walked thirty miles by now. We had followed the trail for about twenty miles. If we came on her in the next mile, he had traveled, perhaps trotting a good part of the way, at least eighty miles, for the caravan road crossed sixty miles south of our camp. The rider had been bound in the saddle perhaps as long as twenty hours, certainly through the heat of the day, and might be an hour's ride further on.

"Omar, we draw close," Timor called.

"How do you know?" I asked.

"By the tracks. These are very fresh."

"I can't see any difference."

"Your eyes are younger than mine—but mine are older than yours." This was a typical Bedouin mot. And I did not really doubt, in spite of its seeming improbability, that although there was no breath of wind to stir the dust, those old trained eyes could see a clearer shaping of the print than at first.

When we had ridden another mile, he called again.

"By Allah, this horseman is no weakling."

"You speak as though you know he's still alive."

"If he's not, his ghost still keeps the beast in good control, in spite of his thirst and his head shafts, enough to drive him mad."

I tried not to strain my eyes peering ahead, because I had learned long ago that an easy glance will catch an obscure object or distant glimmer of light that will escape an intent stare. When the eyes are relaxed, half-seen things signal the brain. I craved the sight of the strange traveler and felt a deep need to discover him before Timor did. This was a superstitious urge and something more. Timor had vested in me the good or evil fortune of the venture; if he were the first to spy the quarry, it would be a sign that fate had not sanctioned the appointment and the main consequences must fall to him. He wanted me to succeed, but he did not look away.

Then, almost before my brain acknowledged the discovery, I raised a triumphant cry.

"There he is!"

At the far frontier of vision a shadow among the shadows flicked and faded out.

"Allah be praised!"

We rode another hundred yards before a speck on my eyeballs became the merest moving smudge in the silvery dimness ahead; then it swiftly took shape as a horse and rider. The latter was leaning forward against the horse's neck, but his head was up instead of lopping; and as we let our horses run, their hooves beat a joyful cadence on the hard ground.

"The horse must be bigger than his tracks showed," I called to my companion.

"Nay, it's a small rider, and that is a strange thing, for the Tuareg are tall people. Even their women are tall——"

The rider had sat up straight. "Timor, is it a woman?"

"My son, I think it is."

In a few seconds more we knew. I rode upon the flank of the trammeled animal and seized his bridle. The rider turned her face full into mine. It was not that of a man or a woman either, or an afrite, but of a girl of about thirteen.

Her left wrist was strapped tight to the pommel of her saddle. Her right arm was fixed in a kind of sling, whereby she could unstop and drink from a water jug hung on her breast. Her ankles had been fastened with a strap running under the horse's belly.

I put my jug to her lips while she swallowed thrice. In a few quick slashes of my kris, I had cut all her bonds. Then the sensible thing would have been to lift her off and set her on the ground, for I saw terror and hope in desperate conflict in her face, and back of these an unbelievable struggle to conceal them both, but I could not keep from bringing her to my saddle and holding her a little while in my arms.

3

Timor broke loose the ivory shafts on each side of the horse's neck. I had noticed now that he was a snow-white gelding, probably a high-bred barb; his saddle was Spanish leather with gold and silver inlay, his cloth of green felt had a heavy fringe of gold threads, his bridle rings were silver, and he wore silver shoes slipped on over his hooves. But Timor had hardly rid him of the last of his load when he toppled down.

Timor opened his mouth and poured water down his throat; then he turned to me with a shaking head.

"He dies even now."

"But the rider is saved."

"I said the rider was a horseman, and even now I do not deny she's stuff of one, to have made him come this far without whip or spur. And we've saved a saddle, bridle, and cloth of no mean worth, not to mention silver shoes fit for El Borak."

"True, true," I answered, not knowing what I was saying.

"A horseman grown might be a victim of *thar* (blood feud), but this child——"

I came to myself, handed down the trembling girl, and laid her on my burnoose outspread on the sand. She looked at me half in dread—my gaunt face in the moonlight appalled and repelled her—half in desperate trust. After letting her drink a little more, I wiped the dust from her face and throat with a wet cloth. The skin was fine and smooth, and in the moonlight appeared a light reddish brown. If she could make a horseman, she was already made a beauty. I noticed now that she wore white cotton trousers, a gorgeous Kashmir waistcloth, and a kind of short smock, richly embroidered, put on overhead without sleeves or sides. This was not intended to hide her breasts, of proper development for a girl in her first flower, but too small for a bride. Her hair was tight-drawn and dressed in several narrow black braids, a delicately fashioned cross hung at her throat, and on her feet were sandals of oryx skin.

I could believe that a faithless bride might be cast forth into the desert for one chance of rescue, ninety-nine of death. There were savage chiefs who laid such punishments on their chattels. I knew, too, that many girls of the backward races married at twelve. I wished I were a free Bedouin, who had never ridden on a horse-of-tree, who could follow *thar*.

The maiden—she was one, regardless of what had happened—swallowed painfully and sat up. I did not try to restrain her, for it was an act of pride. Tears flowed from her long-set eyes—so light-colored in the moonlight that I thought they were blue—down her beautifully molded cheeks. She asked a question in a tongue I did not know. I glanced toward Timor.

"I think she asked if we speak Tamashek, the language of the Tuareg," Timor said.

I shook my head.

"I speak Arabic, also," the girl said in an unmistakable tone of pride. "Are either of you nobles?"

It did not seem a strange question out on the limitless silver desert.

"The elder sits high in our councils," I answered. "I'm a slave, but I was born free and equal to any man according to the Writing which I believe."

"Then I will speak," she went on. "I am Izubahil, descended through my mother from Izubahil, queen to Yunus, Emir of Assode. My mother's husband Mahound, who had taken the name of Rab ed Din (Lord of the Faith) is Emir of the Kel Innek."

I had noticed that she did not say "my father," but thought her usage might be customary among a people who traced descent through the distaff. Timor threw me a triumphant glance. "Kel Innek" were the people of the East whom Timor had guessed were the banished one's tribe. But I could hardly think of these things because of her trembling voice and her effort to hold it firm.

"You are a princess and we pay you honor," I told her. "Now will you eat a little? I have dates in my saddlebag."

"Mahound Emir denied I was a princess, and today I believed him. It may be that proof has now been given—of that you shall hear. My mother was a princess of the Kel Allaghan (People of the Spear), but she is dead." Izubahil clapped her long hands with their beautiful pointed fingers to her face and was convulsed with sobs, but in a few seconds she recovered and again looked me in the face. "It is my wish to tell you these things," she went on in classic Arabic. "Then you will know better what to do with me. Also, I would not have you think I have done some great wickedness, deserving of banishment. When I have spoken, I will, by your mercy, eat."

"As you wish, Izubahil."

"Mahound harkened unto a holy man from Yemen and himself became most holy. He commanded that our women veil and live behind the curtain. When they would not obey and their husbands would not try to make them, Mahound grew greatly angry and killed his brother. To atone for the sin he made a pilgrimage to Mecca, taking with him my mother and me in a great caravan."

Timor interrupted the strange story with a little cough of triumph.

"Having gained more holiness, Mahound started back by way of Suakin." At this point, I coughed to taunt my companion for making at least one mistake. Little princesses could come and go in the night, be saved or perish, but a jest between Bedouins must be followed to its end, like a point of honor.

"You mock me?" the child asked, as though we had struck her.

"Nay, nay." And I bent and kissed her between her straight, black brows, an offense to have me hook-hanged in some parts of Islam, but Izubahil took no umbrage and almost smiled. When I had given her some more water, she continued her story.

"We came by Berber, where dwell my kinsmen of the Sennar, and by the Oasis of El Rab. In due course we passed within sixty miles of the land of Sheik el Beni Kabir, who must be your master."

"Aye."

"It was desert more forsaken and dreary than the Sands of Gidi, whereupon the holy man, who hangs ever at Mahound's side, saw a vision. It was of a lover to my mother, a great lord of Hogar, before I was born. When Mahound reproached her, she said it was indeed true, and laughed into his face like the Princess of Spears that she was, but said I was of Mahound's seed. Then Mahound took the knife that he wears on his left arm and cut my mother's throat, and her blood gushed upon the ground, and she fell dead."

Then Izubahil cleared her throat, causing Timor and I to remember our good jesting, and his hand went up to his amulet, and my heart stood still.

"It was then a question in Mahound's mind whether my mother had lied as to my begetting, for the holy man had turned white, and would not or could not tell. Then Mahound swore that Allah would judge, and ordered that I be set upon my horse of state, with a handful of dates, a square of camel cheese, and one jug of water, the horse to wear the neck shafts that we call the Withholders from Wayside Desire. If Allah preserved me, it was a sign I was of his seed. If I died, it would be only the death of a *shermoot*. And at first I thought I would rather die than be proven of Mahound's begetting, but when the morning turned to the heat of noon, and this to the cool of evening, and this to the cold of night, and the food and water were gone, and my tongue swelled in my mouth, then my spirit failed, and I entreated Messiner (Messiah?) and his enemy Shaitan that I might be found, even if I were made a slave girl to a beggar. It was written that you should find me, and lo, it came to pass. It must be that I am Mahound's daughter, but whether I am or not, I am your protected."

I could not answer for a while, being carried out of myself by her story and its telling. She told it with the grave eloquence to which Arabic is so well adapted—the noble language of poets, singers, and dreamers. It was not her native argot, although no doubt all well-educated Tuareg girls mastered it. She was no more than thirteen. She had been exposed to desert death for around twenty hours, and was just now saved. I knew that the women of the Tuareg were the depositors of their songs and poetry and tales, that they were taught when children to perform in the assemblies, and no Tuareg woman would ever dream of acknowledging inferiority to a man; still I believed that the answer went deeper than this. Mahound's daughter or not, she was an authentic princess of one of the most proud and dauntless races that ever lived.

Then I knew that in bringing her into my life, fate that had always dealt greatly with me, whether for woe or weal, had, after many a winter, moved nobly in my behalf.

4

While Izubahil ate—not turning from our gaze as would a Bedouin girl—I had a chance to contemplate her half-ripe beauty and to dwell upon her in reverie. The moon was still high, and its vast, copious downpour on the desert, like solid silver rain, invoked a mood of mystery and wonder. Without high lights or glare, the light was like the north light that painters love, marvelously softened.

Kerry, an Orientalist, had told me long ago that the Tuareg are one of the purest of the Berber strains, their ancestral whiteness darkened by the sun. They had adopted a mild version of the Arab's religion, but had not mixed their blood, and there were subtle but telling differences between Izubahil and our Bedouin belles. Beauty was no stranger to the daughters of Kabir, but this was richer and more voluptuous. The lips were more full; the eyes, larger and softer, if not as brilliant; the expression conveyed by the countenance in repose, more happy. Izubahil was lighter of skin than Timor, among the most pale-colored in the tribe; but its tints and not its degree of pallor would determine its beauty.

Indeed, I did not think she would be beautiful if her skin were white and her hair golden: the primitive molding of her face needed the pale dusk of the desert where she dwelt and of which she was a part. She was a princess who had never seen a palace. Her hall was a tent or a thorn-enclosed camp under the sky, her wardrobe a bale on a camel's back; she might have owned great herds of camels before her banishment, but her jewels were some silver ornaments and harness trappings. Yet her pedigree might be longer and far more reliable than any in Europe. If an English colonial officer would not admit her to his stuffy parlor—if an American missionary would see her only as a benighted soul to be saved—still I dreamed that a great traveler, a poet, or even a prince of the Valois would instantly perceive her royalty. Perhaps it was far more real than most so-called, since it was not based on trappings and needed none.

The chill of the night caused Timor to gather faggots of camel thorn. I lighted them with my flint-and-tinder; the girl spread her long, shapely hands to the flame. I saw now that her skin was light brown with pale red tints. Her eyes appeared dark blue, her hair raven black. Her developing beauty lay in a symmetry of face and form, more Egyptian than Grecian, but of classic purity. She was already as tall as our tallest Bedouin women, who, like most of our mares, stood fifteen hands; when Izubahil shot up to her full height, she could stand with El Shermoot at sixteen hands. The joining of her long bare arms with her glossy shoulders told me she was clean-limbed as a gazelle.

"Although I am a slave, my having found you on the desert gives me a claim upon you until I deliver you to our sheik," I told her lightly. "Is it not so?"

"It would take ten judges, each as wise as Daniel, to decide the matter, still it may be so," she replied with surprising sprightliness. The Tuareg women were famous for their love of jest.

"If a slave may not address a princess by her first name, surely the finder may dub his foundling what he sees fit. In my native tongue, the name Izubahil becomes Isabel. Also, your eyes and your young limbs are like those of a *ghazal*, which word in my speech is gazelle. So I will call you Isabel Gazelle."

"Iss-a-bel Gah-zaille?"

"Yes. I think it fits you well."

"My mother had a pet *ghazal*—gah-zell—when she bore me in her womb. Do you think it marked me?"

"It could be so."

"I accept the name. And what will I call you, my lord?"

"Omar."

"And the venerable freeman who followed you?"

"Timor."

"Now is it your will that we ride? If we do not, I will fall asleep."

"You can ride and sleep, too, Isabel Gazelle."

"I pray you not to put any bonds upon me to hold me in the saddle. I swear I will stay awake and not fall."

Timor fastened the dead gelding's silver shoes, saddle, and bridle on his croup. The ivory neck shafts that Isabel called Withholders from Wayside Desire he broke in his strong hands. I set her on the neck of my spare mare, mounted behind her, then laid her across my lap.

"I entreated you not to put any bonds on me," she murmured as we started the long trail back.

"Have I done so?"

"What are these?" She touched my arms, her eyes brimming with moonlight in spite of the sleepy curl of her full lips. "Since I am yet young, no doubt they will wear off before I must go to my husband's tent, but I cannot run with my namesake, the gah-zell."

The daughters of the Bedouin and no doubt the Tuareg learn flirtation when very young. Yet I doubted if this remarkable utterance could be called that. She had been giving me quick, furtive glances, no doubt trying to get used to my appearance; and although she had decided to trust me—what other choice did she have?— plainly she found it ugly and most strange. More likely she had performed a courtesy according to the highly conventionalized etiquette of Tuareg belles. A great many gifted but primitive peoples pride themselves on their fluency in the language of love.

"You will run soon enough and too far from me, Isabel Gazelle," I answered.

She gave me a wide smile, wriggled until she was comfortable, then fell instantly asleep.

We trotted the horses for the first hour, but I was so yielding to the jerky motion that my little passenger slept well. When I changed to my gelding, she barely roused, and in spite of the loss and ordeal she had suffered, I thought that the safety that she felt in my arms saved her from evil dreams. My own waking dreams were manifold and strange. Again and again I had the illusion of being under Isabel's protection instead of her being under mine, and when I dispelled it as a nodding man dispels sleep, still the air was sharp in my nostrils and pain zigzagged across my forehead and my body seemed without weight, as in that strange moment when I promised to take the name of Holgar Blackburn and make a good showing for him in Tavistock; and I believed that the spirit of prophecy was upon me—as it has come upon so many dwellers of the desert—and if I would open my mouth and speak, truth would come forth. Perhaps I was afraid to do so. As a morning or a night may be beautiful, so can an hour. It was not perfect, but it was lovely. I did not ask it to stop flowing and stand still; I was being borne down its stream on a voyage of discovery.

The lovely, warm relaxed body across my breast and in the hollow of my arm wrought upon me after a while, arousing a great passion, but it brought no pain or the least temptation to despoil her now. I did not yearn to relieve it, and instead would store it for some enchanted hour to come, for my gift to her, a gift fit for a desert princess, and which such as she could prize.

I was brought back to myself by Isabel's stirring and waking. Her eyes opened, she looked at me without surprise, glanced to the eastern horizon, and said one startling word.

It was *orora* and I could not doubt it was the Tamashek word for the breaking dawn. Since it was inseparable from *aurora*, I mused for a moment on some ancient tie between the wild, nomadic Tuareg and Eternal Rome. Yet it was not as strange as the tie between a Tuareg princess and a former Yankee sailor now a slave. I would not be content with those cold and distant thrills. I would not wait patiently for what might come to pass. If I could, I would force fate's hand. . . .

The night had passed and the moon set while I was in reverie. Now we were nearing the encampment, but I could not slow my horse to a walk to prolong the vigil. I must spur him into a canter and finally to a headlong race with his own shadow, so we could arrive at the tents in a drum-roll of hooves and with yells befitting only a rider at breakneck pace. For the desert had brought forth a new wonder, and the Beni Kabir would never forgive an unsplendid return; and bards living and yet unborn would spurn the tale.

When Isabel saw the distant tents, she sat up and asked me to put her on my croup.

"Is it fitting that a princess ride behind a slave?" I asked.

"I was the captive of the desert and you took me from it, so now I am your captive—until you yield me up."

"That won't be long."

It was no feat for a Bedouin and a Tuareg girl to change positions on a galloping horse. When I let him run, meanwhile whooping like an Indian on the warpath, she adjusted her robe, pressed one hand into my short ribs to help keep her balance, and rode with her left arm akimbo, no doubt a ceremonious position among the Tuareg. I wished I could see her face as we swept by my wide-eyed tribesmen by the cooking fires. I could be sure she would show them only her beautiful profile, as African royalty were wont to do since the first carvings on stone, and her expression would be serene.

Circling the row of thornbush kraals where horses neighed and hounds barked, I pulled up before Suliman's pavilion. Timor and I dismounted and stood at our horseheads; he rose from his carpet, but did not speak until the whole encampment had gathered. Then he addressed Timor first.

"What word, Timor ibn Fareth?"

"None, O Sheik. But the slave Omar has word of what he found on the desert."

"Omar, you have my leave to speak."

I recited the girl's history as she had given it to me, speaking eloquently and punctuating with a finger in the palm of my left hand.

"There is no God but Allah," Suliman proclaimed when I was through. "Izubahil, the slave Omar, your finder, told that you speak Arabic. First, I offer you the shelter of the tents of Beni Kabir and the protection of my scimitar, and of the rifles, pricked and primed, of my followers."

The girl replied with the stately, *"Dakkil-ak ya Shaykhe!"*

"It is a great wonder that you were found, and it would not be so save by the will of Allah, and it comes to me that thereby your daughterhood to Mahound, Emir of the Kel Innek, is proven in all men's sight, the stars of heaven bearing witness, and the evil charge he made has been flung into his teeth; and if we rode swiftly and overtook his caravan, he would acknowledge you before the elders, or they would leave him on the desert impaled on his own spear, for a lying dog." Suliman paused and caught his breath. "But it may be you would not have us do so."

"Nay, O Sheik, I would not."

"For a delicate maiden"—but she did not look delicate to me, sitting straight as a lance on my gelding—"and a princess to be so cruelly cast forth by her own sire for the sake of a base suspicion could turn her love for him to hate. More, she would well fear some other deadly stroke at his lightest whim."

"Yea, that is so."

"What is your wish, Izubahil? Speak plainly without fear."

"I wish to remain with you, O Sheik, and your people, until such time as I wed; then by your leave, I will go with my husband to the tents of the Kel Innek and gather up my camels and donkeys and sheep, and the men of my mother's household who are my servants, and bring them here. For then my father Mahound will not dare deny me, I being no longer his daughter, but a wife of the Beni Kabir, and Allah had spared me not for a day but until I have taken a noble husband, which will indeed cast his lie into his teeth."

"There's no harm in that," the sheik replied, dropping from the classic Arabic of Oman to the dialect. "And I wish my only son, Selim, were old enough to become your husband when the time is ripe, but lo, he has seen only eight suns and may not wed for eight suns more. Even so, there are many sons of Beni Kabir, warriors and riders second to none, of good name, and tall, and valiant, who'll vie for your beauteous hand. And meanwhile you will be in the care of the widow of an elder who has no sons and her female slave."

"It is a great mercy, and also I entreat——"

Isabel paused, and I thought her eyes glimmered in the bursting light.

"Speak, my daughter."

"I ask not to be shut away from Omar, except as is meet, since it was his kismet to find me on the desert, and therefore we've made bond, and he stands closest to me among all your followers, even though he's a slave."

"Truly, he was the instrument of your saving and of our present happiness, and he may be to you as an older brother, as long as is meet. If he were my slave instead of a slave of another, I would set him free. If he were my son of the blood instead of my heart, I would do more than that. But as it is, he or I can do—nothing."

The effect of this on the throng was instantaneous and profound. The Arabs, and especially the Bedouins are an emotional and imaginative people; and suddenly a fact that they all knew, that they took for granted, was seen in a new light. I stood before the sheik's tent, holding the horse that had borne in from the desert this beautiful castaway, a maiden straight as a lotus flower just ere it comes to bloom; of paler color than they; more graced than their own daughters; only a little younger than many brides; more royal in their eyes than any fabled queen of Frankistan or the saki of the Egyptian Khedive. Kismet—or Allah—had moved in my behalf, they knew, but only so far. Now the new-risen sun cast its glaring ray upon us, far off the sand was stirred to hissing life by the morning breeze; about us stretched the desert, the beginning and the end of all things. I did not turn and look behind me, but I saw Suliman's eyes brim with tears, and I knew all eyes that looked upon us were the same.

Their sudden awareness of immutable fate and the wave of sorrow sweeping over us all undermined Isabel and breached the wonderful gallantry that was her last bulwark against exhaustion. I saw her sway and start to topple. Catching her in my arms, I carried her and laid her on the carpet at Suliman's feet. Then rose a vibrant voice, chanting high and clear.

"O Suliman ibn Ali!"

"Ah, Ishmael ibn Abdul!"

At once the bard began his song, the words extemporaneous, set to a melody I had heard only once before, when Ishmael sang of a young tribesman who had been killed defending his mare against a lion.

> Whose tracks are these that lead into the waste?
> Omar looked at them and pondered.
> Who has ridden from the southward into the great thirst?
> Omar saddled his horse at midnight and rode forth.
> With him rode his mullah Timor, wise in the ways of the desert.
> Fast rode Omar, his shadow short beneath him, the white moon
> overhead.
> Fast followed Timor, and the hooves drummed the clay.
> What will Omar behold, what wonder hath Allah done?
> Fast sped the beautiful horses, fast the hours,
> Till they came to the desert's secret heart!
> What is this that Omar spies, far away in the moonlight?

Lo, it is a maiden bound fast to her horse's back.
Now he has cut her bonds away.
Now he has taken her on his croup.
Now he has gazed into her face of matchless beauty.
O the deep wells of her eyes that reflect his own eyes,
O the cup of her lips from which a lover's lips will drink the nectar
    of Paradise.
He has found her, how soon may he have her for his own?
Allah hath wrought him of ungainly form and fearful visage,
Yet appointed him to find her on the desert.
She is not yet ripe for love, but the moon will return
And not fail to return until it looks down and sees her ready,
A maiden and a princess arrayed as a bride.
How soon may Omar take her to his tent for his bride of matchless
    beauty?
Must I answer, O Sheik?
Must I tell you, Beni Kabir?
Never, never, never, never.
For Omar is a slave,
And the bride that awaits him is a chain of iron.

CHAPTER 13

The Wakening

1

NOT MANY months after Isabel Gazelle had come to live with us,
I had a chance to dispatch a long-harbored letter addressed to the
American consul at Gibraltar, and which I had written when my
first missive brought no return.

The bearer now was a Jew, Aaron ben Levi, who sold *dawa* (medicine) throughout North Africa, and who needed bitterly five pieces
of gold. These I paid him—my total store—for his promise to deliver
the letter within two years, or return it to me with the sum. The
Jews we knew were hard bargainers, but once the bargain was
made, they could be trusted to keep it with great staunchness.
Since Aaron was no renegade, I kept a lighter heart in the ensuing
seasons, and my dreams were sweet.

In November, 1814, he returned to our encampment, and when
my eyes sought his across the thorn fire, he shook his head. When

the others were wrapped in their burnooses, we met in the gray moonlight. Pale, he handed me my letter and five pieces of gold.

"I could not deliver it. There's no longer any United States consul in Gibraltar. The consulate doors have been closed and the officer has fled and so have all his countrymen. Even if he were there, it would be useless to give it to him, the people said, because there's no longer any United States."

I waited a few seconds before I spoke. It was to clear my head, put my tongue in good control, and to bid my informant not to speak wildly.

"What causes you to think that?"

"There's no doubt of the war. It was with England, and it began in the summer of 1812. For a while the Yankees made a good showing. But when the English had beaten Napoleon and sent him to Elba, they brought their troops down from the North, from a place called Montreal, and also up the rivers from Virginia. The capital—named for the first president—has been burned to the ground. That much is certain. I had it from one of my nation, one Gideon whose home is in Italy and whose kinsman Judah Touro is a merchant in the city of New Orleans."

"Does Boston stand, and New York, and Baltimore?"

"That I don't know. Gideon had it from Judah Touro that the Redcoats had been driven back from the wild lands in the West, and Yanki fleets on the lakes there—lakes as big as seas—have held their own well. Much land has been laid waste, but Gideon doubts if the old men who fought under Washington have been hanged as was first told, or the young ones captured in battle have been shot for insurrection. For a long while no Yanki ship was seen on the high seas. Lately Gideon has it that small ships, in some numbers, have come out of nowhere to harry the English traders. Now the rumor is that the king will make peace, spare the Yankis that are left, and forgive all treason, provided they swear allegiance to his throne and be ruled by his governors. Whether the Yankis have agreed to these terms Gideon did not know, but certainly there is talk of peace, and the great money-lending house of Bauer of Frankfort on the Main, which is called Rothschild, meaning the red shield, has given out to its agents that the guns will be silent before the Christmas of the Gentiles."

"If there's peace before Christmas—or Christmas ten years from now—you can be sure the Yankis haven't agreed to those terms."

"Think you they would fight that long before surrendering up their freedom?"

I started to say I knew it, but how could I know? Aaron told me, on Gideon's word, that no few Boston merchants of great wealth had connived with the captains of English warships blockading our coast to let their goods through to supply the armies and fleets attacking their own country. But I remembered the Boston men whom I had known, aft and b'fore the mast. I thought of Ethan Allen, with whom Farmer Blood had sat at Sunday dinner, and Anthony Wayne whom my father had seen at Yorktown, John Rogers Clark and Joshua Barney and the silversmith Paul Revere. I had been gone from under the American flag for thirteen years, but I doubted if the ways of the people had changed very much.

When I was in school in Bath we were something like four million. In ten years, we were five million, three hundred thousand—I had proudly told Sophia so—at that rate of gain, more than a third, we must be eight million now. The wagons were winding up the western roads and the flatboats making down the Ohio River when I had left home. By now there were farms and towns, thick or scattered, all the way to the Mississippi. Could I picture a lank frontiersman beyond the Appalachians, wearing a coonskin cap and armed with a Kentucky rifle, bowing down to an English lord?

"England couldn't conquer the land west of the mountains, let alone to the River," I told Aaron ben Levi.

"If you mean the great river that flows by New Orleans, where dwells Judah Touro, one of the great of my nation—it marks only half of the American domain."

"I don't comprehend you."

"Ten—eleven years ago, the American president bought from Napoleon the Louisiana Territory, running clean to the Rocky Mountains. I saw Judah's letter, writ in Hebrew, with my own eyes."

My neck prickled fiercely and my scalp felt too tight and I could not speak.

"You turned red in the face, and now white," said Aaron gravely.

"I can't help it."

"Unwittingly I've dealt you a cruel blow, to remind you how long you've been gone from your native land."

"I needed no reminder. I've kept good count of the days. You only reminded me of how the world has gone forward while I've been away. And the news you gave me is good. I've no fear whatever of America ceasing to be free."

174

"My people wandered in the wilderness for forty years. Yet they came at last into the Promised Land, and waxed great."

"Ah! Ah!"

"You're not a young man any longer—thirty-four or five?—but add twenty years to that number, and you would reach only your full strength of character and mind."

"I'll be free—or I'll be dead—in seven years."

I had told myself this before, but now I had spoken it aloud before a witness, and I knew it to be true.

"I will entreat God to spare your life. Farewell, Omar."

"You've run a great risk, bearing my letter, and brought me news, good and ill, of use to me, so you're welcome to as many of these five gold pieces as you'll accept."

"My friend, I'll accept none. I didn't succeed in delivering your letter, and the gold pieces came to me at a time of need, and I've had the use of them without usury for two years. We Jews are good husbandmen, but it is against our law to reap the corners of the field."

2

I thought to send the letter by some other bearer, but could not bring myself to do so. In the first place, I could find none in whom to put great faith; and I became afraid that if a search was ever made for me, I would not be found. It came to me in my dreams that this desert drama would play to the end without help from any god from the machine. The forces that would free me or destroy me were already on the scene.

The remainder of the year 1814 and a good part of 1815 were the happiest I had spent in slavery. The colt El Stedoro had been foaled in 1812; in this period he grew from a gangling colt to a wondrous chip off the old block of El Shermoot. An uglier three-year-old the Bedouins swore they had never seen—that beautiful Farishti had given him birth remained beyond their comprehension—but they could not keep their eyes from shining when they saw him run. He had neither the soaring motion of his mother nor the headlong charge of his sire: he appeared to progress in a series of tremendous bounds. He loved to jump—no common thing in horses—and no wall of thorns we had yet built, some of them close on six feet, could keep safe the women's store of corn. Running with the other young-

175

sters, he cleared rock piles and dry watercourses as though taking wing.

My duties toward him were light—watering him when his wadi pools went dry, pampering him with camel milk and bread flaps, and tickling his sharp, leaf-shaped ears, almost the only mark of the Arab that he bore. All this was to keep him gentle and in hand. Suliman had forbade that he bear halter, saddle, or rider until he was four. Thereby he should develop strength and fleetness before going into servitude to man.

But there was a far greater wonder in these years than that of an Anglo-Arab colt bidding fair to become the best hunting and stee-plechasing stallion the Beni Kabir had yet to see, and that was a foundling maiden of moving but immature beauty growing to be the most beautiful daughter of the desert they had ever seen. At fourteen she was breath-taking; as she neared fifteen she surpassed, in my fellows' sober opinion, any queen or concubine in Yussuf Pasha's harem, and was fit for a gift from Suliman to the Grand Porte of Constantinople, Defender of the Faith.

I did not measure her by these standards. I saw a tall, slender girl, whose skin was a light reddish-brown, and who was somehow the central and compelling figure in every scene in which she had a part. She took the eye of everyone; it was always with an effort that I took my eyes off her. I felt queerly, even mystically about her. Ordinarily quiet, not constantly singing like the Arab women, occasionally given to outbursts of strange eloquence, she made me daydream that she had come here from some other age or unknown continent, wherein people were happier than in these scenes, and more graced.

She moved so lightly that I could not for a long time believe what Timor told me—that she was remarkably strong. I began to perceive it by the easy way she lifted heavy bales and boxes, or swung pails of water in her long brown naked arms. She seemed to enjoy movement of any kind. It was a common thing to see happiness on the faces of children as they played or went about their affairs, and in this respect she was childlike. The promise of a smile was on her lips almost all the time—it broke and beamed on the least provocation—and although her eyes were beautiful before then, deeply dark and lustrous, then they became magnetic and mysterious as though they gave forth light.

Unlike a child, she was never bashful or timid. Partly this was an effect of her upbringing in a society wherein femaleness was a glory instead of a disadvantage or mild disgrace, and where she was born to high place; partly though, it was self-confidence derived from physical strength and beauty. She paid not the least attention to the Bedouin's taboo against women riding horses—she was forever taking the pet mares for wild gallops around the camps, unbridled and unsaddled and often unhaltered. She made herself at home in Suliman's *mukaad*, ordinarily forbidden to all except the elders and male guests.

She waxed more womanly with every moon. This development would have suited a far more voluptuous form than hers; and seen in relation to her slender body with its taut waist, lithe hips, long, tapering legs and arms, long neck, and countenance carved with a sword, it was at once startling and thrilling. I could not help but beam when kinsmen from the oasis visited the Bedouins, saw her, cried out on Allah, quoted verses by Jamil, but never asked if she were for sale. Sometimes I grinned to see Suliman watching her, stroking his beard and sighing, but the grin died in a chill wave of ill omen, for the sighs meant that the sheik's sixty and more years lay heavily upon him, weakened as he was by capture and torture not long before I met him in Calypso's cave, and he might not have long to live.

What right had I, Omar the slave, to be proud of this tall, dark princess of the Tuareg who graced our camps? I had found her only through the chance that Timor gave me; and I had no real claim on her. But she had made one on me as her protector and companion. She was never very far from me for very long. If I invited her to accompany the old hostler and me on our varied jaunts, she came in joy, not even asking how many nights we must sleep under the stars. If I did not invite her, we had only to ride a few miles to see her loping along behind us on one of Suliman's pet mares. When she overtook us, she would ride into the wind, kick up dust in our faces, then return with her eyes agleam.

"You might as well have asked me in the first place," she would say. "For I intend to stay with you as long as I'm a virgin."

3

So long inured to celibacy, my body and mind adjusted to it, I was not greatly taxed by the presence of this vivid, vital girl, entering into marriageable age, in our lonely bivouacs. Vividness and vitality are essential components of female beauty—the thing itself

177

is bound round with male desire—yet I remained intensely conscious of Isabel's beauty without being tormented to possess it in its full. Partly the answer lay in my profound acceptance—a different thing from reconciliation—of slavehood. I did not feel eligible for a free-born woman's favor. I could not offer her the refuge of my arms because they were chained; I could not endow her with my worldly goods—such as the strength of my body and brain, my prowess, even my whole manhood—because they belonged to another. They did not do so in any law I would recognize, but they did in fact.

However, my attitude toward her was delicately balanced, caused by counteracting pressure, and although it held throughout the year 1815, the third since her coming, it could quickly change.

Just before dawn of a cool and dewy January morning, when Timor and I and our entrancing camp follower were bivouacked on the foothills of the Tibesti, the old hostler rode off to investigate some *khors* that might hold water. As the Sahara daylight broke, Isabel Gazelle made quite a display of waking up—she had been covertly watching me clean my rifle for the past ten minutes—then an even greater show of modesty as she dressed. However, she had managed to give me a view of a long thigh of superb molding as she donned her skirt.

I paid her no obvious attention, and presently she came and squatted beside me.

"What are we going to have to eat today?" she asked.

"Why, doesn't the fare suit you?"

"Bread flaps—camel cheese—dates. I'm getting sick of them."

"It will be different today, because all the dates have been eaten."

"Why don't you spend the day hunting? I'll go with you, and you can shoot a bustard or maybe an oryx. But you mustn't shoot any gazelles because I can't eat them."

"I didn't know that."

"You should know it. It was you who named me Gazelle."

"You've eaten plenty of them before now, and sucked the bones for marrow, and got the grease all over your face. Why have you changed?"

"I haven't changed. I'll eat them other times, but not today. If you're not a good enough shot to get any meat, maybe you can rob an ostrich nest. You ought to find some wild honey, too, so tonight we can have a feast."

"Is this a Mohammedan feast day? I didn't know it."

"No, but it was once a feast day among my mother's followers."

"What was the occasion?" She was waiting for me to ask this.

"Oh, just my birthday."

It would be a base slave indeed who, looking at her and hearing her announcement, would not feel a glowing of heart.

"It was just as proper for the Tuareg to celebrate it as for the Spartans to celebrate the birthday of Helen of Troy."

"You think I've not heard of her, but I have. The Tuaregs are pure Berbers"—this was no longer quite true—"and long ago we had much to do with the Greeks and the Romans, and their stories are written down in Tamashek and many maidens know them. That isn't what I started to say. I wonder how the Tuareg—those who came with my mother—keep my birthday now."

I could not answer lightly. I remembered too well a girl of thirteen cast away on the merciless desert.

"I think many tears will fall, Isabel Gazelle. But they will be dried when you return, the bride of a chief's son."

"It comes to me, Omar, that until then we are both exiles from our native lands, you from Frankistan, I from Tuaregstan."

"Now that is so."

"While among the Beni Kabir, we will do even as they, in their sight, but when we are away from their kraals, or alone together, can't we do as we see fit?"

"There's no harm in that—perhaps."

"You've not asked me, Omar, how old I am today."

"I don't need to ask. You're sixteen."

"More than once, you've spoken of me as a child. Dare you do so any more?"

"Nay, *lilla Kabeira* (great lady)."

"Yet I'm in no haste to marry. The women of the Tuareg are not given in marriage by their fathers when they are little children! We choose our husbands after wooing—being wooed by many young warriors, and often a maiden is eighteen before she settles to the loom. Is it the same in Frankistan?"

"It is something the same. Some of our maidens have many wooers, and take a good while to make their choice."

"Now sometimes we woo for the pleasure of wooing, knowing that the youth is too lowly or hasn't enough camels and goats and donkeys to make a good match." Isabel's voice trembled slightly.

"Does a princess of the Tuareg ever woo—or let herself be wooed —by a slave?" I asked.

179

"I could tell you a story of a young slave, most good to look upon, who fell in love with his master's daughter——"

"Would that I were young and good to look upon!"

"It's true you're not a callow youth. I know you're old enough to be my father. Also your shoulders are too broad for your gaunt legs and arms—to judge from what I can see of them—and no doubt your whole form is ungainly. But didn't the sheik's beautiful mare, Farishti, yield to the great raw-boned El Shermoot?"

I could not resist one wondering glance into Isabel's face. It was grave, and her eyes were wide and bright. I had named her Gazelle because of her litheness and lightness and long clean limbs and melting eyes, but it did not begin to do her justice, for there is no such beauty within human imagination as the beauty of woman, and if I should take the wings of morning to all countries and climes, I would find thousands upon thousands who equaled her in this, but few who surpassed her. At present she squatted on her heels by a dying fire of thornwood in the hollow heart of ultimate desolation.

But a change had come over her since she had first come up beside me. She was no longer flirtatious, and some very real emotion wrought in her was struggling for outlet.

"Farishti did so yield," I answered, quietly waiting.

"Omar, in spite of your years, in spite of you being so gaunt and gangling, I wouldn't be angry if you made love to me."

Then as I was catching my breath to answer, she gave a little wail.

"Liar that I am! The truth is not in me, Omar, and you should take a stick and beat me, but do not, for then I must kill you, and go down to hell. It's not always in spite of those things. Sometimes it's because of those things. Your form is like an old lean lion's—nay, like a griffin's with a lion's chest and head and eagle's legs, and your face carved of rock. Often I can't stand to look at you, yet not once but many times you come to me in my sleep and give me lustful dreams. Omar, I'll save my maidenhead for an elder's son, as is meet. He'll be young and tall and shapely, and laughter and song will be in his mouth, and his face will shine in the sun. With him I may return, his kinsmen riding with us, to the encampments of the Kel Innek, and take my mother's followers and my flocks and herds, and cast my father's lie into his teeth. You will go from me some day, and I can't cook meat for a shadow and sleep beside a ghost. But you said the maids in Frankistan are often wooed by many youths before they make their choice. I can't choose you, Omar, but can't you treat me as though I might? Is there any harm in playing I'm a maiden of Frankistan you want for your wife? Play like my other wooers are richer in camels and sheep, and garments of gold and silver cloth, and many are youths of my own age, and some are as good to look upon as Ishmael ibn Abdul, the singer, but you were born the equal of any—haven't you told me so?—and what you lack in riches and youth and handsomeness you can make up in ardor!"

I took both of her long, dusky hands, their pointed fingers more shapely than hardly any under palace lamps.

"Isabel Gazelle, wouldn't you rather have Ishmael ibn Abdul woo you? He'll sing songs to you that the Beni Kabir will remember a thousand and one years."

"He makes songs in my ears, but you make them in my heart. My heart beats in song when you are near. Don't turn from me any more, as though I was a child, or ugly. If you do, I can't go with you and the old hostler any more, or eat from your bowl, or sleep beside your fire, and I must stay in a kraal of thornbush, out of your sight, until the sheik sends me a husband who'll take me away."

"Isabel, let me speak."

"Speak, then."

"You're not in the tents of the Tuareg, whose daughters make free before marriage, but a ward of the Bedouin. You know what store a Bedouin bridegroom sets upon the virginity of his bride."

"I told you I would save——"

"Fire set in the thorn may spread to the kraals. That is a saying of the desert, and here's a stanza from a desert song you know well. 'If you teach me to love the warm wild honey of Bornu, how will I fare on the hungry hills of Borku?'"

"We Tuareg women aren't afraid of fire. The women of Bornu tattoo their faces and are most ugly, and the hills of Borku grow camel thorn and good grass. You are a *farengi* and a Frank." Then, hanging her head in contrition, "Nay, you found me on the desert and I rode behind you, but you make too much of a few kisses, Omar."

"Do I? We shall see."

Instead I had made too little of them, as I found out when I took them. For Isabel looked wildly into my face and fled, white and weeping.

My next few days were days of waiting—but not for Kismet to move. I was not a Bedouin in heart and soul—I could never embrace Islam—Omar the slave was still the Yankee Homer Whitman. Fatalism is a comforting philosophy, but I was suckled in a more stern creed. Nor was I waiting for any sign or sending to light my way.

It was much simpler than any of these. I waited for Isabel to chart a course. That charting would be by instinct. She knew the desert and its people like her own hand. She had a great capacity to survive—the impulse to conquer and live. She would take risks, but not the kind taken by a fool—of great cost if lost, if won, of trifling gain.

In about a fortnight we came on good grass out from the Wells of El Gamar and drove the herds there. The name meant the Rising Moon, a term of endearment, implying great beauty, among the Arabs, and I wondered idly how it came to be applied to some unreliable wells until I saw tonight's moon coming up above basalt outcroppings eastward of the encampment. One night's sail from full, she shone with an intensity that amazed and charmed me. Perhaps the evening air was unusually dry and free from dust in this area, causing the round lamp of burnished silver to hang so near.

I had wandered out of sight of the camp when I discovered Isabel following on Farishti. She slipped off, and with the moonlight on her face, came up to me. That she was on a momentous mission I could not doubt.

"It was my fault, Omar, that you kissed me at the bivouac in the Tibesti foothills when the moon was new," she said.

"I think it was no one's fault," I answered.

"Many would say it was a great fault—when I'm a princess and you're a slave. Since then I've thought of it day and night. I ran away from you—and now I've returned—to find out something. It may be I'll run away again. If I do, if I get on my mare and ride, it's a sign we must part forever. Then tomorrow I'll go to Suliman and tell him I've chosen Ishmael ibn Abdul, for he sings songs that bring my tears, and he's good to look upon, and the son of a malik, second only to the sheik. But if I give you a sign, you'll know I can't part with you."

"For how long? I ask the question in my need."

"For one year—perhaps two years more. And if then you are set free——"

"There's no hope of that, Isabel Gazelle. You heard Ishmael's song and know it was a true song. Still, if we could be sweethearts even for a half a year, I'd be thankful all my life. Many of the days I spent in the slave pen would be paid for."

"It's those days in the slave pen that may part us now."

"I don't know what you mean."

"Hear me, Omar—and don't blame me for what I can't help. When I first saw you, it was on a night like this. The moon turned the desert into silver. Your face frightened me that night—I can't tell you how much—yet I came with you. Since then I've looked at it across a thousand thorn fires, but it still frightens me sometimes. The men say it turned to stone in your eight years in the Sepulcher —and you have other marks I've never seen."

"They told the truth."

"Are the marks ugly, Omar? If they are, I can't take you for my lover. I'm only a Tuareg woman! Forgive me."

"You shall see for yourself."

I slipped off my aba, baring my gaunt chest and gangling arms. Her eyes slowly widened.

"Omar, they're dreadful marks!"

"Look at them closely."

"The Daughters of the Spear would laugh to think of Izubahil accepting courtship from such a scarecrow."

"Then go quickly and get on your horse and fade away in the moonlight."

"Shall I?" she asked herself.

"Yes, if I'm ugly in your eyes and in your heart."

"I didn't say you were ugly in my heart. You put song into my heart. It will live there always. When you're gone across the desert, I'll hear it still."

"When I'm gone across the desert, I'll love you still."

"The love of a slave?" she asked in a low, wondering murmur.

"Yes. Can't you see?"

"I do see, Omar, and now I'll give you a sign."

Up from my back across my gaunt shoulder ran the black scar of the ox whip. Isabel stood on tiptoe and pressed it with her lips. If the wound were still raw upon my soul, it was instantly healed.

CHAPTER 14

The Sword of Kismet

1

In ensuing months my fellows noticed little change in Isabel Gazelle's and my dealings with each other. Her excursions with Timor and me caused no more comment than before—actually the tribespeople had always been pleased by her attachment to me, as a poetic outcome to my finding her on the desert. Quite possibly there was a bar across their minds against them suspecting a love affair. Ishmael ibn Abdul had told in song how I could never have her for my own, and a princess of the Tuareg would turn away from an ungainly slave, twenty years her senior. If sometimes we yielded to brief love play in the sudden lusts of solitude, that was a matter of course among the unwedded, and of no more moment than a little whirlwind rising and toppling far away on the desert.

They might have guessed the truth from the burning glances she sometimes gave me. A surer sign was shown when she and I had been separated many days by the exigencies of desert life—the women campbound to gather precious myrrh or dye, or for a great spinning and weaving of camel's hair, or the men venturing so far into the Thirst that no measure of food or water could be spared for Bringers of Delight, or entering regions harried by robber Bedouins. The hour that she was free to join me, she would saddle a riding camel and strike out, sometimes eighty miles across hissing sands.

Often she sang to me, fierce songs of the Tuareg warriors or tender lyrics of love, and told me many a thrilling tale handed down by mothers to daughters in her tribe. Once, as I lay with my head in her lap while she combed out my tangled hair with a thorn comb, she recounted an adventure of which she had personal knowledge, occurring only a few weeks before I met her. Its region was the northern part of the Bilad-es-Sudan (the Country of the Blacks), two long days' camel journey southeast of the Nile town of Atbara and east of the river of the same name. On his return journey from Mecca, twenty of Mahound's best riding camels were stolen by the Beni Amer—the dominant tribe—and tracked by a force of Tuareg.

184

In the course of the pursuit a servant of Isabel's mother, named Adem, had encountered a former clansman who had been captured in battle and sold into slavery. Now free and prosperous, he had entertained Adem at his kraal, and in the absence of the other Tuareg, had told him of a strange thing. Of this Adem did not speak to Mahound's men—they were not the Sons of Spears—but he had confided it to Isabel Gazelle.

"On the cliffs separating the desert from the plowed land, there had been a rockslide," my companion told me. "It had revealed a flight of steps leading up, a passage, and then another flight of steps under the cliff. The painting on the wall was like those a fellah had seen far to the north, and which showed it to be a tomb of a Pharaoh living long ago. But while those tombs had been robbed of their gold and silver furnishings, this tomb had not been robbed."

"I'll wager it didn't take long."

"You'd lose the wager, Omar. It's not yet been robbed. The tomb is guarded by spirits of the dead who kill all who go down the second flight of steps. A good many tried to go down in the first years after the steps were found, Adem's clansman told him. Those walking behind would see their torches flicker and go out. When they called, there was no answer, and none of the silent ones ever returned. At last the king of the Beni Amer decreed that no others should try, lest the evil spirits come forth from the passage and kill all the people, so he had many cartloads of rock brought to the place and dumped over the entranceway, closing it forever."

"How long ago was this?"

"Adem said that it had been closed for twenty years, and most folk had forgotten the steps were there."

"I didn't know that any Pharaohs were buried as far up the Nile as Atbara."

"I can't say as to that, Omar."

"Is the country rich in gold?"

"Not now, but long ago, much gold was found. The country was then known as Aphar, Adem told me."

Aphar was suggestive of Ophir, the gold-rich region of Biblical times. The story worked on my imagination and recurred again and again to my mind. That I should hear it from the lips of Isabel Gazelle, who had ridden across the desert into my life, smacked of fate.

"When you return to the Tuareg, will Adem become your servant?" I asked on a later occasion.

Her eyes filled with tears. "He fought for Mama when Mahound was about to kill her, and his body was riddled with spears."

In due course I asked, "Did Adem mention the name of his clansman that he found in the Bilad-es-Sudan?" It would be only a tenth chance. . . .

"Yes, and I had heard of him before. He was Takuba, whose name means 'sword.' He was a great swordsman as well as spear-thrower, and my mother's distant cousin."

"He may be still alive."

Isabel gave me a great wondering glance, then touched the silver cross—with her a pagan amulet—which she wore at her throat.

2

This was early August, 1815. The far-off belated echo of the guns of Waterloo had reached us only a few days before. I had been in slavery over fourteen years, six of them as Suliman's ward, and I had begun to be darkly haunted by the flight of time. It was like that of an arrow that ever missed its mark.

Late September brought one whole day and night of heavy rain, an occasion for great rejoicing among the Beni Kabir. Only the little children slept under such pavilions as we could raise; the sheik stayed up, beside himself with happiness, to listen to its gurgling drums and to drink green tea and barley beer and smoke endless pipes with the elders. Soon after sunrise he rode to look at a near-by wadi. As he rode back, I saw that his face had a gray cast and the skin over its bones appeared taut. Hamyd, his old sais, noticed it too, and stood near as Suliman started to dismount.

But the rein fell from his hand as some awful agony clutched him, convulsing his countenance and form. He could not move or speak—we stared at him in helpless horror—then he stiffened and toppled like a falling palm tree.

Hamyd caught him, carried him into the tent, and laid him on his carpet. A long, anguished wail went up from all the people at the sight, and the elders ran from their kraals to crowd around him. For once I did not stand and wait for a slave's portion. But at my pushing through the pale, gasping, terror-stricken mass, none rebuked me, and some made way for me, because they remembered that on a few other occasions I had given *dawa* of some sort while their hands hung at their sides.

"I speak for the mullahs of Frankistan," I told them. "Stand back so the sheik may have more air."

They obeyed, entreaty in their eyes, but when I turned to Suliman, there was almost nothing else that I could do to help him. His lips and temples had turned blue, his eyes were half open; and I could hardly see his chest rise and fall. When I laid my ear over his heart, I could hardly hear its beat, faint and fast. At my nod to wide-eyed Timor, he ran to get a bowl of moldered horse manure. This I worked until the smell of ammonia came forth strongly, and held it under Suliman's nose. He uttered a coughing sound, and I thought his breathing was a little deeper. When I listened again to his heart, it was still fluttering, but easier to hear.

Then there was nothing to do but watch and wait and pray. My prayers were of different form than those raised to Allah by the weeping Bedouin prostrating themselves on the sand, but their intent and content was the same. Yet the long day passed, the camels went unmilked, the mares nuzzled and shoved us wanting pettings to help some trouble they smelled but did not understand, and the falcons screamed and the greyhounds lay in disconsolate sleep before we could say for certain that the sheik was better. I knew it when the blue tints faded from his face. At midnight he mumbled a few words that we could not catch, then moved up out of trance into slumber.

At dawn he aroused enough to tell us that he would not leave us yet—that the cup of death had come nigh but had passed from him—and we must attend to our work. That night he drank some fermented camel milk and ate a handful of dates—these last a famed restorer of lost strength. I thought of a date seed I had found by torchlight in a black chamber of Calypso's cave, far away where I was free, long ago when I was young.

Thereafter he appeared to mend with thrilling swiftness and surety. In a week he was walking about, in two weeks he took out Farishti for a little canter over the young, thin, narrow-bladed grass which when seen at an angle in certain lights made the ground a delicate green. The Beni Kabir watched him with glowing faces and proud eyes. Behold him, straight in his saddle, guiding the sable-brown mare with the pressure of his knees, controlling her gait with his voice, in his youth one of the greatest riders in all Islam, still a horseman before Allah! They said he rode with green spurs—one of the most cryptic and untranslatable compliments in the Arabic language.

187

In another week his followers had forgotten their terror and blamed his attack on a cramp, caused by his riding in cold rain with a full stomach. Now he looked as well—even a little better—than before. But their need of him was not as dire as Isabel Gazelle's and mine, and that caused her eyes and mine to search deeper than theirs, and then to meet in swift compassion for each other. We perceived something in his face that was not there before. How did we know it was not the mark of death?

In these weeks we hardly dared leave the encampment. In our rare moments of privacy, all we could do was hold hands and say comforting things that neither of us believed. Then came the sheik's word that on the morrow we would break camp to follow the young grass. Wasn't that a sign that the danger had passed? But at sunset my heart fainted at the word brought by his sais Hamyd. Omar the slave was to come at once and alone into his *mukaad*.

"And may Allah be merciful upon us both," Hamyd breathed.

I found Suliman seated on his carpet, resting one shoulder on a camel saddle. He permitted me to sit, then offered me green tea and a water pipe, as though we were to converse on the beauty of woman and of horses, and the splendor of war. I declined these good things once and then again, and he did not offer them the third time, to let me know that this was not a meeting of pleasure, and everything had changed. Anyway, I could not have smoked or quaffed through my full throat.

He raised his hand in some ancient gesture of kings, let it fall, and spoke in classic Arabic.

"O Omar, when a soothsayer of the emir casts his master's horoscope and finds that his days are niggardly numbered, sometimes he does not bear him the evil tidings, lest his master vent his terror and woe upon him. But if the emir is worthy of his throne, he will honor the word-bringer, for thus forewarning him to put his affairs in order and keep the vows he has made unto Allah, and do good works, and, at last, to bring about him his loved ones, that he may gaze once more upon their faces ere he drinks the cup of death."

"*Ah, ah, O Sheik!*"

"Harken to me well, Omar, my son. When the sire of my grandsire was in his fifty-sixth year, he wakened in the night with a fluttering in his left side, in and about his heart, not unlike that in the womb of a young wife when she first feels life. It came and went from the time of the dawn prayers until midday prayers, then suddenly my grandsire's sire was stricken with a woeful pain, in which he groaned pitifully, after which he fell down as though dead. But he did not die then. He lived to tell his son, my grandsire, of both the fluttering and of the nature of the pain, which he said was as if his heart were put into a vise and grievously compressed. This was in the early fall; and in late winter he felt the strange fluttering again. It lasted from the sundown prayers until the middle of the night, then again he groaned pitifully, in great pain, and again he fell down, and this time he did not arise, for the cup of death had been brought to him, and he had drunk it."

"*Bismillah!*" I murmured as Suliman paused. He nodded his head and spoke on.

"Now my grandsire's sire had been a man like to me, in being lightly made, with his hair and his beard growing like mine. But his son, Ibrim, my grandsire, was a man of big bone, taking after his mother, a Kababish woman, and he lived to the winter of his years. But his son, my father, Ali ibn Ibrim, was again light-boned and light-bearded as I am, and in his sixty-fourth year he, too, felt a fluttering about his heart, and in a few hours the great pain came, and he fell down as if dead. And he too walked again—from seeding until harvest—then the fluttering came back, and in a few hours the pain came back, and again he fell writhing, and so he died. And it must be, Omar, that you have divined the tale's end, for you have turned white."

"I cannot help it, O Sheik."

"In your place, I, too, would blanch. I felt the fluttering, coming and going, before midnight on the night of rain, and the pain smote me at sunrise, as you know. In some months, how many I know not, the warning will come again, and—and I will no longer be your protector and stand between you and the chains of iron. The word has gone forth from you and from me that you will return, and it is so written in the stars. But when the door of the Sepulcher of Wet Bones has closed behind you, then the bond is taken up, your debt to me and mine to my pasha have been paid, and if you find a way to break out—perhaps with help of friends from across the desert— I will lift my voice from my deep grave in thanks to Allah."

"What friends, O Sheik? I ask the question in my need."

"Timor is one. If ten or twelve, a number easy to spare from the herding, would follow him across the desert, much might be done. They would have to come in secret some months after you had been sent back, and be a different party from the other, so their faces would not be known. But my pasha is their pasha; to offend him is to offend Allah; the way is very long and the danger great and—I do not know." Suliman began to speak in the vernacular. "It comes to me that Izubahil will help you all she can, which may be more than we dare believe. When Mahound dies—the dog still lives, whining to Allah—she can resume her place among the Tuareg; or if she weds one of their chiefs or becomes the wife of a noble Arab, she'll have certain limited power. True, her people dwell a thousand miles across the Thirst—and no prisoner has ever made good his escape from the Sepulcher of Wet Bones. But remember, there's no desert that can't be crossed at last, no wall too strong to break down."

I longed to make some worthy answer, but my tongue stuck.

"One thing more. Tell only Timor—and if you like, the maiden Izubahil—of these tidings, for my great horsemen are also children in some things, and there would be no laughter or no singing for months on end, and no good talk at the fires. I want them to be happy to the hour of my departure, then when they have wept their fill, to be happy again. And I would you were one of them, Omar, to take Izubahil to wife, and to live out your days as a Bedouin, worshiping what God your soul decrees as long as you keep faith with the bread and salt, for I have learned to love you as a father loves his son."

He raised his hand in a kingly gesture, about to give me leave to go, but instead his eyes turned dark and he made a plea.

"Now leave me quickly, Omar, so you won't see my tears."

3

I saw Isabel's tears when I called her from the cooking-fires and told her the news. There was only a young moon, but it showed them welling in her eyes and on her brown cheeks. She asked me to meet her in an hour at the place we called the Stairway of the Jinns.

It lay about two miles from the encampment, and was an outcropping of some great rock-fold—as though it were a mountaintop rising out of a sea of sand. It towered about three hundred feet, and got its name from a series of receding ledges about ten feet apart, the first two easily gained by climbing broken rock at one side. When I arrived there, Isabel Gazelle had unsaddled her horse and was waiting for me on the bottom step.

"Bring your saddlecloth," she told me.

I did so, and found hers already spread on the flat stone. Near by was a jug of water, and another that I guessed held fermented camel's milk, and a cluster of dates. She took my cloth and spread it on top of hers.

"Will you take your ease, my lord?" she asked.

"Yes."

I dropped down on the cloths and she crouched beside me.

"Omar, I've decided not to marry a youth of the Beni Kabir," she told me.

I nodded and waited.

"There's none of great enough name to be able to do what I want. Unless I've married a chief who can lead a bold and well-armed band to my people's tents—it need not be large, but it must speak for all the Beni Kabir—I'll lose *izzat*, my father Mahound may not repent the lie he told, and he may be able to hold my mother's followers, the Men of Spears, from coming with me on a journey. Ishmael ibn Abdul is good to look upon and is a sweet singer and the son of a malik, but how many would go with him to right the wrongs of his bride, once a princess of the Tuareg cast out by her sire, but now joined to a Bedouin?"

"His brothers and his young uncle. Not more."

"So I've decided to go with some caravan until I join a tribe of Tuareg other than the Kel Innek, perhaps even the Kel Allaghan (People of the Spears) if I can get to their star-far land, and marry a young chieftain. With him and his followers, I'll go back to the Kel Innek and take away my mother's followers, as well as my flocks and herds, and the men will go with me to the desert close by your prison, and with us working from without and you from within, you can break out and go with us on our fleet riding camels far beyond the sway of Yussuf Pasha."

She paused, her eyes fixed on mine. I nodded, but could not speak.

"Oh, don't you believe me, Omar?"

"I believe you, Isabel Gazelle, but it will take a long time. If it takes more than four and a half years from now—when I've spent twenty years in slavery—I'll not be able to go."

"I'll come before then. I swear it by Messiner, my God."

"There's no harm in that," I told her, smiling—yearning to see her smile.

"Omar, do you love me?"

"I do."

"Will you always love me and think of me with joy?"

"Yes, with great joy."

"Do you want me for your own? Your woman—your mate—your

saki until we part forever? Then I'll be your widow whom a young Tuareg weds in pride. And a widow stands as high as a wife in Tuaregstan. . . ."

There was a strange stirring deep in my brain. It was like the ominous rustle of air before the wind sweeps down out of the clouds and lightning flashes. My heart stopped, it seemed, then hammered my side, and I heard my own voice.

"Isabel Gazelle?"

"What do you want? I thought you wanted to come to me, but you're a cold-eyed Frank with water in your veins——"

"I must ask you a question. You must hear me and answer. It's life or death to me."

Her gaze became slowly intent.

"Omar!"

"What if you returned to your people not as the wife of Ishmael the bard but as the widow of Suliman ibn Ali, Sheik of Beni Kabir?"

Her arms slowly rose, her hands drawing in until they covered her face. The strength ran out of my sinews and I felt bitter cold. As we started down, I held out my hand to her, and it seemed I had never known a fear as great as this, but she took it in hers with a little gasp, her long, firm, strong hand with beautifully pointed fingers, but now cold with icy sweat; and tears filled my eyes. Farishti came trotting to her, whinnying, but the gelding made me chase him a short distance into the desert. When at last we were saddled, Isabel turned to me and answered my question.

"If I could go to my people as Suliman's widow, if only with an escort of two old men, Mahound's lie would be cast into his teeth, and I could take away my mother's followers and my flocks and herds."

"If he'll take you for his wife, will you take him for your husband?"

"Yes, until death parts us."

"Then I'll go to speak to the sheik, and I bid you come with me, for I'm a slave and you're a princess of the Tuareg."

"When shall we go? At first light? If we wake him from his sleep——"

"We must go now."

She nodded to the young moon as though to bid it farewell. I led the way to Suliman's pavilion. We found Hamyd drowsing by a watch-fire; instantly he rose, looked from my face to Isabel's, and touched his amulet.

"The sheik is asleep," he said, "but if it's something of great moment—which well I know—I'll wake him."

"Wake him and tell him the slave Omar and the Tuareg maiden Izubahil beg audience."

Hamyd vanished within the tent. We saw the curtain glimmer as torches were lighted, and heard the stir of women setting out water pipes and sweetmeats. In a few minutes Hamyd returned and drew back the curtain for us. Suliman had put on an embroidered caftan, white trousers, and a belt with a golden buckle. I touched hand to heart and forehead as though I were a freeman; he replied and told us to seat ourselves on the carpet.

"I beg leave to speak plainly, and at once," I said.

"*Ah, ah.*"

"In some weeks or months, it's my fate to return to the prison out of which you delivered me, and before I go, I wish to see Izubahil, who has become most dear to me, wedded to one of the Beni Kabir and in his tender care."

"Surely she's of proper age to marry, and, when you are gone, she'll need a husband. If you'll tell me which one of my followers you've chosen as worthy of her hand, I will myself speak to his elder kinsmen so the matter may be pursued."

"I have your leave to speak plainly, so I will. There's only one of the Beni Kabir fitted by ancestry and name and place to become the husband of Izubahil of the Tuareg, and that is Suliman."

Suliman's eyes seemed to change shape in the lamplight, but I could not tell what it boded. He reached for his flint-and-tinder, but Isabel darted forward, took it from his hand, lighted his water pipe, and put its stem between his lips. He puffed until the bowl bubbled with a growling sound.

"A princess of the Tuareg wouldn't be easy to please," he remarked at last. "And since in her own tribe she may say 'aye' or 'nay' to a great emir, let alone a sheik of the Bedouin, I'll ask if she would be agreeable to that marriage."

"O Sheik, as it would be among her people, let it be here," I replied. "Isabel Gazelle, will you answer his question?"

"Suliman ibn Ali, it would give me great joy and pride, and a great hope."

"Spoken like a princess. More, it comes to me that if I die soon, she would bear my name well among her own people, and cast her father's lie into his teeth to rejoice my soul, and—and do other things dear to my heart. But Omar, my son, if I take Isabel Gazelle to wife, not merely as a concubine, it's needful that she be a maiden. That is the law of the Bedouin. Who would warrant it in Allah's name?"

"I'd warrant it, O Sheik."

"It's the word of a slave, but I took it once before, and once before then—in a sea cave in Malta—when you were free. Fourteen and half years have gone by since we ate the bread and salt, and the bond still holds. Omar, she's one of the most beautiful maidens I've ever seen. She is as beautiful as the morning star—you've yearned for her as for the Moon of Ramadan. For the while that I live, she would give me great joy. So I fear that the bride price may be beyond my means."

"It's only that I may ride El Stedoro to the wedding feast." And I could not keep my eyes from filling with tears.

"I'd do more than that. I have a little horsehair band, with brass ends, that I greatly prize, and this I'll present to you, to keep forever."

"I'm your protected, O Sheik."

"Then at sunrise tomorrow I'll declare to my followers my intention of taking Izubahil to wife, and at sundown you shall come for her, at her abode, and you and Timor and the widow her *ayah* will bring her to my tent, and I shall deliver to you the horsehair band. And on the following day, all the Beni Kabir who have followed the grass with me shall feast, and there will be riding, and games, and at that feast you shall ride El Stedoro, and it shall be written by the scribe, and enjoined upon my son, that when again you are a freeman, El Stedoro shall be yours, to be delivered to you at Alexandria whenever you send word. And now you have my leave to go, with this injunction. We have all been weakened by tears flowing from our eyes inward instead of outward, which are the most grievous, and sometimes an evil fate defeats the stoutest heart. Therefore I'll send my sais Hamyd with you as you depart, and he will mount guard over Izubahil until she reaches her abode, and remain to guard her through the night and until tomorrow at sundown, when she's to be brought here and bestowed upon me in marriage."

I knelt before him and touched my hands to my forehead, as was meet, and although she was a Daughter of Spears, Isabel did the same. He raised us up, and kissed us between the eyes, and we went our lonesome way.

CHAPTER 15

Sunlight Through Cloud

1

THAT NIGHT I dreamed of climbing the Stairway of the Jinns, seeking Isabel. It was a perilous and futile climb, and on the summit three men sat waiting for me, with pale, grave faces. They were Enoch Sutler, whom the *Vindictive* men called Sparrow, an Irishman whose real name I never knew but whom I called Kerry, and Holgar Blackburn. To my amazement, all had shed their chains, but I looked and found I still wore mine. They were going away, and I could come with them if I liked. I told them I could not go—I had a watch to keep—at which Sparrow and Kerry smiled strangely and disappeared. When I asked Holgar why he stayed, he showed me that a hole in his chest and another in his back had been stuffed with straw. Then a flock of crows came flying over us, saw us, and darted away in fright.

When I wakened, my face was wet with tears.

I rode hard until late afternoon and did not watch the sun. Just before sundown I donned what finery I had, including a bright headcloth, and Timor decked Farishti with the silver-mounted bridle and saddle, the fabulous saddlecloth with its gold fringe, and the silver shoes that had adorned the Princess Izubahil's horse when she was banished from her father's caravan. We waited for her at her guardian's kraal; she came forth wearing the same raiment she had worn that night, with the addition of a brightly embroidered sash, fastened with manifold knots and bows, quite possibly a gift from the sheik. When she was up, showing only her profile to the crowd, I mounted, Timor fell in behind me, and we led our foundling to the sheik's tent, with the widow and a slave girl, mounted on donkeys, bringing up the rear.

Gorgeous of dress, Suliman received us in his *mukaad*. There was no ceremony; a feast and other acknowledgments and celebrations of the sheik's marriage were to occur tomorrow. He handed to Timor and Timor passed to me the bridal price—in this case a horsehair band with brass ends. By strict Bedouin law, he would have the right to demand its return if Isabel did not prove a virgin. The widow took Isabel's hand and laid it in Suliman's hand.

"*La illaha ill' allah, wa Mohammedu rasul allah!*" Suliman intoned. (There is no God but Allah and Mohammed is his prophet.)

We retired, and as the night deepened, there was high suspense and ill-concealed anxiety among the people. That the gray-beard sheik had taken a young and beautiful bride thrilled them deeply, and it was impossible for the thought to occur to them that it was inappropriate; if the marriage was made good, they would take it as an omen of his long life and their own prosperity. But he was three score and five and was not as strong as most of the elders, and besides that, they feared the chance of accident during her excursions with me. If so, I would not be blamed. It would be only a doubly unhappy kismet falling to me that I could neither have her for my own nor see her the accepted wife of the sheik. Now and then they looked sharply into my face as though to guess my thoughts, but just as often they gazed at me with compassion or even awe.

Few of the men slept much, mostly they smoked and told tales about the thornwood fires; and at the first light they began to assemble near the eastern wall of the sheik's tent. By sunrise all were there, the women squatting further back. Then Hamyd came forth with a sheepskin and hung it out for all to see. There rose a great shout of triumph.

Over my spirit hung a heavy cloud, but not all of it was dark—there was a paleness here and there, as though the sun were trying to break through.

After the morning meal I called El Stedoro by a name he knew, petted him, gave him bread flaps, leaned upon him as I often did, and with one hand on his withers and the other on his loins, leaped high enough that he could feel my weight. He turned his great head to regard me curiously. Presently I leaped powerfully, swung my leg over his back, and caught my hands in his mane.

For some seconds he stood still, greatly astonished by the situation, and somewhat alarmed. I spoke to him in gentle tones, but was not able to reassure him, and in growing panic, he pranced and broke into a run. Still he never knew real terror. My voice and my smell were strongly associated in his mind with coddlings and petting and care, even with safety from unknown perils, ever since he was born. The weight on his back was new and frightening, and he tried rearing and leaping to throw it off, but like all blooded horses, he landed with springy legs, so I was in no danger of falling. He took another dash, but with my knees and by shifting my weight, I turned him back toward the encampment. As he slowed to avoid running into the kraals, I slipped off.

He ran a short distance and stopped. I walked slowly toward him, calling. When he turned and came toward me, his lips working for corn flaps, the breaking of El Stedoro was done.

I rode him with a halter on short jaunts in the course of the morning, and in the afternoon showed him a saddle and put it on his back. When the other Bedouin had mounted, we fell in with them and made a dashing sweep about Suliman's tent. By now Hamyd and his other attendants had fixed a carpet with cushions before its door; and the sheik and his bride came forth in new and gorgeous attire. When they had seated themselves, the men rode round and round, howling like red Indians and performing feats of equestrianship. Some sprang in and out of their saddles, rifles in one hand, at a full gallop; others rode standing, or picked up scarfs; and although I did no tricks, both El Stedoro and I came to honor in the display. When we dashed out into the desert, the gray stallion wanted to pass every horse in front of him and refused to be passed by any. In this band ran some of the swiftest horses ever bred by the Beni Kabir—sable-brown mares and geldings with white points that moved in a soaring motion light as gazelles—but the great bounds of El Stedoro invariably brought him to the lead and, if I had let him tire himself, he would have left the others in his dust.

There followed a sword dance performed by eight youths, a beautiful and frightening sight. It ended with the star performer turning cartwheels—so we called the feat when I was a boy in Maine—at dizzy speed, hurling himself over with one arm while he held a short sword, its point to his breast, in the other.

Then the great metal trays were brought forth, laden with banks of rice and heaps of boiled meat. The elders dined first, and Suliman left his seat to pass among them, sometimes handing one of them a tidbit. When the young freemen had feasted, we slaves had our turn. But as he gave me a hucklebone, supposed to be lucky, I was suddenly carried far away.

A movement of his hand had caught my eye. On its blue-veined back was a slight cut that might have been made by a knife a few hours before, deep enough to have stained the sheepskins of the bridal bed. I could not doubt that it was self-inflicted and that he meant for me alone, of all his wedding guests, to notice it and perceive its meaning. The message was for me. Only two others—himself and Isabel—knew the secret.

Its effect on me was profound. I could not bear to glance at the still, beautiful face of Izubahil, my foundling Isabel Gazelle, but I looked into some strange, far country of the soul I had never seen before. Now Ishmael ibn Abdul began to sing a marriage ode, his clear voice ringing out to the silent throng, but I hardly heard him, because of a song making in my heart.

Suliman ibn Ali, Sheik el Beni Kabir, you've kept troth with me from the eating of the bread and salt even to now. I did not call the provost when I found you hiding in Calypso's Cave, but that was no cost to me. Years passed before I sent you the token from the Sepulcher of Wet Bones; you had only to say to yourself that kismet had brought me to that pass, that you would like to help me and would do so if it came your way, and put the matter by. Instead you traveled hundreds of miles across the Thirst in my behalf, you brought great influence to bear, you brought me forth, you let me live again.

I have lived again. Although you could not set me free, I have labored with my fellows, rejoiced or mourned with them, fought the desert, rode, eaten bread that tasted like the bread of freedom, drank from the desert wells, sat by thorn fires, beheld the sun's rising and the sun's setting at the desert rim, watched the moon in her courses, and gazed upward at the stars. It came to pass that again I knew the glories and the pangs of love, far deeper than before because I had been divorced from beauty so long, and by then its least finding rejoiced my heart, and this was a mighty finding. I did not find fulfillment, but not through your denial, only Fate's.

Suliman, my captain, you have only a few months to live. For that time I have bestowed upon you the desert's gift to me, and whatever beauty of bliss you may find in her, take it with the full wish of my heart, by the proud endowment of my soul. If I begrudge you that, I have not come through the Valley of the Shadow of Death, and my soul is lost.

2

In mid-March, 1816, when Suliman and Isabel had been married five months, he ordered an oryx and gazelle hunt with greyhounds on a thorny plain on the western border of the Oasis of Baeed. The hounds had run at sunrise and killed when Suliman made me a curious address. Riding up beside me, he extended his hand. When I put forth mine, he clasped it warmly.

"Omar, *sahabti* (friend), I've taken great joy in Izubahil."

He gave me a wonderful smile and rode on. The strange thought came to me that Isabel Gazelle might be with child. I did not believe it enough to dwell upon it now; more likely in his elation over the good hunting he had been moved to tell me something long postponed. A few minutes later the hounds flushed a fox that quickly earthed; then they had a glorious run after a white oryx, whose horns bent back like sabers, only to lose him in the heavy thorn. For an hour or so in mid-morning, we rested the dogs and horses at a water hole; and we had hardly saddled when a joyful cry went up. Half a mile across the plain browsed a small herd of addax, long-legged, brown-maned, spiral-horned antelope who will lose in dust all but the swiftest hound or horse.

When the race was underway and I was holding in El Stedoro for a final spurt, again Suliman brought Farishti on my flank. "Let the gray jinn go," he shouted. "If you don't, his dam will shame him even now. On, on, Farishti, moon of beauty! Teach your great, gangling son how a lady runs!"

I loosed my rein and thrust my heels into El Stedoro's side. He bounded forward, but Farishti was so fired by Suliman's fervor that she would not be passed. Three full furlongs the gray stallion and his beautiful dam ran abreast, and since the track was perfect and the day cool, our hard-riding chasers had never seen such flying hooves, and yelled their joy.

Then the stallion's youth and greater gifts let him forge ahead. When we had gained two lengths, I cut away from her to come up behind the greyhounds, but Farishti kept a straight course. To my amazement, Suliman had dropped his reins and rode with his head bowed.

"*O Sheik!*" I shouted, in sudden terror.

His arm rose to touch his forehead in the grave Arabic salutation. Then it fell limp, and he swayed in the saddle and pitched down.

A wail rose from our rear, and the young riders as well as some of the elders sprang off without checking their madly running mares. In a few seconds they had gathered about their fallen chief, gazing at him in a great silent sorrow whose like I had never seen. As I crouched beside him, only a few gave any sign of hope. They remembered that my *dawa* had helped him after his previous fall, but now he had a different look from then and seemed to lie closer to the ground. When I laid my head on his chest, I could not detect the slightest stirring within, so I took a handful of dust and held it in front of his lips. Not one grain was blown away.

"Slave though you are, you were as a son to him, and if it comes to you to speak, speak," an elder told me.

"It comes to me to say this. I believe that our sheik was given a warning of his death this day, and he led us to the hunt so he might die when riding hard after hounds in the pursuit of game, a sport that he greatly loved and which we love; and so we could be happy with him to the last."

Farishti came up then, whinnying, and nudged Suliman with her muzzle. I thought then that the weeping men might bind his body in her saddle, but instead they passed it up to an elder's son, who rode with it in his arms. With Farishti following us, whinnying pitifully, all rode fast for a mile or more, then the rider passed his burden into the arms of another youth. So the young men took turns until we came in sight of the encampment. I had hoped one of them would choose me for the office, a last service to one I loved, for although I was no longer young, I was far stronger than any of them and rode the strongest horse. Perhaps because I was a slave, more likely because his death put an end to my place in the tribe, I was passed by.

Now the elders took Suliman's black burnoose, and spread it on Farishti's back and fastened it well. With light blows of a rope they drove her ahead of them, and when the penned horses whinnied to her, she trotted into the encampment. At once there rose a woman's cry, and then, as we rode in slow and solemn file, the sound of wailing came to meet us on the desert. As we came up to the kraals, all the women save one were weeping and smearing dust and ashes on their faces and hair. One, beautiful Izubahil of the Tuareg, my foundling Isabel Gazelle, stood white but dry-eyed, and no one had ever seen her head more high than as she walked to the bearer of Suliman's body and took it in her long arms. For a moment she stood there, holding it against her breast.

"I am Izubahil, widow of Suliman ibn Ali, Sheik el Beni Kabir," she said, looking into the elders' faces. "It is my command that a grave be dug, not in the village and not in the oasis, but on the Hill of the Broken Pillars overlooking the desert, and ye are to gather here in white raiment an hour before sundown, that we may lay him there."

She turned and bore the sheik's body into his tent. Thereafter events appeared to move with gathering speed and fatefulness. By mid-afternoon the grave was ready; as the sun pitched, we climbed the hill, four young men bearing the bier, with Farishti shaking her head and whinnying behind; before the light failed, we had completed the strange task, including covering the new-turned dirt with a cairn of stones. That night was given to mourning. The women wailed and the men wept; and in the flickering light of the thorn fires, Ishmael ibn Abdul sang a death song of noble eloquence and beauty. But it was no more moving than the strange, wild outpourings of the old horsemen who had followed the grass with Suliman for nearly half a century and could hardly bring themselves to believe that he had gone.

In the morning Izubahil—for she had not yet returned to Isabel Gazelle—spoke with the elders in Suliman's tent. Soon the word passed as to their plans for the Beni Kabir. Osman Malik, Suliman's cousin, and Isabel would be joint guardians of Suliman's son Selim until he came of age; and Osman would lead the people alone until such time as Izubahil returned from a journey. With her would go the widow who had been her *ayah*, a female slave, twelve riflemen of name, and camel drivers and tenders to make up the caravan. It was her purpose to return to the Kel Innek and establish her birthright and bring away her patrimony. Meanwhile, six freemen led by Timor and with the help of a few followers and slaves would escort me to the prison from which Suliman had brought me, according to his bond with Yussuf Pasha and with me. The two missions could make a joint caravan for part of the distance, then go our ways.

Almost before I knew it, these plans were underway. Although we used only a minor fraction of the Beni Kabir's great stock of riding and baggage camels, still the caravan stretched long, and was strong enough that a band of acrobats, with marvelously trained hyenas, fell in with us at the Baeed Oasis for the journey to Wau.

By not any great count of days or many swoops of the Black Falcon Night, we came to the village, the parting place for the two missions, and of Isabel and me. I had spoken rarely and briefly to her throughout the journey—this was proper in the eyes of our companions, since there were strangers with us—and as the time neared to go our ways, we stood at the door of her small pavilion in full view of our fellow travelers. Her sword-hewn beauty was never more moving; her eyes were dry and burning. Now we must make an assignation of last hope to me.

"Omar, I've counted all the days before the day that I can surely come to you," she told me. "With good luck, I could come sooner—but the luck isn't always good. So that day is far off."

"I hoped you could say one year," I answered. "Is it two—or three

201

—or five? Unless it's within five years of this coming June—that makes twenty years of slavery—it will be too late."

"Five years? O Messiner in Paradise! Omar, it's five months! Am I a land tortoise making across the Igidi Desert? In four months and a few days begins the Month of Ramadan. At the end of that month will rise the Moon of Ramadan to break the cruel fast, and all the guards will be on the hills to catch the first glimpse of her. If you can, file off your chains, for they would slow your running and rattle in the dark. Your fellow Jeem will have files of Damascus steel; if he's not alive, they'll be hidden under the tree of the rook's nest. You and he make eastward to the first wadi beyond the oasis. Hamyd told me it's a secluded place, only a mile from the prison; there will be an old marabou there, with a stick fire, and the fastest riding camels in the droves of the Kel Innek. Once there, you're safe. I swear it in the name of my foremother, Izubahil, wife of Yunus, Emir of Assode. By my teats, in five years of famine I, too, would be dead!"

The outburst was low pitched, but it rang in the still dawn.

"I love you, Isabel Gazelle."

"I love you, Omar, and my love will make atonement, only a moiety of what is owed, yet more than you dream, for your years as a slave. Am I not the Daughter of Spears? So go in hope. Admit not one black devil of despair. I'll come, Omar. Hear me? I'll come if I'm alive, and if death takes me before the day, someone will come in my place. Is it a bond, Omar? I give it by this *barraka* (magic) that I wear at my throat and don't understand."

"Truly, it's a bond."

"The rising sun has heard me, Omar, and he'll dry my bare bones if I lie. I've spoken it in the morning breeze, and it will remember, and unless I keep faith, it will mock me by every thorn fire until I lie down and my mouth is stopped with dust. Now go. I'm the widow of the Sheik el Beni Kabir, and it's not meet that I should weep over a scarecrow with a stone face. But when you are free, I'll be free with you for a certain space. Then I'll weep to my heart's content."

3

I left her and went down toward the Sepulcher of Wet Bones. Day after dogged day we had pushed on or rested in the shade, night after moonlit night we had followed pilot stars or, in the deep dark, slept; and the long empty miles had fallen away behind us. We did not hurry to my chain, nor did we loiter. But on the day that we saw the plumes of the oasis against the burning sky, Timor drew his camel beside mine, and put his hand in mine. Thus we rode for about a mile. All who saw us wept, even slaves and camel drivers from Baeed whom I had not known till now, but Timor and I were two old hostlers, inured to blown dust and sand, so our eyes stayed dry.

We reached the stockade late in the afternoon, and there was a darkness in my soul that would not pass away, no matter how Isabel's farewell rang in my ears. It seemed more concerned with Sparrow, Kerry, and Holgar Blackburn than with me, and the dream I had dreamed of them was upon me again, just around the corner from my conscious thoughts and fears. The quarry master's scribe came out of the groves to meet us, showed no surprise or hardly interest in my return, and made an entry in his book. At once the smith welded shackles with chains to my wrists and fixed them to the iron rings I wore on my ankles. They were somewhat lighter than before, but that was no comfort to me because it only meant they were shorter, and so I had less arm and leg room. Then a guard I had not seen before led me around the building to look at the iron hook.

I started to ask a question in Arabic—stopped—then asked it anyway. If, after six and half years among the Beni Kabir, I did not confess to speaking their tongue, I would be suspected of some design. My concealing it before, as though it were a tool I had hidden away for some hour of need—seven years of silence depriving me of some little fellowship with the other prisoners—had come to precisely nothing.

"Is this the same hook I saw before?" I asked. "It looks like it."

"The same one, although not quite as sharp. But that's no comfort to the meat when it is hung."

In the dusk rose the awful sound of chains clanking in unison, faint at first, but growing louder. Torches flared, and the dust-smeared file trudged through the gate. The fore guard was called Majid, he who had taken Caidu's place after Holgar had danced a *dance macabre* with his chains; and I hoped to see Ibrim, the least cruel of our wardens, bringing up the rear. Instead I saw a brutal-looking European, his bared chest matted with reddish hair, who had come here since my departure.

Then I must stand with a face of stone while my whole skin prickled and crept. Several of the chained marchers were Negroes, and one, still in deep shadow, had a familiar look. In an instant more I knew. He was James Porter, called 'Giny Jim, and he had come upon evil days. I had not the least doubt that he recognized me, but he made not the slightest sign.

Then the rear guard, whom I took now for a Slovak or a Pole, showing powerfully built and even more brutal-looking in the lamp light, spoke to his fellow and then came up to me, grinning, and asked me if I spoke German.

"No, sir."

"But you're Omar, known as Sittash," the man went on in corrupt Arabic.

"Ah."

"I'm Otto Effendi. I've a little account with you. It's stood on the books before I came here. It appears that on your last day here your workmate, known as Kerry, jumped off the shard dump and killed himself."

"True, he did!"

"He shook hands with you before he jumped and you didn't jerk him back. When it was reported to the quarry master, you were charged with negligence of duty and neglect of property—you could have saved a slave past his prime but still worth a hundred dinars. But the master had already put you in the sheik's care—he did not want to offend his noble guest—so he postponed the punishment until you returned."

"What is it, if you'll kindly tell me?"

"Not the hook. You're too good a workman. Also, your record had been good as to violations. However, you're to be taught a lesson. Forty blows of the kurbash—twenty on the sole of each foot—with the blunt side. Come with me to the block and I'll give them to you now. They'll be to welcome your return to the Sepulcher of Wet Bones."

In the midst of terror I thought of something, and a wave of happiness washed through me. Isabel had promised to come for me on the new moon of Ramadan, in a little over four months from now. It was possible that unforeseen circumstances would prevent it. Perhaps Jim and I could not do our part—his being chained and no longer having the run of the grounds increased our difficulties and dangers manyfold. Yet I was committed to the attempt, and Jim would go with me. I would go to any lengths not to be taken alive, and Jim would join me. If this, too, failed and we were brought back, we would surely be hung on the iron hook—both of us together, most likely, a sight for the prisoners' sore eyes—for that was the punishment for attempted escape, not to be slacked if the slave were worth a thousand and one dinars.

What did it mean? Why, it meant that in about four months our slavery would end! I would not have to stay the few years remaining of the twenty-year term I had set as the ultimate limit. By a bright road or a dark road, I would go forth. If I took the dark road, Captain Phillips's last command would remain unobeyed, a great wrong to God and man, but I would have done my best and failed, and all the *Vindictive's* company would be in the same boat.

4

Yet on the one occasion that Jim lost heart—the night watch had been doubled because of the desperate actions of several prisoners—I did not remind him of this certain outcome, and instead used subtlety to encourage him.

"I wish we could make a good try, when de time come, but it look to me like we ain't even gwine make a good try," he told me, whispering in the dark.

"I'm not worried about that," I answered. "It's what will happen afterward that worries me."

"What you reckon, Cap'n?"

"Isabel will bring help to us, and we'll do our part. There'll be risk of getting killed, but none of getting caught—and I feel it in my bones that we'll live and go free. But what then, Jim? How are we going to start to obey Cap'n Phillips's orders? Maybe we could do what Sparrow said he could do—run up and kill—but that wasn't what Cap'n said. Two penniless jailbirds against the high and mighty, and a trail fifteen years cold!"

"Cap'n, is 'at what you studyin' about so hard lately?"

"Aye."

"It ain't how we gwine break out?"

"I'm thinking of two or three ways and will choose the best."

"Well, then, I ain't gwine to let it worry my mind no mo'."

"No, don't worry about that."

But in bracing up Jim, it turned out I had not concealed as much as I had revealed. For the first time I had put in words some plain facts that I had long ignored and would continue to ignore until Jim and I were free or until they, too, were shadows. I knew that I had told a truth that had haunted me, under my more urgent anxieties, for many years.

"As for how we gwine go 'bout de duty, I won't study 'bout 'at neither, 'cause I wouldn't get nowhere in fifteen years mo'. All I know is, you got to get high and mighty, too, for a fightin' chance to win."

Jim, too, had spoken truth.

The days crept on, the nights sped by, and the time to strike for freedom grew near. Jim and I had had one strange stroke of fortune in the cruel death of a Negro for the murder of his teammate. His body had been left to hang on the iron hook until it would fall; and as a consequence, all the prisoners had moved the black burnooses on which they slept from that end of the building. In the dead of night in this clear coast, we prepared a means of exit under the wall.

To dig a tunnel through the hard-baked earth with no tools but hand drills would be an impossible feat in the course of one night. But one night we removed a third of the necessary dirt, replaced all we could, and scattered the rest. On the next night we easily took out what we had packed in, dug some more of the hard dirt, and refilled the hole. Out of the nightly period of three or four hours that we could give the task without slackening our next day's labor, a continually greater part went to taking out and replacing loose dirt; even so, we delved further every night, and in six nights only a shell of solid ground remained to break out. We need not fear someone stepping on this shell and finding loose earth beneath it. It lay directly under the hook where some grisly carrion still hung. There was hardly more risk of one of the prisoners venturing near our digging place.

By careful testing, we discovered that we could not be seen by our prisonmates so far from the watch lamp; and we took great care not to rattle our chains.

The day that the cruel fast of Ramadan was to end, we quarry slaves were brought back to the prison half an hour earlier than usual so the guards could repair to the high ground to watch for the new moon—the Moon of Ramadan whose first glimpse signals the feast. From within the walls we heard their joyful cries; and Jim and I looked at each other across the darkening room. Shortly the prisoners grew quiet. The night darkened, and the stars shone brighter as the moon set. We waited till every form was still, then crept to the wall.

In less than an hour we had scooped out the loose dirt from our passage; then, crawling in and stabbing upward with the drills, I broke the shallow crust that still penned us in. In a moment more we stood outside the wall, holding our chains so they would make no sound. Jim knew a quick route toward the rook's-nest tree—he had learned every footpath in the oasis in the days before Zimil died from a fall and he had been sent by a jealous foreman to the gangs.

We came up into the hard-packed road leading to the quarry. There was no reason to expect any traveler here at this time of night, and in our awful urgency we did not take great care with chains. Had their occasional low rattling carried far? I must ask the question when I heard one stone knock another far up the path. It might be a stray camel or donkey or even a wild night prowler venturing this close to the reek of man, but it might be a man in some venture of the night.

"He comin' dis way," Jim whispered.

"Who could it be?"

"He wearin' hard sole shoes lak Otto de guard."

We had time to hide, but very little room. The greatest safety lay in the thorn thickets, some of them shoulder high, growing beside the road; just beyond lay naked ground whose dim, illusive starlight would surely disclose black shapes. Jim found a refuge about ten steps up the road from the one I chose. As I crouched behind a thornbush, I reached down and found a stone as big as an orange and held it at my shoulder ready to hurl in a short-armed throw.

I died for a time, it seemed, and the world died with me, and nothing was left but the darkness, the watching stars, and the sound of footsteps drawing nearer. Time neither sped nor crawled: its passage was apparent only in the increasing nearness of the traveler. My eyes grew strangely relaxed. I made out his shape far beyond any vision less keen than a night hunter's. He walked briskly, with his head high, and on the opposite side of the road from the thickets. I thought that he was watching them out of the corner of his eye.

Such alertness was natural enough by a walker in this lonely place at night. His mission might be easily guessed by some object—I took it for earthen jug—under his arm: likely it contained a liquor forbidden good Mussulmen, but which he had got hand on, concealed at the quarry, and had now retrieved to drink at tonight's feast. This was instantaneous perception—he had not yet come opposite Jim. As he did so, I detected not the slightest change of his step or suspicious action.

But as he passed on, his head turned a little toward the thickets, so that he kept a narrow field of vision over his shoulder. Now he was in ten feet of me, and I hurled my stone.

It struck him in the belly and he fell hard, like a butchered camel. Instantly Jim and I had crouched over him, ready to strike him with our chains if he tried to rise or to call for help. But he could only groan and tremble.

"Jim, can we bind him and gag him and put out of sight till we can get away?" I murmured. But I knew better than that.

"They'll come lookin' for him when he don' bring 'at booze, so I gwine kill him."

I could not bear for innocent, great-hearted Jim to be the one of us two to take human life. And that was the reason, not forty blows of the kurbash on my bare feet, that I quickly picked up the stone I had thrown, struck quickly with it and with great force. In a few seconds or two more, we had sped on.

"Cap'n, le's don't stop to file off 'em irons. Le's run as fast as we kin, and not mind 'at noise."

So we ran like burdened camels running toward water after great dearth on the desert. Jim knew the shortest way; we had hardly got our second wind when, from high ground overlooking the wadi, we saw the beautiful yellow flicker of a thorn fire. We ran toward it, our chains clanging. Soon there rose beside it a man dressed like a wandering mendicant, but these profess poverty, while picketed near the fire were three of the most noble riding camels I had ever seen, beasts of great price. "Ick, Ick," he told them in a low voice, and they straightway kneeled. I could hardly believe they would let us mount, with our jangling chains, and smelling as we did of the prison and of human blood, but if their strange dignities were offended, they gave no sign; and at once Jim and I were hoisted to a giant's height.

Our leader took up the wadi until it leveled off, then across the desert. I saw that he was guiding by the great star in the east that the Arabs called Azazel, but when we had crossed a rocky ridge, we turned due south, toward the caravan road from the oasis to the military town of Misda. Long before we gained it, a company of camel riders bore down on us from a hillcrest where they had stood vigil. As they swept around us, I saw that they numbered about twenty, and all but one of them wore black veils. The bared face was only a pale blur in the darkness, but it caused a painful swelling of my heart and a great exultation of my soul.

One of the men passed me a robe, a cap, and black slit facecloth; another gave Jim the same. We put them on the best we could over our irons, during which our smoothly running camels never changed

pace. Before long we came upon the road, and when we had followed it southward about an hour, we met a small caravan of Fezzan
Arabs hastening toward the oasis to celebrate the feast of Ramadan.

"Who are you?" their captain called in Arabic.

"The Tuareg," our veiled leader answered.

"Bismillah! The Men of the Black Veils!"

They would tell tonight of meeting the Abandoned of Allah, and
on being questioned might remember that the garments of two of
them seemed awry, and a clanking sound rose as they rode past.
But we would not be traveling this road if it would lead us into
danger, and my fear passed away like a puff of smoke in the cooling
breeze, and only joy remained.

We turned off in about an hour, and to my surprise struck, not
west toward Tuareg country, but southeast. For three hours more we
kept a steady gait, guided by the stars, until we came to a little
wadi and followed it down to a well-pitched camp by an abundant
water hole. Here fires of thornwood and dried camel dung blazed
cheerfully, two small pavilions and one large one had been raised
against the sun, and white-veiled men picketed the camels and
tended fires and cooking pots.

I lost sight of Isabel before I had one clear glimpse of her face,
but her orders were being forthrightly carried out. Two white-veiled
men with files began to cut away my irons; two others were removing Jim's. The chains fell and rattled on the ground. The iron rings
on my ankles, never letting me go for more than fifteen years, soon
lay impotent on the ground.

Presently a Negro slave girl came forth from the largest pavilion
with some garments which she passed to Jim and me.

"Izubahil sends these to you, to take the place of your rags," she
told me in Arabic. "Also, a little way below the big water hole is a
smaller one, and since you and your companion are foul and stinking
from the prison, and since it is the custom in Frankistan, you have
her leave to lave in it. But she bids you not stay long, for to be
immersed in water causes a man's strength to wane, and he's likely
to die from fever."

"Tell Izubahil I won't stay long."

"Afterwards the black effendi may go to the cooking fires. To you,
Izubahil will speak."

When we had laved and scrubbed with sand, Jim put on white
garments sometimes seen on Negro travelers from the East. I dressed
in a kind of loincloth under a resplendent deep blue Kashmir robe

not greatly different than some of the barricans worn by rich Arabs. There was no headcloth or face veil, no cross-handled sword and dagger that the Tuareg invariably wore. Plainly Isabel had no idea of arraying me as one of her tribesmen, no doubt good policy by a capable princess.

When I returned to the fires, I found her seated on camel's-hair cushions in front of the closed doorway of the large pavilion. At once she rose and showed me her profile. She had gone a little farther from childhood since I had seen her last; her manner was more grave and ceremonial. She was dressed in a sleeveless, sideless jacket and tucked-in skirt, as when we had first met. Her beauty was the same I had seen in manifold dreams.

She turned her eyes on mine and began to speak in Arabic.

"Omar, you're no longer a slave. You've escaped from slavery and shall never return to it as long as you ride with the Tuareg. Do you think the Tripolitan dogs could catch you now? If they discovered your flight before butter can melt in the sun, and some *barraka* (magic) brought the quarry master and his guards straight to this camp on camels as fleet as ours, do you think they'd show themselves beside our fires? Not when they are guarded by the Sons of the Spear.

"Will they not send to Misda for a great company? What if they do? We've already ridden sixty miles from the prison; before they can bring the Mamelukes, we will ride three hundred miles. Will they guard the water holes? What if they do? Give us dew-wet fodder for our camels and we can cross the Igidi Desert with no drink but their foaming milk. They will be as jackals trying to catch the white gazelle with back-bent horns. They will be as vultures trying to catch a falcon.

"So until the stars pale, we will rest here, in the cool, and then vanish like shadows in the desert."

She paused for dramatic effect—I could not and never wanted to forget that she came of a people as poetic and language-loving as the shepherds who roved the hills of Judea with David for their king—then she began to recite an ancient writing.

"*Let him kiss me with kisses of his mouth, for his love is better than wine.*

"*A bundle of myrrh is my well-beloved, and he shall lie between my breasts.*

"*Lo, the winter is passed, the rain is over and gone, and the flowers appear; the time of the singing of the birds is come, and the fig tree puts forth green figs.*

"My beloved is mine, and I am his; he shall feed among the lilies. Until the day break and the shadows flee away.

"Awake, O North wind, and come, thou South, blow upon my garden, that the spices thereof may flow out. Let my beloved come into the garden and eat his pleasant fruits.

"Make haste, my beloved, and be thou like to a roe or to a young hart upon the mountain of spices."

Her eyes shone, and with the promise of a smile she held out her hand to me while with the other she drew open the pavilion door.

BOOK THREE

Forging of Weapons

CHAPTER 16

Fall of the Chain

1

THE NEW moon of Ramadan had waxed but half her fill when we passed beyond the last vague border of the Pasha of Tripoli's dominions, out of danger of pursuit. For the first time I saw what true-bred, well-trained riding camels could accomplish as ground-coverers when expertly ridden and managed. Our band of forty-some people had over two hundred beasts. Every day one camel in five carried riders, two in five bore light loads of baggage, mainly grain and water bags, two in five ran free. The baggage-bearers were always offended and tried to bite their wallahs; those running without burdens were the most nervous; those that carried the black-veiled Tuareg, the most proud. Traveling in the early morning hours or, later on, by moonlight, with ample rest for man and beast, we sped five hundred miles in seven days.

Thoughts can fly faster than that, and sometimes mine turned back, for a few troubled minutes, to the Sepulcher of Wet Bones. The keepers would not have taken lightly the breach Jim and I had made in its boasted inviolate walls. The Pasha in Tripoli would thunder his rage, heads would roll, new rules and regimes would be enforced; but I did not think that the prisoners would have it much harder than before, because otherwise their output of beautiful marbles would be diminished, which would lighten the Pasha's purse. Perhaps the greatest impact would be made on the prisoners' souls, whether for good or ill, I could not reckon. Some might be encouraged to attempt escape, only to die on the iron hook. A great many might dream of escaping and hold to that dream to the dreadful last.

During this week of flight an Arabic-speaking Tuareg told me some news of the outside world, no hint of which had reached me in the prison. In the preceding year a strong flotilla of warships from Frankistan had bombarded Algiers and forced the Dey to surrender prisoners. Of late the Pasha of Tripoli had broken treaties made with these same Frankistan captains some dozen years before, again harrying their ships, so he, too, took terror at the sight, since he thought their power had been broken in Christian wars. In the upshot, both of these pirate kings and the Dey of Tunis to boot had begged mercy from "the terrible captains with blue eyes" and had sworn by Allah to give wide berth to all their vessels.

I wondered what captains these were. Some captains from U.S.A. had treated with the Pasha about twelve years ago. Frankistan was a general term for Western Europe and beyond. . . .

"From what tribe of Frankistan did the captains come?" I asked my informant.

"I didn't hear that, Omar."

"Were you told the color of their flag?"

"Ah! Ah! It had a blue square in one corner, with sixteen stars, and red-and-white stripes to the number of thirteen."

"Why, I know of that nation," I remarked when the Tuareg warrior peered sharply into my face.

"And you too have blue eyes!"

So all was well with my native land! Wondering what it would be like to be homesick again, I rode on with my good companions. On our eighth day of flight, generally southward but veering a little eastward, we came on some good wells in a lake bed grown to camel-thorn, in striking distance of the caravan road that Mahound had taken on his return from Mecca. Now we must take new bearings, and chart a course.

"It would be well, and pleasant, to rest here for five days," Isabel Gazelle told me as we sat by a dying thorn fire when the camp had stilled. "Then we will strike the road to ride either east or west."

She was grave, and her eyes were big and bright. "Is it a hard choice?" I asked, well aware she was leading up to something, hardly daring to guess what it might be.

"It won't be hard or easy either, for I'll not make it. It's for you to say. For as long as you want me and can stay with me, I'm your woman. These Tuareg, the Sons of the Spear who followed my mother and now follow me, will take you where you wish to go and do what you desire. If we go west, in due course we'll come to the tents of the Tuareg. But I know you wouldn't stay longer than the second caravan making toward the Christian settlements, if indeed you don't join the first."

"How did you know that, Isabel Gazelle?"

"Because for many moons I've watched your face—when I could bear to look at it—and lately have lain all night in your arms. The Beni Kabir say you will follow a great blood feud, but I doubt if it's business of the blood. It may be to go on a pilgrimage to—what can I say? It may be to cast some lie into its teller's teeth. It may be to raise a cairn of stones over the bones of your brethren whom you greatly loved."

"It's all three of those things, but especially the raising of a cairn of stones over the bones of my brethren whom I loved, for the peace of their souls wherever they may be, and the peace of my soul, and to vindicate my survival in the sight of God."

She swayed to me then, this beautiful young woman whose lineaments and form looked as though carved with a sword, this daughter of the merciless desert, and I felt her tender lips warming with the warmth of life and transfiguring with love my jagged face of stone.

2

Isabel Gazelle fed the fire and brought squares of camel cheese, a handful of dates, and a wooden bowl of fermented camel's milk. This was to tell me it would be a long time yet before we went to bed.

"Behind the little Christian settlements of the Rio de Oro, the Sultan's Mamelukes raid to catch slaves, and his ships rake the seas," Isabel told me. "I never want you to hide again, or run. So what if we journeyed eastward to the tents of the Beni Kabir? It would be a fit thing for me to dwell among them until my husband's son becomes a man, and you could ride El Stedoro while I rode Farishti. But I might as well ask the moon to ride backward across the sky."

She spoke cheerfully, plainly having still another string for her bow. I was almost sure what was forthcoming, but life with Isabel Gazelle was one continuous adventure of surprise. . . .

"What if we went still further east?" I asked.

"After many days we would cross the Libyan desert and come to the Nile. Beyond lies the Atbara River and the lands of the Beni Amer, fiercest of the Beja. But my mother's cousin, Takuba, of whom I told you, has become a great chief among them; and he would be of help to you when you try to rob the lost tomb of the Pharaoh."

Now that she had come out with it, I felt belated wonder. I wished I had no more need for buried treasure than the Tuareg or the Beni Kabir. Isabel and I could live together on the desert until one of us died and dusky sons and daughters could live after us. Our sons would be great cameleers and horsemen and hunters; our daughters would be beautiful and proud.

"I've never mentioned robbing the Pharaoh's tomb," I remarked to Isabel.

"Your eyes did when I told you about it, your head on my lap."

"Now I'll tell you why I must have gold—much gold. Two tasks have been laid on me by my captain. Many years have passed since then, and the trail is cold. Without gold, I can't come close to the doers of the crime or enter the same doors or even speak to them, for would they hire one with a face like mine for a body servant? My fellow Jim and I are long forgotten and unknown and unarmed. Also, I'll need gold to build a cairn of stones in memory of my brothers."

"Much of that, too, I knew," Isabel answered. "Suliman told me you would need gold—he said it's king in Frankistan. I myself have seen how with trade goods bought with gold, the captains of the slave ships can buy whole villages of black men and women, sometimes whole tribes, and carry them away over the sea."

"Did Suliman think the tomb might contain gold?"

"Yes, for those tombs downriver, beside the Gezira desert, gave up gold—as much as a donkey-load in the times that men remember."

No doubt she meant the pillaged tombs along the Fourth Cataract which various travelers had described, insignificant compared to many in Lower Egypt. I had retained very little of this lore; but I did recall that dark-skinned savage conquerors from the Nubian deserts had more than once swooped down on the luxurious courts and sat the golden thrones like camel saddles. Might one of them be buried in Egyptian splendor on his own steppe?

"You told me the king of the Beni Amer had rock dumped on the tomb entrance to close it forever."

"Yes, so the demons wouldn't come out and kill the people."

"Wouldn't we have to open it on the sly?"

"I think we could hunt elephants, as though to get ivory."

"Do you think the demons that guard the passage will kill me?"

"I asked Suliman about that. He said he had never seen anyone killed by a demon. Perhaps you can find some kind of *barraka* to keep you safe." She paused, collected her thoughts, then went on in great earnestness. "There are many other dangers, but none in our own camp—you can be sure of that. If you brought forth gold to load ten donkeys, not one of the Tuareg would take a grain."

"Now, that's a wonderful thing, and will you tell me why?"

"To start with, they know very little about gold. They've never dealt with it or judged things by it, and the thought of it doesn't make their hearts beat fast. They count wealth in camels, horses, donkeys, and sheep. Besides this, I'll tell them a story they'll believe and love. It won't be true and yet it won't be wholly a lie. It will be, that a prophecy has been made, long ago, that you shall come to this tomb and seek for gold that was put there for you by certain gods; and that other gods are arrayed against you and will try to kill you, and your quest for it is like the great quests of old. With that in their hearts, they'll vie with one another to help you find it, and get it out, and bear it away. Remember they are sons of the desert—they love a tent more than a palace, one fleet she-camel more than a drove of plow beasts, a tale more than a feast, a verse more than a silver bangle, a dream more than a victory, the young moon with a star beside her better than a field of durra, and a princess they deem beautiful best of all. And aren't you her finder when she was lost in the Thirst—long her lover separated from her by the curtain of the sheik's tent—and at last her husband?"

"*Ah! Ah!*" I murmured, trying not to break the spell of prophecy suddenly come upon her.

"We loved each other with great passion, yet I made marriage with the sheik," she went on in a beautiful soaring tone. "I would have given him my flower, not in begrudged due, but in joy and pride, for I'm a princess of the Tuareg, and I'd taken him for my husband; but that was not to be, for causes forever secret between him and me. And that did not keep him from being a husband to me in his heart and mind. And lo, he gave me of his wisdom, and of his truth, and of his greatness as much as I could bear."

Something was coming, and I did not know what it was. My neck pricked fiercely, tinglings ran up and down my spine and across my back, the air was sharp in my nostrils, the fire burned with strange, sharp cracklings, the stars leaned down. I looked at Isabel Gazelle, and again she was Izubahil of the Tuareg, and beauty was upon her beyond my comprehension, and something more than beauty, something born of the desert or the night.

"When I went to dwell in his tent, I was a child. I knew the joy of living and loving, of work and play, of peril and sweet escape, but I knew no evil. I did not know that it dogs the soul of a man like his shadow follows his form. It was Suliman, my husband, who taught me to fight it tooth and nail, so it might not fasten upon me or upon anyone in my heart or in my charge."

"I am in both," I answered, "so tell me what I must do."

"What I say now is what Suliman bade me say. I—I could not have thought of it myself. I was the one appointed to free you after fifteen years of slavery. If besides that I give you a sword of gold to fight your battle, you must promise never to use it in revenge."

"I don't know what you mean."

"How can I tell you when I can feel it only in my heart, not in my head? But it is a great thing. Unless you live by it, your soul will die."

"You've set me free, and if you also give me a sword of gold, I'll never use it in revenge. I'll take no blood price for the wrongs done to those I love and to me. I'll do only what my captain bade me with his last breath."

"Do you swear it by the bread and salt we've eaten together?"

"By that, and by my love for you, and by my soul."

"It's by my love for you I ask it, which is all I know."

Suddenly she was sobbing in my arms. Over the eastern hills the moon rose shield-shaped and red, and the jackals raised their voices in eerie cries. But there was only one sign that I believed, prophetic of my future days, and it was of love that would guide and guard me still. It was the sign of her lips on mine, her tears upon my face.

CHAPTER 17

The Challenge

1

WE CAME from the raw desert into a steppe rimmed by purple hills. Thorn and acacia thickets became a commonplace; some of the watercourses had little rivulets among the rocks in the cool shade of the heavy growth of the wadis; water holes were no longer hard to find. No few sheep, camel, and cattle drovers followed the grass, sometimes in bands no larger than a patriarchal family. But the fodder was not as good as it used to be, they told us, and the steppe not as broad. In their grandsire's time they could range far east and north where now stretched burning sands.

Although we had entered what was called the Country of the Blacks, the people we met were not Negroes of any kind we knew, being slightly built men of brown or reddish skins, broad between the eyes, with straight high noses, pointed chins, and sparse beards. The children's hair showed wavy; the men wore it fantastically dressed. Invariably there was one or more in the band who could speak Arabic. Only a few had heard of the Tuareg, starfar on the western Sahara; almost all knew of the horse-raising Beni Kabir. The most immediately exciting feature of the country was its numberless and varied kinds of animals. As soon as we got into partially wooded lands, we could hardly believe our eyes.

Crossing the Nile on ancient ferries, we went forth into the bush without great trepidation. Most of the robber bands were small and poorly armed, and far weaker parties than ours went about their business, largely unmolested, savages as well as thieves being restrained by fear of battle, fear of reprisal, and fear of breaking that oldest and greatest of all laws, moral and economic, to live and let live.

The plain was largely steppe, broken by thorn and acacia thickets and occasional clumps of wadi thorn and dwarf mimosa trees; tall trees I did not know and dull-green thorny jungle filled some of the watercourses. Many kinds of antelope and gazelle thrived on the coarse herbage. We must keep our guns loaded for rhinos, watch for snakes, approach no big water hole without looking out for crocodiles; burn night fires against lions and leopards, and be ever ready to turn out for elephants.

We saw several cows and calves and young bulls, none with ivory worth the taking, on our first day east of the Nile. On the second day we had distant views of several lone bulls, and toward evening came close to colliding with a herd of thirty or more elephants, led by a monster whose height I might have guessed in feet, but having horses on the brain—as all men do who live by them for a few years —I took pleasure in reckoning him at thirty-six hands. That was twice as tall as the largest Clydesdale draft horse. I could not believe his weight to be less than six tons.

Yet he, his cows, some young bulls, and several calves were making through the thorn forest like so many clouds of smoke. By staying downwind, we did not wake their rage, and they let us pass.

"Collecting ivory, if only as a screen for robbing graves, will be excellent sport," Zoan, the intrepid Tuareg chief, remarked with a boyish smile showing through his veil.

Three days from the Nile we came to the Atbara. Only trickles and pools remained of the late summer floods that had brought down whole trees from the Ethiopian forests, the flotsam of villages, dead herds of cattle, and drowned elephants. We crossed the deep-scoured bed, and in half a day's journey came to the village of Takuba, Isabel's kinsman, a Tuareg of the Kel Allaghan, who are Sons of the Spear.

He dwelt in a house of baked mud with a tiled roof; his kraals spread far and wide, bursting with cattle and sheep, goats and horses, and the thatched-roofed huts of his serfs dotted the plain. He was away on his pastures when we arrived, but when the shadows longed, we saw him coming on an excellent sable-brown mare— one bred by the Beni Kabir unless I missed my guess—his face hidden behind the black veil of a Tuareg nobleman. His bearded scribe was riding beside and a little behind him, and his Negro sais brought up the rear.

At sight of his black-veiled kinsmen he uttered a great cry of "Sano!" and spurred his horse. But before he could greet them, his eyes fell on Isabel, and then he could hardly keep his seat. The Tuareg were haughty and stone-still with strangers, debonair in times of stress, and I had not lately seen a man so overcome. His hands dropped to his sides, and he blurted out a question in the Tamashek tongue. It contained the name "Izubahil."

She made some warm answer and, hurrying to him, put her hand in his. It was as though she wished to show him that she was Izubahil in the flesh. Deeply moved, he dismounted and kissed her between the eyes, as might an Arab elder. During the grave talk that followed, he glanced at me with friendly interest. Then while his slaves passed tobacco and barley beer to the company, he led Isabel and me into a dim room with whitewashed walls.

Their conversation was in Tamashek, Isabel interpreting as tersely as possible. Granting that my *barraka* was of great power, yet he believed the demons guarding the tomb to be invincible, and he would counsel me not to meddle with them in any manner; but plainly it was my kismet to do so, and no man can fight his kismet. A hunting party could well choose as its base camp the bank of the Atbara close by the buried and almost-forgotten stairway. But there was one obstacle that must first be overcome. This Isabel repeated to me in direct translation.

"The king of the Beni Amer won't let foreigners hunt ivory in his dominions without his consent," Takuba said. "If I ask him to come here—his kraals are a day's journey southward—he will do so, and decide the matter, whether yes or no. You have a fearful face and an ungainly form. This will go against you, but Izubahil wouldn't wife with you if you weren't strong and brave, which Simba—the name means Lion in the tongue of his mother, a slave trader's daughter from Mombasa—demands of every man receiving his favor. Also, he shall hear that you were born free and equal to any man in your tribe, according to the Writing, which Izubahil has told me, and which will please the king."

A runner to Simba's kraals sped on his way. For three days we travelers rested and were richly fed. Then midday brought a swiftly moving dust cloud that soon disclosed a band of fifty riders on good but not pure-bred Arabian horses. Less than half had guns, the rest carried spears either of iron or, longer and fully as formidable, bamboo sharp as bayonets and hardened in fire. They wore woolen robes, and their hair grew in a fuzzy mop, projecting above the forehead and standing brushlike all over the head to the nape of the neck. They were lightly built men, not as tall as the Tuareg, with glowing reddish-brown skins. Patently they were horsemen and nomads since time out of mind.

Their king was more like Zoan than anyone I knew. Not more than thirty, he had a like grace of movement and an equal beauty of countenance; his body was wonderfully put together, and he did everything, whether only to give me his hand, with the same magnificence. I thought that his life, crammed with adventure, was as poetic and thrilling as Zoan's.

To my great joy, he spoke Arabic—many of the Beja did so, and Simba's mother, being a slave trader's daughter, was probably almost pure Arab—greatly augmenting my chances of winning my point. Whatever business I had with him, he wished done at once. He chose for our meeting place the shady side of the house with his followers and the black-veiled Tuareg seated in a semicircle in easy hearing. Benches were provided for him, for Jim and me, and for Takuba. With no trappings of royalty but a black-maned lion skin over his shoulder and a slave with a palm-leaf fan to shoo off flies, he listened impassively to my host's plea in my behalf. Meanwhile I could read nothing in his face, but afterward he turned to me such brilliant eyes that I became at once fascinated and on guard.

"Omar, your face would frighten vultures from their meat," he remarked in a casual voice.

"So does a lion, O Simba!" I responded, my head screwed on well today, as Maine folk used to say.

The response pleased the listeners who could understand Arabic, and it was immediately translated into Tamashek and into Tigré, the language of the Beni Amer, behind many dark hands.

"And to judge from your form, the mutton was lean last year," the king went on.

"It was fat enough, but I fed on addax, which only a hunting leopard can catch—or a very lean lion."

"If you fed on addax, you must know how to ride a horse."

"Yea, Simba Pasha."

"Yet you are all mounted on camels."

"We came a long way across the desert."

"Think you that your best rider might ride with one of the better riders among the Beni Amer?"

"It might be so."

"Then I'll tell you of a custom of the Beni Amer. Sometimes when traders come up the Nile or from Mombasa, we go forth to get ivory. But the elephants ruled the land before the first men set foot here and are kingly still. Thus it isn't right that we should dig pits for them, and slay them by base stratagems, or even kill them at a distance with rifles until we've proved ourselves in a more even match. So the first bull must be slain by two horsemen, armed only with bamboo spears. Sometimes the bull does not fall; instead, one or both of the riders are scattered in pieces over the plain, and others take their place. Now, if one of your band will ride with one of my band to kill the first bull elephant—each helping the other in his need according to our custom—I'll give you leave to hunt in my domains. But if none of you will so prove himself as a rider and elephant fighter, I refuse your plea. That is my word, not to be recalled, and you may give me your answer when the double-tongued repeat it to our followers."

When this had been done, a wave of excitement swept through the throng. The Beni Amer looked exultant, the black-veiled Tuareg drew their veils closer, always a sign of deep feeling, Isabel Gazelle turned pale, and Takuba gazed from me to Simba in perturbation.

"We have no horses or bamboo spears, O Simba. But if you will supply them, one of us will gladly stand the test."

"Will you appoint him now? He may have his choice of all our mounts, which tonight will be well fed and rested for tomorrow's run. But by mercy of your gods, choose well. Meeting *Tembu* in the tusks—so the ivory buyers call him, teaching the name to all peoples under the sun—is not a game for women and boys."

The answer to this was easy. The black-veiled Tuareg were camel riders without peer, but not one, even Zoan, was a finished horseman. All were masters of the spear, their tribal token, but a little close thinking told me that a bamboo lance was quite another thing from the long iron spears of Africa; it was only a thrusting weapon and no good, from lack of momentum, for throwing. Certainly it was on horsemanship that the elephant fighter's life would hang. As to handling a long bamboo, at least I had clubbed rabbits going full tilt.

All this was open and shut. Still that did not account for my not dreading the encounter. I was a sober man of purpose, not a *beau sabreur* like Zoan. Perhaps the answer was deeply rooted in superstition. I would not be killed because there was no one else to do a hard, long, dirty job in the Book hereafter. Perhaps I had learned to be reconciled to the inevitable.

"I, Omar, aspire to the honor of hunting with the chosen one of the Beni Amer," I said with ceremony.

"*La illaha ill' allah!*" This great Arabic watchword was meant to impress his men. "By my mother's milk, I'll not be outdone. So I myself choose myself to be your fellow of spears! And Tembu had best drink deep tonight, for tomorrow we'll give him a hot race for his life or ours."

I grinned at Zoan, to which he made sheepish reply, and I was able to look Isabel in the eyes, for they were ashine with pride in spite of a worried drawing-together of her dark brows. But there was one of our hearers at whom I could hardly bear to gaze, seeing too well in fancy the heavy trouble, surging up from his heart, in his black face.

2

For tomorrow's race, I chose a horse from Takuba's paddock, a bay with white points, with some rough barb in her. Her sloping shoulder muscles, arched crest, rounded barrel, and clean, hard pasterns made me remember horses of free and easy movement; her quarters were magnificently rounded for great driving power. Equally important in this race, her small, high-held head with small mouth, melting purple-brown eyes, and far-apart pointed ears hinted at Arab wits. Her top gait was not nearly as fast as El Stedoro's, but she could gain it sooner. Indeed, I had never known a horse with a faster start. She could turn around on a prayer rug—a rather impious saying of the Beni Kabir—and when running up to dangerous holes and corners, she kept her head well.

Her name was Mariyah, after the beautiful Coptic concubine of Mohammed, and no doubt given her on some Arab's stud farm.

When the cooking fires had expired, Isabel drew the door curtain of the tent, bringing me a cheroot and a bowl of palm-toddy Takuba had supplied. Lighting a smoke for herself, she took a seat just out of my reach.

"Tonight I sleep against the wall," she told me.

"Why?"

"Tomorrow you must ride hard for your life. Your horse must be well rested, and you the like. The least diminishing of your strength might give Tembu victory."

"Show me a youth of twenty, who's my equal in strength. If you can, I'll show you a young bull elephant of twenty who can match old Tembu, with his scars and blunted tusks, whom Simba and I will fight tomorrow. Can a three-year-old stallion match a six-year-old except in a short race with a jockey-sized rider? Not in hunting or in battle or in getting colts of great heart. By our giving to each other, my strength tomorrow would not be diminished the least jot. Are you afraid that our happiness will anger the bad gods, and tomorrow they'll set gopher holes in my mare's path? Isabel, I know these gods —I've taken their measure—for although they can maim, they can't

224

kill, for King Death retains that power alone. To the devil with them. I defy them."

"Don't talk so, or I must run to you and hold you tight and fall. Yes, I schemed to please those very gods, but that was not all. I know of the great strength that's been given you for some task not meant for me to know or share—still I can't believe it until I feel it ever renewed. I wanted you to long for me tomorrow as I once longed for one swallow from a cool well I had barely tasted the night before. Then you would live to come back to me. Are you and I from the dim alleys of a great city where folk are only half alive, or are we riders of the desert? You saw El Shermoot with Farishti in the wasteland, but have you seen a maned lion and his mate? Takuba has, and told me of the burning. Think you he would spare the hunter who stood between him and his beloved?"

"Sometimes my eyes are dimmed, Isabel Gazelle, and I can't see the signs and wonders, and I too become half alive. Sleep with your head on my arm, so I may waken and look into your face, and watch you breathe, and wonder at the mystery of life, and drift into sweet dreams."

3

It was morning before I knew it. The sounds of fuel gathering and firemaking were queerly muted; and when I went out to water Mariyah, I could not fail to see the sober mood into which all the men had fallen. The black-veiled Tuareg bowed to no man, but they laid their long, dark hands on my shoulder as I passed in reach, and the Beni Amer touched their foreheads when I went by. The white-veiled Tuareg groomed the bay mare until she shone in the sunlight, filled water casks, and sharpened the long points of twenty or more fire-hardened bamboo spears.

But when I looked anxiously at Jim, he gave me a big grin. His heavy trouble over the risk I must run had lightened in the night.

Takuba, walking about with his gray-bearded scribe, beckoned me to the kraal on the excuse of showing me a young and likely foal. After I had looked at her, the elder addressed me in fluent Arabic.

"Omar, I speak for my master, Takuba, or by his leave, out of the lore I have myself gathered in this bush for two score years."

"I am your protected," I answered.

"Five times in my years among the Beni Amer have they played this game. Once the two players who began it, ended it. On three occasions, fellow tribesmen took the place of the players who fell. In these three fights Tembu killed one, three, and five, all good riders and spearmen, before he fell. In the fifth race he killed eight, whereupon the Beni Amer gave up the hunt and returned to their tents, knowing that they had somehow angered the gods. It might be they would have never hunted so again if, on the following day, they had not found the body of the great man-killing Tembu, bearing four broken spears."

I thought of something—a hard problem—and could not at once reply.

"Now hear this truth of Tembu. He can run with great swiftness, but he can't overtake a horse on hard, open ground. So don't let him decoy you into heavy thicket, which he can break down like a landslide while you plunge in one place. His sight is dim, but his ears are great traps for the least whisper of sound. Fight the battle with all your might, and with a warrior's joy, but never cease to take care, or you'll not fight again."

He touched his hand to head and heart and fell silent. To my wonder, Takuba drew aside his veil a little way, so I could see his face. I did not know the full meaning of the gesture, but it cast a solemnity over all that the scribe had said.

As the men broke fast, a brief ceremony was performed that struck me as being far more important than their laughter would indicate. One of Takuba's slaves brought out on a tray a little cake of durra meal, and a bowl of cow's milk. At once Simba's close kinsmen, no doubt leaders of his tribe, took hold of him and brought him, he feigning reluctance, to the offering. Meanwhile the black-veiled Tuareg did the same to me, I, too, pretending to hang back. Then both of us broke off and ate a piece of the bread, and in turn drank from the bowl.

Of course the bread contained salt, and the sharing of the milk might have symbolized a closer brotherhood than that of war—even that we were brothers of the breast. One thing was certain—he would not desert me during the day's strife, and would not hesitate to risk his life in my behalf. Beyond any doubt, I would do the same for him.

Assembling to go into the bush, the black-veiled Tuareg cameleers took lithe ease on Takuba's horses. Jim rode a white gelding, and being truly black with grizzled hair, he made a fine appearance. When I swung up on a spare horse to rest Mariyah, I took a bamboo spear and dashed in front of our tent until I met Isabel's gaze, then lowered and raised its point in salute—an act of ceremony that made the Tuareg throw back their heads. In reply she made a little formal motion with her hand.

Our party made for a hill about five miles from the kraals, overlooking a brush-grown plain. As we were climbing it, I dropped back from beside Zoan to come abreast with Jim.

"Jim, if I'm killed, the Beni Amer will expect one of our men to take my place," I told him in English.

"I was thinkin' about 'at," he answered.

"None of the Tuareg are horsemen, although they're good with spears. You've ridden the horse-of-tree, but not the four-legged kind for many years, and you're not a spearman either."

"When I was a young'n in 'Ginia, sometimes I rode out hosses for Ol' Mas', but I wasn't no real hostler, and bless Jesus know I ain't never had one of 'em spears in my hand."

"Yet if I fall out, I think the Tuareg would give you the first chance to take my place. But they won't think less of you if you stand back—they know you're not a horseman—and anyway, they're not your judges. At a time like that, you'll judge yourself the best you can in the sight of God."

"If you fall out, Cap'n, I gwine take your place. I can't stop to figga whether it right or wrong, wise or foolish—I just gwine do it. We're the last two alive of all 'em who sailed on the *Vindictive*. Just like you'd spell me in a hard job, I'll spell you."

I nodded my head and rode on.

CHAPTER 18

Appointment in the Thorn

1

ATOP A little hill, the sharp-eyed Beni Amer did not take long to spy elephants. Most of them were young bulls and cows, their ivories too small to be of worth; but away in flat-topped woods of stunted mimosa roved three big elephants, any of which looked fit for our first kill. Not only their heavy tusks, but their association, aloof from the herds, indicated that they had outlived their youth, and were evil-tempered hermits. The woods showed open, with no thick thorn, as favorable ground for the game as I could ask.

We rode toward them, and when no more than two furlongs down the wind, Simba and a companion made a circling dash for a better look at them. When he dropped back beside me, his black eyes were shining.

"I've rarely seen three finer bulls together," he told me. "It must be that they chose one another's company as might three champions in a host. The least of them, Tembu Sheik, is about two score and stands six and a half cubits. The middle one, Tembu Khan, is ten years older and a good seven cubits at the shoulder. The great one, Tembu Emir, has as great a frame as any Tembu I've ever seen, and if he were as massive as the others, would weigh forty *gislas* (seven tons). As it happens, he's gaunt as you are, which we know by now doesn't mean he's frail. Although three score and perhaps more, I believe he'll be fast as his own sons of thirty. Truly, he's so much like you in so many ways—you should see his lean face carved of rock —that we would have named him Tembu Omar, save it might have caused you to die in his place. His tusks are short but of exceeding weight—I'd guess them at four ngomas each (one hundred and eighty pounds). We believe he once fell into a pit and was raked with a sharp stake hardened in the fire, for he bears a great scar on his side—and didn't you fall into a pit when you were young? So if it's agreeable to you, we'll choose him for our quarry."

It would be more sensible to take the first one that came handy. To try to separate the giant from his vast companions would be to carry folly beyond all bounds. My brain knew it and told my thudding heart; still I would not, even if I could, interfere with the plan. I told myself I would lose face, but the real reason would be that I would break a spell. I did not know what had cast it over us all. I knew only that if once I began to count odds, to measure folly, to make compromises, and to alter rituals, I would find myself little and alone in the lap of terror. I was committed to a certain role in an antique drama of blood and death, the same as Jim was.

Then an unearthly light broke upon my mind, but whether the visions it disclosed were truths of life or mirages of the desert I could not tell. My survival or my destruction depended on how well and how valiantly and how luckily my companion and I rode. Then when all was said and done, was it not a test of horsemanship? Could I try to dodge it or mitigate it, when I had been delivered from the Sepulcher of Wet Bones to ride seven years with the Beni Kabir? What of the two great prizes I had won thereby? Was I willing to give them back as undeserved?

"Tembu Emir will suit me well," I said.

"Then you shall try for the first thrust while I divert his attention. Don't come full alongside, for he'll turn and strike sideways with his trunk. Cut across his rear at an angle, the spear entering in front of the thigh. Meanwhile, we'll try to cut him off from his two friends, but look out for them well."

He went on to give me final instructions and advice. As soon as I had struck, I should try to draw the bull's attack so Simba could come up on his rear and likewise strike. Both shafts would then be sunk or broken or lost, so as soon as possible we must take others from the outlyers. The right arm lifted high was a signal to come up. Straight out from the shoulder warned of hidden danger.

Our horses were brought up, sweating with excitement. While the spear holders posted themselves in the open, Simba and I cantered toward the quarry.

In a few seconds I made out their gigantic shapes, then saw them in vivid detail among, not under, the mimosa trees. All three were waving their trunks, feeling for scent, their great ears spread. Tembu Sheik and Tembu Khan stood side by side, as mighty and magnificent as the herd bull we had met in the thorn; Tembu Emir was a little in front, and a strange cold thrill came over me at sight of him, for I knew we were in each other's fate since we were born.

2

Simba had seen him with less searching eyes than mine. Instead of three score, he might not be any older than Tembu Sheik, who was about two score; and the gauntness of his vast frame and his craglike head were not the wastage of years, but the burning-away of fires. Simba had spoken of a scar running up his side. Instead, it was a ridge a foot wide standing out several inches, white as leprosy, the dreadful mending at last of a gash that must have barely missed ending his colossal life. How many years ago did you fall into the pit, Tembu Emir? Have you kept the count of days? Were you a young bull then, in your first love affair? Didn't you know that little beings with cunning brains and hearts full of hate dig pits in which sharp-pointed, fire-hardened stakes are set, and screen them well, in your cool dim forest paths?

I do not believe you are native to this ugly sun-baked bush. I think you were born on some snow-capped mountain far to the south. And why did you choose this place, close to the desert, so far from your green hills, to dwell in exile with two brave companions? Must you come here to meet someone?

Simba did not tell me of the two other scars you bear. Both are rings about four inches wide, above the right forefoot and left hind foot. Looking closer, I see what may be vestiges of similar rings above the other feet. When you lay close to death from the wound in your side, did your capturer weld on great iron rings and fasten you with four chains to posts, veritable tree trunks, deep-driven in the ground? If he could tame you, he could sell you to a king. What other king in Africa could ride so high?

A moment ago I burned with fever, shivered with fear. Now both have passed off, and a deep quiet is in my brain, as though waiting instruction, and wonder and pity are in my heart for great hearts such as yours, and for small, fast, frightened hearts wherever they may beat.

You and your two companions see us advancing.

But you do not seek battle with us, your rage is not yet aroused as we ride up on your flank. You move in long, swift strides, but not as fast as running horses on this open ground, and soon we pass you. Then we turn in your fore to perplex and anger you. You stop, again stretching forth your trunks.

As we ride in opposite ways to encircle you, you turn back and forth and around, shuffling your feet. The first to tire of the silly game is Tembu Khan. His trunk drops, and his only movement is a heavy swaying from side to side. Suddenly his trunk rams out on a downward slant, and he utters a blast of rage.

Wildly riding, Simba cuts in front of him. Tembu Khan does not know Simba is trying to separate him from his mates. As I press the others close, the dauntless horseman decoys him further and further from the arena. In a moment he comes cantering back, while Tembu Khan continues across open ground two furlongs distant. He has not been able to vent his wrath, and it has turned cold inside of him, and he is balked and beating sullen retreat.

Tembu Sheik and Tembu Emir have been tried almost beyond endurance by my riding and shouting, fury is breaking within them, and at the sight and smell and sound of Simba returning to torment them, they trumpet in unison and rush forth. But Tembu Sheik cannot keep pace with his gaunt captain; he is not as battle-tried or as resolute, so my riding on his flank deflects his aim. As he veers toward me, I see my chance for my first blow in my war with Tembu Emir.

For it is between us only, great kinsman. We have found each other after many years of waiting. I do not know who you are, unless you are Death. You look like Death and you shake the earth like Death.

I look somewhat the same, Simba said. Am I marked to die on your tusks, or will I conquer you and clear you from my path and myself kill in your place? The issue is very close.

I veer in my course, across Tembu Sheik's fore and toward Tembu Emir's flank. For the first time I give spur to Mariyah, and she dashes forward at top speed. In my right hand is the nine-foot lance, with a needle-sharp yard-long point hardened in fire, made of male bamboo, easy to grip and light to wield. I allow for Tembu Emir's shuffling run—so much faster than it looks and frightening to behold, as though some raw, crude force of nature had taken animate shape and superhuman wrath—so that I may cut across his rear at an angle, as Simba bade me. The vast gray shape looms close in front. I rise in my saddle and thrust the spear forward and outward, so that the point enters in front of his great driving thigh. We are riding fast, and my thrust is strong and swift besides, so the point enters its full length. A second later the shaft strikes a tree branch and breaks off.

Tembu Emir, why don't you turn on me and seek revenge? Do you not know I have given you a grievous and perhaps a mortal wound? On and on you charge, trumpeting; don't you see you can never catch that sure and daring rider? This is too easy, kinsman.

Simba rides in a great circle as I rush up to draw your charge. But now there comes a change in the tenor of events, hardly discernible at first, but perhaps of great moment before the course is run. The happenstance of Tembu Sheik falling in behind his leader prevents Simba from completing his circle and planting his spear; but it is some design of action, an intent we cannot yet guess, that causes Tembu Emir to continue on his course, paying no attention to either of us. For the first time our spear holders must change ground to keep in touch with us. I take the opportunity to ride up to one of them and rearm. By now the two monsters are three hundred yards off. They have slowed down to a swift walk, but do not veer right or left.

Simba and I ride after them. Watching our chance, we cut in between the pair, and by dashing back and forth in front of him, I bedevil Tembu Sheik into charging me. When after a hundred yards' run he gives up the chase, Simba's yelling and dogging drive him to another charge that carries him an equal distance into the mimosa woods. Our purpose is to get him out of the way; then we will give short shrift to his wounded comrade. Running away from the woods into the sun-baked plain, he cannot escape us now.

As we wheel away from Tembu Sheik, Tembu Emir strides a low hill. At once Simba raises his right arm and rides after him full pace. He remembers now what lies on the other side; but he is too late; and he had better rest his horse for the trial ahead.

It will be a mighty trial. Over the hill lies forty or fifty acres grown to heavy thorn bush and trees. Wounded, dying perhaps, the Death King of the Elephants has gone there to take revenge.

3

Sometimes my night dreams of adventure and conflict, usually involving hard riding or hard sailing, turn suddenly into nightmares. So it was with my fight with Tembu Emir. At the close of one tense but exhilarating moment, I was riding down a kind of avenue through the thorn bush looking for the monster, my main anxiety that we would lose him altogether, Simba skirting some thickets on my flank. At the beginning of the next moment I had run up on him and was instantly in desperate flight from him and seized by terror more profound than any my conscious brain had hitherto known.

It was unmitigated terror, unlit by hope. Countless thousands of men have felt its seizure in the second before they died: very few have lived to remember it because it can be caused only by danger so enveloping and extreme that escape therefrom is preternatural. I saw him suddenly in what had seemed, the instant before, an unmenacing stand of thorn trees. There he loomed, vast, dark, his ears spread, but his trunk down, the most terrifying animate shape known to man, with the possible exception of a charging whale at sea.

His seven tons were poised to obey a signal from his brain. It came, and he rushed forth with an unearthly blast of sound, and the place I had thought safe was a death trap. The brush thickened ahead of me; his charge cut off my retreat. He came from my left while my spear was on the right hand; anyway, I never dreamed of using it in self-defense, my mind denying admission to the useless notion. I began the action of checking and wheeling my horse, knowing well it was too late. He swung the hammer of many hundredweight. I was in easy reach, and there was not even time to tumble off my horse out of his first aim.

But I lived on. It was some seconds before I knew what had saved me—the only thing that could—a thing at once true to life and in-

232

ordinately strange. Somehow he had mistimed his blow, and it had missed clean. Before he could recoil and strike again, I had completed the turn and was out of his reach. An instant later I was riding full-tilt down the avenue I had just come up, with Tembu Emir in furious pursuit.

Then there was no longer any pattern to the fight, any art or science, and its nightmare likeness grew. In every case that one of us was free to fly, the other was penned in. Sometimes we were both in frantic flight between and around the thickets. You would have thought our horses would go crazy and bring the chase to a quick and bloody end. They stopped, wheeled, turned, dodged, or ran with incredible swiftness. It must be that Mariyah often acted on instinct, and her response to my unconscious signals, such as shiftings of my weight and pressures of my knees and heels, was so complete and swift that she appeared to do my will the same as my own hand. For my part, I had never ridden as well. That much the gods gave. Mariyah and I had become, in a very real sense, a centaur.

In the deeps of my mind the elephant became very Death. I dreamed that when Death comes, he shows vast and dark, sometimes with a terrible hammer that can strike in all directions and, in some eerie fashion, in his victim's image. I dreamed that Death was a mirror in which our own shapes melt away. Death was my great kinsman. He had come with a craglike head and a gaunt body bearing awful scars. But when he had taken other shapes, I had sprung out of his reach. In the blazing sunlight between the thorn I dreamed of escaping him again.

Amid low bush that slowed but did not trap me, Tembu pressed me so closely that his shadow fell across me, but I rode on. Looking back, I saw Simba cross his rear on a bold dash and thrust with his lance, but the point broke off when it had barely pierced the skin. Still it stung the monster, for he turned from my pursuit to chase his tormentor, who more than once had interfered in our affairs. I saw no danger of Tembu catching him, since the course was fairly open, and in the same glance saw my chance to deal a telling blow.

It was my first chance since the battle had moved to the thorn, and to judge from Mariyah's snorting breath and the sweat foam on her sides, I might not have another. She wheeled and darted on a slanting course until we were sixty feet behind my enemy, and about forty on his right. Then we cut in to strike.

Perhaps the drum of Mariyah's hoofs on the sun-baked ground warned him. I was poised to strike and leaning forward when he turned, in the opposite direction from what I might expect, bringing him up parallel to my course. There could be no doubt of his deadly intention—to strike me with his trunk as soon as I came abreast and in his reach.

I had no time or room to veer further to the left and away. I was committed to my stroke, and I gave it the instant his great side became vulnerable, far more forward than the other, slanting toward his vitals, and with the swiftness of Mariyah's run and of my thrusting arm. In the same instant, Mariyah began a wheeling movement to flee Tembu's vengeance, but she was too late. The outstretched trunk made a scythelike, sideways sweep, aimed low enough not to pass over our heads. Its end struck her in the throat a handsbreadth under her jutting jaw. I heard heavy bone explode into splinters as she pitched down headfirst.

I went over her head and tumbled and rolled to the edge of the thorn. The shock of the hard fall saved my life in the next few ensuing seconds because I could not obey the fatal instinct to spring up and try to break through the brush, and instead lay still. So Tembu Emir did not see me yet. Screaming, he rushed upon the still quivering horse. I saw what no man could forget as long as his mind lived.

Tembu lifted his foot that was two feet thick and set it down on the mare's chest. With a fourth of his weight he smashed it flat with a horrid sound. Lowering his head, he drove one of his tusks through what remained of her torso, lifted it clear of the ground, then heaved it over and on the other side of the thicket by which I lay. I was reviving now; if Tembu turned his back to me I meant to try to crawl away, trusting to his blasts of rage to hide the sound. Instead he moved to the front of the half-obliterated carcass, which brought him up facing me. Lopping his trunk around the broken neck he pulled it till it stretched to ghastly length; then the head broke off. This he dropped in sudden indifference and fell silent as in deep thought.

That silence let me hear the drum of hooves. Simba was riding hard and close in and around the thorn clumps, trying to provoke Tembu into charging him. But the monster did not look at him and appeared oblivious of his presence. He began to shift his feet and move a little back and forth, the end of his trunk close to the ground.

He showed no anger now, only preoccupation with one train of thought, concentration upon one goal. But as the moments passed without gain, he began to be puzzled, then perplexed, and finally deeply anxious. Was it so? Was my mind wandering? Once he bowed his head in a curious way, then shook it as though to clear it of a mist. Moving slowly, he neared the bush beside which I lay, touched it with the quivering, probing fingers in the orifice of his trunk, then turned his head to sniff the ground about three feet to one side.

Now he showed what I thought was joy. Taking a brisk step, he sniffed the ground carefully but confidently for about six feet in a straight line. I realized at once that I had passed that way in my rolling tumble after being thrown from my horse, but in the opposite direction. He was back-trailing me. And now he came to the place where I first touched ground. Here the trail ended.

He searched the ground in vain. Then with a long sweep of his trunk he picked up the scent where he had first found it and again followed it to its end. For a moment he stood motionless, his trunk dangling, his ears laid back, and, I thought, his eyes closed. His vast frame swayed slightly as might the strongest blockhouse in an earthquake—a different motion than he sometimes made just before he charged.

Now Simba rode up on one side, shouting. He was taking a most terrible risk to come in so close on an almost exhausted horse: had Tembu charged him, he would have surely pinned him among the thorns. But the monster only half turned, curled his trunk, and uttered a warning blast. Then, so strangely floating into this nightmare world into which I had been cast, came Simba's voice.

"Omar! Omar! My horse has given out, but I'll get another, and a thirsty spear. There'll be another rider, the best in your band, to take your place. If you yet live, we'll try to help you. If you're dead, we'll avenge you. All of us will die before we'll forego revenge."

But I scarcely heeded him. My whole mind was fixed on two circumstances. Both might be straws to clutch at ere my nightmare ended in darkness; and taken together, they were only the stuff of hope. Yet my numbed spine tingled with rekindled flame.

As Tembu had turned to trumpet at the horseman, I saw that the small, dark red trickle down his side from the frontmost of his two deep wounds was hidden under bright red froth. And as he turned back to the hunt, he reeled so heavily that only by a sideways thrust of a forefoot did he keep from falling.

The time had been running out for one of us ever since the fight began, and for one of us only a few grains of sand remained in the glass, and of late I had felt almost certain that I was the one. Now it was as though a coin had been tossed and was still spinning. Now it had become a game of chance played by the great gods.

I had ridden well today, but it was not yet decided whether I rode well enough to win and ride on. Tembu had fought well, but it was already decided that he would not go forth from this patch of thorn to pursue his loves and hates. He did not even ask it of his god. He asked only for a few minutes more—less than a minute, perhaps—to search out this little piece of bloody ground, find his fatal kinsman, strike, and die unvanquished. But it may be this would be denied him. The ancient writing would presently be shown.

If I can live to gain my feet and give one bound, I can escape. Still I dare not move: at the first flicker of movement his dangling trunk will whip and strike fast as a python. Once more he sniffs at the tainted ground without avail. But he has nailed his flag to his mast-head. And now as he starts back toward his starting place, he becomes aware of a strange and startling thing. The scent grows stronger as he nears the bush, instead of weaker. No longer will his brute brain mislead him. He thinks he has found the path to glory that beastlike man and manlike beast must seek, forever in vain.

Tembu Emir has found it too late. The spinning coin falls, the wheel turns no more. One of his hind legs suddenly gives way; while his front legs stand like pillars yet, he drops on both hind knees. Still his trunk probes the ground between us, but before it can touch me, it sags in weakness terrible to see. As I roll back and spring up, it lifts once more.

But its speed slackens as it ascends, instead of gaining to become the whizzing hammer of doom. It stops, and its end droops beyond the noble arch. I am running now, but as I gaze over my shoulder, I must stop and wait. The trunk falls, the head lowers, the tusks drive into the ground beneath the mighty weight.

He does not see me now. He has forgotten me. He beholds only the vistas of his birthplace, not this sun-blasted land at the desert edge, but green forests on the slopes of a snow-crowned mountain. He has never heard of pits dug in his paths, in which sharp fire-hardened stakes are set and cunningly screened. He knows no hate and no vengeance. He is forever safe from evil, forever free.

CHAPTER 19

Sepulcher of Dry Bones

1

WHEN THE Beni Amer had departed, the Tuareg built kraals close to the Atbara River where low cliffs divided the silted land from the desert. Here Isabel and I raised our tent; from hence rode out black-veiled hunters to the elephant grounds to lay low the giants with bullets and take their ivory. This hunting also was not due sport for women and boys. Unless the ball found the brain, no larger than a washbasin in the gigantic head, the monster did not drop, and instead fought or fled.

Thus it seemed unlikely that all the hunters would in time ride back to Tuaregstan, but those who did not had played a great game, and lost.

In seeing us settled in our encampment, Takuba walked with me near some broken cliffs where a hot spring bubbled up, giving forth a smell like rotten eggs and another smell, very faint, of a fumelike sort. Just above this, a rift in the strata caused by a fault had been filled with broken rock.

To remove the obstruction would take weeks of labor by many hands and might easily tell our secret to passing shepherds. I hoped to tunnel through it, and started digging in the afternoon. By the midday following we reached the boulders that had blocked the fall of broken rock. Creeping down between them with a torch, I found the rift that had revealed the stone steps, and following it a little, soon the flight itself. It led up instead of down as in the tombs Kerry had described, and ended at a jagged hole in what was once a brick doorway sealed with plaster.

Beyond the flickering gleam of my torch showed a corridor of more than man's height and something like five feet broad, bored out of the solid rock and disappearing into darkness; and on the wall a fresco painting that thrilled my heart.

The figure was of a lean, brown man, unbearded, of the cast of feature of the Beni Amer. He wore a crown and was driving a chariot. Beside the horses stood a supernatural being with a man's body and a jackal's head, Egyptian beyond question. On the body of the chariot were two interconnected heraldic devices, representing an asp and a vulture, well-known emblems of the two kingdoms of Egypt and Nubia.

Was this one of the conquerors who had swooped down with his hungry horde on the effete capitals at Luxor or at Thebes, and founded dynasties over the joined kingdoms? Such an emperor, disdaining the lush and alien land where stood his palace, could have willed that his corpse be returned to his native desert. And if he had absorbed Egyptian religion during his reign, he must also have believed in the afterlife that it promised—almost a continuation of the same life, Kerry had said, in the silent, treasure-strewn palace of the tomb.

All of the next day we spent in widening the aperture, concealing it behind thorn, and securing the surrounding rocks from falling in. On the following morning Jim and I, with Isabel wide-eyed in our wake and a few adventurous Tuareg standing guard, began our first sally into the corridor beyond the broken door. I had wiggled my big shoulders through the gap and had walked on about thirty feet when I had my first encounter with a demon of the tomb. But she came of a different litter, and was of more solid stuff, than those that had snuffed out lights and human lives in the black beyond.

I think that my eye had fallen on her when I was yet several paces distant and had mistaken her for a long narrow shadow on the floor along the wall. Holding my lamp high and gazing intently ahead for taller dangers, I came fully upon her before we suddenly recognized each other as enemies. She was a dark-colored snake, fully nine feet long, lying perfectly straight with her tail toward me. Only when my leg drew in her easy reach did she raise her wicked-looking head. Probably because she was sleeping off a heavy meal, she had not fled or warned me of her presence. Torpidness in her yet and my sudden stopping had delayed her lethal stroke.

The lull would not last long. She was becoming more awake and more dangerous every second. No one need tell me what she would do if I moved; if I ever read a subhuman mind, it was hers. She watched for that motion with coldly glittering eyes. She only wanted proof that I was alive—she must not break her teeth on wood or stone. When she became sure, she would strike.

I was flexing my muscles for a desperate leap when a soft voice rose behind me.

"Stan' still, Cap'n."

It was Jim's voice and he stood on the other side of the broken door. Yet the tone, urgent in the extreme, was hopeful.

Then I saw a darting flash of light and an instant later heard a most strange sound. The sound was of the great snake in her death throes. I had leaped back before I perceived what had caused the swift glimmer in the gloom and now the flailing and beating of her head and body against the floor and the wall. Clean through the swell of her neck thrust the foot-long blade of Jim's knife.

The rapid, frantic bumping against stone, as by a green bamboo rather than a hard club, and most like a prayer rug being beaten to rid it of dust, changed to dry rustling, shuffling sounds. The spasmodic movements of the snake's body became slow and finally almost silent. Jim had come through the broken door and drew his breath hard beside me.

"Jim, I didn't know you were a knife-thrower."

"Yassah."

"Were you saving it for a surprise—such as this?"

"No, Cap'n. I was goin' to show you when we'd git around to it. It ain't anything much—not one time befo' did I have any use for it, 'cept the night we met Otto comin' down de road when we was runnin' from de jailhouse, and then I didn't have no knife. I kin take a man in de throat at thirty feet and maybe forty, but it still ain't no good agin' a gun, and it won't stop no big animal such as a lion. I reckon it might stop a leopard if it landed jes' right, but he could do a lot of clawin' till de blood choke him."

"How did you come to learn it?"

"It wasn't nothin' but a game 'tween me and Zimil. We was forever throwin' at coconuts and sech as that. I got pitty good, but I never come nigh to beatin' him. In three throws he could cut the stem of a cluster of dates clean off."

"It's been a good while since then. How did you stay in practice?"

"It don't take no big lot o' practice. It's like swimmin', or like handwritin' for them that's learned their letters. But I throws sometime, jes' to be doin' somethin'."

I wished that I could have known Zimil, Jim's Negro pard and workmate on the plantation before he died from a tree fall. But I might as well wish to know every man on earth, for everyone was as unique as he, and as impossible to know. I could only guess at my old shipmate, Jim.

I stood in the dimness, struck silent by the thought that each one was part of God or had broken off from God.

Takuba had testified to Isabel's account of the demons guarding the tomb. When the grave robbers had descended the second flight of stairs, watchers had seen their lights dim out and called to them in vain. But there could easily be ascending steps further on, rising above the heavier-than-air gas that settled in the hollows. If the burial chambers lay above that level, our venture would be immensely simplified. If they lay below it—but that was to borrow trouble when we had enough on hand.

When I brought a brightly burning lightwood torch to the top of the flight of steps, I was given a surprise. Instead of a narrow passage, I looked down into a pillared hall, about thirty feet wide, at least fifteen feet high, and far longer than my torch could show. The pillars began about fifty feet beyond the steps on a yet lower level, with some kind of a ramp between, and could easily form a colonnade for worshipers approaching a shrine. On the whole, the discovery augured well. Most royal tombs in Egypt were associated with temples.

Half seeing, half imagining, I got an impression of a large sculptured form against the wall on one side of the colonnade. Also, some long shadows lay crosswise of the room beyond the third pillar. I could not guess what caused them.

My first chore was to provide an easily portable air tank. Every sailor had heard of children swimming with cattle bladders: the jump of the mind to elephant bladders of twenty times their content was an easy one. When it was inflated with air, I could open or shut the duct by pressure of my fingers and breathe through the reed. I did not make the mistake of inflating the two bladders with human breath, scant of life-giving oxygen. With patience, I contrived a crude pair of bellows out of antelope skin and soon had two bean-shaped air bags, big as bushel baskets, which the Tuareg eyed with admiration and amazement. They did not see what possible use I could make of them in fighting demons, but they would have liked to have them for playing ball.

The Tuareg had strong, light picket ropes which Jim spliced to make a hundred yard—fifty fathom, as we used to say—life line. For light I would have to depend on a reflected beam from a fire fed with mutton tallow, since my candle-lamp would expire in the hall of demons. There was no getting out of going alone; Jim must handle the rope and I refused to let Isabel descend the first flight of stairs. Since the Taureg would not help me and only increased my cares, I sent them buck-hunting on the plain, and I wished with all my heart I could go with them.

Yet the moment came when Jim held the life line coiled in his hand, its end fastened about my waist. I was to jerk it like a biting fish every third step; if he did not receive the signal, he must haul in. One of the bladders was fixed on my back, the other proved so awkward that I left it on the landing. From my belt hung an old cavalry pistol, cocked and primed, the pride of one of the Tuareg. Isabel fed the fire.

I descended the steps with my candle burning bright and true, my black shadow jumping ahead of me. Here I began to get a faint and occasional whiff of the rotten-egg smell I had noticed exuding from the hot spring and, I thought, traces of some other fumes. Below the stairs the floor had a downward slant, and although I had expected it, I could hardly force myself on. Then the floor leveled, and I passed three pairs of pillars which seemed constructed of stone rather than rock-cut. Since I took the walls to be limestone, it seemed likely that much of the temple space had been a natural cavity which the builders had reshaped and enlarged.

The long shadows I had seen by my first dim searchlight proved to be three steps, each a foot high, again descending. As I took the first, my candle-lamp dimmed. On the second it whisked out, as though blown upon by the breath of death; but the rotten-egg smell, which I thought was from some sulphur compound, was not strong yet, and the fumes I had barely detected were much stronger. At once I slipped the reed of my air bag into my mouth and loosened the vent. On the bottom step I drew a little of the gas into my nostrils. The sulphuric smell had become suddenly very strong.

Only a few feet beyond I came on the outstretched skeleton of a man. Beyond this, all vision ceased, except for a far-diffused reflection of the fire on the chamber walls. However, there were other lights, very dim and ghostly, puzzling me greatly. They were more like a luminous mist that darted horizontally a few feet from my torch, then vanished. I thought they were some dim sort of will-o'-the-wisp.

In trying to take more shallow breaths, I felt dizziness and a faint nausea. I was a little short of air, it seemed, but I did not believe I was taking in any of the gas, or its rank smell would have warned me. Two patches of pallor were human skeletons lying side by side, as though the treasure seekers had been walking hand in hand when death felled them with one blow.

Then a wave of darkness passed across my brain and I suddenly realized I was losing consciousness. Instantly I dropped my useless lamp, and holding my nose with my right hand, took a deep breath from the bag. Meanwhile I turned and started back, reeling in the darkness like a man sodden with drink. Still I had felt no pain or terror, only dread and deep gloom, now strangely fading. It must be that the Death who laired in this black hall was of a kind sort.

I had come close to him, but his shadows lifted as I breathed through the tube. Hope returned to me, almost like light in my dimmed brain, when, too weak to jerk on the line, I felt it tighten. I was being hauled by strong hands; now I could lift my feet without heavy labor. What if I should fall? The heavier-than-air gas filled the hollows like water. My head was above it, on the steps and the steep incline, but I would drown if I lay down.

Against my orders, Isabel came halfway down the outer flight of steps to grasp my hand. In a few seconds more I was in the upper passage, gulping the fresh air. I felt as alert as though newly wakened from restful sleep. Still, I could not be content till the blue sky arched over me once more.

"Did you see any demons?" asked a white-veiled Tuareg skinner, overcome by curiosity.

"I couldn't see any because my lamp went out, but I wrestled with them, and although they forced me to turn back, the gods who wish me to have the gold kept them from killing me."

"Will you try again or turn away defeated?"

"Assuredly I will try again."

"Now that is good news."

"And you, Akasani, are the bastard dropping of a she-ape," Isabel told him in sudden fury.

Yet Isabel, too, would have been shamed almost past bearing if I gave up now. Not bravery, but necessity, drove me on.

A little of the poison was in me yet, for I slept a while after the midday meal. In the evening she and I rode forth to look at game and to clear my head a little. When we returned, we found Jim whittling a stick with his big knife before our pavilion door.

"I been studyin' about 'at gas," he remarked when I crouched beside him. "What you reckon caused it?"

"There's a fault in the strata, and an earthquake or some other disturbance caused a breach that let through hot water and gases from

242

deep within the earth. That was sometime after the hollowing out of the temple. Some of the gases were forced up by pressure into the hollow space, and I think there are two kinds, one smelling like rotten eggs and the other having faint fumes I can't identify. There's been nothing to disturb them these thousand years, and I think they lie in layers with the rotten-egg gas, the heavier, at the bottom. I think that's the killer, but if there's a gas between it and the air, it would kill, too, in time, because it will put out fire."

Jim considered briefly, then spoke. "They seek they own level like water do?"

"Yes."

"How many feet do you reckon you went down befo' you got your head under?"

"I was holding the lamp a little higher, or on the level with my head. Counting my height at six feet, the gas is between eight and nine feet deep at the foot of those three steps."

"A man can walk fifty feet and back, holdin' his breaf," Jim went on.

"Certainly he can."

"Supposin' we made about six ladders about fifteen feet long. I could cay in one, set it up agin' the fust pillar, and come back and get another. When I got short of air, I'd climb one already set up. You come along behin' me and fix lights on de top of every one. It would be jest like swimmin' underwater and comin' up when we need air. We can bof do 'at."

I stopped and thanked my stars for Jim.

"Fine," I said. "But it would be like walking underwater without knowing how to swim."

"'At's right. Cap'n, you reckon all dat quarryin' of de rock was for to make a tomb?"

"I think so, but I'm not sure."

"A sepulcher ain't nothin' but another word for tomb, is it, Cap'n?"

I nodded.

"Wouldn't it be queer if we could even up part way for de Sepulcher of Wet Bones by what we find in de Sepulcher of Dry Bones?"

"It would be another turn of the wheel of fate."

3

Jim and I made seven ladders of light, strong acacia wood, and to the top of each we cut a notch for holding a candle-lantern. These

Jim carried down into the temple and set up in turn, climbing one of them when he needed fresh air. I came behind him, lighting the lamps.

The glimmer from a middle ladder disclosed the sculpture I had half-glimpsed, half-guessed before. It was a seated figure of a god or king, the hands resting on the knees. The head bore a round cap or crown, the forehead a projected seal or emblem, and the chin a square-cut beard. The form was fully twelve feet high and lighter colored than the limestone walls. Two pairs of pillars, set opposite to each other at right angles to the colonnade, approached the statue.

A little farther on we came on four other skeletons, representing stronger fellows than the first three, but not strong enough. One had clutched a Spanish sword with an intricately worked silver hilt. One had put on a devil mask to conceal his humanity and frighten the demons away, and it was a queer adornment on his naked skull above his bleached bones.

Beyond the sixth ladder, we found three steps leading up, identical and on the same level with those we had descended into the fatal pit. Jim raised the seventh against the last pillar of the colonnade and the light I fixed showed a ramp leading to a flight of steps the same as at the opening. These we climbed boldly, lighting an eighth lamp at the head of the stairs. Now the little flames made a strange and beautiful bridge across the whole dark gulf of the temple. Their beams did not quite meet, but the darkness never quite parted them: there was a kind of a pale yellow mist between.

Carrying a lamp, I led my companion into a passage apparently identical with that leading into the temple; just beyond stood a plaster-sealed doorway. Grinning, Jim raised his ax. I nodded, and he began to break away the plaster. Underneath was a panel of some very hard wood. The ax rose and fell, the blows echoed and re-echoed against the stone walls, and the hole through the wall rapidly widened. In a moment more I had crept through, Jim close behind me.

We had come out in a rock-cut room, no more than eight feet square, empty except for two black statues, about three-fourths life-size, standing sideways to the wall and close beside it, facing each other. They were carved in obsidian by an expert hand to represent men very like the Beni Amer of today; since one of them had a sword and the other some sort of halberd, I took them for soldiers. They could easily be typical of the fierce desert tribesmen who had followed some Sudanese conqueror into Egypt.

As I was noticing these things and marveling over the realistic carving of the faces—as though the sculptor had picked and perfectly portrayed two members of the king's guard—there came a dim stir in my brain that almost, not quite, brought forth some associated experience. The memory escaped, and I did not pursue it, since a profound dejection had begun to take hold of me. The room appeared the dead end of a great subterranean enterprise itself as dead as the stone. Where was the king's coffin and his gold?

Jim went tapping here and there with his ax head. I examined the floor and cast my light on the ceiling. Presently he turned to me, the whites of his eyes glinting.

"Cap'n, how long has it been since we lit 'at first lamp?"

"Not much more than an hour."

"Well, sah, I reckon we better go back and blow out 'em lights and start agin tomorrow. I got a headache and de pessimism. Maybe tomorrow it won't look so gloomy as it do now."

"I think it will look even gloomier, but both of us are tired—we're not as young as we were, I guess—so we'll call it a day. But remember, Jim—we're both free."

" 'At's right." Jim squared his shoulders.

I let him go out first, and before I crawled through the opening, I turned to look again at the two black statues. Again there came a little stirring deep in my brain, and after a few seconds' intense concentration, I captured the memory that had escaped me before.

"Come back a moment, Jim."

"Aye, Cap'n."

"I've finally thought whom those two statues reminded me of. When I went to the Navy dockyard in Valletta, there were two jollies, with fixed bayonets, standing guard at the gate. They faced each other that same way."

Jim's eyes slowly rounded. "Cap'n, do you reckon?"

"If there's a hole in the wall, it's between those two statues."

While I held the light, Jim looked carefully at the stone. A lateral crack ran from behind one statue to behind the other about three feet from the floor; it curved like other cracks and appeared indistinguishable from them. Jim took hold of one of the statues and, with a big heave of his shoulders, moved it about a foot to one side. Its side and pedestal almost touching the wall had concealed a perpendicular crack, running straight from the floor to intercept the other. In a sudden frenzy both of us heaved on the other statue. To our great joy we found another perpendicular crack, forming what might be the straight-sided, crooked-topped rim of a stone panel.

Where the crack was widest, Jim inserted the blade of his ax and pried. The edge of what was no doubt a facing began to emerge. In a few minutes it was free—a slab of limestone two inches thick which Jim set aside. Within were clay bricks laid without mortar. We had a little trouble loosening one of them because of their tight fit; thereafter we took them out with ease. The hole grew rapidly bigger and less dark.

"Go first, Jim," I said.

"No, sah, if you'll 'scuse me."

So I went through first. Jim was alongside before my mind could make the least sense of what I saw.

A long object occupying the full width of the room, perhaps ten feet, suggested to my mind the bottom half of a mummy case, but this was only because I was in an Egyptian edifice. There was no real resemblance, and nothing else to see but its contents and the bare walls. About two feet wide, with raised ends, it was crowded with fifteen or more wooden manikins about two feet high. One stood in the rear with a paddle-shaped stick, all but one of the rest faced forward with poles in their hands; one, a seated figure, bigger and finer than the rest, and evidently the master, faced the rear.

"It pertend like it's a real big bateau, with a lot of men to pole it." Jim remarked.

"Yes."

"You said 'em 'Gyptians was buried wi' things they thought they'd need in the nex' worl'. Do you reckon 'at king wanted a boat and men to take him across some big water, like de blessed River Jordan?"

"That's about right, I think."

"Is 'at de king settin' in de bow?"

"I think that's the captain. The boat hasn't taken off yet—you see the steering oar and the poles are still out of the water. She's waiting to take the king when he's ready."

"Accordin' to 'at, he belong to be still in de tomb."

"I guess so."

"Well, I'd like to know where he at. This here is the solidist-looking rock we've seen yet."

I held my lamp high. The room had been hewn out of solid limestone. There were no cracks in the walls or ceiling, or the least indication of anything beyond. Jim took hold of the boat and shoved it

246

out of the way. The part of the floor it had concealed was as solid as the rest.

"We'd better go back before the lights go out," I told him.

4

In the following days of search, we found no hidden exit from either the boat room or its antechamber, and the tapped walls gave forth no hollow sound. Without a qualm I washed away the splendid fresco painting of the desert king in his chariot, in the feeble hope that the paint might conceal a trap door or inset stone. The rock-cut wall was inviolate.

The conviction grew upon us that if a burial chamber existed, its opening was concealed somewhere in the gas-filled temple where we could never find it.

Then there came the night that I was hurled up out of a dream by a startling realization. There was a part of the passage easy to search at which we had not even glanced—the outer stairway leading to the broken door. I rose at once, dressed, and wakened Jim. The light was only beginning to clear, and close by in the thicket we heard a leopard cough, a sound like a dull saw drawn across a board. The sand grouse were flying to their water holes as we crept down our well.

The flight consisted of twelve steps about a foot high. We began our search at the bottom, fearful of finding any opening so low down, but more likely, we thought, to find nothing. But we had climbed only four when Jim looked at the one above and gave a little grunt.

In a moment he had his ax blade between the tread of the fifth step and the riser of the sixth. Plaster cracked and broke away; and a big grin broke on the black face. I lifted what was only a limestone facing on clay bricks. The tread of the sixth step was a similar facing; we continued to remove limestone slabs, vertical and horizontal, lightly plastered to bricks, till we came to the tread of the ninth step. This proved solid and continuous with the stone.

We removed the unmortared bricks, to find that they had rested on a heavy grating of wrought iron, supported by stone projections left when the stairway shaft had been quarried out, and level with the tread of the fifth step. It was as free from rust as though newly smelted, and had a fantastic design of snakes and birds—again the asp of Egypt and the vulture of Nubia if I judged aright. As Jim and I stood on the fifth step, it took our combined strengths to lift it by

247

one edge, wheel on the stairway, and set it to one side. Now the treads of the fifth step and of the ninth dropped away in sheer cliffs into darkness. Between was a gap the width of the stairs and three feet across.

I fixed a string to a candle-lamp and lowered it into the pit. It burned well until about four feet from the floor, then suddenly went out. Since my hands would be in reach of Jim's and the drop was an easy one, I decided to go down. The corridor was plainly rock-cut and more narrow than the main passage into the temple; its floor appeared level as far as I could see. After making several tests, I was sure that the gas pool reached midway up my chest, still too high for comfort.

When we had broken our fast, Jim and I prepared for a first sally. Again I must leave Jim to handle a life line tied about my waist, although certain I would not need it, since the floor inclined a little and my lamp burned well. Sailors once, used to bawling in a heavy gale, we had no trouble making ourselves heard. Following the curving passage, I fetched up against what seemed another solid wall.

I was sure it was not solid. Although most of our findings made very little sense, a cunningly hidden passage leading nowhere made none at all. Anyway, there was some way around it. When Jim came with his ax, we found a suspicious looking stone about ten paces back from the dead end and dangerously close to the floor. Jim had only to push against it to make it turn. The aperture revealed was barely wide enough for my shoulders.

Holding his breath, he knelt down and put the lamp through the hole. Immediately he sprang up. In the wan light his face looked gray.

"Cap'n, you won't like to see what's in there."

"Well, I've seen what I didn't like before now."

"It's the Sepulcher of Dry Bones, sho 'nough."

I kneeled and looked in. The room was on a lower level than this passage and larger than any we had seen except the temple itself, so my candle-light did not disclose its farthest walls. But it showed the floor, not strewn, but heaped with skeletons two or three feet deep in a jam like cordwood. I could not doubt that there were two hundred, and there might be four hundred.

I rose and we made our way to the open air. Under the burning sun the gray cast passed slowly from Jim's face. My dank blood stirred again, but I felt a great heaviness of heart.

"What you reckon now, Cap'n?" Jim asked at last.

"Jim, if you tried to keep your direction as we were making up the passage, where do you think we fetched up?"

"I don't think we was very far from 'at big statue at one side of de temple."

"I had the same impression. Well, that could explain all those skeletons. There's probably a hatch of some kind between the temple and that room. Maybe the rites included human sacrifice. Maybe the god was given a libation of blood from a slave's neck. Afterward they pitched the corpses into that vault. If they offered only one a year, on some especially holy day, they could pile up four hundred in due time. Time moved slowly in those days. The Egyptian religion endured without much change for three thousand years."

There fell a long pause. Jim looked straight into my eyes.

"Cap'n Whitman, you got somethin' more 'n 'at to tell me, 'cause I see it in yo' face, and I'd like to have you git it over with."

"I've become convinced that the digging isn't a tomb at all. It's only an underground temple. I guess the painting at the entrance represents the king going down to worship; the cult probably dealt with the mysteries of death—the Jackal-headed god would bear that out. Maybe the boat we found symbolized some hope of the future— the soul's journey to the next world. And if that's the case, which stands to reason, we're wasting our time."

"Why do you reckon they went to all that bother to hide them passageways?"

"It was a secret cult. There have been thousands like it."

"So we better take to iv'ry hunting sho 'nough?"

"Until we can find a better way to make some money."

When I returned to camp, Isabel Gazelle was drying elephant meat on a stick rack over a smoky fire. After one glance into my face, she caught my hand, led me into the tent, and drew the curtain.

"What's happened?" she asked.

I told her of the charnel-chamber we had found and the conclusions I had drawn. She made an astonishing reply.

"If you looked only at bones, the world would be an ugly place."

"I'll look at you instead."

"At me before you leave me, and at trees growing before you chop them down to burn, and at gazelles before you shoot them to eat, and at great elephants before you kill them to take their ivories. None of that is evil. Suliman, my husband, told me about evil, such as had made Mahound cut my mother's throat; and killing of slaves to please a god would be terrible evil—worse than that Mahound did, although I can't tell you why. I know that evil dogs a man's soul as his shadow follows his body when he walks toward the sun. But if you look only for that, you'd be sorry the world was ever made."

"I take great joy in you, Isabel Gazelle. I'm ashamed that I came in with a sick face. I'll find some other way to get the gold we need. What does one defeat count, compared to having you?"

She had grown more beautiful in these months of our bridal. I could almost believe that her beauty had waxed in the last few days. Surely this was an illusion, yet I could not dispel it, and felt bewitched.

"Don't tell me how many days longer you'll stay with me," she said, as though she had read my mind. "Let me know the day before you go."

"I'll postpone the telling as long as I can."

"Once I thought I could hardly stand to have you go—that I might get on a horse and ride into the desert until I died—but that's changed."

"I'm glad to hear it."

"I'll have someone to love from the moment that you leave."

"So soon?"

"Omar, do you know what day this is?"

I did know. I still kept the count of the days begun when I first went into slavery. But Isabel counted days according to the changes of the moon.

"What day is it?"

"It's the fifth since the full moon, and I've not yet gone to make my bed beside the wall."

I caught my breath. "Perhaps it's only delayed——"

Laughing happily and almost wildly, she threw her arms around my neck. "Then what of the drawing of my breast, and the sharpening of every taste and smell, and the happiness in my heart? Omar, I'm sure! You're a lean old lion, and this will be your cub."

My heart swelled, and it must be that my soul exulted, for I felt a lifting like that when I had dropped my chains.

"I wish we could return to the tents of the Beni Kabir and live among them all our lives."

"No, when the time comes, you'll go across the sea, and you'll be to me as one who's drunk the cup of death. Suliman told me so, and it will be so."

"Can't we go there and stay until the babe is born——"

"I think you'll never see him except in dreams. And for the little while more before we part, we can't go to the tents of the Beni Kabir, because you'll be busy taking gold from the Pharaoh's tomb."

"What do you mean? I told you it's only a temple——"

"Didn't Jim Effendi tell you that the Sepulcher of Dry Bones weighs in the balance against the Sepulcher of Wet Bones? His vision was true. Today you've proved that he gave it the right name. You think the countless bones you saw were those of men sacrificed to some god of stone. I think they were killed for an evil dream of a wicked king."

"What dream?"

"The taking with him of his gold into the Hereafter."

"They were the men who had cut through the stone and built the tomb?"

"By his command, they were shut in one of the rooms they made, and the door sealed."

5

At present I did not dwell upon Isabel's conceiving. I needed a quiet hour—when we were alone, perhaps when she was asleep on my arm and I could look into her face, or when her arms were about me in a tenderness akin to that my babe would know—in order to contemplate the common wonder, the unsolvable everyday mystery.

I called Jim and told him Isabel's explanation of the charnel-chamber.

"I wish we could make it up to 'em mens, somehow," Jim said.

"I wish so, too."

"They was slaves, I reckon, and I was a slave once, but Ol' Mas' set me free."

"He did?"

"After 'at I worked wif freemen, in fair weat'er and foul, and when de time came, I fought beside 'em. I reckon they was the freest men who ever lived in de worl'."

"There were none more free that I know of."

"We bof been in Africa a mighty long time. We ain't heard de church bells ring in de little ports we stop at, and see the people goin' back and forf. But someday——"

"When that day comes, we'll do what two men can."

We had been walking slowly from the camp to the sepulcher. Now our step quickened, and our excitement rose to the pitch we had felt the first day. When we arrived at our cache, Jim got out a piece of carpet I had brought from the tent when we first began our digging, and which we had used for catching rubble as we widened the well.

"Cap'n, I want to try somethin'," he told me. "'At bone room is nigh de passage end, and we left de do' open. Don't you reckon if I fan real hard at de opening in de stairs I can blow in fresh air and drive some of de poison into de bone room?"

I answered without thinking. "It won't hurt to try."

So when we gained the stairway aperture, Jim stood on the fifth step and fanned vigorously with the rug. After about ten minutes, as I sat on the step with my legs through the aperture, the inkling came to me that instead of facilitating our afternoon's work, we had quite likely bitched it. Whether or not Jim had fanned out any poison gases, he had certainly disturbed their layers, which alone had permitted us to penetrate the passage.

To test the air, I lighted a wisp of grass and dropped it into the aperture. As I did so, a possibility which hadn't occurred to me was dawning in my brain. Then there came a terrific explosion.

It happened in the passage over which I hung, and it blew me clear out of the aperture. Amid that deafening blast, I was hurled against Jim, and we both careened down the steps. Actually that fall saved both our lives, for it carried us below the level of the broken outer door which a second later became a three-foot cannon mouth emitting a prodigious charge. We were still tumbling when this second explosion, many times greater than the first, put out our sense, as a gust of wind puts out a light. There must have been flame above us, but we did not see it. There must have been sound beyond imagination, but we did not hear it. The solid rock must have quaked, but we did not feel it—we were not blown to pieces because the solid rock-cut steps down which we tumbled raised an unshatterable barrier between us and the blast.

How long we lay stunned, we never knew. When once more I became aware of time and place, Jim and I lay sprawled at the foot of the steps. Some of the rocks we had braced had fallen, but a jagged hole remained, and through it came a gust of wind blowing into the temple. I heard its rush and saw dust flying into the aperture and instantly disappear. Enough light came down so that I could make out Jim's face.

"We better git out o' here, Cap'n," were his first words.

"I'll give you a boost and you pull me out."

We were both used to taking sudden action. But we had hardly begun when the truth burst upon me. The demons were all dead. Nature abhors a vacuum, and the air rushing into the temple was taking the place of the lethal gases that had passed away in flame.

Jim's fright passed off and wonder took its place. The gale blowing into the aperture died away in a gentle breeze. The air smelled very fresh.

"It's a mighty big wonder we alive," Jim burst out after a moment or two in which we stood tongue-tied, with our arms dangling, as men do after a severe shock.

"We wouldn't be if we'd got down into the passage with lamps in our hands."

"Did stirrin' up dat gas wif de carpet fix it so it would blow up?"

"I think so."

We gazed off across the plain toward camp. Isabel and her Tuareg came running. When they saw us, we thrilled to their jubilant cries of "Sano! Sano!" Isabel did not pause in her gazellelike pace, but if her followers had seen terror in her face, she had either shed it or hidden it by the time she dashed up to me and took my hand in hers. Around the black veils of the Tuareg, their skins still looked gray.

"What was the great thunder, O Omar?" an Arabic-speaker asked. "We heard two claps, the first one very loud, the second shaking the earth."

"We used some very strong *barraka* on the demons," I answered, "and blew them all to hell where they belong."

That quick retort and the Tuareg's happy laughter when it was repeated in Tamashek cleared the muddle from my brain. In a moment or two more I had found a reasonable explanation for what had happened and could propose it to Jim.

"It must be that the gases in the new passage couldn't explode until they were mixed with air," I told him. "The fanning did it, and when I dropped in a bit of burning grass, they blew up. Why didn't they mix before now, when we were walking about in them? Certainly we stirred them up a little. Well, in the temple I thought I saw very dim lights dart horizontally from my lamp—maybe small quantities had become mixed with air in the right proportions, but not enough to set off an explosion. That might be because the heavy

253

gas at the bottom, smelling like rotten eggs, was an explosive kind, but it was cut off from the air by a layer of some noncombustible gas, not quite so heavy, lying between. The explosion in the passage blew out some door into the temple and mixed the gases there. In not more than two seconds the mixture became explosive and the heat—or maybe sparks—set it off."

"Look like we was workin' in a powder magazine de whole time."

"It amounted to that, and we weren't much smarter than those poor devils asphyxiated in the temple twenty years ago. But any gas that didn't burn was surely blown out by the blast. I see no reason why we shouldn't go down."

We waited a while longer, throwing in burning grass and sniffing at the apertures. The grass burned up and out and we could smell nothing but fresh air. Then Jim and I put lines about our waists and entrusted the coils to the dark hands of two black-veiled Tuareg. If we ceased to shake the rope every three steps, the holders must haul, but my light heart told me that the lamps would burn and we would be able to breathe.

We walked up the steps, along the passage, down the second flight and the ramp, and through the colonnade. The lamps never flickered as we descended the three steps into what was once the pit of death; when we came to the side aisle approaching the statue, we saw that it had been knocked over backward by the force of the explosion, leaving a ceiling-high gap in the wall. Perhaps our hearts stopped beating as we came to the fallen giant and cast our lights into the room beyond; then they leaped.

It was though a tornado had swept through a palace. Idols and images of all kinds, and couches, chairs, stools, tables, and chests lay strewn in ruin or smashed against the wall. A chariot with its wheels blown off lay on its side. An elaborately carved bed, almost intact, stood on its side. A harp hurled by the blast had fallen over the head and around the neck of a hawk-headed idol.

And amid the ruin, everywhere, and as far as our lantern beams could cast, came up the glimmer of gold.

CHAPTER 20

Harvest

1

JIM AND I moved about the room in silence, picking up objects, putting them down, gazing, wondering.

The body of the chariot had heavy plates of gold. Wooden chairs with feet representing the hooves of bulls and couches whose sides were carved to represent animals, still warm and slightly charred from the explosion, had golden overlay or decoration. From the broken lid of a chest I picked up an intricately worked golden panel that weighed thirty pounds, and the floor was littered with such chests spilling their contents of clothes, cosmetics in alabaster jars, myrrh, wigs, and withered flowers that blossomed in some summer thousands of winters gone. In gold-inlaid cabinets or strewn on the floor lay countless scarabs of gold, lapis lazuli, and beryl; ivory wands; rackets and balls used in games; jars of ointments; gold collars and rings; swords and daggers with jeweled hilts; golden caskets containing perfume in vials; jeweled amulets and ornaments; and golden seals. Cups, bowls, pitchers, and pots in gold and silver or enamelware, glass and pottery whole or broken, and figurines in green and blue enamel lay everywhere under foot. We could not move without brushing against some treasure.

Twisted out of shape by its impact against the wall was a golden bowl, too heavy to lift, held by four servants four feet high, cast in silver. Two fallen statues of the king—the likeness to the fresco painting at the entrance was unmistakable—were of black stone with breastplates of gold and face wrought in sheet gold with crystal eyeballs and jeweled irises. Human-headed, hawk-headed, ram-headed, jackal-headed, crocodile-headed, pig-headed, hippopotamus-headed, and lion-headed gods and godlings lay in profusion, mostly with gold decoration. Lying in one corner was the foot-high form of a leopard carved in black stone, on whose back stood a two-foot figure of the king as heavy as lead and presumably in solid gold. There were life-sized golden hawks, but the prettiest ornaments we had yet seen were a pair of song birds, also wrought in gold with inlay of jewels to imitate their colors, on an ivory perch.

255

We had no time to look at the bright fresco paintings showing farmers sowing and reaping, fishermen with nets and spears, hunters with bows and arrows and boomerangs, cart makers, armorers, butchers, and cooks; but we gazed through two apertures that had been broken outward by the blast. One, reached by a step, opened on the charnel-chamber. The other, a wide doorway on the floor level, gave a glimpse of a golden throne, a gold-lidded chest about which stood four female figures in black stone decorated with gold, a large screenlike object of gold overlay or solid gold with gods and goddesses in relief, and a burst-in door beyond.

"We'd better go up, now," I suggested to Jim.

"If we seen any more, I reckon we'd be struck blind," he answered.

I looked at my hands, and they were empty. I had picked up dozens of treasures and put them down. Before we left, I chose a golden bird with lapis-lazuli inlay, Jim, a golden cabinet of elaborate workmanship full of myrrh. When we came to the stairway pit, only the two line holders waited there. Isabel and her Tuareg had moved to the shade of a thorn tree about a hundred paces distant. But when they saw us, they came on the run.

"So you've found the gold!" Isabel exclaimed.

"Yes." I started to say, "Thanks to you," but all of us knew that.

"How much is there?"

"We've seen many donkey loads. There may be as many more."

She turned and spoke in Tamashek to her kinsmen. They nodded and smiled on me, glad that Jim and I had defeated the Kel Acouf (demon people) and I had come into my heritage, and they admired the golden bird and box that they passed from hand to hand, but they did not seem greatly excited. Then one of them asked a question that sobered them all. They watched my face anxiously as Isabel translated it into Arabic.

"The men wish to know if now you break camp and go to your own place."

"Are they in haste to return to Tuaregstan?"

"They are never in haste except in a race. They have never had such hunting as they have here, and they are afraid it will be cut short."

"Tell them it will take weeks to get out the gold and melt it into bars and many weeks more to get it safely to the sea."

Isabel gave a happy little toss of her head as she repeated this. The Tuareg smiled beneath their veils.

I could not match their calm and did not try. On the other hand, only Isabel divined my intense excitement. She saw to it that I ate bountifully at supper, the good meat and millet washed down with fermented camel's milk—such care as she had given Suliman when there were weighty matters on his mind—still I went to bed not expecting to sleep. But her sweet warmth against my side and child-like breathing and my glimpses of her face in the watch lamp lulled me, giving me a still, deep happiness which, when I lost it, no gold could buy; and my soaring fancies flew home.

Isabel and I liked to go to sleep in the first clear starlight and be wakened by the rush of dawn. Today I rose when a first glint eastward showed the shape of the hills, called Jim, and shared with him my rough breakfast of dried elephant meat. My fancies were again wild, for I thought of how many dawns had cracked since a cruel king had furnished his palace of death—close on a million, perhaps—and this present dawn, so like all the rest, was the one that his astrologers should have bid him beware, because it would usher in the day of his darkest dread.

We lighted our lanterns and went down. With hardly a glance at yesterday's finds, we made through the door into the throne room. What we had thought was a screen might be some kind of shrine, bearing a frieze of gods and goddesses worked in massive gold. The throne itself was an armchair made of some very hard wood, with plates of gold bearing the emblems of the asp and the vulture. The four goddesses we had seen surrounding the chest were likewise of wood, with draperies and hands and faces and hair wrought in sheet gold; and the cover of the chest was a wonderful piece of the gold-smith's art, showing snakes intercoiled. Within were porcelain jars containing black human hair and what I could not doubt were nail parings. To judge from their quantity, they had been saved from every clipping of the king's hair and beard, fingernails and toenails over a score or more of years. Great Pharaoh, did not the thrift begin after you conquered Egypt? I cannot imagine a desert ruler setting such store, lest his lean tribesmen laugh.

When we came to the door beyond, we did not question but that it led to the funeral chamber. Our lights showed first four alabaster jars, whose covers bore human or animal heads. Within were cloth packets, only one of which I opened—revealing what I thought were human entrails, preserved with aromatic drugs. Against the west wall —and I had looked for it there, because of some instruction I had long ago forgotten—and occupying more than half the room, stood the sarcophagus, a block of gray quartz weighing many tons. The top had gold handles, but it did not seem possible that Jim's and my combined strength could move it. We found a stone idol that would do for a block and the pole of a chariot with which we could pry. Marble tablets recording the king's glories made excellent wedges, and within an hour the huge case was open.

Inside lay a bronze coffin, man-shaped, the upper half of its lid wrought to portray its inmate. The arms were molded as folded on the breast, the hands, apparently solid gold, holding what I took for a flail and a sickle; the face was a mask in sheet gold with crystal eyes. The asp and vulture emblem was shown in inlay on the forehead.

This lid opened readily to reveal an inner coffin, precisely like the first except for being slightly smaller and wrought in solid gold. We raised its 400-pound lid. Our first find was a great quantity of linen cloth. Beneath lay a hard object, its shape suggestive of a body, swathed in cloth. As we cut the bands, a shrunken human form began to appear, still half-hidden under breastplates of gold. These, too, we removed, along with golden bracelets and necklaces and amulets and sandals of beaten gold and gold stalls on the fingers and toes; so at last we gazed upon the mummy of the king.

The torso and limbs had shriveled almost out of human resemblance; but the head was remarkably preserved. I was quite sure I could identify the face as the same as we saw in the fresco painting and which had appeared on the statues and the sheet-gold masks. The lips appeared thinner than in living faces, the nostrils somewhat drawn, the whole bony structure more visible; but many human faces, including my own, were as gaunt. Its type was of that I had seen in the Beni Amer, broad between the cheekbones, with the high Hamitic nose and pointed chin. The skin, like theirs, appeared reddish-brown. I could fancy him a great horseman and hunter, a born commander, brave, haughty, superbly intelligent, as sure of his destiny as was Alexander, and as without pity as Genghis Khan, Tamerlane, or Attila the Hun.

It came to me with a start that he had emulated none of these because he had lived and conquered before their time. Neither Herodotus nor any other Greek historian recorded a Nubian conqueror of Egypt later than 660 B.C. His name had once thundered through rich, populous Egypt; the princes and the priests trembled at it as they had never trembled at the name of Osiris. Now his name

was forgotten and these leather-encased bones were the last of him
and he had left his gold to me.

Jim and I came up to rest under the same thorn tree that yesterday
had shaded Isabel and her Tuareg. We needed to obtain a calm
something like theirs.

"Cap'n, how much gold do you reckon it all come to?" he asked
when we had sat and smoked.

"What's your opinion? You used to guess a lighter cargo within a
hundred weight."

"'At coffin weigh a clean ton. De gold in de bronze coffin and de
screen and de throne and de statue on top de leopard is a ton mo'.
And 'at's not even half."

"It's close on it, though."

"If it was lead—and I can figure lead better 'n gold somehow—I'd
say it would catch five. And wif 'em 'Gyptians caying de golden bowl,
a good ton of silver."

"That's no trifle, either."

"Cap'n, you reckon that's as much as one of 'em English lawds has
got?"

"Some of them have much more—in land and money—but some
not as much."

"I heard 'em talk about a million dollars. I don't know what 'at is.
Would de gold bring a million dollars?"

"Twice that much—maybe three or four times—when we can get
it into a Christian port, but that part's not going to be easy. About
twenty-five baggage camels could get it to the coast if we could stay
clear of robbers; then it would have to be loaded on Arab dhows.
A good many are pirates already, and almost all would turn pirate on
a moment's notice. The nearest Christian port that can be reached
from the Red Sea is Cape Town in South Africa—several weeks' sail."

"Then we got to move it on the sly, somehow. We got to make out
like it's something else'n gold."

"When I was a boy, we painted copper pennies with quicksilver
and tried to pass them as half-dollars. But we never fooled anyone."

Jim laughed at that—his deep-throated laugh that was one of the
joys of my life, and my heart was suddenly light. Jim and I had found
a king's treasure only yesterday. There might be a third as much gold
as was fetched to King Solomon every year from the mines of Ophir

—six hundred and some talents of fifty-eight pounds each—and quite possibly the gold-rich northern Sudan was itself Ophir, for some regions of it still bore the name of Aphar. If we let ourselves be saddened by the hard problem of transporting it to a Christian port, we had been ill-picked to find it. Fate, having dealt with us so terribly or splendidly since we were young, deserved better of us than this.

For a fortnight Jim and I worked happily underground, separating gold and silver from the wood or stone it had adorned and piling it up for removal. The riddle of its shipment remained opaque as ever. Then an incident of the camp cast the first beam of light.

Another patriarchal family of shepherds had paid us a visit, their band including a small Negro boy, probably a slave, whom they treated as one of their own blood. Apparently he had never seen an elephant tusk at close range, and on looking at one of our growing pile, he was surprised to find that it had a hollow end. This hollow became smaller throughout almost half of the tusk's length, but the tusk was a large one, and he was able to insert his whole arm. Still unable to hit bottom of the curious cavity, he dropped in a handful of stones.

As soon as our visitors had gone, I poured water into various tusks from a pot containing a half-gallon. The larger tusks took the whole amount and more, tusks as small as forty-pounders would hold a quart.

Gold was eighteen times heavier than water. Since a pint of water was a pound the world around, a quart of gold weighed thirty-six pounds. Ivory varied greatly in density and hardness: big tusks that looked about the same size often varied twenty pounds in weight. An ivory buyer would of course investigate a tusk unusually heavy for its size; a porter or a dock hand would curse and ask no questions.

I wondered where I could buy five hundred tusks of mature bulls.

On the following day Jim, Isabel, and I, with a few Tuareg who wished to go for entertainment, rode twenty miles across the plain to Takuba's kraals. We had not the slightest compunction in leaving several tons of treasure in easy reach of Isabel's followers and clansmen; their well-tested loyalty to her was hardly more of a restraining force than their natural reluctance to go underground and, strange as it might seem, their diminished interest in the hoard now that the demons guarding it had met defeat. The Tuareg must either work hard or play hard or ride hard. They could not endure inactivity for very long.

Isabel addressed Takuba in their native tongue and gave me his reply.

"Takuba says that about three hundred miles south of here, where the Blue Nile joins the White Nile, the land juts out into the waters in the shape of an elephant's trunk, and thus it is called Khartoum, which means an elephant's trunk in the language of the people living in that country. Every year a great fair is held there. This year it will begin on a new moon following the next new moon, and will last for two moons. There will come down from his capital, Sennar, on the Blue Nile, Akbar, who is king of the Fung, the mightiest of the tribes, who trace their descent from the Juhayna Arabs. And since he is over-lord of the Sudan, he takes a tax from all goods bought and sold, but also he keeps out robbers. It is at this fair that the lesser kings sell their stores of ivory as well as slaves, which are bought by traders coming up the river from Egypt, or down the Blue Nile from Ethiopia, or down the White Nile from the Country of the Naked People; these traders are not blacks but Arabs, some of them from Mombasa and some from Zanzibar. And there is one trader, whose name is Kamel Malik, who lives in a tent as fine as Akbar's and will buy or sell a thousand slaves or ten thousand tusks without spitting once."

Far away in the camps of the Beni Kabir I had heard of Kamel Malik of Mombasa, the king of the traders.

"What money is used for this buying and selling?" I asked. "It can't be shells on a string!"

"Nor cows or sheep or camels," Isabel replied with some wonder when she had talked to Takuba, "but any silver money is good, as are also bars of silver to the weight of two hundred rupees, of which Kamel Malik keeps a great store."

Two hundred rupees equaled twenty English pounds—hence a bar of silver weighing about five pounds avoirdupois.

"Ask Takuba if any gold is used in buying and selling."

"Takuba says that gold is sometimes brought from the Beni Shangul, which is a land of mighty mountains far up the Blue Nile," Isabel reported shortly. "It comes in bars or in skin sacks of golden pebbles and dust, and it is told that men from afar will buy it at ten times its weight in silver, but this Takuba cannot believe."

This was good luck of no surprising sort, provided that Takuba had some of the silver bars in store and that he would lend me one. Being subject to Simba, king of the Beni Amer, he took care not to ask what I wanted of it or why I needed a pan or pot of cast iron. This article was not on the premises. I told Isabel of the stumbling block, for she liked to share in my small as well as big affairs here in Africa. She conversed with Takuba and quickly found the answer.

"The silversmiths of Agades melt silver, not in an iron pan, but in an earthen jug. Takuba thinks you need a round bowl, made of well-baked clay, which he can have made for you at the village. Around the top will run a band of wrought iron, from which three strong spikes stand out. With the bowl will come three strong pipes of wrought iron to fit over the spikes. Thereby the bowl may be lifted even if the milk you pour from it is as heavy as melted lead."

"Such a bowl would exactly fit my needs. Ask him also to buy a dozen ax heads of the hardest kind, and a dozen hammer heads as heavy as a man may swing, and if he can get us three or four anvils, they will be most welcome. All this will cost several bars of silver or a drove of cattle. Tell Takuba that I will repay him in due course, and that I am his protected."

Our next task was to build a blacksmith's forge, which did not tax us greatly, since we had an abundance of brick and the wherewithal to make a big pair of bellows. This we set up near camp, proposing to tell any innocent shepherds who came by that we used it for melting lead and casting bullets; in thickets near at hand we dug pits for quick concealment of more questionable gear. The obtaining of charcoal was an easy chore. The natives made it by leaving a vent in a stack of wood burned under a covering of moist earth. The product, if heated long enough, was almost pure carbon.

It took a deal of bellows pumping, patience, and a pile of charcoal to melt the thirty or more pounds of silver in the pot; but at last it looked like dirty quicksilver and gave forth a bluish light; with this we cast five silver bars hardly distinguishable from the one we had borrowed from Takuba. With a better arrangement of our fire bricks and a two-man bellows, I believed we could melt fifty pounds of silver or gold a day.

When the tools arrived, I had Zoan divide all his men into two work crews to labor on alternate days, the free day spent in hunting. While the white-veiled Tuareg made charcoal, pumped the bellows, or carried burdens, the haughty black-veiled nobles who had the duty hammered and hacked wonder works of gold and silver into pieces small enough to fit our pot. Avowed to war, pillage, and the chase, scorning labor of any sort, they surprised me by their ready assent to the task, working more cheerfully than Isabel could well explain. Apparently the demolishing of the beautiful objects appealed to them. Deep in their souls, perhaps, they were vandals. Perhaps that had to do with their being such good hunters and warriors—perhaps they hated civilization and all its works. But I guessed in the dark. . . .

3

In six weeks' work, we had smelted a ton of silver into specie bars and five hundred pounds of gold into ingots similar to those brought from the mines of Shangul. Thus we had five hundred pieces in all, itself a treasure dizzying Jim's mind and mine, although the Tuareg regarded it with complete calm. These bars and ingots I distributed among the score of black-veiled Tuareg and ten of the white-veiled who would accompany Isabel and me to the great Khartoum fair.

The day came that we left Jim and some white-veiled Tuareg at our prosaic-looking camp and struck southeastward on our fleet riding camels into the bush. The beasts had put on fat in their long indolence and suffered throughout the first day's ride; after that they found their gait, and the Tuareg shouted verses in their praise and the long miles sped behind them. Every one of those miles brought forth wonders to see and hear and know. The greatest in the long run was the people following the grass with their cattle and sheep or dwelling in little villages in minute islands in the wilderness. They were at everlasting war with the lions and leopards and hyenas that preyed upon the flocks and herds; the elephants that raided their gardens and pushed down their huts; and the antelope and wild pigs that broke through their fences. Yet striving and surviving still, weeping or singing or laughing, they retold man's story, from its beginning in the swollen bellies of the young wives to its strange end in a new-dug grave. But we, ourselves men, short-sighted as our kind, looked with bigger eyes and quickened breath at lions, leopards, hyenas, elephants, antelope, and wild pigs.

Good fortune rather than good sense—for the Tuareg were loath to yield the trail even to evil-tempered rhinos—saved us from fights, and we ate bountifully of various bucks, including the succulent eland, as big as an ox. Avoiding regions where robbers might lie in wait, we took six days to gain the Blue Nile, then camped for the night on its eastern bank amid other caravans from the Tigré country. Before we crossed on the big dhows that served for ferries, I donned the full dress of a sheik of high rank, found in a bale from the Beni Kabir and once worn by Suliman on an official visit to Yussuf Pasha.

I wore it to please Isabel, for certain satisfactions and amusements of my own, and as a stroke of policy.

Accompanied by several black-veiled Tuareg, I paid a ceremonial visit to the king of Sennar, overlord of a vast territory. Instead of kneeling to him, I clapped hand to head and heart, a bold stand for an Arabic-speaking *farengi* to take. If I had resources to back it, I should get on well. If a penurious adventurer, I would more likely be impaled on a Fung spear. When I presented my tokens of respect to the monarch, he gave me a smile and the promise of his protection. They were five bars of silver and one small wedge of gold worth at least two thousand rupees or two hundred English pounds. No doubt Kamel Malik would hear of me before the day was out.

When I had changed ten silver bars for twenty skin bags, each containing a hundred silver rupees, our whole band went sight-seeing. There was no sight in Africa quite like the great fair at the interflowing Niles. A deserted promontory and a goat pasture had become and would remain for about two months the greatest city on the continent south of the Sahara.

Back from the bazaars rose the tents and the kraals of hundreds of native kings and chieftains with their attendants and trains. There were brown or reddish Hamites from north and east, coal-black Negroes from the steaming equatorial cornlands, and lean, storklike men, fully as black, with sharp noses and thin, cruel lips who leaned on their nine foot spears and were the scourge of the peaceful cultivators. These bargained with Arabs in flowing robes, bearded Jews, Armenians, Persians, and no few turbaned Indians for beads, baubles, and finery, tools and weapons, parasols, rugs, cloth, and toys. One whole quarter of the bazaar was a food-and-drink market. Among the dried and salt meat, fruit, nuts, grains, locusts by the basketful next to homey beans and pumpkins, and Indian and Turkish sweets, I saw a cask of salted herring bearing the strange word "Boston," and how it had found its way over a thousand miles up the Nile was beyond my wit to guess.

There was a heavy traffic in ebony and ostrich feathers, both in demand in the great unguessed outside world, but when all was said and done, this was a slave and ivory fair. To judge from the pens that I saw—only a fraction of the total number—ten thousand men, women, and children were being offered for sale. Almost all belonged to the pure Negro tribes, mainly peaceful cultivators from the deep south; the lean nomads were too fierce to please the catchers' fancy. Only a few wept or wailed; some were desperate and must be confined; mainly they appeared stunned. I wished I could finish my business quickly and be gone.

It should not take long. Ivory was heaped like cordwood beside most of the larger pavilions; it filled a good many yards of the Arab merchants; and almost every peddler had a tusk or two in a store. Very little was new ivory, and I believed that less than half had been obtained by elephant hunting; the main had been found at the scene of some monster's death on the plains or in the bush. Hence, most were long-dried, and a great many the heavy tusks of old bulls. On the second day of my stay I visited the beast fairs, picking out with the Tuareg's help about two hundred baggage camels for later purchase. On the morning of the third day, alone except for Zoan in his most stately garb, I went to an immense pavilion, hardly second in richness to the Sennar king's, the abode of the king of the traders, Kamel Malik.

Zoan and I were immediately ushered into his *gulphor*. Kamel himself appeared in a moment or two, a notably handsome Arab of my own age, grave and dignified but far from austere, and employing stately Nahur Arabic instead of the Kalam wati, the vulgar tongue. By now I was used to the shocked first glance of those I met—a quickly hidden consternation in their faces—yet I did not expect to surprise it in the highly disciplined countenance of a notorious slave trader. It passed off, and his eyes narrowed slightly as I replied in the same language. He was wondering who in the devil I might be.

A slave brought coffee and sweetmeats. Thereafter Kamel and I spoke of hunting and war, but we did not mention the beauty of women and of verses because we had not broken bread or salt. Then there fell a little pause.

"Kamel Malik, I wish to buy ivory for export to Europe, and since I need a large quantity, I would like to buy from some merchant rather than the natives."

"That would save time, effendi," Kamel replied, smoothing his small, silky beard. "Also, the merchant who sells you a large quantity at the source of supply should be willing to deal at a modest profit. Would you state an approximation of your needs?"

"I am considering ten tons of large bull tusks, well seasoned."

"For such tusks, I am paying eighty rupees per ngoma. For ten tons of seasoned tusks, I would ask ninety rupees per ngoma."

"If I should double my purchase, how much less would you ask?"

"Two rupees less—eighty-eight rupees."

"If I should triple it?"

"If you buy thirty tons of large dry tusks, to be assembled in my yard within five days, my price would be eighty-six rupees, eight annas."

"Because of the civil wars in Egypt, I'm afraid to ship ivory down the Nile and wish to take it to Suakin on the Red Sea. That means a dangerous journey overland. If I buy from you, what help can you give me in safeguarding my purchase?"

"I can stamp each tusk with a certain seal respected by all and feared by a great many."

"I've heard of that seal. From Suakin I expect to ship my ivory in dhows to Cape Town, whence it can be trans-shipped to England. Such dhows are often untrustworthy, and those seas are infested with Arab pirates. Is there anything you can do to lessen the danger?"

"For a price, yes. Every year I ship goods worth many lakhs of rupees with almost no loss by theft. The Emir of the Hadarib, who owns the mainland at Suakin, is an old friend and a distant kinsman. The greatest fleet of dhows operating on the Red Sea and along the western shores of the Indian Ocean belong to my associate Saad ibn Hassan; all bear a crescent moon in a square of stars painted in white on the bow. His charge for transporting ivory from Suakin to Cape Town will not exceed four hundred rupees per ton. This is at the shipper's risk. No one in Africa can insure you against shipwreck, which Allah forbid, but I, Kamel, have ways of protecting my own and associates' shipments from pirates and robbers. May I ask if you read Arabic as well as you speak it?"

"Not as well, but I can read it."

"If you will pay me ninety rupees per ngoma for thirty tons of heavy tusks, one and one-half ngomas and up, I'll give you my testament, sworn before a cadi, Allah bearing witness, to recompense you half the amount of your loss from robbers or pirates sustained from the border of the Emir of Hadarib's domains to the dock at Cape Town."

"I've already acquired some ivory by hunting. Although it won't be covered in the insurance, will you instruct your agents and representatives to see that it has the same care?"

"All the ivory that you ship would have the same care."

"Thirty tons would come to——"

I expected Kamel to reach for the paper and inkhorn on his desk—instead he answered instantly. "One hundred and twenty thousand rupees."

Smiling over his feat, he handed me pen and paper. Since a ngoma was seven and one-half kilabs of six pounds avoirdupois, my patient figuring arrived at the same sum. The amount was twelve thousand English pounds and close on to sixty thousand Yankee dollars.

"If I deliver the ivory to Saad ibn Hassan's docks in Suakin after ninety days, and before one hundred and twenty days, need I wait long for shipment?"

"Not more than two weeks."

"I would like to pay half the sum in three hundred silver bars of two hundred rupees each, and the other half in thirty ingots of gold of two thousand rupees each."

"That will be quite satisfactory, effendi." Kamel beckoned to a slave to fill our coffee cups.

Living up to Isabel's graphic tribute to him, he had not spat even once. But I, too, had dealt largely with speed and aplomb and, unless I missed my guess, without going far wrong. Considering my lack of practice, I had every right to pride as well as hope.

CHAPTER 21

Rendezvous

1

OUR RETURN journey was no fine six-day dash through the bush. Besides our riding beasts, we had nearly two hundred baggage camels, each to be watered, fed, loaded with upwards of three hundred pounds of ivory, marched a score or more miles daily, unloaded, picketed, and protected from lions—all by one hundred and fifty black Swahili tribesmen whose labor we had hired from Kamel Malik. The Swahili and the white-veiled Tuareg did most of the daytime tasks, while the black-veiled Tuareg and I stood the night watches. By taking turns at catnaps, we were able to keep our eyes open and our rifles primed beside the watch fires.

When I came off watch at midnight at our second day out from Khartoum fair, Isabel was awake to give me supper and to enjoy a cheroot with me beside our cooking fire. The small red blaze could be scorned or circumvented by a bold prowler, but a radiant moon, our old well-loved companion, illumined the barren ground for a comforting distance about our bivouac, and we listened to the night sounds with no sharp apprehension. Hyenas wailed or sobbed or broke into horrid laughter; elephants trumpeted far away; lions uttered rhythmic grunts as they paced the plain, and one, balked and hungry, silenced all other sound by his furious roars.

"His name among the Arab traders is Simba," Isabel said thoughtfully. "In Tamashek his name is Zaki. What is his name in the speech of Frankistan?"

"Lion," I answered.

"When my son is born, I'll name him Lion for your sake."

"That's a good name. But what if the babe be a girl?"

"I don't think it will be so. At the moment he was conceived a dog-jackal—his voice is deeper than a bitch's—barked on the desert. But if it is so, I'll name her Gazelle, for my sake."

"Either one would suit me well."

"Omar, what was your name in the speech of Frankistan? You told me, but I forget."

"Homer Whitman."

"Omar?"

"Breathe into Omar as you say it, and slur it a little."

"Will you return to that name when you go to Frankistan?"

"Not for a long time and perhaps never. I can do my work better under another name."

"There's no one there who would keep the secret? Some old woman who loved you, or a child who's grown up since you went away?"

"I have no one in my homeland any more—but I have everyone."

"What do you mean by that?"

"I couldn't tell you very well."

"What name are you going to take?"

"Holgar Blackburn."

"What does his name mean in your speech?"

"I don't know what Holgar means. In Scotland 'blackburn' can refer to a dark stream or it can mean something burned black."

"Is he dead?"

"Yes, with no one left to mourn him. Also, he's as long from home and forgotten as I am. But I promised to do well by him there, in payment for the use of his name."

"Did Holgar look like you?"

"Not especially, but that won't matter after all these years. I have some marks he didn't have——"

I stopped, remembering he had a mark that I had not, fixed on him before he left home. It looked like an X and had been burned into the back of his hand for stealing a meat pie from the kitchen of the workhouse master. I recalled his face as he told me.

"I know every one of your marks," Isabel said, looking away. "Perhaps I should get one more." I told her about the burn.

"Do you think anyone would remember it after all these years?"

"No, and Holgar's bones have been picked eleven years, and I've been marked enough."

We lay down and began to drift into sleep. One of the last sounds I heard was the cough of a leopard not far off in the bush—a grating sound like that of a saw on a rough board. He had been attracted by the smell of meat, but he dared not come into camp to snatch and make way with it—the smell and sound of man, and occasionally his shadow, and the dying coals of the fire balked his desire. If driven to white-hot fury, he would have charged a whole body of spearmen, but he was only vicious-tempered now. Isabel, lying in the hollow of my arm, did not speak or rouse, only lay a little closer to my side.

At bright noonday on the ninth day of our journey, only a few miles from its end, I heard a similar sound. It, too, was in near-by thorn; again it was an expression of rancor, and on this occasion it was caused by our caravan approaching close to the beast's lair. I was so sure that he would slink away, scowling, into the long grass that I hardly tried to get a glimpse of him; and instead I gazed back to a scene of moonlight. Its only connection with this scene was a leopard's cough, but for some reason I did not yet know, it returned with a living vividness. I saw again the open moonlit ground before the tent, the dark bush beyond, the dying fire, and, close beside mine, Isabel's beautiful face lovely in surrender to sleep and dreams. From thence I remembered our leaving the fire, and before that, our low-voiced talk. Touching on the future and the past, it had sorrowed both of us a little; but suddenly it seemed to have some importance that I had failed to perceive. I did not know what it was— I wished I did know. . . . Something had been said that must be well weighed. . . . It was as though the gods had listened. . . .

The gods! If there were no gods in the sense I meant, there was a mystery of life and fate that only fools deny.

This swift train of memories and thought had interfered with my taking an accustomed action—swinging out a short distance from the thorn where I had heard the leopard. Also, I failed to consider that the sound rose downwind from our course, so if he stood his ground instead of slinking off, my camel would not know it and warn me by her alarm. I had led the caravan on about fifty yards, when, again, once more, I encountered death.

He came rushing forth from the thicket in a different and diminished form from his awful aspect among the mimosa trees. He ran low to the ground and at stunning speed. So far he did not show beautiful and bright in leopard kind, for he burst through the shadows of the thorn, and yellow and brown grass obscured his adornments. Nor did he come straight to me like my beloved. I rode high upon a camel out of his easy reach. Also, he let pass one of the white-veiled Tuareg on a belled mare close behind mine.

The next in file was a coal-black Swahili, naked except for a waist-cloth, leading a refractory baggage camel. I did not know his name, but I called him Kongoni because when he was wonder-struck at anything, he had a foolish look that reminded me of a somewhat absurd-looking buck common on these plains, known to the blacks by this name. Far from a fool, he got along well with our beasts, perhaps because he was as gentle with them as with his milk cows in his native village. Altogether, he was one of the most useful men we had hired from Kamel Malik.

It was this man on whom the leopard rushed. I did not see them meet because my camel caught sight of the beast and whirled in panic. Unable to aim—knowing it was useless to try—I slid off her back, my rifle in my hand. Only a second or two had gone by since my last view of the scene, but the issue I had instantly divined was now made clear to all beholders, and the stage had been set for the drama about to unfold.

The Swahili and the leopard whom he called Tui waged no ancestral war. If he had his way, the black man would be dwelling peacefully in his village on the thickly peopled coasts, raising millet and lentils and pumpkins and groundnuts. When the leopard attacked him, he knew terror, but no fury to change almost to glory in the blaze of battle. Unless someone saved him, he would die.

Meanwhile some deep-seated instinct made him shield himself the best he could. Knowing Tui's way of hanging to his victim's shoulders with his front claws while he scooped out his guts with his rear, he dropped to his knees so the beast stood on his hind legs before him. Bowing his head, he hid his face in his arms. Although the leopard raked his back and shoulders and bit his arms, he had not yet attacked his vitals. If Kongoni would be patient, help might come, and death would pass him by.

I saw red stripes instantly appear on the glistening black back in the wake of Tui's claws. I saw the leopard shine like living gold. But I could not shoot without great danger of killing my kinsman, and in running near for a clear shot, the beast saw me.

In a sudden great revival of his pride and power, he left his inert prey and rushed at me. Not half my height as he ran, weighing about the same, he was no larger than a half-grown lion, smaller even than a lioness, but he remembered now how he slew cattle and buffalo, even the heavy-horned bulls. When he saw my arms come up and one of them extend long and gleam in the sunlight, he knew me for his mortal foe. Perhaps he smelled my purpose as plain as I saw and heard his.

There seemed hardly time to aim and pull the trigger, and I did both too fast. He appeared to stumble and roll over, but instantly was up again and rushing on, his speed and fury undiminished because one forefoot hung useless. The sudden, miraclelike sharpening of every sense that comes in battle let me see it plain. I saw it in great joy. It seemed a small impairment of my enemy's powers, but it served to increase my already great physical prowess, perhaps to match him or to win. I recognized it as my mainstay in the coming storm.

I knew all this without thought. It was in my heart and every motion that I made. I dropped my gun, but there was no time to reach for my knife; my hands must meet the upspringing beast. He came up from the ground in a long bound, straight for my shoulders, but he did not succeed in getting the deadly clutch upon me that he intended. The claws of one front foot drove deep and caught in my shoulder, but the broken foot balked his intent, and before he could sink his teeth in my neck or face or rake my belly with his rear claws, I broke his hold and flung him to the ground.

His recoil seemed instantaneous. It was a terrible thing to find him back this soon, again clinging with one set of claws to my shoulder, flapping his broken foot back and forth in frantic fury, his snarls right there in my ears, his fangs so near my throat. I caught him by the leg and jerked out its hook from my flesh, but I did not hurl away the beautiful blazing beast to leap on me again. Enduring the horror of it, I fell with him.

Somehow he turned as we pitched down, so that he landed with his back feet under him, but his upper body sideways under mine. An upward heave of his loins broke my hold on his sound leg, and in a furious upward sweep, the claws raked my face. But by letting

271

go of the broken leg I forced my left elbow into his neck, pinning down his head. With my right hand I gained a grip on his unbroken leg. He tried to break it by violent throes, but it was like iron.

At once he rolled his lower body on its side, so he could rake with his hind claws. I pinioned them with my limbs, and for the time being, he was helpless. But I was making a great expenditure of strength. It was being tested beyond any test it had ever stood.

Moving my knee forward, I pressed it into the beast's short ribs. His snarls turned into furious growls as the pressure increased, then into a sound very like a scream. There was a low sound, then a softness. The rib had broken. Glory swept through me as I continued and even increased the pressure, by what strength I did not know.

A shadow moved at the corner of my eye, and, turning my head, I caught sight of Isabel and a black-veiled Tuareg running up, the latter with his blade bright in the sunlight. They had not been tardy in coming to my help—the time seemed long since Tui and I had first embraced; but the count of seconds was still few, and some of these they had wasted in breaking through the press of panic-stricken camels. The Tuareg warrior saw the quick shake of my head and instantly understood—far better than I—my need to kill him by naked power. Isabel stopped with a gasp. I wish that I had cast away my visions and looked into her face. They were far and terrible visions of Death.

Isabel moved her foot, and a stone lying about eight feet away rolled close to my side. I remembered my flight with Jim from the Sepulcher of Wet Bones, another who would keep me from my goal if I let him live, and my picking up a stone. I could not pick this one up as yet, because my right hand pinioned the beast's sound leg, and my left elbow was jammed into his neck to hold down his head. Even so, I had a better chance to get it than my knife, far out of reach and under the weight and tension of my loins upon the leopard's loins.

I worked my right arm until its elbow pinned down the leg I held, then, without relieving the pressure, forced it sideways against the joint. Under these conditions I could not get a good purchase on it and must try the utter and ultimate strength of my forearm. It was a tremendous trial. Blood gushed from my nostrils and a weak tooth crumbled in my jaw and it seemed my brain would burst. But the spotted leg slowly bent until I heard it crack.

Still holding down the gaily spotted head, I reached and got the stone. As though he perceived my intention, the leopard's eyes fixed on mine in absolute defiance and infinite hate, and I knew now that he was death in gorgeous masquerade, and in the green depths of his eyes I saw hell.

I pounded the rounded dome above the eyes until it was soft and blood oozed up through the fur. The last tension passed from the hot body beneath mine. Then I rose, staggered about, retched, and sobbed; no proud black-veiled Tuareg dared put forth his hand to help me, lest the gods strike him blind or witless, and Isabel stood as though carved with a sword in stone. At last I braced myself and wiped some of the blood from my face and felt the deep scratches there and traced with my finger the track of one deep-driven claw, like a groove cut, full across my cheek.

Then I turned to my woman and held her eyes with mine and spoke.

"Isabel Gazelle, I said to you some nights ago before our cooking fire that I had enough marks already and wouldn't bear any more."

"I remember well."

"I rebelled against fate and have been taught a lesson. As soon as I'm well enough, we'll make a little cross out of gold, like the letter we call X, and fix it on the end of an iron rod and heat it red hot. Then you shall brand me with it on the back of my right hand, the same brand worn by Holgar Blackburn. I promised to do well by him in Tavistock, and no one must suspect I'm not he. Also, I have other tasks better done in his name."

"I knew you had weakened that night, but could not bring myself to tell you so. I'll put a black burn on your hand, as is meet."

CHAPTER 22

Desert Farewell

1

THE FANGS and claws of lions, leopards, and hyenas bear deadly poison from their putrid kills. Wounds therefrom must be treated as soon as possible; and almost always when they are severe,

273

and often when they are slight, no treatment can save the victim from mortification of the flesh and swiftly ensuing death.

Wherever Kongoni's skin was broken, the Tuareg rubbed in salt. The gashes and deep clawings on his back and shaven head were packed full of salt and sealed with melted tallow. He did not utter a sound during the treatment—watching his face, I could not detect the slightest sign of pain—so I could be glad for my own stone face when my turn came. Isabel had me stripped naked and treated in the presence not only of the Tuareg, but of the Swahili tribesmen. She wanted everyone to bear witness that a *farengi*, whose life was in her womb, could bear pain as well as a native son.

Then the men made crude but reasonably comfortable litters to bear Kongoni and me into camp. In three days my scratches had healed and my deeper cuts were mending well. But a raging fever came upon Kongoni, and many of his wounds bubbled and frothed with putrid gas. One of his tribesmen made medicine for him by walking about shaking dry seeds in a gourd, and that night all his tribesmen ringed his pallet to chant or shout or wail or strangely gesticulate while the watch fires leaped and the hyenas howled on the plain and little jackals barked in frenzy, but when the sun came up at last, Kongoni's life was gone like the flame of the fire that had become ashes, where they knew not, no more than I. What remained they carried far enough on the plain that I would not hear the merry-makers, and left it there. They had hardly turned their backs when the first king-vulture glided down, lighted, and hopped wildly.

It seemed that I wrote down his name in some book of my heart.

I made certain gifts to the Swahili and they returned to Kamel's compounds. The Tuareg and I went to work to melt gold and hide it in the tortuous hollows of the tusks. As I had foreseen, the process of pouring in a little at a time, letting it cool, and adding more was expedited by our setting up two or three score tusks; with the black-veiled Tuareg taking daily turns at demolishing the wonder works and the white-veiled Tuareg helping with the smelting, we stored away about half a ton a week. I was not content to leave the precious lading unsealed, lest a piece unfused with the rest should fall out on a boatman suspicious of a tusk's weight seek to explore its hollow, or a smuggler of jewels or rare drugs use it as a hiding place.

Remembering that the Beni Kabir used some sort of glue that became stone hard, I asked the Tuareg if they had knowledge of its like. They assured me promptly that they did—with horse or camel hooves and lime they could make a viscid mass which hardened to resemble bone. Enough hooves of this sort would be hard to find; would the great horny nail of elephants serve instead? If so, they could collect all that a man could carry from one kill.

Experiment proved that the substance was better than horses' hooves for my purpose; the glue when hardened was a dirty white and had the feel and, according to the Tuareg, the smell of ivory. The compound required careful mixing and preparation, but half a pound poured on top of the gold sealed it as though the fiber of the tusk had grown around it. The danger of its being discovered was cut in half.

In nine weeks we could boast of a great piece of dentistry—putting gold fillings in four hundred and twenty-five teeth—but the joke was not worth cracking to the Tuareg, who knew naught of dentists and whose glimmering teeth wore down, but never rotted out. Before demolishing Pharaoh's inner coffin of massy gold, Jim repaired the bed found standing on end in the outer treasure chamber, the gold decoration of which had long since gone to our pot. Softening it with the linen found in the sarcophagus, he politely, if not reverently, laid therein the Pharaoh's mummy. Beside it he put the alabaster jars that contained the viscera and a beautiful enameled vase into which we had poured his store of hair-cuttings and nail-parings.

We poured the molten gold of the coffin into a hundred and forty tusks, almost all we had left that were not split or unsuited to the purpose. Counting what we had spent at Khartoum, our total harvest was about one ton of silver and only a couple of hundredweight short of six tons of gold.

I had thought to save a little gold for branding my hand, but without any reason within my mental reach, I decided to use iron. Jim chiseled off a little from a horse's bit, heated it in the fire, and hammered it into an X, each leg of which was about an inch and a quarter long. This he fixed to a bronze rod that had carried a hawk head for some ceremonial use; and alone with him and Isabel, I heated it in the coals of our cooking fire. When it was dull-red hot, I laid my right hand, palm down, on a piece of firewood.

"Isabel, will you put the mark on the back of my hand? The pain will be sharp, but nothing like as long as I'll give you a few months from now."

"You mean the pain of borning our babe? You won't give me that pain. The babe himself will give it to me, in his desire to come forth. He kicks me even now in his impatience."

"He's a lusty babe."

"It's a good thing there are new ones to fill the emptiness when the old ones go away. If it weren't for him, I couldn't burn your hand with the red iron, the sign of your parting with me and taking a new name in a distant land."

"The iron's ready now."

"That's for me to decide. Omar, do you remember what my husband Suliman said when he appointed one of his men to shoot a horse whose leg was broken?"

"Yes, he asked if the man would bungle it. If so, he would do it himself. Then his clansman answered, 'If I bungle it, O Sheik, I ask that the next bullet be mine.'"

"Omar, my beloved, if I bungle the hard task appointed me, I ask that you burn me in the face."

"It's for me to decide your punishment."

Isabel dried the back of my hand with a cloth. Then she fanned the coals until the iron was not dull red but bright red. Then in one smooth movement she took it from the fire and touched it firmly but quickly to the back of my hand. The pain of the flesh was severe, but the worst of it quickly passed. In my soul was travail that must be very like the unseen agony of those who die in sleep.

2

The day came that I returned to Takuba all our borrowings except a final one, thirty bondsmen for camel drovers and baggage wallahs on our journey to Suakin on the Red Sea. They would not come back empty-handed. Besides the wage I paid them, they would bring to Takuba as a parting gift—the only one he would accept—two hundred baggage camels I had bought at the Khartoum fair.

Then with our long file of laden camels and their tenders, the Tuareg and Isabel and Jim and I made north and east until we struck the great caravan road running between Berber and Suakin, on which travel countless Mohammedans from the great bend of the Nile back and forth to Mecca. The moon that was old when we began was again a silver bow when we came into the cut that the Khor Baraka—the River of the Blessings—makes through the mountain ranges flanking the sea. On our last day we traveled a narrow sandy wasteland running north, to pitch our camp below a large sand dune close beside the town.

Within the town, thronged with Arabs and white-robed Bejas of many tribes, merchants and pilgrims, I sought out Kamel Malik's factor and was courteously greeted. He brought me to the Suakin agent of Saad ibn Hassan, who said he was expecting me and that two of his master's best dhows would hove into port before the moon came full.

In our days of waiting, all our party except the borrowed baggage handlers sat long hours in the sun, silent until one of us remembered an incident, thrilling or strange or funny, to tell in a rush of words. We lived again our flight from the Sepulcher of Wet Bones, the great battle with Tembu Emir, and my embrace with Tui, whose claw had left an indelible track across my cheek.

But in the swift-sped nights, Isabel and I dreamed, not of these scenes of violence, but of incidents of little moment and passages between us that we thought we had forgotten. And often, it seemed, we would both dream of being lost from each other, on lonely roads that would never meet again, and we would waken and hold each other close and kiss, rejoicing that the hour of parting had not yet struck.

It would strike soon. The two ships came into port and discharged their cargoes. On the day that my ivory was to be stowed twenty black-veiled Tuareg went down to Saad's wharf and formed a line from the yard where our camels were unloaded to each vessel's hold in turn, their camel whips in their hands; and with my telling the dock master that they were savages from the Great Thirst who would flay alive any stevedore who dropped or broke one of my tusks, there was no doubt that my ivory would be handled with care. I saw the whole lot brought aboard without a single mishap. The trouble that fate, or fortune, whatever name fitted her best, could have caused me did not develop. Because Kamel's purse would be lightened if any of the ivory were stolen, it was put under stout guard.

"My porters declare your tusks the heaviest for their size that they ever stowed aboard a vessel," the dock master told me when he came up for his *backsheesh*.

"They come from a mountain district where the soil is heavy with iron, and I chose them for a special use," I replied with premeditated cunning. "But here is a sack of rupees, half of them for you, and half divided equally among the porters, with which to buy balm for lame backs, or bhang for weary spirits."

The drovers we had hired returned to Takuba's kraals with the baggage camels. The ships would sail on the morrow's sunrise, taking advantage of the offshore wind and a rising tide that would help to lift the ship through the perilous two-mile passage between the harbor and the open sea. There was no getting out of Jim traveling on one ship and I on the other, in the way of a merchant and his factor when his goods required two bottoms—otherwise our seeming carelessness might lead the unwatched crew into temptation. Isabel Gazelle decided not to come to the dock among the polyglot throngs, but to bid me farewell at the desert rim; and of course her Tuareg would stay with her.

Tonight we feasted, sitting in a ring, and as the moon climbed Isabel related in Tamashek, an Arab-speaking Tuareg whispering its translation in my ear, the great desert love story of Zoan and Zara. Why did she not recite it in Arabic? Her followers knew it fully and by heart, I, only its gist. The answer eluded me, but I sensed the propriety of the act, its high-mindedness and what I could only call royalness. Isabel Gazelle was never anything less than a princess.

When the story was over, Zoan, namesake of its hero, rose and spoke to me, Isabel herself translating.

"Omar, you have a little band of horsehair, with brass ends, that you greatly prize."

"Yes, I do. The hair was plucked from the mane of a great stallion."

"We have made a bracelet for your wrist out of hairs from the tail of Tembu Emir, whom you slew in battle in the thorn. Fear not that in wearing this you will anger the soul of Tembu and it will cast its great shadow upon your soul. Tembu's soul will be proud that you so honor the great fight he made. Also, we have drawn forth the claw of Tui that made the long mark on your face and set it in a little silver that you and Jim Effendi overlooked, and hammered out a small silver ring which we fastened to the setting, so you may wear it on a chain. Fear not that the soul of Tui will make war against your soul. It, too, will be proud that you so honor his ferocity and his bravery, whereby in his last breath he gazed into your eyes in implacable defiance!"

"I will wear both with pride. And I wish I had a gift for you of the same fitness."

"Omar, we have taken as our gift something that you cast away. It is the chains that we chiseled from your limbs. We will take them with us on our journeys on the desert, and hang them in our camps, and when we look at them, we'll remember the slave who rode with us into freedom, and who loved our princess and gave to her his seed. Thus always we'll rejoice at our own freedom, and fight to the death to defend it, and never again buy or sell or hold any man or woman or child in slavery."

"My heart swells at the tidings, Zoan, and my soul exults, and I cannot hide my tears."

"There's no reason for you to hide them, brother. Now we of the Black Veil and our kinsmen of the White Veil go into the desert to pass the night. You have only to call loudly or wave your hand in the firelight, and we'll return. But if you do not do so, we'll not see your face or hear your voice again except in dreams. Farewell, Omar."

"Farewell, Zoan."

With his left hand he touched me on the face. With his right he drew aside his veil so I could see his face. When he had turned away, another Tuareg made me the same salutation of farewell. All the others followed, these tall dark men of the desert with high-bred faces and equestrians' hands and forms and graceful movement—the black-veiled Tuareg and then the white-veiled Tuareg, their eyes bright with tears.

When they had gone, Jim gave me his slow, heart-warming smile.

"Cap'n, I've had mighty lively times with 'em Tuareg mens, and I reckon I'll spend the night amongst 'em, talking it over."

"If you like."

"When de morn start coming up across de bay, I'll sing out."

"Aye, aye."

"Isabel Gazelle, I might not see you no mo'. I'm mighty thankful for all you done for Cap'n and me, and for de love you gave him in his loneliness, and I'll pray de Lawd for you to be happy when us gone."

"I'll pray to Messiner to take good care of you." Her throat was suddenly full.

I led Isabel back to her seat before the fire. After a moment or two I asked, "Why did the Tuareg leave the camp tonight?"

"Do you remember the night we left camp, intending to spend it on the Stairway of the Jinns?"

"Yes."

"We didn't do so, because it came about for me to marry Suliman. I told the Tuareg of it, and of how we were parted. Tomorrow we'll again be parted, forever. The wheel of our fates had made another complete turn, and they thought that the night of solitude we lost should be restored to us before you went away."

"Did they tell you so?"

"No, but I, too, am Tuareg. Besides this, they thought that if I must weep aloud, it would come easier if they weren't here."

"I wish I could pay my debt to the Tuareg."

"You have paid it, in full, by leaving me with child. They had great admiration for you before they met you—I'd told them enough that they considered you a true chief—and it's greatly increased since Tembu tried your horsemanship and Tui your strength. They think that if I bring forth a boy, he'll have great strength and become a great rider. That, with his courage, which is as much a part of every Tuareg as his flesh and bone, will fit him to become a chief of the Sons of the Spear. If I bring forth a girl, they think your fearful visage will cause her to turn toward beauty as a flower to the sun, and she'll become greatly beautiful, to bring joy to our whole clan. And although they'll miss you and mourn you more than you know, they think the prospect of these things coming true is much better if the baby begins life as a Tuareg, and knows no other life, and isn't touched by the ways of the *farengi*."

"Now that's a strange thing, but I don't deny it's a true thing."

"In what way is it strange, Omar?"

"There are those in Frankistan who would condemn me past forgiveness for leaving my woman with a child I'll never see, to be brought up as a desert nomad."

"Such folk are blind or mad. It's not the babe who needs care—it's you. Beside the pain of parting from you, I can hardly bear to have you go back to your cruel world now that you're no longer young. The life of the Tuareg is a life of peril, but no matter how few his days, those days have been full. He has journeyed far and ridden hard and hunted and fought and loved women and seen the desert in the moonlight as well as in the dust storm, and known the beauty of poems and of stars. Our daughters are freeborn and can't become chattels to any man's hate. So think of him with joy. If he's dead, he'll have laughed much, and been well-loved, and won many victories before he died. If he's alive, he'll be growing tall and strong, brave and proud, a rider and warrior and hunter and a lover of our maidens, or if she is alive, she'll be growing tall and strong and beautiful, worthy to mate with and to mother a rider and warrior and hunter. We trace through the distaff. So do not doubt your babe will be a Son or Daughter of the Spear!"

"I'll never doubt it, Isabel Gazelle."

"But how can I think of you except with terror and pity, as you dwell in the great city shadowed with hate and fear? So I'll tell you my farewell wish. Gratify it if you can, for the sake of the love we bore each other, and will bear each other to the last. When you've built the great cairn of stones over those you loved who were lost—when you've done what you must do, according to the bond—go back to the life you lived when you were young and which you so greatly loved. Sail the tall ships. Do battle with the sea and make him serve you. Ride the horse-of-tree."

"I'll do it if I can. It will be my heart's desire. Have you any other heart's desire to tell me? The hour grows late, and I want you in my arms."

"I want you in my arms, my beloved. Although I'll wed again, some youth with light in his eyes and laughter in his mouth, my arms will yearn for you still. Yes, I have a heart's desire I've not yet told you, but its fulfillment will be on the lap of fate. I want you to marry some woman of Frankistan who'll remind you of me."

"There must be one, and when the time comes, I'll try to find her."

Then we went into our tent and left the door open to the moonlight. Once more I knew the fullness of her beauty and the victory of her love in the reuniting of her flesh with mine, and then the strange dream of love and the vision of immortality that it wakes as I gazed into her face as she lay in childlike slumber in my arms. Sometimes I drowsed, but mainly I kept vigil over her while the moon sailed westward down the sky. Long after midnight I fell into deep sleep, and it seemed that I was sinking into death when Isabel wakened me with a long kiss. The joy it gave me flowed through me in a great, sunlit wave, and it did not die away because the dawn had not cracked, and we could have each other one more hour.

It seemed an hour out of the world. At its end I knew that our so-brief mating, to be followed now by forever parting, was not a defeat but a victory to enrich our stay on earth, the price of which was heartbreak. When I had heard Jim call, and a few minutes later he asked me a question, low-toned, standing beside the ashes of our fire in the chill dawn with his eyes on mine, I knew the answer.

"Cap'n Whitman, is it needful 'at we go?"

"Aye, it is, James Porter."

I returned to Isabel, who stood in the doorway of the tent, and once more the jagged flint of my face was aglow with her beauty, redeemed by her kisses, and wet with her tears. She was still standing there as Jim and I started down into the town, and as I touched my hand to head and heart, she replied with the same gesture. On the dock Jim and I shook hands before we went aboard, and just before sunrise, the two white-bearded captains ordered the hoisting of the lateen sails. As the dhows moved out from the dock, jerkily and yet uncertain of their bright-red wings, but slowly gaining headway, the sun heaved up and glimmered on the bay.

It cast a reflected glow in the west. Against that glow I made out the shape of a sand dune, alone in that part of the coast, and on its top a minute figure. I could not doubt that it was Isabel, if only by the tallness and straightness of her posture. Standing on the deckhouse, I waved my arm.

It came to me that she waved in reply. Long after distance hid her from my sight, I was sure she watched our bright-red sail on the blue sea. But at last it also dimmed, grew small, and began to drop below the horizon. With her eyes I saw it fade. It was as though I had died.

Instead of death, Isabel, you brought me life and freedom. Now there comes upon me a greater strength of will and purpose than I ever had before, and I buckle on the sword that you gave me, the strange, strong sword of gold. If you could know its wielding in the days to come, you would not be ashamed of me. I will not flinch from its use in behalf of those I loved, or in fear of my foes.

I will be true to you, Isabel Gazelle. In memory of you, I will be a captain worthy of the name.

BOOK FOUR

The Sword of Gold

CHAPTER 23

King's Country

1

WINDS BLEW, sails filled, heathen stems cut the water much like Christian stems. Hardly nine weeks after our departure from Suakin, the two dhows rounded the Cape of Good Hope into view of Cape Town. I went below to don some of the garments I had bought at the moribund Portuguese settlement at Sufala. I had not tried them on until now, and to my amazement I had forgotten how to put on a shirt, tie a lace, or fasten a button. When I had finished the labor, we were putting into port. My heart stood still at the sight of a church like those of the old Dutch settlements on Long Island Sound and at what looked like a village green.

Most of the white men I saw on the wharfs were bearded Dutch, soberly dressed, but not as quaintly as I. When the dhows had docked, Jim came and stood beside me, dressed in a flowing aba. We waited motionless and silent, remote and apart from the people passing by.

Two young Englishmen, one dressed in what must be the latest London fashion and the other in the undress uniform of the Royal Navy, stopped to gaze at the dhows and spoke in something near to my native tongue.

"What do you make of yon scarecrow in Don Quixote's clothes?" the more languid and elegant of the pair asked his fellow.

"I don't like the cut of his jib."

"It's true it would frighten the little ones from their porridge, but he's no kind of Dutchman I've seen, and that black with him is from back of beyond. I think they must have come from Mozambique."

"There—or from the tomb."

The pair laughed and walked on. A few seconds later I saw them both gazing seaward, patently to avoid speaking to another young Englishman walking briskly in my direction. The newcomer did not let them know he felt or even noticed the slight, but he could not hide from me the bitter set of his lips or the stiffening of his stride. Fair-haired and blue-eyed, rather delicately made, he walked like a horseman. His clothes, once good, had worn almost to shabbiness. He stopped near me, ostensibly to look at the dhows, then turned suddenly, as by a feat of will.

"I say, can you speak English?" he asked.

"I can."

"I had a feeling you could. There's a hint of English stock about the eyes. Good God, but you've been through hell."

"I don't know that country." But I once saw its fires in the eyes of a leopard dying in my arms.

"Please don't resent my speaking to you. I'd like to ask you some questions. They might benefit us both."

"You can try."

"Is this your first visit to Cape Town?"

"Yes."

"You've been in the Bush a long time. Longer than any renegade I've ever seen. Most men couldn't have lived that long in the Bush."

I did not answer.

"The word's out that those dhows are loaded down with ivory—something like forty tons. By any chance could it belong to you?"

"There are thirty-six tons, and they belong to me."

"Jove, what a joke on Sidney! I mean the fine buck that just snubbed me, along with Ensign Wells. Sidney is a kind of office boy to the governor. If he'd known you had thirty thousand quid of tusks, he would have been the first to make you welcome to this latest jewel in King George's crown."

"I didn't know either I had thirty thousand quid of tusks."

"They'll bring forty pounds per hundredweight from the buyers here, but the pot can't call the kettle black. I came to that ivory like a cat to a pan of milk."

"Before you explain that, I'll ask you a question. When you speak of King George, do you mean George IV?"

"Sir, there isn't any George IV—yet. George III is still king in name, although he's mad, and the crown prince is regent."

"I can hardly believe it. George III was king twenty years before I was born——"

"That's about right. You're not over forty. He came to the throne in 1760 and has worn the crown nearly sixty years."

I liked the young man's earnest way.

"Now I'll explain the questions—whether or not I justify them," he went on. "If you're a stranger here, I can serve you until you get acquainted with the town. I can help you order more suitable clothes —arrange good quarters for you—find you good servants—run your errands. I'll charge you for it, of course—I need the money very badly—but I won't rob you."

"What's your name?"

"Alan Ridgeley."

"What will you charge me per day?"

"I'd like to ask a pound——"

"That's not too much if I engage you. You seem an educated man of good family. Why do you need such work?"

"I got into trouble with the military, and my brother, who's a lord and controls the purse strings, booted me down here. Now he's written me I can come back or go to the devil, but he's through with me. I'm trying to live until I can work my way back on a ship."

"You're engaged. Your first duty will be to find the harbor master and see about the unloading of my ivory. I want it put in a warehouse that can be locked and guarded. Is there a bank in Cape Town?"

"The Bank of Amsterdam had a factor here for fifty years. Now the banking is done by Baring's, in London, hand in glove with the East India Company. You haven't told me your name, sir."

"Holgar Blackburn." It came easily to my lips and I had the sense, intangible and strange, of speaking truth.

"You've got to be from someplace, in filling out the forms."

"My last address was a workhouse in Tavistock. I ran away when I was fourteen."

"Well, I'll get the worthy."

The harbor master, Mr. Barneveld, was as Dutch as his name. He did not offer me his hand—as though he feared I might crush it in mine—but he welcomed me to the port in broken English and promised that a work crew of thirty Hottentots would unload my ivory at once. I asked that great care be taken that none of the tusks be dropped and broken.

"If one of dos Kaffir drop yus one, I give him hunnerd lashes on his black back," the master said.

"That won't mend the break," I answered, at which Alan looked at me in some surprise.

2

When the tusks had been stored, Alan took me to a kind of boarding house catering to officers and travelers. A pink-cheeked Dutch girl looked at me with dismay, but rented me one of the best rooms and set a small table for me, away from the long board, in the dining room. Of many pointed reminders of my frightening appearance, this was the most sharp so far; but it did not pierce my skin. It came to pass that Jim took the dishes from the waiters' hands and served me himself. He asked to do it through some law of his own, and I made no protest.

I slept that night in a deep, clean featherbed, Jim on a cot in the anteroom. In the morning I bade Alan request the presence of an East India Company official, an officer of the government, a merchant of standing, and a minister of the gospel at an important meeting in the warehouse. Alan's eyes asked if, after all, I was mad.

"I can't promise they'll come," he told me.

"I'll present each of them with a bottle of the best schnapps in town, and if any of them find the matter beneath his notice, I'll give him half a ton of ivory of my own choosing."

He looked at me and rubbed his chin thoughtfully. "I doubt if you'll have to pay up."

I felt sure that curiosity, if nothing else, would bring the four witnesses whereby my possession of the gold would become a public fact. Meanwhile I had Jim borrow a saw used by ivory workers for cutting billiard-ball pieces. When the four men arrived, worthies all, the minister was boyishly excited, the merchant and the company official were more impressed than they wished anyone to know, and only the government officer, Mr. Gerry, took a superior attitude. However, he bowed politely enough when Alan introduced me, and no one wanted to be caught listening to the witticisms he whispered behind his hand.

"Now, now, Mr. Blackburn," he said to me. "You've asked us to come here, and we've obliged you, so oblige us by making the business short. What's all this mystery about?"

"Will each of you gentlemen be kind enough to select one of the tusks from the stacks? My factor, James Porter, will lay them to one side."

This was done. The four tusks were laid in an open space in the warehouse. When I nodded to Jim, he began to saw one of them about where the hollow ended in solid bone. Near the center the saw-blade met an obstruction. This he sawed around and broke off. Each part of the tooth now showed a small yellow core that glimmered in the shadowy room. Jim dug around each with his knife. He extracted two hunks of gold, one about four inches long and the shape of a goat horn, the other twice as long and more like a bullock's horn with a blunted end. The two pieces, a total weight of about twenty pounds, Jim laid in my hands.

"Sir, do you know what these are?" I asked Mr. Gerry, putting the objects in his hands.

"Good God, they're gold," he answered.

"This is no time to take the Lord's name in vain," the minister intoned with great solemnity; and in spite of my heavy heart—longing to be back on the Atbara—I could not help but grin.

The gold passed from hand to hand. An intent, almost anguished look was on every face, and the staring eyes looked glazed. No one spoke a word as Jim began sawing the second tusk. This time he bethought himself and cut nearer the base of the tusk than before, about at the top instead of the bottom of the deposit, an ivory-saving process that had not crossed my mind until now. By breaking the cement and chipping the pulp, he soon loosened the gold and brought it out in one nicely curved and tapered piece. He had begun on the third tusk when the banker, breathing hard, got himself in hand.

"Mr. Blackburn, are we to understand that *all* those tusks have gold in 'em?"

"Every one."

"Then there's tons of it."

"Between five and six tons, I think."

"Why, damn, that's half a million pounds!"

"I don't think it will disturb the even tenor of Alex Baring's bank in London," the merchant remarked.

"He's Mr. Alexander Baring, if you please. Sir, if I may ask, whose gold is it?"

"Mine."

"But can you prove it?" Mr. Gerry asked. "That's what I want to know." He looked to the others for approval on this well-taken stand.

"He doesn't have to prove it," the merchant, Mr. Walters, remarked with some acerbity. "Possession is nine points in the law—even government officials are supposed to know that. Unless someone can prove he lifted it off him—and it had better be a white man, not some naked heathen—he can keep it."

The banker meditated a moment and wiped his face with his handkerchief. Everyone waited for his pronouncement.

"What Mr. Walters said is perfectly true. Mr. Blackburn has brought his gold into an English port—beneath the English flag—and common sense tells me he brought it out of the Bush, where other men have made their fortunes. Mr. Blackburn, do you care to tell us the source of this gold?"

"A mine in a native state on the Upper Nile."

"Mr. Blackburn, I've not the slightest reason to dispute your owner-ship of it, and I won't. I'll accept it, and give you drafts on Baring's Bank in exchange. I'll have company workmen get it out of the tusks, working in guarded shifts, and will have it in our main vault before dark. Also, I wish to be the first to congratulate you. You—whom the Honorable Alan Ridgeley told me began life in a workhouse in Devonshire—are now one of the rich men of the Empire."

I wondered if Alan had gained face in these last few minutes along with me.

"I have a request to make, Mr. Blackburn," the minister broke in. "The first Christian symbol your eyes lighted upon as you returned from exile among the heathen was the bell tower of my church. The building needs new roofing. Will you contribute the contents of merely one of these tusks—what I estimate as twenty pounds of gold —to that cause?"

"No, sir, but I'll give a ton of ivory, worth nearly as much."

"A tablet will be set in the wall, acknowledging your gift for all time to come."

I mused on Holgar Blackburn's name being inscribed on that tab-let, and what he would think if he knew. The scene changed, and again I was under the iron hook in the wall of the Sepulcher of Wet Bones, and Holgar was speaking to me in a voice hoarse with long-ing.

"*Ask if they'll let you do it, Big Yank. . . . Those bully boys of Sidi's are edgy and will bitch it sure. . . . You're strong as a lion—*

and you ought to see one jump over a six-foot boma with a man in his jaws. . . ."

That scene seemed the present reality and this the dream. But it slowly faded, and I was back with Jim and Alan and the four worthy burghers of Cape Town who were talking in low, awed tones.

3

By Alan's arrangements, the best tailor in Cape Town worked all night at making me a proper-looking broadcloth suit, but he would not have it ready in time for my call on the governor, Lord Charles Somerset.

The invitation brought by a uniformed Negro was, as Alan put it, virtually a command. Disturbed over the figure I would cut, Alan wanted me to borrow more suitable clothes from some of the burghers or buy some second hand; I told him not to worry, since I would feel perfectly comfortable in my old-fashioned rig. Actually, I wished I could care a little about royal governors' opinions of me except as it served Jim's and my future undertaking. It would be better for me if I winced within when a now familiar expression came into people's faces at sight of me: I could then believe I was one of the people, instead of a stranger from some other world on a fated mission. More ominous than indifference was a secret satisfaction I had begun to take in these responses. It could mean that a shadow that dogs every man's soul had caught up with mine—but I believed it meant something else.

After waiting in the splendid hall of the castle, I could not help but grin, for the secretary who came to escort me into the governor's presence was none other than the foppish young man who had remarked on my appearance on the dock. Of dim imagination, he had made the almost incredible mistake of failing to connect his scarecrow with the fabulous Mr. Blackburn. At sight of me, his jaw dropped.

"Are you ill?" I asked.

"I've seen you somewhere, sir."

"Is that any reason to lose your aplomb?"

"No, sir."

"Perhaps the governor has little children I may frighten from their porridge."

"If you tell him I said that, I'll get the sack."

"I doubt if you'll be brought into any conversation involving half a

289

million guineas." For I thought of other outlanders whom his careless contempt could sting.

"I'm properly rebuked, so please let it go."

A gray-haired man of patent distinction, elegantly garbed in black plush, Lord Somerset received me civilly enough. Also an experienced diplomat, he did not at once ask me the question that was the purpose of my summoning; and as he spoke pleasantly of Devonshire, I thought to put one to him. Truly, I could hardly find the courage. There were two possible answers, one as likely as the other; and the difference to me would be immeasurable. The question had risen often to my mind in the early years of my slavehood, but I had learned to set it aside—rather, to distract myself from it. Ever since I had Isabel it had been only a haunting deep in my brain. Even if the answer was No, I still could not have Isabel again—I could not return to Africa, to joy and safety and complete freedom—but how changed would be the whole future pattern of my life; with what scope I could set my course!

Is Sir Godwine Tarlton alive?

I did not ask it in this form. I waited my chance. . . .

"I dare say you've had enough of the country and will live in London," Lord Somerset was saying.

"Perhaps so. I've no one left in Tavistock."

"You'll enjoy the sporting life, I know. I could give you letters to several good fellows. Do you know anyone there?"

"No, unless some of my boyhood friends have gone there. One of our local squires went there to live when I was a boy, but I can't recall his name. Then there was a bigwig from the next shire who spent most of his time in London—I saw him at Bodwin, and his being a captain in the Royal Navy impressed me greatly. It's just possible you know him. His name was Tarlton."

The blood did not rush to my head; the floor stayed solid under my feet; my voice sounded a little strained, but not enough to attract the governor's attention; I doubted if there was any visible change in my face.

"I don't believe I recall him," he answered after a polite, thoughtful pause.

"Perhaps he's long passed to his reward."

"By any chance do you mean Lord Tarlton?"

"I think not. This gentleman might have been a knight——"

"Lord Tarlton was a knight before being made a baron—Sir Godwine Tarlton was his name then—and now I think of it, he had a long career in the Navy. Why, I admire him intensely. He was the only gentleman of high position who refused to meet that upstart, Beau Brummell. The Prince of Wales was put out with him for years, but came to realize he was right, and when he broke with Beau, what did he do but elevate Tarlton to the peerage! At least that was the story—quite in keeping with our Regent's character—although of course Tarlton's service against the Americans, in that little ruckus of 1812, was the official excuse."

"Is he as rich and prominent as the country people thought?"

"One of the first gentlemen of London. A great sportsman, he wears his sixty years like a younker."

I had known it all the time. My soul had confided there was no need to ask. He looked, not like an eagle, but like a phoenix, that ever rises laughing from the fire.

"You have a highly individual countenance, Mr. Blackburn," Lord Somerset remarked.

"That's a mild way to put it."

"Ordinarily I am good at reading faces. It's part of my training as a servant of the king. I must confess that yours baffles me. Some expression passed across it a moment ago, but again it's like—what shall I say——"

"Please say what comes to your mind. It won't offend me, you may be sure."

"Flint, with one gouge of a chisel across the left cheek. But 'tis better that, than to look like every Tom, Dick, and Harry. In some pursuits it might be an advantage."

"That of a professional pugilist, perhaps."

Lord Somerset laughed nervously. "I see you're plain-spoken and your feet are on the ground. I'm sure you'll get on well in the sporting world of London. As to Lord Tarlton, I could give you a letter to him, but being so very English, he's a bit aloof."

"I won't take any letters, thank you kindly. Since I'm humbly born, I'd better make my own way."

"Now I think of it, Tarlton and you might get on famously. Mark you, he's a great blood. Although his title, Baron Tarlton of Grindstone, is quite new, his lineage is ancient. But he conforms to fashion as much as he pleases, and no more. He flaunts his bastard son in the best society. To put it in a nutshell, he lives by his own law."

Now that Lord Somerset had mentioned his son, there was no reason that I couldn't speak of his daughter. But I did not.

"Grindstone, did you say? That's an odd designation."

"It was his own choice, largely speaking. It is often so with newly created peers—or else the king suggests some appellation out of sentiment. As I remember it, Grindstone is an island near North America that was the scene of a sea battle between his ship and an American vessel during the Rebellion."

"That's very interesting. And since you've given me so much of your time——"

"There's one other matter I wish to mention. If I send a secretary to your lodgings, will you draw a map for him showing the position of the mine that produced your gold? His Majesty's government would like to know, in view of future developments."

"Sir, it was in Southern Nubia, a country that's been mined over for thousands of years. My gold was a small deposit overlooked by earlier seekers, and there's no use to search any further."

His face flushed with anger, but as he looked upon my face, he did not speak. A moment later he gave me a cold but not stinted bow.

It might be I could now explain the deeply troubled satisfaction I had found myself taking in my gaunt form and stony visage, but the explanation appalled me as much as the fact itself. Perhaps I perceived at last it could be used as a weapon against my enemies. Along with my sword of gold, it might help my cause.

But when the need of my heart came round, what would I do for friends?

CHAPTER 24

In Remembrance

1

My impulse and temptation was to keep Jim near me all the time. I felt a distinct loss when we were out of sound of each other's voices; when he had been away, my heart lightened to hear his step. So two ghosts might feel in a throng of living—or two of the quick cast by shipwreck on an island of the dead. The fact remained that in the immediate future he had more important work to do than being my counselor and servant.

When dealing with English-speaking people he was at a disadvantage because of his color and dialect. The fact remained that he had come far from the simple man whom I had known aboard the

Vindictive; the ordeal in Africa had developed his resources, his mind had broadened, his character had strengthened, and the struggle to survive had taught him subtlety and cunning. He spoke the Kalam wati—the Arabic vernacular—fluently. In Berber dress he would attract no undue attention about the docks of Malta. The Arab-speaking emigrants and migrants would probably suspect that he was not of the Faithful; but he could catch many a fish with a silver hook.

I was a marked man, and he was not. This was another and clinching reason why he, not I, must undertake a necessary mission in Malta. And it was in view of parting with him at Lisbon for several months at least that the idea came to me to engage Alan as a general secretary and agent. He knew London well, had had a good deal of experience in English upper-class society, possessed an alert, keen, although not powerful, mind, and seemed to me honest and capable of such loyalties as I would require of him.

"Would you care to tell me about the scrape you got in?" I asked him one evening in my quarters. "As you said to me when you first questioned me, you might find it to your advantage."

"I'd rather someone else told you. You might get a truer account."

"I'll take a chance on yours."

"I had a commission in an old and rather swagger rifle regiment. I hated the whole business, and especially fighting. A good many people say I was afraid to fight, and it might very well be true. Especially I hated fighting the Americans in 1812. My grandpa, the first Lord Ridgeley, was born in Virginia, and he had stood with Chatham and Wilkes and Barre in '76 in the Colonies' defense. Still, that may have been only my excuse to get out of a dirty job."

Alan paused, as if to ask me whether to go on. I nodded.

"Ever since we lost the War of the Revolution, we've pretended we didn't lose it and those great states are still our plantations and the Americans are a pack of rebel dogs. I doubt if we—the English Upper-class, I mean, to which I was born—will ever get the notion clean out of our heads. Yet by bad luck my regiment was under General Ross in the raid up the Patuxent River on Washington. By the worst of luck, I was ordered to command a detail to set fires. I refused and was court-martialed for disobedience and cowardice. The cowardice charge didn't stick, but I was cashiered for the other, and might have been shot if the burning of the capital hadn't begun to smell bad clear across Europe. The London bucks wanted me hanged for a traitor. I was expelled from all my clubs and my old schoolfellows erased my name from their rolls. I could have helped Napoleon escape from Elba without incurring such wrath from my own kind."

"What's its real cause? Hatred of the American Republic?"

"In a large measure. The toffs don't like the idea of English people —they think of Americans as English—getting along well without a king and all that pertains to a king. The idea of freedom and equality in the American sense of the terms is obnoxious in the extreme—the swain no longer doffing his cap to the squire—Tom no longer a cut below Dick and Dick three cuts above Harry—with wealth and personal achievement taking the place of rank. Often the feeling's merely resentment or pretended scorn. Sometimes it's deadly malice. And I'm afraid it will last a long time."

Plainly Alan was trying to answer my questions fully and intelligently. No doubt he suspected what was in my mind, but still he put a damper on his hopes. I could see it in his face.

"You told me that you hoped to work your way back to England," I said. "Have you any employment there?"

"I hoped to find some. I love the island dearly. I don't think I'm cut out for a colonial."

"Would you like to work for me in a position of secretary? I would expect you to live at my establishments for the time being and travel with me on some of the journeys I intend to make, so your salary of three hundred guineas a year would be largely found."

He turned pale in the face, then red. "It would be heaven," he answered.

"Then you can start tomorrow."

"I will—if after I tell you something—give you a warning—you still want me." He was trembling so he could hardly speak. "Although technically speaking I belong to the aristocracy, I'd be a liability to you instead of an asset in the matter of you getting on in English society."

"I don't want anything from English society except what I buy and pay for. English society will want nothing of me except my gold. I can assure you, you won't get in my way."

"That settles it, Mr. Blackburn."

"My factor Jim, yourself, and I will sail from Cape Town on the first England-bound vessel having accommodations for passengers. Make the necessary arrangements."

Early in October we put out in a fine East Indiaman of eight hundred tons burden. My hired cabin was nearly as large as Captain Phillips's on the *Vindictive;* Alan and Jim had cubbies larger than the little room where I had first slept aft the mast. Neither fast nor yare, she was staunch and steady; and without once heaving to in heavy weather, we made Lisbon in forty-five days. Here I gave Jim a money belt, a letter of credit on an English bank in Syracuse, and some long-mulled instructions. Wearing western clothes of a plain sort and with Arabic raiment in his chest, he set sail for Gibraltar on his way to Malta. I did not expect to lay eyes on him for six months at least and probably a year.

2

Sailing on, we passed Cape Finisterre and the very waters where we had lost Thomas Childers, whereby I had become bosun and Ezra Owens had signed on the ill-starred ship, the last comer, the next of the last to die of all those gone. The last time I had seen this land was in the spring of 1801—the days already numbered before I should go into slavery—and this was the year's end, 1817. Our next landfall was Ouessant Island, which we rounded to enter the English Channel; and on a raw, chill, gray morning in early January, 1818, we came up on the tide to London.

While Alan attended to our baggage, I walked across the dank-smelling wharf up to the street. My clothes tailored in Cape Town and my hat and greatcoat bought in Lisbon proclaimed me a man of substance, although not yet of fashion, so only a few urchins, ready to run, remarked openly and pointedly on my appearance. "Coo, 'ere's Jack Ketch, dressed like a toff," cried one, more imaginative than the rest. Most passers-by gave me troubled glances. No beggars came near me.

I hardly noticed these expressions. All my thoughts and musings and perceptions busied seeking an answer to a vital question. I had come here in smoldering anger against England. It seemed to have no bearing as yet on my attitude toward a little knight I had once known, which was cold as a stone; but it would worry Captain Phillips if he knew of it. The fact remained that twice within fifty years English soldiers had ravaged my native land. In the first war they had hanged our patriots and employed red Indians with scalping knives to murder our frontiersmen, and in the second war they had burned our capital to the ground. In the years between the Royal Navy had impressed our seamen and the bigwigs of the government had treated us like dirt beneath their feet. Although I remembered pleasantly most of the Englishmen whom I had met in the hospital at Malta, I recalled too clearly some high-handed doctors and arrogant officers. Now I wanted to go and look at some plain English people. Maybe they would mitigate the bitterness in my heart.

So I walked about and watched them—sailors, deck hands, costermongers, shivering pinched-faced clerks, custom officers, merchants, housewives with market baskets, artisans with their tools— an endless eddying river of humanity in the streets and alleys. Although an occasional lordling in his coach or carriage seemed not to care whom he ran over and the high-handedness of some of the officials reached the point of insult, I got over my feeling of being in enemy country. The governor of Cape Town had spoken of Lord Tarlton as being "so very English." I did not think he was a perceptible fraction as English as an apple-cheeked woman selling "Irish lice." On the whole the people seemed as kindly disposed as the folk of Naples or Syracuse, almost as polite as the Maltese, and as warmly human as the crowds at the Khartoum fair.

I need no longer fear dissipating my energies and emotions in the coming struggle. By the bearings I had taken, I could chart my course.

Until now I had considered going to Tavistock as soon as London tailors could array me suitably for my mission there. Now I decided to wait until I had completed more pressing business in America, then undertake all my English affairs in unbroken order. My preparations went forward swiftly. During my absence Alan would undertake various missions.

"Keep in mind that my favorite sports will be gaming, steeplechasing, fox hunting, gunning, and cockfighting in the company of the best bloods in England," I told him.

He gave me a great wondering glance.

I was greatly tempted to take passage on a Yankee ship. In the end I chose an English vessel, with no very good reason other than that most traveling Englishmen did so, and for more practice in English ways.

Then up rose Beacon Hill, crowned by a great edifice of red brick, and the tower of Christ Church on Copp's Hill, where hung the lanterns that sped Paul Revere on his famous way; but the city had spread and grown so, I would have hardly known it; and my heart could not lift in pride because of its load of loneliness.

"I have no one in my homeland any more," I had told Isabel, "but I have everyone." I had hardly known what I was saying and did not know my meaning, and maybe the words were empty. Maybe the people had changed in this long while and some great dream had died. Maybe the righting of one old wrong as far as it could be righted by two men's mighty striving was a hollow dream.

Standing on the dock, I began to hear familiar accents and to see faces reminiscent of those I had known in my childhood. From hence I re-embarked for Newburyport, at the mouth of the Merrimac River, and after that I knew I had come home.

Long sharp ships, to the yare manner born, were a-building in her yards. About her docks hung codgers and lobsterers with crinkled eyes and red faces who spoke with a nasal twang. Men as lean and light of movement as the Tuareg, with something of the same grace of gesture and even beauty of facial bone spoke together of sparms and bowheads, crow's-nests and harpoons, and the "grounds" off Greenland, but these grounds were icy-blue and icy-cold. There was such a thing as aristocrats among human kind, and there they stood. Of all the great equestrian orders, they lived the most daring and beauty-flooded lives. Riding the most gallant of horses-of-tree, they hunted Leviathan.

My main business in Newburyport was to seek Sparrow's sister Bessie and his aunt, Calesta Peck, and, if I found them, to give them an important message. I could not find Calesta, she having gone to lie in the churchyard eight years before. But I found Bessie, a small, tidy woman with quick movements and a lively countenance, and the ghost of Sparrow rose before my eyes.

I told her what Sparrow had said—that he had never done any great wrong, such as murder or treason, and he loved her to the last. Without explaining my dealings with him, I assured her that he had lived and died true to his flag, his ship, and his mates. Then it came to pass that my first raising of a cairn over the bones of my shipmate could be an especially notable one. Bessie and her husband and little ones had lately come upon hard times. The brig *Molly Stark*, of which they owned half, had been lost off Hatteras; just before then they had rashly gone into debt for a share in another vessel building in Putnam's Yard. I arranged for them to pay this debt, buy a controlling interest, and name her the *Enoch Sutler*. Thus his name would be remembered on the seven seas. Bessie wept in grief-torn joy as I made my lonely way by the budding elm trees.

At an inn in my native town of Bath I heard the name of a living man that caused my face to burn as though I had come into a warm fo'c'sle from a winter gale. It was none other than Joshua Tyler, the second officer of the *Vindictive* until he left us to take command of a Salem sloop. Having married Mary Greenough, sister of George and Will Greenough, he had been persuaded to quit the sea and take the position of harbor master. Here was another besides Jim and me who knew our every yard and spar. Appointed to his berth, I had bought some of his clothes and worn them when I sat at meat with Sir Godwine Tarlton.

In the morning I waited on Captain Tyler at his office, finding him somewhat stouter than I had seen him last, and not as graceful of movement or keen of face. That was natural enough—he had not been whittled down by the knives of the wind for many a winter— but no one could doubt his high intelligence and character, and he looked much younger than his forty-five years. At sight of me his eyes became slightly narrowed and sharply alert—often the first response of those whom I came on suddenly—then filled with thought. But it got him nowhere, and soon he let it go.

"My name is Holgar Blackburn, and I've an account to settle with some sailors' families living in these parts," I told Captain Tyler. "The men were lost nearly twenty years ago on a vessel you had served on, as second officer, and I hoped you might know them. She was the *Vindictive*."

He sat so still that it gave the effect of a start. I thought there were little pluckings by his spirit inside his brain. But my face did not change under his searching gaze, and his visions faded away.

"Pardon me, Mr. Blackburn. I had divined somehow you were going to speak of the *Vindictive*—one of those promptings no one can explain. As for the families, I've kept track of them as far as I could. I did so out of natural feeling. We were under a great captain. We had a friendship crew."

"In Gibraltar there occurred an incident I'll mention briefly. The ship's crew, roaming the waterfront at midnight, saved the life of a traveler who'd been set upon by footpads, and took him aboard to mend his hurts. He swore that if the chance ever came, he would reward them generously. Since then, fortune has been kind to him, and he would like to give half a tithing, in equal shares, to their surviving kinfolk."

"Do tell!" remarked Captain Tyler. He spoke softly and without emphasis, yet adequately expressed his profound astonishment.

Perhaps the end of the story I had told was not very likely. Perhaps most men, however rich, would never forget such a rescue, but the glow of gratitude would have dimmed in these long years, the list of names misplaced, the good resolve undermined by the habit of self-partiality, the effort enfeebled by time. But I remembered Suliman and a horsehair band; whereby I looked straight into Captain Tyler's face, and my voice had the ring of truth.

"The sum is ten thousand dollars," I announced, essaying a businesslike tone.

"To be divided among the men?"

"No, sir, that sum is apportioned to each of the fifteen souls aboard the ship when she touched Gibraltar. In the case of those who've left no needy kindred, the money is to be used for an appropriate memorial. I have dealt directly with the heirs of Enoch Sutler, and will do the same as to James Porter and Farmer Blood."

"*Farmer* Blood." Captain Tyler's eyes became very bright.

"I think his shipmates called him that."

So I read off the list, my voice holding steady. The money would be well spent in every case. The Greenough boys would be remembered by a school for orphans of men 'fore the mast. Only when I came to Ezra Owens's name was Captain Tyler at a loss. He had never been able to find one kinsman or friend of this fourth from the last to die. Yet perhaps his soul, the soul of a windy man of common birth, a former jailbird, might have been the haughtiest soul of us all.

"If I'm not mistaken, he wanted to be a doctor," I said.

"He did. You speak truth. Good God, he did."

"Will you take the trouble to have a tenth of the sum spent on some monument to him—say a public drinking fountain, suitably inscribed, in the city of Philadelphia—and divide the rest among nine poor boys of promise who wish to study medicine?"

"None of the cases will be any trouble to me—only very great pleasure. I'd like to make one comment. You know that the man given my berth—Homer Whitman—was not on the ship at the time you mention, but was lost with the rest."

"I've heard as much."

"Perhaps I shouldn't have used the word 'know.' Sometimes those whom we mourn as lost, return. Mr. Blackburn, may I dare speak what comes into my heart?"

"Aye, sir, you may."

"My heart is faint, and I fear I'm white in the face. It seems to me there's a little change in your face, too. Sir, I believe you're Homer Whitman, returned from the grave."

I drew a long, aching breath. "Do I favor him in any way?" I asked.

"No way that I can see with my eyes."

"Is my form like his?"

"Not in the slightest. He weighed one hundred and sixty, all bone and muscle."

"What of my voice?"

"I don't—know."

"Could his face have ever come to be like mine?"

"Not by any course of event I can imagine. If it bore the stamp of great guilt, I could believe it—for who knows what awful guilt may come to lie on a human soul? Instead, it is like the face of Lazarus."

"Lazarus lay four days in the grave."

"I think you lay there four years or more. But that's my last word on the subject. I'll follow your directions, Mr. Blackburn, as well as I'm able."

I had one more pilgrimage of great joy. It was to go by riverboat and a good plug to Poultney, Vermont. I had never seen a lovelier spot than the valley of the Battenkill River, flowing to the Hudson. Near by gleamed Lake Catherine, a deep-blue jewel in the green hills; and with the rich valley land producing grain, potatoes, honey, and apples, the upland pasture cropped by cattle and sheep, maple groves for sugar, and birch and beech and hickory and butternut woods to range and hunt, it was no wonder that Farmer Blood grew to a mighty man.

Sitting at the farmhouse dinner table with his still-vigorous parents and numerous brothers, sisters, and kinsmen, I heard how his mother, the one to say, wished his money disposed.

"My son Ethan—Farmer, you call him, and I reckon it fitted him well—would be mighty proud if you'd send it to the Quakers to use in fighting slavery."

My neck prickled fiercely, and I could not speak.

"You see, Mr. Blackburn, Vermont was the first of the states to forbid slavery," the patriarch told me, as though I might think the proposal a foolish one. "My son Ethan was mighty proud of that; and I don't doubt he boasted of it, 'mongst his shipmates."

"Yes, sir, he did. But aren't any of his kinsmen in need?"

"They're not, and if they were, they'd get in and scratch," Stella Blood answered. "If they become truly bad off, we others will pitch in and help them. None is rich, but all of us have enough, and the young'ns have hope and opportunity galore. You can give me five hundred to save for a rainy day—I'll pass it out where it's most needed and 'twill go the farthest. The rest we'd like to send to the Quakers and to Doctor Rushmore's Society in Pennsylvania, in their fight for all men to be free."

To be free! Suddenly I was looking again into the face of Zoan, chief of the Tuareg. He had told me that the chains I had worn would be hung in their camps on the desert, to remind them of how I had been a slave, and in token of their pledge never again to hold their fellow men in slavery. But I could not look upon these eager faces here about me, because my eyes had overflowed with tears.

Farmer Blood, we will fight on till Captain's gone—and he will never leave us in this world.

3

I had been off watch awhile, but now I must go back. On the excuse of a sight-seeing with a little fishing on the side, I chartered a lugger with a well-salted crew of four. At my whim, we cruised eastward across the Bay of Fundy, northeastward along the long Nova Scotian coast, northwestward through the Gut of Canso, and a hundred miles north until we lay off the Magdalen Islands, looking like a pair of leg bones on a chart, rough, chill—thinly peopled by fishermen, wood cutters, and shepherds. One of the islands was named Grindstone. I decided to go ashore and stretch my legs.

"A kinsman of mine, Cap'n Ezra Fairbank, was lost off this isle when I was a babe," I remarked to a halibuter on a dank little dock.

"Do tell!" he commented politely, an exclamation that I had thought confined to New England.

"He was captain of the Yankee privateer *Saratoga*, and he fell foul of the English sloop of war, *Our Eliza*. The Yankee was sunk with all hands."

" 'Pears like I heared about that fight from some 'n."

"Do you suppose there's anyone on the island that would remember it?"

"*That*, there is! Uncle Jake Tate can remember everything that ever happened here since Wolfe came into the Gulf to take Quebec, and before that, I reckon. Would you like to talk to him? His house is not five minutes' walk from here."

We found the old trawler sawing wood, and my first satisfaction lay in his firm, ruddy face, keen eyes, and youthful movements. Actually he was about seventy-five—by that reckoning he had been a youth of sixteen when Wolfe died on the plains of Abraham overlooking the Saint Lawrence, so young was America, so short was her history compared to the story of the Nile.

"Uncle Jake, this gentleman wants to know if you remember a sea fight off here, between an American privateer and an English sloop of war during the rebellion."

"As though it was yesterday," the gaffer answered briskly. "I and my three boys climbed yon crest to watch. We didn't know their names at the time, but we found out later they were *Our Eliza*, under Cap'n Tarlton, and the *Saratoga*, in command of Cap'n Fairchild."

"Fairbank, sir."

"Thank 'ee. 'Twas a slip of the tongue. Cap'n *Ezra* Fairbank, if my memory fails me not. 'Twas a hard-fought fight. They lay broadside, laying it on."

"When the *Saratoga* went down, did *Our Eliza* put out boats to pick up survivors?"

"The *Saratoga* didn't go down during the fight where we could see."

"What?"

"Mark you, I had to leave the lookout 'cause of some duty, but my boys stayed up thar. The *Saratoga* struck her colors. That was what we heard later. But my boys thought it was the sloop of war what asked for quarter. The two ships had got out a good way and a light mist had come up; still it was hard to believe my sharp-eyed sons had made a mistake, and you could knock us all down with a feather when the news came in. I had to lam my oldest son, Matt, for holdin' out that the Yankee had won—he being so certain he 'sputed the post boy. But neither ship was sunk. They quit firing and lay side by side awhile, and I got back to the lookout in time to see the Yankee making east with the sloop about a sea mile in her wake. They passed clean out of sight."

"East?" I heard myself ask softly.

"Why, yes."

"If the Englishman had won, why didn't he and his prize make west?"

"I reckon he meant to round Cape Breton Island down to Halifax."

"Where was the wind?"

"Out of the east, and right brisk."

"Would the English captain take his prize into the teeth of a contrary wind instead of running full sail into Quebec?"

"'Tis odd when you think of it."

"If the Yankee had won, she'd make eastward hard as she could tack, get out to sea, and double back to Boston."

"That may be so, but *Our Eliza* came to port—in Halifax like I told ye—and the *Saratoga* was never seen again."

"The story was that *Our Eliza* sank her in the fight."

"Well, she didn't. That much I know. What I pictured was, she was leaking bad and her seams gave way and she went down all of a sudden, soon after me and my boys lost sight of her. It amounted to the same as her going down in the fight, and 'twas the way the story got out, and I reckoned Cap'n Tarlton didn't bother to set it straight."

"No, sir, it didn't amount to the same thing, because the prize crew Tarlton had put aboard would have gone down with her."

"Yes, unless he rescued 'em, and if he did that, he'd have picked up some Yankees, too."

The old bright-blue eyes confronting mine had become deeply troubled. I waited patiently. I thought Uncle Jake Tate would have something more to say.

"I'll pass on to you something my youngest sister told me," he went on at last. "She got it from a beau of hers, Sam Lincoln, trapping on Saint Paul Island. He said two ships came out of the west, and all of a sudden the foremost one, a three-masted Yankee, blowed up in one big burst of flame. He thought her powder magazine had caught fire somehow."

"How did he know she was a Yankee?"

"She was flyin' the Stars and Stripes from her masthead. But the vessel follerin' didn't show her colors."

"What happened then?"

"The hindmost ship started to the scene, but soon turned broadside to the wind and fell off a ways. After a while she swung about and tacked up thar, but she didn't put out no boats—there was no use, I reckon—and went on her way."

"Didn't it occur to you they were the same ships?"

"Yes, sir, but by then the news was out that the sloop of war had won, and if they was the same ships, the Yankee wouldn't be flying her flag—that is, if the news was true, and who could doubt it? Marthy said he'd seen the flag as plain as day. Also, the victory ship would stay to the wind'ard of her prize, and again it was the Yankee windward of t'other. I puzzled about it for a while, but let it go."

"Did you ever talk to Sam about it?"

"I can't say as I did. I only seen him two or three times after that when we didn't have no chance, then he moved to Saint John, in New Brunswick."

"Is Sam Lincoln still alive?"

"*That*, he is. The last time I heared."

"If I paid you a hundred dollars now, would you come with me on the lugger and try to find him, with another hundred if you succeed, and pay your own way back?"

"*That*, I would."

"Then get your kit bag, and we'll put out."

Uncle Jake Tate proved a most engaging companion on our voyage into the Bay of Fundy. He had the kind of memory that had made Kerry the fascinating consort and mentor that he was to me—far-ranging, ready, positive, and sharp as things seen by lightning. Opposed to that pleasure, the business we were on begloomed my spirits and haunted my dreams, and of all the towns in Canada I wished least to visit, it was Saint John, called Parr Town in my infant days, and settled by Tories who had quit my native land in order to keep their king. But the haters left alive were growing old now, perhaps they were a little mellowed and had not passed the hatred to their sons.

I did not go ashore and instead tried to sweeten my imagination, not with an ounce of civet—the unforgettable proposal of an aged, mad king—but by fishing for chicken halibut in the harbor. Meanwhile Jake moved spryly, getting track of Sam Lincoln the first afternoon, finding him the next morning, and bringing him to see me in the cool of the evening. Sam had begun life as a trapper and hunter, given most of it to trawling, and now earned his bread making dories as fine as Yarmouth's. A man cannot train his hands without schooling his mind. I could not want a better witness than this tough-grained, lean, quiet-voiced Canuck, the survivor of sixty-five winters, none of them mild.

In reply to my questions, he repeated to me what he had told Jake Tate, but my hearing it first-hand made a deal of difference. I, too, saw the Stars and Stripes flying in triumph over the foremost of the two ships, then, all of a sudden, the vessel bathed in fire.

"What day was this, Mr. Lincoln?"

"The day after Christmas, 1781."

"Are you sure?"

"Just as sure as I'm sitting here. Pa and me hadn't much of a Christmas dinner, and I'd thought to get some heath hen with my fowling piece. 'Twas why I climbed the hill."

"Did you ever hear that the *Saratoga* and *Our Eliza* fought on Christmas Day?"

"Yes, sir, I did."

"Could you escape the conclusion that they were the same ships?"

"They answered the description, and I couldn't doubt it."

"How did you reconcile that to the report of *Our Eliza's* victory heralded through the empire?"

"I couldn't reconcile it, but I was a poor trapper in the back woods, and if I said anything, who'd listen to me, and wouldn't I be going against the king? I reckoned them lords of the government had seen fit to hide the truth to cheer the people up after Cornwallis's surrender."

"Have you since imagined what might have been happening when *Our Eliza* started to run down to pick up survivors, then came broadside to the wind?"

"I knew there was no hand on her wheel, but I let it go at that."

"Thank you for your information. I'd like to pay you a hundred dollars and assure you it will make no trouble for you or Mr. Tate. This was a private inquiry concerned with sentiment."

My two informants accepted their fees, looked at me with sweat-beaded faces, and went their ways. I thought to fish awhile in the morning before I turned back, but it would take a deal of sunlit water to burn the shadows of these long-ago events out of my eyes.

Present your sword to your conqueror, little nobleman. You have fought a good fight—only two of your white officers are left alive—the crude Yankee skipper has never seen so great an aristocrat—he is greatly impressed by your courtly manner—he will not want to be outdone in courtesy. Surrender him your sword, and he will give it back. You need never wear it again except in ceremony. You can carry a little stick.

He will parole you because he doesn't know what is in your heart. He will parole also your two officers, for Cornwallis has surrendered, and the war is almost over anyway, and he doesn't know they are two Loyalists from Maryland who had fought their own countrymen. Your lascars will be confined to quarters; he will not be so rude as to put them in irons. The prize crew that he puts aboard your limping *Eliza*, outsailed and outfought and bound for the bottom if the fight had gone on, have orders to treat you with the greatest deference and to deal kindly with your crew of dark-skinned mercenaries. That a great aristocrat would break parole was unthinkable, let alone lie awake all night, planning, plotting, hating. . . .

Little lord, great lord, the stars fight on your side! On the morrow the *Saratoga* blows up in an empty sea, out of sight of land except for what you deem an uninhabited island. When the prize crew aboard your beloved *Eliza* start to run down to pick up survivors, you see your chance. Their guard over your lascars was too trusting to be strict. They are half out of their minds over the sudden loss of their mother ship. And one command in that wintry rattling voice of yours brings your long-haired heathen swarming up the hatch with such weapons as they can seize. You are a born commander, pretty little fellow, or you would not captain a sloop of war at twenty-four. You lost your command for a little while—you lost your ship to a Yankee hooker manned by chaw-bacons fighting their king—but now you're again on her quarter-deck, calling orders in that terrifying voice.

The Yankee lubbers, taken by unbelieving surprise, fight desperately. For a little while the ship lurches with the wind—as Sam Lincoln perceived from his lookout, there's no hand on the tiller. But the rebel swine are outnumbered and soon overwhelmed. Order is restored. Dark hands are on the wheel. The ship's bow swings into the wind, and she can now resume her eastward sail, but not to a Yankee port in captivity and disgrace. She can make for Halifax with her flag flying.

The trouble is, a few, a mere handful of the prize crew are still alive. Some are wounded, some surrendered to overwhelming numbers. What's to be done with them, pretty little lord?

Why, that's an easy riddle, sink me if it ain't. These aren't prisoners of war, but mutineers to start with, traitors to the king. Hang 'em to the yardarm, every rebel bastard, then weigh 'em by the heels and heave 'em overside. Don't waste good canvas and hemp keeping out conger eels and sea lice. And may God deal the same with all their like!

And thereby only some dark-skinned Indians, who can't speak a word of English, will ever know the truth. But you know it, Captain Tarlton, and also your two officers. They changed into Barbary pirates. What did you change into?

CHAPTER 25

Runaway's Return

1

WHEN I TOOK ship for Plymouth, England, out of New York, and watched the shores of my native land draw away distant and dim, I did not know when, if ever, I would lay eyes on them again.

From Plymouth I made up the North Road by stagecoach, lay the night at Callenden, and on the following day went by chaise to Tavistock. It was a pretty town, my adopted natal place, lying at the edge of Dartmoor in the valley of the Tavy; and what remained of the Abbey of Saint Mary and Saint Ruman, now used as a public library, was an impressive sight. It had been founded by Orgar, Earl of Devon, no doubt Holgar's namesake in the tenth century. On my telling the parish clerk that I wished to pursue a genealogical inquiry, he let me consult the records.

By no great search I found the short and simple annals of the Blackburn family. Bruce Blackburn and wife Anne, emigrants from Wiltshire, were listed as tenants to George Russell, Esq., whom I took to be kin of John Russell, the great Duke of Bedford, the largest landowner in this part of England. Holgar was their oldest child, and when I read the date of his birth, the short hairs rose on my neck. It was on Monday, December 25, 1781, the very day that proud *Our Eliza* struck her flag to the upstart *Saratoga*.

It had only happened so. It was not by the devil's scheming. Perhaps Anne Blackburn's baby had been born before midnight of the twenty-fourth or in the early morning hours of the twenty-sixth and she had told a little lie to win for him some special notice from the curate. Yet it came to me with a little cold shiver in my soul that the linking of the two events would prove of use to me before my course was run.

Holgar had had five brothers and sisters born about two years apart. I took note of their names and need never consult the record again. In the winter of 1793 there came the smallpox; these five and their parents had been wiped out in one fell swoop. Shakespeare comes to haunt the mind. That phrase brought up the rest of the quotation, as fitting to this case, all his *pretty chickies and their dam* had been taken from Bruce Blackburn before he turned over and died.

Below, in a different and more elegant handwriting than that of the other entry, perhaps no less than the rector's very own, I read:

"This family suffered more from the disease than any other in the parish. Since it is well known that God employs such maladies to punish the wicked, and since Bruce Blackburn was of a stubborn and rebellious nature, often failing in respect to his betters, and leading his fellow tenants in public demonstrations of discontent with the wages paid them by their masters, let this be a lesson to all who are tempted to the same iniquities. God's mercy was shown in His sparing of the oldest son, Holgar. Over his parent's objections, he had been sent to lodge with another tenant five miles distant, to help with wood-cutting. He will be given a home in the parish workhouse, there to be taught honesty, humility, and industry, whereby he may grow to worthy manhood."

When I returned the records to the clerk, I pointed out the entry. "I was interested in this birth, because it's my own," I said.

The little gray man read it over, then looked at me with unbelieving eyes.

"*You* are Holgar Blackburn!"

"That's my name."

"The same that ran away from the workhouse twenty-three years ago?"

I showed him a burned X on the back of my hand.

"You've had a hard time—I can see that—yet you've come back in a costly carriage, wearing fine clothes!"

There was no righteous indignation in his face over this upset, not the least malice, only a wild hope.

"Why not?" And I glanced at a handsome gold watch that I had bought before leaving London and wore fixed to a gold chain by a horsehair band.

"You don't mean, do you, sir—please pardon my presumption in asking—you've come home *rich*?"

"I stink with money," I answered, grinning into his eyes.

"Oh, will you stay awhile here? Will you let some of the gentry see you, and his reverence, and his grace the Duke? Oh, if you'd not be averse to making a vulgar show—gold flung about like water—a coach and four—servants bowing and scraping—maybe a great festivity to celebrate your home-coming. Oh, you don't know how 'twould do my heart good!"

"Yes, yes," I cried to him, as though speaking to a heart-hungry child. "Wait and see. It will be the most vulgar display of wealth the shire has ever seen."

2

The Sepulcher of Wet Bones was a far more terrible institution than the workhouse from which my name-giver had run away, but the two had similarities. The inmates of both labored from dawn to dark on barely sufficient food; they were whipped for any real or imagined offense, herded like animals, and their humanity insulted at every turn; and, after long terms in either prison, their bodies, minds, and souls were permanently damaged. Sunlight flooded our roofless palisade most of the day, but it barely crept through the broken or dangling shutters of the three-story ramshackle tenement where, by average count, forty aged or ailing men and women or destitute children lived a dim half-life.

Mr. Peters, the parish clerk, was about to be retired from his office with a modest pension. More eager to please me, who might reward him, than to avoid angering some of the local bigwigs who had never exchanged a cordial word with him, he did not hesitate to tell me that the house was owned by a Mr. Hudson, the son of the wielder of the branding iron in 1795. Now counted a gentleman, he did not condescend to hold his father's office, but rented out the ruin to a board of guardians for a hundred pounds per annum, about three times its worth. Also, Mr. Peters was not loath to institute some further inquiries. Thus I learned that a good farm of three hundred and twenty acres close to Holgar's birthplace, with two rambling houses whose combined room was greater than the present tenement, was being offered for sale for three thousand pounds. After driving out to see it and liking its lay, I asked Mr. Peters to engage me an honest lawyer.

I did not stay for the completion of the business, but would be present at its upshot; on arriving in London I straightway sent Alan to see how it fared. During his absence I lived at the Albion Hotel, saw the town, and looked at various houses from which I might choose my London abode. The owners, solicitors, and agents whom I met in this connection invariably started at my appearance, but treated me with an intense kind of respect.

Alan returned from Tavistock in a fortnight, pleased with his attainments. These he recited to me in his terse way.

"I gave the old clerk, Mr. Peters, a hundred pounds. The lawyer you hired, Shirley, paid thirty pounds earnest money on the Marwood farm as you directed him. Then he wrote the workhouse guardians, offering it to them for twenty years at one guinea rental a year. One or two were quite ill over cutting Mr. Hudson off from his hundred quid per annum for his ratty tenement—one raised the point that clean quarters and healthy farm labor instead of picking oakum would pamper the paupers to their ruin—but the worthies damned well knew what the rate-payers would say if they refused the offer, so they accepted it with all the grace they could muster. I paid the balance of the sum and got the deed in your name. The paupers are going to move in on July first. The fete is scheduled for July fourth, as you wished it."

"Do you think you can complete your other arrangements on time?"

"In half the time. Money makes the mare go, as the saying is. Mr. Blackburn, does it occur to you that July fourth is a rather odd day to hold a great fete in England?"

"I don't believe it will worry those who come to the party."

"I request that you give it on the third."

"Well, what the Americans celebrate on July fourth is an outgrowth of an English idea. The Great Charter antedates the Declaration of Independence and is of similar stuff. Your request is granted."

The party was upon us almost before we knew it; but Alan had done his work well. Everybody in the parish was invited by bill and proclamation; people from neighboring parishes would not be turned away. No one need bring food or drink, no hats would be passed or subscriptions solicited. By sunrise our tables were spread and pavilions erected, with fifty footmen brought from Plymouth and Bristol to serve ham, bacon, cheese and bread, cakes and cookies, and iced tea, lime-and-lemonade, coffee, and French chocolate without stint. Besides these good things, there had come by stagecoach, wains, and carts three bands, one of them decidedly Dutch, the best troupe of acrobats touring England, jugglers, clowns, mimics, ventriloquists, and magicians, an excellent dog-and-pony show, Toto the Diving Dog with ladder and tank complete, hand-organists with their monkeys, and several marionette shows including the immortal Punch and Judy. Six-horse teams had brought merry-go-rounds—and I remembered a carnival on Malta which Sophia and I had visited and fled. There were no dancing bears because I could not look at the pitiful brutes. No ale or stronger drinks were served because this

310

party was for children and for those who might return to childhood for a little while.

The walkers began to stream into the grounds soon after sunrise. Families from as far as Launcestan arrived in farm wagons, and strange-speaking shepherds with their fey-looking wives and wide-eyed little ones came riding shaggy ponies or behind them in high-wheeled carts from the wild wastes of Dartmoor. By noon the bright-eyed laughing throngs moving from one merriment to another numbered a good five thousand. Not one so far ranked among the gentry; the whole crowd could be lumped off with dreadful insolence and sacrilege as "The Great Unwashed." But I had forgotten of late that little children could be enchanting. My cold heart glowed again at sight of youth and maiden, graced by God, often made gawky and awkward by the supercilious gazings of their betters, but in this hour beautiful beyond words, walking hand in hand. All this was man. It was the earthly body of God.

I stayed out of sight as much as possible, hanging off the fringes of the crowds and in easy reach of Alan if he needed instruction. My happiness was as full as some remembered from long ago and in the beauty-haunted hours with Isabel, and often I had a far-away feeling of sharing it with Holger Blackburn, gone somewhere beyond all the deserts and all the seas. Yet he remained part and parcel with every child who played, every parent who beamed. The mystery was deep and moving in my soul.

A clown doing tricks of legerdemain before a delighted throng caught sight of me away on the outskirts and, having not the slightest notion who I was, beckoned to me.

"Come up and join us, Mister Stork," he called jovially. "The gov'-nor asked me to find out how much bacon you've hid in your hat!"

"That's my secret, and I'll keep it," I shouted back.

"Come up unless you're a-feared," the clown persisted. "Ain't that a rabbit you've poached, wigglin' under your coat? Make way for him, friends. Why, blast me, I think he's Dick Turpin, the famous road knight!"

The bright-faced crowd parted obediently. It occurred to me to wave and walk away; then I remembered that I stood for Holger Blackburn, and I had promised to make him a good showing in Tavistock.

But as I advanced, the laughing throng grew still. The clown's face fell as I neared him; then a little girl's voice rose clear and pure as the notes of a flute.

"Mama, is en a ogre?" she asked in cheerful curiosity.

I laughed at her; then the crowd shouted with laughter. It had hardly stilled when a young woman raised a shrill cry.

"Coo, 'tis Holgar Blackburn hisself!"

"Why, so 'tis," some deep-voiced countryman, a natural leader, broke forth in the breathless hush. "Folk, let's give en a cheer!"

They gave it with great vehemence and in the English fashion, and since they counted me one of them, the name they shouted at the end of the three hip, hip, hurrays was Holgar only. But a giant young farmer, in rollicking humor, was not content.

"Once more," he yelled, "and see that ye name en right!"

Again the cheer roared forth, to be heard a mile,

"Hip, hip, *hurray,*
Hip, hip, *hurray,*
Hip, hip, *hurray,*
OGRE!"

Afterward the people laughed loudly but nervously. I wished I could tell them that I perceived their delicate motive, that they had done a wonderfully considerate thing which most of their betters could not have conceived, that there was no danger of my misunderstanding their great sociability and philanthropy. Perhaps only the lowly—and a few of those so high that they need not always stand on guard—can be truly sociable. Look to these to learn good manners!

I could only laugh with them, wave my long arms, and walk away. Afterward I grinned over a curious sequence of names—Homer, Omar, Holgar, Ogre. Fate loves conceits of this sort, I thought; she is fond of puns and witticisms of all kinds. But very rarely does she complete a first-rate poem. So often her composition begins with a noble stanza, then falls apart.

3

The guardians of the workhouse arrived in a body. It was their duty, and they did it, and I grinned at their three-horned dilemma: their necessity of showing one another disapprobation of this sort of goings-on, their anxiety not to offend me, and an irrepressible human and boyish desire to share in the fun. They had not brought their wives or daughters; dash it all, there was a limit to what could be expected of them; and it was best that I understand this right from the start. It turned out, however, they were not properly supported in this virtuous stand. Not one of them was higher than a knight; while nothing less than an earl, with his countess and his children and two nurses and a footman, arrived presently in a coach, and the whole kaboodle ranged the grounds, eating free lunch and seeing the shows with every sign of delight. Before the afternoon was over, there was a definite sprinkling of nobility and gentry amid the throng.

One gentleman, a bluff sort with no nonsense about him, sought me out.

"A damned fine thing you're doing here, Mr. Blackburn, and I don't care who hears me say so," he told me.

"Thank you, thank you."

"I'm that Sir Thomas Wilson-Walch, whose name you may have heard—if you saw it in the public prints, it had B-a-r-t-period written after it. We can't keep our names out of the newspapers these days, and why should we try? After all, the common sort have a natural curiosity about our sort."

"Our" could have a flattering meaning in this case, but I decided not to stake on it.

"You're quite right, of course."

"There are some, Mr. Blackburn, who look down on men who've made their own way, but I'm not one of 'em. My hat's off to 'em, sir. What they lack in the little refinements, they make up in grit and pluck. I, for one, welcome you back to your native land."

"That's very good of you, Sir Thomas Wilson-Walch."

"Are you planning to buy a seat here? A country seat, I mean."

"Not at present."

"What are you going to collect? Almost every man of means I know collects something—in the way of hobby, y'understand."

"I hadn't thought about it yet."

"It occurred to me you'd like to acquire a collection already made —save you a lot of trouble and time. Now I've made a collection of walking sticks and canes. I've every kind you could think of—sword canes, sticks from every country in the world, canes carried by kings and conquerors I paid a pretty penny for, I'll tell you that. For instance Richard III. He was an English king of three centuries and more ago, and a bit crippled. I have an oaken walking stick with a silver handle with his monogram on it plain as day. I dare say you've never heard of Tamerlane—the name means Timur the Lame—but he was as renowned in his day as Napoleon. I have his favorite crutch—

ivory with a gold knob, with a dragon engraved on it. It happens my sons and daughters have taken other hobbies and I've no one to leave this priceless collection to, so I asked myself, why not sell it to Mr. Blackburn?"

"What price would you ask, Sir Thomas?"

"Now that's a joke, Blackburn—a man of your wealth asking the price of anything! Just say you want the collection, and there'll be no trouble about the price."

"Would it be under a thousand guineas?"

"Not much over that, I'm sure. Although you'd not believe it, one of my canes is made of rhinoceros hide and looks like amber. There's another——"

Suddenly the grim fun was over. I remembered a whip made of rhinoceros hide, known as the kurbash. It had repeatedly fallen with an awful sound when there came to the real Holgar Blackburn an impulse he could not resist.

"I'll take all you've said under advisement," I told the baronet. Quickly retreating, I left him flushed with anger.

No ghosts were made to rise and walk by this nincompoop; the momentary sharpness passed away; and having been shown a valuable sample of what was waiting for me, I could try to steer clear of the main. What told upon me far more was a glimpse I had of a young girl—about eighteen, I thought, in the company of a slightly younger girl, a boy of twelve or so whom I took to be the latter's brother, and a tall, erect elderly man, with a finely chiseled face, who I did not doubt belonged to the nobility. It was the girl's carriage that first caught my eyes—I could almost believe she had acquired it from carrying water jars on her head. On gazing at her idly, I thought warmly of Sophia. Then as I looked at her in growing pleasure and surprise, she reminded me of Isabel Gazelle.

It was not merely a matter of a long free stride and a high-held head and the childish way she beamed on the performers. I could not doubt that she was of ancient lineage, her form and face and dress indicating good breeding and wealth, but I thought she was highborn in the only sense I believed, as are poets and men of high bravery and women of great beauty. It was a mystery of the spirit's manifestation in mortality. Her linking in my mind with the tall brown maiden who followed me at the Wells of the Rising Moon did not fail because of her bright blondness. Many English blondes appeared colorless, as though bleached instead of tinted; on this girl color had been poured as on the feathers of a golden pheasant. She shone in a crowd or would glimmer in the forest, and she was always a little conscious and proud of it, as was Isabel of her royalty.

I watched her with flooding joy until she happened to catch my eye. Her face fell as had the clown's, so I quickly turned away. But later I asked Alan if he had seen her, and if so, what was her name?

"No one could help but see her," he replied. "No, I don't know her name, but I can find out. She was with Lord Bray's granddaughter—the Brays live near Milton Abbey—I suppose she's visiting her."

"It was idle curiosity, so don't bother to inquire."

The last of the day's events was most strange. It happened late in the afternoon when the throngs were thinning out, and its meaning that I grasped seemed only part of a greater meaning beyond my ken. I stood among some trees, out of the way of the crowds, when a farm wife of about forty, ordinary-looking to a casual glance, dropped behind her children and husband and came to me with a hurried step. I noticed now a deep sensitivity in her face and rather strange wide eyes.

"Mr. Holgar Blackburn?" she asked.

"Yes."

"You're not, you know."

"What?"

"Holgar lived neighbor to us. We were only childhood sweethearts, but I never loved anyone as I loved him. I knew his walk. It was like no other. I know he's dead and you've taken his name, but not his riches because he could never have none."

"What are you going to do about it?"

"Nothing. I won't tell nobody in this world. I don't know what your reason is, but I know it's a good reason. Good-by."

She turned quickly and vanished in the throng.

CHAPTER 26

The Baring of the Blade

1

IN THE Weald, on the border between Kent and Surrey, by the village of Hudleigh, and not far from the fashionable resort of Tunbridge Wells, lay the manor of Elveshurst, the most desirable of all the country seats which Alan had surveyed. It lay only thirty crow-flight miles from London Bridge. It contained five thousand acres, a thousand of which were in crop, the rest being wild pasture, forest, and ponds. Several streams offered trout fishing and otter hunting, and these debouched into a short, bold tributary of the Medway, the best salmon waters hereabouts. Water fowl were abundant in season; snipe used the fens in great numbers; and the seat was famous in seven shires for its countless coveys of partridge. Since time immemorial, the Carronade Hunt, whose M.F.H. was Squire Hudleigh of Hudleigh, had counted on Elveshurst for its strongest foxes and best runs.

Its price was so moderate that I saw little chance of loss. Still I did not close the deal at once, for Jim was enroute to England. He arrived in early August, looking fine and fit and almost venerable in his old-fashioned broadcloth suit. At the Albion Hotel after supper, I asked him to tell his story in his own way.

"The fust thing I done was to send word to the Beni Kabir to take El Stedoro to Alexander, like the old sheik promised you. The last thing was to go to Alexander, to see if he'd done come. He had, and I fixed for him to be shipped on an East Indiaman comin' into London in about two week."

"How was he?"

"He looked mighty big and raw-boned, and he wa'n't no beauty, but I never seen a hoss cay hisself like he do."

"He's six years old and ought to be getting into his prime. Did you hear any news of the Beni Kabir?"

"The only one I talked to was Zaal, the sheik's nephew. He say the people all doin' fine."

"I don't doubt they are."

"Now I'll tell you what I found out at Malta. I hung around the Turkish quarter till I got acquainted good. Pretty soon I heared of a Greek, what dey call Paulos, who used to be clerk to de harbor mas'. In 'em days he made a lot o' money on de side. One of de Turk hint 'at he make it passin' on to spies whey de ships gwine when dey leave Malta. Paulos, he take to smokin' bhang and down in de gutter, but I go see him and buy him some bhang but not 'nuff to satisfy him. When he want mo', I get him to talk pitty good. His mind clear as a bell when de bhang take hold, he 'member heap o' t'ing. De main spy was a Spaniard workin' for de French. But wif my keepin' at him, I find out dey was a Maltese, dey call him Julius,

316

who spy for de reis effendis in Tripoli, Tunis, and Algiers. De bad luck was, dis Julius, he daid."

"There was bound to be some bad luck. Go on."

"When Julius hear something de pirate want to know, he send word by a real fast boat, who make out she a Dago fisherman, to Linosa, de island 'at lay only a night's sail if de wind fair. All de pirates pass by Linosa, and de Dago's pard, he signal from de shore wif mirrors or lights plain as writin' on a paper. Sometime when it look safe, de pirate come up to Gozo in de night, not two hours' run from Valletta. Murad Reis, he done it the day before we sail. De Dago done carry him word 'at de huntin' gwine to be good."

"How do you know, Jim?"

"De Dago 'fess it if I give him a hundred pounds. But if I ever tell de provost it was my word agin his. And 'twas de Dago 'at tell him to watch for us by Aegadian Island."

Jim looked down, unspeakable sadness in his face, twirling a ring he had made from the Pharaoh's gold on whose seal he had engraved the letter V.

"Did the Dago tell you who sent the messages?"

"He say he know mighty well it was de little lord, but he can't prove it. De one who deal wif him was de Maltese dey called Julius, and he daid."

I thought of something like a distant move in a game of chess.

"How did you find out Julius was dead?"

"I didn't have no easy time findin' it out. Dago thought he was alive somewheres. De Greek Paulos, he say Julius went to Syracuse, and maybe he die in de plague, but he change his name 'fore then, and Paulos didn't know for sho. I went to Syracuse, lookin' for him, and it was jus' a piece of luck I run into a Turkish opium peddler who knowed Julius. He say Julius git away from de plague but was stabbed to death and robbed in Athens. He seen his corpse wif his own eyes."

"Did you tell Paulos or the Dago?"

"No, Cap'n. Bof of 'em would be too glad to know it."

"Is there anything more?"

"A small dark young man meet Julius about t'ree o'clock in the morning of de day befo' we sail in a wine shop in Notabile. De Dago say he was de lord's son, Dick."

"Had Harvey Alford, Sir Godwine's aide, anything to do with it?"

"Dey was a young Englishman, wif yaller hair, mighty handsome, who come along and hang outside de wine shop when Dick talk to Julius."

"What was the name of the wine shop?"

"De Don John of Austria."

"Did you ask leading questions? Was there any likelihood of the Dago telling you what you wanted to hear and pay for?"

"Not one little bit. I say to him, 'Who tol' Julius we was coming, and where we was gwine? Was it de Greek Paulos, clerk to the harbor mas'?' Dat was what I say to him, not to give him no lead. He say to me, it wa'n't him dis time. It was de little dark man who do de runnin' back and fort', and de word, it come from a English captain who carry a little stick instead of a sword. He wore powdered hair and he walk wif his feet straight in front of him. How do Dago know? 'Cause he saw him once talkin' to Julius. Later on, Julius he brag about dealin' wif de big gun. He say de big gun give him a hundred guineas, beside what Murad Reis send him."

"Then what was your decision on this part. Say it in plain words."

"In plain words, Cap'n, de little lord, his name Sir Godwine Tarlton, betray us to de pirate as sho as God's in heaven, and his son help him."

"Had he ever betrayed any other American ships?"

"The Dago say he did, but he can't prove it."

"Could he understand why?"

"Once he tell Julius dat dey gwine be another war wif what he call de Colonies—to make 'em come back under de English flag and all de ring leaders in de rebellion hung by de neck—and de more ships de pirates capture, de fewer for de English to have to fight. But Julius say 'at only a 'scuse. De real reason was, he hate Unity States wif poison hate."

"Then half of the duty Cap'n Phillips laid on me is done."

"Aye, sah, the truf's been 'stablished, as he done told you."

"The other half was, if he's guilty, to bring him to lawful judgment. Do you think it can ever be done?"

"Cap'n, as far as bringin' him to de bar of justice in de cou't, de Ribba Nile will freeze over bank to bank befo' we can do 'at."

"I never really hoped we could do it. We were in prison too long. Jim, do you know any other kind of lawful justice operating on this earth except that of the courts?"

"No, sah, unless de Lawd lean down and do it. What dey call de unwritten law ain't law at all."

"I don't know of any, either, but there may be such a thing. Long ago the Greeks had a goddess whose name was Nemesis. Her name came to mean punishment by the gods. They had some reason to think that the gods punished evil—perhaps there was some law of nature operating that we don't understand—it may be that great evil brings its own punishment. Many noble minds have accepted that belief. I don't deny it."

"I reckon 'at's what I meant when I said de Lawd lean down. But he don't always seem to, and 'at's where de trouble lie. I can't bear to t'ink of 'at pretty little cap'n who came on de boat 'at night, wif his stick and his powder hair and his voice wif de east wind in it. De blood of our boys is on his little white hand, de black of de treachery in his soul, but what he care? De hate of freedom in his heart—for 'at what he hate when he come down to it; he want men to be his slaves, not his brothers. You swore you wouldn't take no vengeance on him—like trackin' him down and killin' him. But Cap'n Whitman, can't you do nothin' toward rightin' de ter'ble wrong?"

"I'm going to try. We'll stay in England until we succeed or have to give up. I'll seek the acquaintance of Lord Tarlton—for that's his name now. He shall see much of me."

As Jim gazed into my face, his eyes grew slowly round.

2

It was no great feat for an upstart with a sword of gold to hew his way into the sporting world of England and even to the fabulous province of the London buck.

To begin with, it made no small stir in the Weald when I bought Elveshurst. Moreover, my neighboring nobility and gentry soon perceived me as an unpresuming soul, knowing my place, never known to push, respectful to all, and generous with my salmon and trout waters, snipe and duck marshes, and peerless partridge cover. Mention was made that I shot quite well myself—actually, wing-shooting with shotguns proved an easy adaption from rifle-shooting at moving game from horseback or camelback, and I had no nerves to make me flinch or fly off—but I never flaunted the skill, invariably gave my guests the best butts or walking-up, and hung modestly in the background. Meanwhile the breakfasts served before the beats, the refreshments between, and the lunches brought smoking to the field were the best that clever Alan and our highly competent kitchen staff could furnish.

Any farmer who wished could ride with the Carronade Hunt, and in addition to a great gray stallion that only my hands and tenants ever saw, my stables housed half a dozen well-chosen hunters. But I did not presume to a pink coat, was far from a thruster, and never rode over crop; so no untoward attention was drawn to the fact that almost always I was among those present at the kill.

The gray stallion had made the journey in good fettle. When I met him in Portsmouth he sniffed me uncertainly for a few seconds, then began to whinny in an agony of emotion. Presently I slipped my hand between his jaws. When he closed gently upon it with his great teeth, I knew that our long parting had been bridged and our old bond held yet.

The lords and gentlemen who hunted or angled or shot at Elveshurst began to say I was not a bad sort, considering my beginnings. A few remarked on my having done a rather handsome thing at my birthplace, in the way of the new workhouse; and it was quite decent, the way I kept my ugly face from being conspicuous. Seeing that I did not embarrass them by seeking invitations to their homes or any acquaintance with their womenfolk, they treated me with great civility when I ran across them in London.

Here I kept a rather small, quite elegant menage on Charles Street. Meeting a fellow fowler at Tattersall's, where I hung a good deal, he offered to nominate me for the Jockey Club. The turf as well as the game room was always a leveling force in English society, and this club prided itself on a man-to-man fellowship; still it numbered many a fine buck. Among the names I read that of Dick Tarlton. Although a lord's son, he was not listed as "honorable." Breeders and backers of horses think well of established stud.

Whether I would be elected would make a good bet—say three to one against—at White's. In my favor, I knew a horse from a hayrick, picking up several tidy bits at Tattersall's auctions, and had shown a good fellow at turf and paddock. Also, I had the backing of several horsemen of no mean ilk and name. What appeared most against me, my face and form and the story of humble birth, actually told for me in the upshot, since my admission to the club was such a conspicuous demonstration of true sportsmanship and a rebuke to rival clubs.

Swiftly upon my election, I was caricatured in the *Universal Magazine* as a skeletonlike jockey riding a bony nag, Jim following as my groom, in a desperate race against General Smith, an upstart who had made his fortune in dubious ways in India; the goal was the glittering doorway of the Brighton Pavilion, favorite resort of the Regent. Actually the shot missed its mark. Several gentlemen stopped me to express their indignation at the "vicious" attack and to praise me for keeping my head well and my feet on the ground. It was quite possible that had I sought election in one of the great gambling clubs such as White's or Brook's, I might have obtained the honor.

I continued to frequent Almack's Assembly Rooms in King Street and Saint James Coffee House, where anyone with a shilling in his purse could put it to hazard. Here I played deeply but carefully, and no one observed that my opponents were invariably men of great wealth, who need not quail at their losses—this in respect to my own desires and in memory of the one who had armed me with a golden sword. Still, it did not take long for me to become known as a ready gamester. I preferred faro, since it presented the most difficulty to the sharper, but was agreeable to basset and macao; and for fast play, sometimes bewildering my opponent, there was nothing better than the dice box and old-fashioned hazard.

While I waited in this strange ambush for my prey, I was asked to join another club—perhaps the strangest in London. It was called the Ugly Man's Club, exactly what it purported to be. Only those deemed of remarkably ugly visage were invited to join; great corpulence or emaciation or any other mark of disease disqualified the candidate; scars were disparaged unless natural ugliness set them off. In the way of social position, members ranged from an earl of ancient name, one of the great noblemen of his age, through a Jewish rabbi, to a low-born, high-minded gunsmith. Gaming being forbidden at the meetings, bibbling kept in bounds, our main entertainment was conversation, the most eager and frank, and quite possibly the most stimulating, to be heard in any London club. I did not know why, unless during this brief breach of loneliness, every man let his soul flow free.

Every man but one. Enjoying the talk and sometimes taking part in it, I remained alone as when I walked the streets in fog.

When I cast my accounts at the end of the year 1818, I had good reason to be pleased with my progress. I had not yet laid eyes on Lord Tarlton or made the slightest effort to do so, but our paths were drawing closer and they would surely cross before long. I had seen Dick Tarlton at the Jockey Club and at race meets, small, dark, carelessly dressed, and remarkably young-looking as far as I could tell from a distance; and with no apparent effort I had learned much of his goings and comings, his affairs and his ways, to stand me in good stead in our future dealings. Never mentioning the name of Harvey Alford—wishing I need never hear it—dreading any involvement with him and wish-thinking him innocent, still I had happened to hear that his wife's name was Sophia, and darkly knew we would soon come face to face.

My losses at gaming had been slight, considering how deeply I had played—amounting to not much more than the hosts' fees for "services." At the turf I was a slow but steady winner, and might have won heavily had I been willing to show my hand.

I could read a pedigree as well if not better than most; my eyes and instincts were fully as sharp in viewing horseflesh; and my great advantage lay in perceiving an animal's mettle just before a race. This was something Timor had taught me. He had pointed out the signs a thousand times—the eagerness of glance, the set of the ears, the carriage of the head, the arch of the neck, the spring of the step, and, curiously enough, the movements of the tail. Often the impression ran contrary to all my other judgments; yet if it were strong enough, it usually picked the winner. Sometimes it failed utterly.

Yet it was at gaming that I bared for the first time the edge of my golden sword.

3

I had come into Almack's late at night. Some desultory playing went on, but the main event, bursting on my pupils still wide from darkness, was a dice game between a heavy-set, florid man of my own age, suggesting a country squire lately drawn to the lights of London, and a small, superbly dressed, elegant little figure of a man whom I would know in any passage of years or sweep of distance. Some of the arresting vividness of the scene may have been a trick of my eyes; but some was an effect of brilliant lighting and part was its innate drama, apparent to all the people in the room. These watched with locked gaze in silence. An old man's hand jerked back and forth every time the younger player, he who had dared contest Godwine, Lord Tarlton, shook the dice box. The aged Dick Vernon cackled in senile glee. A magnificently built yet effeminate-acting youth laughed shrilly whenever the little lord won, meanwhile gazing at him with sickening ardor.

After the first impact of the scene on my unready eyes and brain, I turned cold and picked up its details with great care, one by one.

Lord Tarlton sat in a large, luxurious chair placed sideways to the table, and his white hand, looking almost tiny emerging from lace cuffs, rolled the dice with a graceful motion over its right arm. He wore a black coat and knee breeches of a somewhat antique style, glossy dark blue hose, black slippers with silver buckles, and a white satin cravat adorned with one large pearl. A Malacca walking stick leaned against the left arm of his chair. He need no longer powder his hair, and worn rather long and brushed back, it called attention to the beautiful structure of his head and face. His small prim mouth bore the merest suggestion of a smile. I could not see the winter-sky blue of his eyes, but their gaze seemed only half attentive to the game. The thing that set my spine a-crawl was his look of youth. There were no lines on his face, no hollows under his eyes, no loosening of the skin on his cheeks and delicate jaws. It was as though Age had not dared lay hand on him.

His opponent, if I could call him that, sat in a straight, plain chair squarely facing the table. Something went on in his face that puzzled and then frightened me. I could soon identify it as conflict between bravado and terror. As he took the dice box, he postured unmistakably—showing the crowd that he, too, could be lordly in his own fashion—but when he counted the pips I saw a rounding of his eyes and a tension around his mouth, as though he were gazing past the immediate moment to some future he dared not believe. No doubt he had had too much to drink, but the symptoms were not strong enough to impugn his opponent's sportsmanship in the crowd's sight. Anyway, who could question any conduct of such a great aristocrat as Lord Tarlton?

"Who's winning?" another newcomer asked an acquaintance in my hearing.

"You can guess, can't you? Lord Tarlton's already into him for a thousand guineas, and Bozy's just matched it, all or nothing."

"He'd better shed that silly grin."

"Let him have it. It may be his last."

I had heard of Bozy—his last name was Barnes—as a shallow player and would-be buck. Tonight he had got beyond his depth, and I wondered what pressures had made him do so. He rolled with a last trace of bravado. His eyes glazed with hope as he looked at the pips; although I stood twenty feet away, the whispers told me almost instantly he had thrown an eight. It was one of the easiest points to make; but he threw thrice more without it coming up, or the deadly seven either. Then he breathed into the box, shook it prayerfully, and rolled out the little cubes of bone.

He looked at them and turned white. "Seven," someone intoned. When he had set the box down, his arms dropped to his side.

"An unfortunate throw, my friend," the little lord said gravely.

Bozy Barnes could only shake his head.

"You owe me two thousand guineas, and it's for you to say whether we play on."

"Two thousand guineas! Good God in heaven. Oh, I'll match you once more. This can't go on forever."

"All or nothing?" Lord Tarlton asked quietly.

"Yes, yes."

"I must remind you that twice two thousand guineas is four thousand, no trifling sum. But of course, it cuts both ways."

"I'll play. I said I would."

"Then be so kind as to pass me the dice box."

Lord Tarlton took it, dropped in the dice, shook them once, and rolled them lightly on the table.

"My lord has thrown a ten," a self-appointed scorekeeper announced to the now-breathless watchers. It being one of the hardest points to make, I could almost make myself believe he would not succeed and that a seven would come up instead. There was something very like beauty in his face as he played for his point, one easy roll after another. I had seen it once before when he had toasted *Our Eliza* in Lepanto Palace.

"Four," the announcer intoned, " . . . six . . . two . . . five . . . *nine!*"

Lord Tarlton paused, glanced at his watch, wiped his lips with a silk kerchief, and gave a little smile to the beautifully built youth with the effeminate airs. Then he dropped the dice slowly in the box, gave it one violent, vicious shake, and threw.

"*Ten!*" the announcer shouted.

Lord Tarlton leaned gracefully in his chair as he waited for Bozy Barnes to speak. The latter could only shake his head, his pale face beaded with sweat.

"Does that mean you don't care to play any more?" the nobleman asked in his softest voice.

"I've nothing left to play with. I'm ruined."

"I'm sure you've enough to meet the obligation, or you wouldn't have played." There was just a trace of a wintry rattle in the sound.

"I'll meet it. It will take me a few days. Be a little patient with me, my lord, and you'll get every penny."

Meanwhile I had moved quietly through the gaping throng to the table.

"Lord Tarlton?"

His eyes moved slowly to mine. Not a trace of expression came into his face.

"That is my name, sir."

"I seek the honor of taking Mr. Barnes's place for one cast, all or nothing."

"You wish to hazard four thousand guineas against Mr. Barnes's debt?"

"Yes, my lord."

"Sir, I've not the pleasure of your acquaintance, and perhaps you'll not take kindly by my knowing who you are from previous description by others."

"My lord, I'm quite used to that."

"I regret that your cognomen slips my mind."

"It's Holgar Blackburn."

"Then you're the one without fail. Why, sink me if I wasn't in Cornwall, staying at my first wife's family seat, when you gave your fete in Tavistock—and the report brought to me was, it was a jam up. Since then I believe you've bought Elveshurst and the best rough shooting in sixty miles of London. If so, I don't doubt you're financially competent to play."

"My lord, I'll write an order on Baring's Bank beforehand and put it in the stakeholder's hand."

"Why, blow me down, that's plain dealing, what I like in a man. Take Bozy's seat there, and we'll roll for high dice, and the one that wins will take the box to win or crap."

There was not a sound, not even a wheeze from old Dick Vernon gazing at me with bleary eyes, as I took the seat. The Greek god with Cupid's airs stared into my face, as though trying to frighten me.

"My lord, if it meets your favor, we'll throw high dice for the main sum."

"One cast?"

"Yes, sir."

"Well, I've risked more than that on a single shot. Will you roll first?"

"Gladly."

The dice rattled in the box and rolled out. I had shot an eight.

" 'Tisn't very good," I told my adversary, restoring the dice to the box and handing it to him. "My luck has been but middling ever since my birthday, happening on Christmas."

His hand paused briefly. "On Christmas, say you?"

"Yes, my lord, and since Christmas fell on Monday on the year that I was born, I should be 'fair of face.' "

He sat gracefully but very still. I wondered if others saw an obscure change of expression.

"You're about forty-four——" he ventured.

"No, sir, I'm thirty-seven according to the book. I was born on Christmas, 1781."

"So?"

But he shook the box too hard and the dice rolled out before he was ready. By the laws of chance that could not increase or decrease his chances of winning by the least jot. Yet he hated himself as he looked down and saw he had thrown a four and a three.

"That would have won for you, my lord, if we were playing hazard," I remarked.

"Now that's consolation worth having." He turned to Bozy Barnes, standing there gaping; the east wind was in his voice again and his pupils looked immense and black.

"Sir, you may pay your debt to Mr. Blackburn."

"No, he needn't," I broke in.

"What in the devil's hell do you mean?" Lord Tarlton demanded.

"I wish to call it square, as the Yankee saying goes. You've lost nothing but your winnings of the evening, I've lost nothing, so why not share our good luck with our friend?"

"I can't do it," Barnes stammered. "It's not sporting——"

"I played your turn for you, sir, and it was my pleasure to win for you, and you'll offend me if you refuse, and by heaven, I'll challenge you to a duel!"

"Then I'll not refuse! No matter what the bucks say about me. I thank you and bless you——" He covered his face with his hands.

"A touching scene," the little lord remarked. "We haven't seen its like since the late Beau Brummell—pardon me, I believe he's still alive—won fifteen hundred pounds for Tom Sheridan. Mr. Blackburn, are we to consider you a candidate for the Good Samaritan?"

"No, sir, but I thought you'd misjudged his condition, or you'd not have played with him."

"Why, blast it, you're a cool one. Twenty-odd years my junior, and spending most of your life 'mongst naked savages according to what I heard, yet better able than I to judge drunk or sober. You used a Yankee expression just now. Maybe you've Yankee wits as well."

"My lord, I hope you won't take me to task. If you're the Lord Tarlton whom I think you are, I came nigh to being named for you."

"How did that happen, if you'll tell me?"

"I wasn't christened for two months after my birth, and if some great feat of arms in the war with America had happened on my natal day, my father intended to name me for its hero. The first report was, you'd sunk a Yankee vessel on the morning of that day. But when he chanced to discover that the *Saratoga* went down late on the following day, I lost out on the honor."

The little lord drew his breath to speak, then let it go and stared. Perhaps this roomful of bucks and their hangers-on had never seen him stare in quite this way before. Its suggestion was too powerful to resist. One pair of eyes after another fixed on my face. It had no expression they could read; it seemed roughly carved of flint, unfinished and jagged, with a deep chisel stroke across my cheek. Yet when they looked back to the elegant figure in the big chair, there were strange questions never raised before in their searching eyes.

"You astonish me," he remarked at last—perhaps the first guarded words he had spoken in many years.

"But may I yet gain the honor of your presence at Elveshurst before very long?" I asked. "Snipe and duck are plentiful, the partridge have not yet paired off, and fox scent holds well in our damp woods. And if your son Dick and your son-in-law Mr. Alford would care to come, they'd both be welcome."

"We'll welcome the invitation, Mr. Blackburn."

"Then I'll bid you all good night."

In making for the door I must pass the young Adonis who had eyed me with such fury a few minutes before, and I was half afraid he might strike me. Instead he looked into my eyes with a revolting smile.

CHAPTER 27

Echoes Resounding

1

UNTIL AFTER my game with Lord Tarlton, I had never questioned Alan about him or shown any interest in him. While this was vaguely in accordance with my general strategy, on the whole it was a secretiveness I could not entirely explain, shot through with superstition. But when I told Alan of my winnings, he fell easily into discussing the little nobleman.

"It's not often that he loses—I'll tell you that," Alan said. "Even in games of pure chance such as yours last night—well, it's as though the dice don't *dare* go counter to him. And if anyone succeeds in beating him, that fellow had better look out, for Tarlton's going to get it back twofold—tenfold—once a hundredfold."

"His manners last night were most agreeable."

"I've seen them when they weren't! Still, he's a great blood. It's generally agreed that the Hanovers are upstarts compared to him."

"If you think he's going to seek revenge, you'd better tell me about him. Has he a family?"

"He has a daughter by his first wife, a lovely woman who married Lieutenant the Honorable Harvey Alford. Since Alford sold his commission in the Royal Navy, they've been living in Cornwall at an old seat, Celtburrow, that his wife inherited from her mother's family, but have very recently come to London. Tarlton has also a natural son, Dick, somewhat older, whom you may have seen at the Jockey Club—a terrific horseman and a rather hard case. His mother is Countess Isabel of Harkness, and it was quite an affair even in the good old days, when bastardy was rampant."

"Has his daughter Sophia any children?"

"No. By the way, did I mention her name? I don't recall doing so."

"I've heard it somewhere."

"You have very sharp ears, sir, and a remarkable memory. I was going on to say that about twenty years ago, Lord Tarlton—Sir Godwine Tarlton he was then—married again. As I heard the story, he was on leave from duty at sea and fell in love with a girl from Jersey—no family, no money, but with great beauty and dash. He left her at Celtburrow while he served in Malta: the affair was kept very quiet. Later there was talk of her leaving him—perhaps she liked the lights of London—but she was drowned in a boating accident."

"Perhaps I heard her name also," I said with a tingle along my spine. "Was it Elizabeth?"

"It was Elspeth, the Scotch form. And his other daughter is named Eliza."

"His other daughter——"

"Elspeth bore him one less than a year after the marriage. I've heard she's the apple of his eye, and he keeps her tucked away in the old pile, in fear of some young blade making off with her. I dare say he'll bring her out before long. I doubt if he can hide her much longer, for she's about nineteen."

I doubted if any young blade would make off with her without Lord Tarlton's consent. He would smile a little smile—and Eliza would obey him. I was haunted more by thoughts of a beautiful girl from Jersey, without money or name, married to the pretty little knight, going to bed with him, delivered of a child by him, then going to bed in the sea.

2

Two days after the game, I received an invitation brought by a powdered footman to attend a rout given by Lydia White, whose fetes were as famous in London as the debaucheries of old Q., who lately had passed to his reward. Certainly this notice taken of me was the direct result of my exploit at Almack's; whether someone wishing to meet me again had proposed it to the famous dame, I could only guess.

The affair began with late tea, to be followed by a play. I skipped both of these and arrived at the mansion in time for the spread. Through a vast doorway I saw an elegant little man with white hair, carrying a little stick, and walking with his toes straight in front of him like an Indian. On his arm was a woman who signaled her beauty to me across the great glittering room and down the years.

Her hair was dusky, and presently the lights picked up a gleam in its midst that I took for a wreath of pearls. I did not go near her yet, but watched her walk, and thought of her long coming up the beach, barefoot, with her boots in her hand. That was midsummer, 1801, before I came two-and-twenty. This is late winter, 1819. I had not seen her since except in flickering dreams.

When she and Lord Tarlton had dined, they took chairs near a faro table in a game room almost as large as White's, adjoining the ballroom. But they did not play, and after they had greeted some of their friends, I strolled toward them.

It was as though I walked into the past under deep cloud. Old scenes, old signs, returned to give strange dimensions and meanings to these scenes and signs. I saw Sophia's beauty then and I saw it now, the last a culmination of the first, its outgrowth in a harsh climate. Not many others in the throng perceived it at all, I thought; but I had loved her with great passion and I loved her still in my heart. Her beauty was the kind transmuted and not destroyed by fire. It had greatly changed, but not dimmed in the long years.

I could not see that she looked much older. Poignance and not time had remolded her lovely face. The curved line at one corner of her mouth, deeper than on the other even then, had become a cruel mark. The smile that I occasionally saw, that had touched me in such strange ways, came more commonly now—almost every time Lord Tarlton spoke to her. Her eyes that had appeared lighter of color than her pale olive skin, brightened still more by dense black lashes, had darkened. She still walked with lonely grace.

As I came nigh to Lord Tarlton, I gave him a grave bow. He had not noticed me until then, or had pretended to overlook me—for I had come to doubt his naturalness, a quality everyone seemed to attribute to him—but now his gaze fastened on my face, and he looked pleasantly surprised.

"Why, it's Mr. Blackburn, or you can blow me down. Pray stop with me a minute, sir, if you've the time. I didn't know you frequented these petticoat affairs."

"It's my first one, sir, and an eye-opener," I answered, pausing politely.

"You'll excuse me not rising, since I've years on my back, but my daughter shall rise, if I may have the pleasure of presenting you to her. Sophia, here's the buck who took me for four thousand guineas. Mr. Blackburn, Mrs. Harvey Alford."

Sophia had observed me before Lord Tarlton spoke. I had seen an expression of dismay come into her face. Now she rose lightly, and as her eyes met mine, it must be that certain memories, strangled like unwanted babes, stirred and plucked at her spirit, for she blurted out an ill-mannered question.

"Mr. Blackburn, have we met before?"

"I apologize for her, sir," Lord Tarlton said quickly with his pale, faint smile. "She was raised on the moors of Cornwall and has not been schooled in the niceties of polite behavior."

"I spent some years in a workhouse and am ignorant of the art, so I must ask the reason for the apology," I said as Sophia flushed.

"Since it didn't offend you, I'll ask you let it pass."

"It did not, nor does your apology, which, of the two, is the blunter reminder of my disturbing appearance."

"Why, sink me, Sophia, but he's a man of spirit, and I'd swear, a man of the world! Anyhow, you've come up in the world since those days you speak of. May I praise your language? It's not Tavistock rustic by a long shot—in fact, I listen in vain for any note of the West Country I know so well—and what could I expect, when you've been gone so many years?—but it's as good as Boston Yankee when it comes to grammar, and your accent is much like it, which I'm told is second to none. Now sit down a minute, if you'll favor us."

"I'm the one that's favored." I took the nearest chair.

"Sophia, here's a man of parts! He's made himself one, along with a million pounds, and ain't that proof of what the Americans maintain?"

"That's twice you've mentioned America, Papa, without Mr. Blackburn showing any interest in the subject. Perhaps polite behavior requires you change it."

"You said something like that before a long time ago. Where in the devil was it? Anyhow, Mr. Blackburn, I'll get on with what's on my mind. At our gaming t'other night, you made a remarkable statement. That the engagement of my ship, *Our Eliza*, with the Yankee *Saratoga*, occurred, not early on Christmas morning, but on the following day. I didn't wish to discuss it before that crowd—we English are too mortally afraid of blowing our own horns, sometimes to the loss of our fair deservings—but 'twas an odd misapprehension, and my curiosity was aroused how you'd fallen into it, or rather how your pa did. I'm an old-fashioned sailor who looks well to the log, so pray humor me."

Sat he well in his chair as he spoke, with no sign of strain. His voice was low and pleasant to the ear; his face looked serene; a common man who had made a trifling mistake could be flattered at his friendly interest in it. But I had been expecting the question and I saw him jiggle the walking stick lightly held in his white hand.

"My lord, I don't think it was ever questioned that the battle between the two ships occurred on Christmas morning. The report was, that the Yankee vessel didn't go down till the following afternoon."

Sophia was watching me with oddly guarded eyes.

"She didn't, damn me!" the little lord broke out. "Sophia, was I under the table all that time? Pardon my levity, Mr. Blackburn, and let's get on with this queer business. Did the report say that the Yankee was leaking and finally foundered?"

"No, sir. She blew up."

He stiffened slightly, and I saw the white knuckles of his hand holding the cane.

"Now what kind of a Yankee lie is that?"

"It came from Canada, sir, if I'm not mistaken. Perhaps it was a letter from an old friend. I'd have to look it up and see. It's still in my possession."

He hesitated, then spoke against his will.

"After all these years?"

"It was among a few trifles I took with me when I ran away from the workhouse. I saved it because—well, somehow I had gotten the idea it was important. My father spoke several times of publishing it, but I think was afraid to do so. Actually, I can't recall reading it after reaching the age to understand it. But if you are interested in it, in the way of a side light on the battle, however mistaken, I'll gladly look it up."

"Pray don't trouble yourself. I won't indulge idle curiosity that far."

"It would be no trouble, my lord. I myself would be entertained, perusing the old document."

"I'll give you better sport than that, before long, with the dice."

"Sir, wasn't the battle fought in an east wind?"

"Why, yes!"

"Off the coast of Grindstone, a Canadian island. I remember that much. Also that the vessel went down off Saint Paul Island, one hundred miles eastward."

"As my daughter suggested a while ago, let's change the subject." With great elegance Lord Tarlton took snuff.

"Your pardon for carrying it farther than you wished. No doubt I dwell too much on ships going down, having sailed on one that went down. Mrs. Alford, the dances I knew before I went into exile are out of fashion, and I may not partake of the waltzing, but I hear it's a pretty dance to watch, and if Lord Tarlton will excuse you, I request your company, a little while, in the ballroom."

"I accept with pleasure." She rose with a kind of spring that I remembered.

"I've not excused you yet," the little lord said gravely. "Mr. Blackburn's manners are better than yours. By God, they're better than I'd expect of a rough-and-ready miner; I'll praise 'em along with his language. But I will excuse you, for I've some things to think about, at comfort and leisure."

The wintry rattle had come back into his voice, and his eyes were blue ice.

"Among others, pray consider coming to Elveshurst on Tuesday to stay until Saturday, bringing as many of your family as can come," I said.

"Thank 'ee kindly. I'm fond of sport when it's that and no more, and I'll answer you soon."

I gave Sophia my arm. As we walked across the brilliant chamber into the ballroom, her other walkings at my side rose up from the dim dark past, and I could hardly believe they did not haunt her, too. Once we had walked hand in hand up a long beach. Once we had followed a clifftop path toward a witch's cave. Once we had climbed steps to a minister's house with a little parlor and an organ and a picture of the king; and there came a bleakness on my soul and sorrow past any healing in my heart. Why do I think of you now, Ezra Owens? Do I wish Sparrow and Jim and I had played the game you proposed, and which, at my stern refusal, you played alone? If I had, I would have never found Isabel Gazelle. I would have never ridden with the Beni Kabir and found fellowship among the Tuareg. But what did you find, Sparrow, except agony and death?

Yet you died proud, as did all the *Vindictive* men who died, and the debt is on me, and I'll pay it.

3

I led Sophia to a high-backed sofa out of hearing of anyone. For a moment or two we watched the dancing—lovely at its best, only a little pitiful at its worst, the posturings of the fops and the ladies of fashion made up for by the innocence of a few yet young who had somehow been included in the rout—tall, gangling boys and pretty wistful girls; and the German music was romantic and yearning.

"Do you enjoy dancing?" I asked Sophia, whose eyes had misted with tears.

"I've never done much of it. Papa told the truth when he said I was raised on the moors. The old house is near Bodmin. Perhaps you know that's not very far from Tavistock, which Papa mentioned as your home."

"I've been near Bodmin." It was true—long ago I had told Sophia of our putting in at Boscastle and seeing Bodmin moor. Holgar also had visited the region. As an urchin, he had seen Celtburrow and Sophia's grandmother. He had told me so in prison.

"I'm wondering if you could have been the boy who stole flowers from our garden when I was a little girl. You know how impressionable children are—how they remember little things. One of the gardeners caught him and was going to flog him, but my grandmother rescued him. When she asked why he had done it, he said he couldn't help doing it."

"An irresistible impulse," I remarked.

"Grandma said he was from near Tavistock and his name was—Holgar."

"I was the one."

"Good heavens. But I only saw you through a window—you couldn't have been more than ten. That couldn't account for my feeling I'd met you before."

"Not very logically. Do you still have the feeling?"

"No. . . . Yes, I do."

"That's a queer answer."

"I've been trying to deny it—why, I don't know. What queer things go on in our minds! They play tricks on us, don't they? Well, I have an irresistible impulse—as you put it—to tell you something. I heard what happened at Almack's. Papa told me, and my husband, Harvey, told me, too, as he heard it from a friend. It's very unusual for Papa to lose, and he took it especially hard. I mean, it jarred him more than you would expect—more than I can quite account for. Perhaps your giving the money back to the poor oaf—and suggesting he wasn't in condition to play—made it worse. I hate to go to social affairs without Harvey—I lean on him much more than I should—and he was engaged tonight—but I asked Papa to bring me, and the real reason was, I wanted to speak to you."

"What made you think I would be here?"

"Well, you'd attracted attention, which is never lost on Lydia White."

"Did you think your father had asked her to invite me?"

Sophia's eyes darted to mine. "You are very—perspicacious. Yet your guessing that makes it easier for me to tell you what I wanted to tell you. It was to advise you not to play with Papa any more. I suppose you think that's very odd behavior in a daughter—to a stranger."

"No, I can't say that I do."

"I say it. I can't offer any explanation except you gave the money back—and Harvey said it saved the man from ruin—so I'm on your side in this affair, instead of Papa's. I was sure he was going to entice you into a game—whist, most likely, at which he's deadly. He knows how to goad his opponents into rash play. Once he took ten thousand guineas from a man to whom he'd lost only one hundred—it took that much to balm his hurt pride. I'll try to be honest—I don't think hurt pride is the right term, but I don't know what to call it. Papa is a very complex man. I shouldn't say he's vindictive——"

"Vindictive?"

"It's a rather hard word to use."

"Its root is vindicate, to claim or to defend or justify. In olden times it meant to set free. The old meaning of vindictive was only punitive, not revengeful."

She sat very still, her lips parted, her eyes fixed on my face. Then she came to herself with a start.

"Pardon me. Someone told me that—something very like it—a long time ago. It was an American sailor—his ship was named the *Vindictive*. How strange that I'd remember."

"In getting back at a player who'd won from him, would your father use loaded dice?" I asked.

"Oh, you've no right to ask me that, when I came here to warn you. Yet I opened myself to it. Papa is incredibly lucky with honest dice—I suppose lucky is the right word, since it must be pure chance. The devil doesn't help people. No rational person believes that."

"I can't say. I don't know the nature of evil."

"Well, I've told you what I intended to—if Papa knew it, he wouldn't hit me, but he'd be angry and make me very sorry. And now I feel it was—unnecessary."

"Why?"

"I felt it even before I told you—but I went ahead. This situation is different than I thought. I've decided Papa didn't intend to get you to play tonight. He had Lydia ask you for some other purpose."

335

"Can you guess what?"

"No."

"Do you think I can?"

"Yes, I think you know. I think, too, that you're capable of looking out for yourself, and I've never thought that of anyone before—in connection with Papa. Yes, I did think the same about another man —a long time ago—but all the dice went against him, and he's dead. Now please take me back to Papa."

We started back through the throng. Her dark red lips that I had loved were pale, and her eyes looked haunted, and she wanted to say something more. Only when we came in sight of the little lord did she blurt it out.

"Maybe you can do more than just look out for yourself, and that frightens me."

"That isn't very plain."

"When you talked with him about the sea fight, it wasn't just talk and it wasn't self-defense, which is all I'm used to in people who deal with Papa. It was attack."

"Did you think so?"

"Instead of taking sides with you—because you were in the right at Almack's—I may have to take sides with him."

"Could you explain that?"

"You've come here out of Africa. You deal with things that happened long ago. You're bringing back to life things that are dead. And you see—I'm afraid of those things. I want to shut out the past. It's dangerous to all I have left."

I wanted to say, "I'll never harm you, Sophia," but I could not. We were almost in hearing of Lord Tarlton. And it might not be true.

He was playing a sociable game of whist with two ladies and a gentleman of high station. He smiled at Sophia and bowed his head to me.

"So you're back! The game's tight, so sit down or what you will——"

"Thank you, but I'm otherwise engaged," I answered.

"Then, Sophia, wait a bit, and play my next hand. Blackburn, I'll accept with pleasure your invitation for Tuesday next, and I'll speak the same for my son Dick and my son-in-law, Harvey Alford, unless you hear to the contrary."

"That's good news."

"I accept also, Mr. Blackburn," Sophia said clearly.

"Oh, blast it, Sophia, Blackburn doesn't want ladies around, for rough shooting in winter weather."

"On the contrary, you'll be very welcome," I told her quickly. "It's too early for angling, the sport you love, but you can look over the water, and later the salmon will be as fat and sporting as those you used to take on the Cornish moors."

"Sophia, you've been boasting, if not lying," the little lord remarked.

"Oddly enough, I've done neither," Sophia answered in low tones. "Pray come early, all of you, so as not to miss any sport."

Their eyes fixed on my face. The gentleman waiting Lord Tarlton's play uttered a nervous laugh. I bowed and departed.

4

Lydia White's rout was on Wednesday. Before the week was out, three incidents of varying unusualness became linked in my mind and excited my imagination. None deserved the merest mention in the newspapers, although there might be a handful of people in London who, if they knew of it, would muse over the first of the three, hold it in their memories all their lives, tell of it perhaps when they grew old, and even write it down in books.

Walking the cold streets late Thursday night, I thought to take refuge from the bleak and biting wind in a coffee house in the Poultry. As I turned toward its glowing door, three young men emerged and came face to face with me under the streetlight. Two hurried on, but the youngest, no more than twenty-four, stopped and stared, and a most strange expression, beautiful and touching, came into his face. I saw it was a remarkable face, flushed now with wine and, I suspected, with fever. Also I noticed he was dressed rather shabbily as well as inadequately to the weather.

He addressed me in poetry,

What doth ail thee, scarred knight,
Alone and palely loitering
The sedge is withered by the lake
And no birds sing.

At once he hurried after his friends. Instead of entering the inn, I walked on. The verse haunted me, and I wanted to be alone with it awhile. Recalling it with care, I soon fixed it in my memory.

On Saturday afternoon I had a caller who sent in the name Walt Chalker. I had heard it before in some pleasant connection and told the haughty footman to conduct him to the parlor.

"I'll tell you right 'ere, 'e's not a proper person to be let in the front rooms," the servant remonstrated. "He ought to be made to wite in the entry."

"It's too cold to wite there with 'im," I replied, "so kindly show 'im in."

As I opened the parlor door, a shrill outcry, as from a termagant, appeared to ring out behind me.

"Come on back here, hubby, or I'll whack ye with this here broom."

My visitor laughed boyishly at the start he had given me, and instantly I recognized him as one of the star performers of the fete I had given at Tavistock. There he had put on a most realistic Punch and Judy, as well as feats of ventriloquism with a manikin dressed as a jack-tar between shows. Small and swarthy as a gypsy, he had a wonderfully mobile countenance. Although no doubt humbly born, he was not afraid of footmen, had an easy manner, and when he wished, could employ good English.

His business with me was not to beg or borrow but to seek employment. This was his slack season; and the next time I entertained my friends, he would like to show them what he could do. If only gentlemen were present, he would take off the House of Commons acting on a motion to do away with itself, the show being somewhat ribald. If ladies came, a more refined act could be substituted, mainly of ventriloquism and imitations. He had served his turn on the stage and could bring back David Garrick and Colley Cibber from the grave.

I pressed a guinea upon him and asked him to hold open the following Wednesday. Yet the idea of employing him in my solemn pursuit was so distasteful to me, smacking of artifice and dangerous as well, that I had little intention of doing so and probably would not have, except for the chance opening of a book on rainy, darkling, lonely Sunday afternoon. For the first time since I was in the hospital in Malta, I read Hamlet. The prince's stratagem in employing the company of players to disclose the king's guilt struck me with peculiar force; and suddenly I was ashamed of my false nicety. Was I playing a sociable game of whist with Lord Tarlton and his lieutenants, or trying to carry out Captain Phillips's orders at any cost or by any means at hand?

So when I had talked over the matter with Jim, I sent for Walt Chalker and told him exactly what I wanted him to do. Was he capable of it, without histrionics or indignity or exaggeration?

"I reckon this is something mighty close to your heart," he said before he replied.

"Yes, sir, it is."

"Well, I never told you so, but what you did at Tavistock was close to my heart. I, too, was a workhouse boy."

"I'm glad you told me."

"Even at the time, the gentlemen may guess it's a plant, the best I can do, and they're almost sure to, afterward."

"That doesn't matter."

"I'll do my best, and you won't be ashamed of yourself or of me."

"That's all I need to know."

5

Jim and I took carriage to Elveshurst on Monday to make ready for our guests, a cart behind us bringing a large quantity of iced delicacies hard to find in the Weald. Lord Tarlton, Sophia, Dick, and Harvey Alford arrived by coach-and-six on Tuesday afternoon with a maid and valet in attendance in addition to a footman on the driver's seat, and a man-of-war's man, the little lord's man Friday, riding his favorite hunter. Until I greeted them, I had seen Dick only at a distance and Harvey not at all since my return, and I could not help but expect great changes in seventeen years, eight months, and several days.

That is about the age of a locust native to Maine. After seventeen years of sleep and perhaps dreams in his secret place, he comes forth full of vigor and appetite. But Dick and Harvey had been out and around and alive; fools or physicians by now, and looking into their faces, I was baffled and perplexed. I could read almost nothing there because almost nothing was there to read. Dick was a projection of Lord Tarlton, of darker skin, careless instead of meticulous of dress, weaker and hence less dangerous in the long run, more dangerous in any one crossing; he would be more likely to strike out recklessly, while his father would bide his time. I could not doubt that he was a formidable rider. Recklessness and cruelty do not make a finished and rounded horseman, but can win many races. He looked at me with ill-concealed disdain.

I remembered hearing that he had never married. Loving him and wishing to retain him, Lord Tarlton had no doubt frowned on the notion—or else given it his pale, terrifying smile. He had never loved Sophia and was glad to get shed of her, but had got his price for her just the same—a young man whose appearance and manner and name fitted him for his entourage, and whom he had expected to use. This last had not worked out very well, I thought. He was not too strong, but too weak, and Sophia had somehow interfered. But she, too, could make nothing of him except a companion in desperate loneliness; she had not even been able to have children by him, perhaps because of a yearning for suicide. Lord Tarlton looked at him with barely concealed disdain.

But there was much to read in the face of Pike, the little lord's body servant. He had the voice, the strut, and something of the spruceness that the Royal Navy imbues in its petty officers. His heavy-lidded, three-cornered eyes, suggestive of a swine's and somewhat common to pugilists, were of stony blue; one ear had been battered out of shape. He was inclined to glower at all except his master; at him he gazed with a kind of dumb worship and the dull visage became wildly animated when the lord addressed him. He was not very tall but of great strength and endurance; he had a short bull-neck, heavy jaws, a squat nose, stiff sandy hair cut short, hairy wrists, and short, thick, powerful hands. Lord Tarlton ordered him about in a somewhat brutal tone which evidently reassured the man and which he loved to hear.

Along a lagoon followed by water fowl in their evening flight, I had built half a dozen dry platforms, with reed-enclosed sides—duck-blinds, as they were called in Maine. After refreshments, my guests changed to rough clothes, and with their guns and gillies—the latter of my supplying except in the case of Pike, who attended his master—they got into the shelters to shoot high-climbing widgeon, darting teal, air-boring prochard which come and are gone with incredible swiftness, and noble, wary mallards.

I had given Lord Tarlton the best blind, and, taking the next one in the row, let pass all ducks making in his direction. To compensate for this flattery, I fired only at those he had fired at and missed, not only calling attention to these misses but frequently "wiping his eye," in the parlance of hunters—a trial to his temper and self-control. My only motive was pleasure. It was good sport to confuse and needle him—until sport would be over and work began.

The five guns brought down twenty-five birds in an hour's shooting—good fare for all hands. Harvey proved to be high gun, and perhaps for the first time in many years, Lord Tarlton was low.

These trivia passed from my mind when, at eight o'clock, I met with my guests at dinner. We five who had dined together in Malta had met once more about a glimmering board, and what long-laid ghosts rose up by sympathetic magic? No one knew but I. Sophia glimpsed them just around the corner of her eye, and her eyes grew haunted and her face pale except for a crimson circle on each cheek. Still she could not make out their shapes or hear their whisperings.

The dining room of Elveshurst Hall could not compare in splendor with the great chamber of Lepanto Palace, but had somewhat the same style. Although the spread of plate and crystal was not half as fine, it picked up and mingled the countless gleamings of candles, causing a kind of aura over the lace cloth. No fault could be found with my meat and drink as to quality or variety. The service of my new-hired, high-paid footmen from London was as skillful as that of old family retainers. In all this I took grim pleasure.

"How did this pleasant manor come by its name?" Lord Tarlton asked when his face was flushed with wine.

He spoke softly, but silence set in, and Sophia brought her hand quickly to her lips, as though to hold them closed. Only she and I, I thought, remembered the asking of a similar question in regard to Lepanto Palace by her Yankee lover in a scene of hate and evil remote in time and space; but there came a groping within the lordling's brain, to judge from his indrawn eyes; and Dick's eyes glittered with excitement he did not understand.

"My lord, I believe that *hurst* is a West Saxon word meaning 'wood,'" I answered. "No doubt they thought that these woods were peopled by elves."

"Why, I like your learning the lore of the country, or you can blow me down. You ought to put down roots here—marry and found a house. You'll reap some of the harvest yourself, and your grandchildren and great-grandchildren will be great in the land."

"He must have his portrait painted, too," Dick said, the devil in him raised by the wine. He looked with exaggerated seriousness at Harvey.

"I'd advise Lawrence," Harvey replied in a weighty tone.

These two being up to their old tricks was an unexpected development that cast a new and eerie light on the whole scene. As though time had really rolled back, reality became hard to grasp and the mind wandered strangely. This was so with me and, I felt sure, with Sophia; and she was more haunted than I because she remained in the dark. Nor was Lord Tarlton's mind at rest. He had drunk more than either, and a sense of power, with its accompanying arrogance, crept through him; but there was something in the wind that he

341

scented and did not like. He had only minimized, not yet overborne, the awkward fact of my knowing too much about the sea fight. He did not want to be bothered by it now—not now, when the three of them were getting drunk together on a rarer drink than wine—but he dared not forget it. He believed I did not know enough to make him any trouble, even if I should try. The fact remained that I was a rich man of unknown aims who showed no fear of him. He had more respect for money itself than the younger men, which comes with age, experience, and disillusionment.

It seemed that I knew the brew these three men were sharing in dreadful fellowship and glory, and it was evil. I did not know evil's nature or its substance, but I had learned to recognize some of its aspects. Wherever three or more are gathered together, there is an altar and a god; and the congregation of these three was ancient and terribly wicked. It belonged to the devil as surely as the bond between the *Vindictive* men belonged to God. I thought it had begun with their joint denial of the first law and platform of God, which by some mystery may be the essence of God—the brotherhood of man. There are many who mocked it and despised it, and since proof of it ever rose before their eyes, they came to hate it with a deadly hate.

The United States, breaking with feudalism, had been dedicated to that law and was an experiment in its practice. Although it fell woefully short of the ideal, yet the ideal remained; the run and ruck of Americans felt it in their hearts; no other nation in the history of mankind was so nobly founded and offered such good evidence of the law's truth. Its faults were the faults of individual men, not of evil concepts passed down from the sad, dark past. Those who held by those concepts, who did not want the humbly born to raise their heads, those whose own preferments became endangered by men walking free, and the greedy, the hateful, and the base found in America a mighty enemy and hence a positive object of hate. Within Lord Tarlton's cankered soul it had turned into malignance neither sane nor insane, but inhuman, and of the stuff of evil.

I thought I knew when it had happened. With one terrible act he embraced evil, as not a few, but a frightful many, had done before him. It had proven the key to power and place, almost to godhead it seemed to him, and he had come to love it and glory in it. Dick had been suckled in its creed. Sophia had had the protection of her grandmother and the wild moors inhabited by beasts and birds and a few shepherds' families who had no dealings with evil. Harvey had been a proselyte, I thought, and not a very staunch one. His loss of an uncle and an estate in the Revolutionary War had prepared him for the doctrine; he had been under Tarlton's thumb and was a snob of the silly sort without real self-faith, and was, in fact, self-dubious, like so many English snobs. Sophia had kept him away from his master and fellow as much as possible; but again, in their company a great scorn came back upon him, he sat in the high seats, he knew the thrill of power and immunity to punishment; in his face was half-hidden mirth that only his brothers could share or even understand.

Lord Tarlton had made at least three other converts, if I guessed right. Two were American Loyalists who had become Barbary pirates. One was Pike who, although humbly born, was allowed a share in the glory.

This was the second time, once as Homer Whitman and now as Holgar Blackburn, that I had become their laughingstock, antagonist, and, they hoped, their prey. What seemed uncanny coincidence confused me a little while; then I perceived it was not this at all. It was merely the recurrence of event under almost identical circumstances. Before they saw me as an upstart Yankee, one of a hated nation, who dared presume to equality with them and who had got in their way. Now they saw me as an upstart Englishman, one of a class tolerated as long as it was servile, but hated monstrously when it tried to rise, one who lately had made too bold and had got in their way. I did not think they consciously recalled the dinner at Lepanto Palace, but I could not be sure; certainly Sophia was haunted by its memory, and it made unrecognized suggestions to the others. The outcome of that dinner had been a triumph. The Yankee sailor and a good number of his ilk had their hash properly settled. Something told them that Holgar Blackburn's hash would not go unsettled very long.

6

"Have you gone into the genealogy of your family?" Dick asked, with overdone gravity.

"Not yet."

"You should, by all means. It's quite possible that your paternal ancestors had a coat of arms. If so, you'd be perfectly justified in reviving it. If some branch of the distaff had one, you might get permission to adopt it. Or possibly the king would award you your own."

343

"The last would be my preference—to start fresh."

"There's the true Englishman for you," Lord Tarlton cried. "He don't want to wear borrowed plumes. When he's hauled himself up by his own bootstraps, he'll honor those bootstraps, by God!"

"Harvey, what do you think would be a suitable device?" Dick asked.

"A lion rampant, certainly. That would mean his fortune was made in Africa, infested with lions. A miner's pick could be emblazoned on the shield, and a shock of wheat to indicate strong, upstanding yeoman stock. A proper motto is most important—what do you think of 'Blackburn bears brunt'?"

"That's awfully silly, Harvey," Sophia broke in.

"What's silly about it? Doesn't a coat of arms granted in the year 1819 deserve as much care as one of three hundred years ago?"

"How about 'Blackburn bears brands'?" I asked. "I've one on the back of my hand."

"I doubt if you mean that seriously," Sophia said. "Just the same, it's a good motto—too fine a motto to put on a coat of arms." Her eyes were too bright.

"I thank you kindly. Lord Tarlton, you suggest I marry and start a family. In your opinion, should I take a girl in my own class, the sturdy yeomanry, or try to marry into the gentry?"

"I'd say, betwixt and between. In the old days we had franklins—above yeomen, and not quite gentlemen. Certain people in trade and in the so-called professions have the same rank now. Then there'd not be such a gap as to mar felicity, and yet the children would be started on their way."

"You don't think there are impoverished ladies—real ladies—open to marriages of convenience? If she were a widow, she might have children whom I'd make my heirs. Or possibly she might have a well-born lover who could attend to that. Surely I shouldn't complain if thereby I could found a house of honor in the shire!"

A hush fell over the board, and the mock-sober faces changed expression.

"I don't think you're quite in earnest, Mr. Blackburn," the little lord remarked.

"Our host's a bit of a wag," cried Harvey, who was getting quite drunk.

At that moment Jim, dressed in sober black, filled my champagne glass. This was according to his rule. When the hired footmen had served the others, I turned again to Lord Tarlton.

"My lord, as the ranking person here, will you offer the toast of obligation?"

"I'd be pleased to." And when we had risen with him: "To George III—old, mad, but still the king!"

When we had seated, I rose again.

"I would like to have you join me in a toast to the head of the other great English-speaking nation of the world. To James Monroe, President of the United States."

"Oh, that happened before!" Sophia burst out.

"What in the devil do you mean?" her father demanded.

"The other dinner. You can pretend you don't remember it, but you do. You asked Homer and he came. It was exactly like this. It's come again."

"Are you mad?"

"I'm not far from it."

"Pardon my daughter's erratic behavior, Mr. Blackburn. I think she refers to a dinner to which I invited an American seaman with whom she thought she was in love. His name was Homer—yours is Holgar, enough like it to jog her memory—and quite true, he offered a toast to his president, perfectly proper conduct. A few days later he was lost at sea—which she took rather hard."

Still without rising, the pretty nobleman reached for and fondled the ivory knob of the light cane leaning against his chair.

"Yes, sir," I said.

"Now for this toast you offer. I must remind you that after the toast to the king, it's customary to drink to the Regent. However, Mr. Monroe is the acknowledged head of a state with whom the king is presently at peace, and if you wish to vary the procedure, why, we'll rise and join you."

"Thank you, I do."

"Then I'd add this—may he lead the Yankees in the way they should go!"

"You said that before, too," Sophia murmured.

"You must harbor a deep admiration for Mr. Monroe," Lord Tarlton said when we were seated.

"I know very little about him, my lord, but I greatly admire America."

"After the Americans have waged two wars against their rightful king? That takes a good deal of tolerance."

"I take it that all the people of my class admire America, and most of them wanted her to win."

345

"You amaze me. I wonder how they'll feel after the third war. Then we won't be busy with Napoleon, and the outcome may surprise all admirers of America. I remind you that no revolt against the throne ever endured for long, from the peasants' uprising under Watt Tyler, through Monmouth's, through the Civil War, clean down to the peasants' rebellion under Washington. The latter has lasted forty-two years. That seems a long time—but the mills of the gods grind slowly. We shall see."

Dick sprang to his feet, his face darkly flushed.

"I drink to a ship that did her part in teaching traitors a lesson," he cried. "To *Our Eliza*."

"I'll join you in it, but let it go at that," Lord Tarlton replied.

"I remember meeting one of her crew," I said when the table had stilled again.

Again it stilled until the nobleman spoke. "Is that possible?"

"He was an East Indian who had settled in Africa," I went on. "Before then he had been a lascar, serving under you on the sloop of war *Our Eliza*. He had learned to speak English and told me of the battle."

"He did?"

"Yes, my lord."

"Is that where you got the impression that the *Saratoga* sank on the following evening? For I thought you said it was some sort of letter——"

"I had disremembered, as we say in Tavistock."

"I doubt if the expression is Devon. It sounds more like Yankee."

"Puran told me that two other survivors of the fight were in Africa," I went on. "Both were American Tories who became officers under you. One, Hamed Reis, became a pirate captain under the Sultan of Morocco. The other, called Murad Reis, served the Pasha of Tripoli. It was he who ambushed and sank the American schooner the *Vindictive* off the Aegadian Isles. Her course had been betrayed to him by someone in Malta."

Harvey turned slowly pale, Dick had a witless stare, and I could not look at Sophia. But Captain Godwine, Lord Tarlton, sat gracefully in his chair, a look almost of beauty on his face, his lips pursed a little, as though from thought.

"You've picked up some odd stories in your comings and goings about Africa, Mr. Blackburn," he remarked at last.

"I'll try to remember them in detail on a later occasion."

"If I'm not mistaken—Sophia will correct me in that case—the *Vin-*

dictive was the ship on which her suitor—the one she called Homer —was lost."

Sophia stared at her plate. "Shake not—your gory locks—at me," she gasped, her hand at her throat.

"If you can't talk sense, Sophia, please don't talk at all."

"Then I won't talk at all. I never have." She leaped up and ran away, weeping.

"Didn't you speak too harshly to her, my lord?" I asked. "She was merely quoting Shakespeare. You remember the speech, I know— Macbeth's to the ghost of Banquo."

"I remember it well. You're a very cultivated man. Now if you'll excuse me, I'll see about my daughter."

With his cane in his small white hand and his feet straight before him, he walked out of the room as might a phoenix newly risen from ashes.

"Now there's nothing to stop us from having a good old-fashioned brandy bout," Dick told Harvey.

CHAPTER 28

Ghosts Walking

1

THE BOUT had lasted only a round or two when both contestants took the count, one with his head pillowed on his arms on the table, the other gently sliding from his chair to the floor. The hired footmen lugged them to their beds. Jim did not have to touch them.

They were down at nine, helping themselves liberally to the kidney pudding, fried herring, curried eggs, and other breakfast dishes, none the worse for their dissipations, indeed, remarkably fresh of face and bright of eye. It was doubtful whether they remembered some discomforting remarks I had made at the dinner or wondered if they had dreamed them. Sophia looked wistful and touching and quite beautiful. It seemed that she kept away from me when I stood alone, but invariably came up when I talked to Harvey in ill-hidden protectiveness.

Lord Tarlton appeared in half an hour, blaming the years on his back for his tardiness, but by all sign impervious to their weight— graceful, pretty, and courtly. No concern over last night's events appeared to cross his mind. He spoke of the good food and the fine wines without mark of study. I could be sure he would not speak of the long past until again I raised the subject; and only if he were brought to bar before a jury of his peers need he answer questions. But he could not deny that terrifying possibility—he did not know my weapons or my intent—and I was not troubled by his seeming complacence, and felt an inkling that all went well.

My guests had dressed for the field. When I had placed them in butts behind a hedge in a stubble field, a line of boys beat out a wide strip of partridge cover, flushing out the coveys which settled in thick woods. Their task was now to close in, and advancing slowly and carefully under the direction of the keeper, to drive them over the guns. Each guest had a pair of double-barreled pieces and a loader. As before, Lord Tarlton was attended by Pike.

"Blackburn, aren't you going to set us a good example?" he asked when I hung back of the butts.

"I may shoot a little when the drive's well underway."

"In the meantime I'll ask a favor. I shot badly yesterday afternoon —I didn't think I was flinching from the trigger, but perhaps I was. Will you seat yourself about ten feet back of Pike and watch a few shots? I think you're gunner enough to spot my fault."

"I doubt it, but will try, with pleasure."

I did not sit down but crouched, and not more than six feet behind the stocky tar. Firing at the first flight, the nobleman jerked at the trigger, missing with both barrels.

"You flinched rather badly that time, my lord," I said.

"I was afraid so. See if this is not better."

Firing again, he flinched at the first shot, but got off the other smoothly and dropped his bird. As flock after flock came over, he shot with varying smoothness, cursing when he missed, greatly elated when he killed clean, meanwhile questioning me as to his form. It seemed a remarkable exhibition of his personality and, under ordinary circumstances, I would have found it intensely interesting. But these circumstances were not ordinary; and I gave him only the outer fringe of my attention.

A scene pregnant with terrible event may have a strange beauty. Covey after covey of partridge broke from the woods in search of shelter; trustfully they flew until they came suddenly in sight of the guns; at this betrayal by their familiar haunts, they swerved in terror, some of them surviving to fly again, some darting into the unseen swishing pellets. I remembered the grapeshot's terrible sound as it broke over a deck. I saw the birds ineffably alive, borne swiftly on God-given miraculous wings, and I saw that life end, all over in an unguarded and undreamed instant, innocence and beauty ceasing; and I heard the thuds on the frost-hardened ground. The shots rang out with a kind of festiveness. Two of the shooters became wildly animated, calling back and forth, but the naked trees stood one and one, incommunicant with one another, and looked drear.

I felt sure the moment I was waiting for was near. It was not undreamed and unguarded like the instant of the partridges' sudden darkness and downward pitch. Lord Tarlton had fired one barrel and was holding the fire of the other until a target offered; Pike had finished loading the alternate gun, but was fingering the hammer and mumbling to himself.

He turned his head and spoke to me.

"Your honor, have ye got a penknife?"

"Yes."

"Loan it to me, your honor." Meanwhile he was turning toward me, the gun held in both hands. "There's a piece of trash stuck——"

At that instant I struck the barrel of his gun with mine. It was too late for him to stop the quickening action of his hands, and both barrels roared almost simultaneously. The charges struck the ground fully thirty feet distant. The man turned yellow-white and almost dropped the piece. He did not speak nor did I, but Lord Tarlton spoke. Without looking over his shoulder, he talked in a tone of chill reproof.

"You blasted my ears, Blackburn, and I wish you'd warn me, hereafter, before you shoot."

No doubt he prided himself on that speech, brilliantly conceived and perfectly delivered. He had pictured himself repeating it to a coroner in what would appear as a commendably forthright account of a fatal accident at a cut-and-dried inquest. Dick would be sitting among the unimportant witnesses, looking very grave; at this point he and Harvey would exchange solemn glances.

"I didn't shoot, my lord."

Now the little lord turned and looked. His eyes were round, as he had never intended to let anyone see them; his pretty mouth was drawn; his delicately tinted cheeks had paled. One of the barrels of his piece remained cocked and primed, so I held mine handy in my arms for him to see. He did not know that by some law I did not understand, but must obey, my gun was unloaded.

"What the devil happened?" he burst out, but though he spoke with vehemence, there was no wintry rattle in his voice.

"Pike fired both barrels by accident."

"He did, did he? Did the charge come near you?"

"Not at all."

"You stupid dog," he cried, turning on Pike. "You careless swine! Take that!"

Lord Tarlton struck him in the jaw, then kicked him in the knee.

"I didn't go for to do it," Pike yelled.

"Nobody said you did, you clumsy fool."

There fell a slight pause. Lord Tarlton kept from looking at me, but he waited for me to speak.

"No, Pike, nobody said you did," I said.

"But I've told him a thousand times——" Snatching up his cane that was always close at hand—today it was a light rattan—he cut the fellow thrice across the shoulders.

"What's the brabble?" Dick cried, running up.

"Pike was careless with my gun and has been punished for it."

Dick made no display, and I was reasonably certain that the event had taken him by surprise. That need not surprise me; the pretty nobleman found pleasure and also played as safe as possible in plotting alone, acting with trusted tools. He loved a *fait accompli*. Pike rubbed his jaw, his knee, and his shoulder in turn, his doglike gaze fixed on his master's face. I doubted if I had impressed him with my ready and swift guard—exactly what had happened had fogged over in his mind—but from now on he would take more pains not to bitch his master's business. Didn't en larrup him right! Wa'n't en a daizy!

2

"While you're getting on with the sport, I'll send for a round of brandies," I suggested. And when Pike looked at me, grinned, and wiped his mouth, "There'll be one for you, too."

For it would be too grim a joke to soothe the little lord's upset nerves and neglect his bully boy's. But I did not go at once to the refreshment wagon. Instead I made for the line of beaters about to enter a second strip of cover and spoke privately to the keeper. Thereby my guests would have dull sport the rest of the drive.

I did that, and then had nothing to do of any profit or comfort. While I had run no great risk in my sudden craving for direct and violent action, the course had been ill-charted, and its outcome empty. My hopes had taken a great fall. I was in no mood to believe that my future strokes would be any more telling. To play cat-and-mouse with my great enemy was wildly exciting; but often the game itself made me forget the goal; and the devil laughed. If he struck again, again the blow would be indirect, stealthy, unpunishable. He was too cunning, too secure, to be frightened into desperate attack. Unless I could find his Achilles heel. . . .

My thoughts were interrupted by a movement in the brushwood down a little road. Then into the clearing rode one of my grooms with a young lady in a stylish riding habit. I perceived at once that he was taking her to the shooting butts; but what her errand might be, important enough to bring her here in person, I could not imagine.

She had not yet seen me, for I stood in shadow, while the pale winter sunlight showed her plain. My first impression was of bright color. Her horse was a bright bay, her skirt buff, and her jacket green, and the hair unhidden by her low-crowned hat was glimmering gold. Then I was astounded to realize I had seen her once before. That occasion was so utterly dissociated with this one that I could scarcely believe my eyes. It was at the fete I had given at Tavistock nine months before. She had ranged the grounds and enjoyed the entertainments in the company of an English lord and his family. I remembered her coloring, high as a golden pheasant's. Alan had named the people she was with, but did not know her.

She caught a first glimpse of me and spoke in low tones to Perkins, the groom. "Aye, en's the master," I heard him answer. Then as she looked straight at me, intending to speak to me, I saw the same expression of dismay come into her bright face that I had seen when she returned my glance before.

She got rid of it and rode up to me. I touched my hat.

"I recognize you now," she said. "You're Mr. Holgar Blackburn. I saw you the great day at Tavistock."

"I saw you, too," I answered.

"Well, I've done a cheeky thing, but I couldn't help it. Didn't you invite me to come down here with the others? Sophia—Mrs. Alford—told me you did."

"I invited Lord Tarlton and his family."

"Papa said I could come, and then they slipped off when I was at dancing school."

"You must be Lord Tarlton's daughter Eliza."

"Of course I am. I thought you recognized me, too. I'm Eliza Tarlton. I went with some other people to Tunbridge Wells and then rode over alone. But if it's inconvenient——"

"It's not inconvenient, and your coming has given me great pleasure."

"It won't give Papa any, or Dick, but I want you to tell them what you just told me."

Still another memory came, dim and pale, one which at first I could not quite seize. But that was because it had come so far in time and space; and in a second or two it glazed like the morning star on the deserts of Baeed. Far away on those deserts, long ago when I was yet a slave, a beautiful young girl who looked to be carved with a sword liked to ride with old Timor and me. When we slipped off from her for what we thought was a good reason, it was not long before we saw her following us. She would ride into the wind, kick up dust to blow in our faces, then join us with a toss of head and a wide smile.

Eliza Tarlton reminded me of Isabel Gazelle.

"I'm sure you're mistaken about your father and half brother being displeased."

"Dick's jealous of how Papa loves me. There's no harm in telling you—you'd see it yourself in five minutes—everyone knows it. But Papa wants to keep me a little girl. He's penned me up at Celtburrow and hardly ever lets me come to London. I dare say he's old and eccentric—though he seems young to me—and desperately afraid something will happen to me. Did you ever hear of anything so absurd?"

She seemed anxious to ingratiate herself with me. Talking rapidly in a gay tone, she had been looking about her, taking in the scene with sparkling eyes, patting her horse, listening to the desultory shooting. But as she asked the question, she gazed again into my face.

Her eager expression swiftly faded. Her gray eyes widened.

3

Beautiful beyond denial, with the generosity that beauty gives— like to that which bravery gives—she looked for beauty's reflection everywhere and wanted to find it in everyone. Since my appearance distressed and dismayed her, she made a special effort to be sociable, her eyes skipping me the while. As she talked with great girlish animation, I had a chance to drink her in.

I was not surprised that Godwine, Lord Tarlton, had sired two beautiful daughters and that neither of them looked like him in any perceptible degree or hardly like each other. In contemplating and in observing him, I could never feel that he loved woman—that would have stood between him and evil—and the few he had ever pursued since his affair with the Countess Isabel had been great rarities whose conquest fed his vanity. Sophia's mother had been of the ancient house of Linden, Eliza's mother Elspeth had come from the isle of Jersey, had been poor and of obscure family, yet had dazzled everyone, a tremendous prize. He had won her in his custom of winning prizes, but not cheaply: he had given her his great name. To her babe he had given the name of largest bearing upon his soul of any in the world with the possible exception of his own. The first ship over which he held absolute command, whereby his devouring lust for power was first relieved—a ship that made the winds of heaven serve his will, that buffeted great gales and soared across the vast, dark, fearsome, unplumbable deeps of ocean —was named *Our Eliza*. The baby was My Eliza.

The wild moors about Celtburrow served her as they had served Sophia. But a great difference had lain between their conditions of confinement. Sophia had been kept there so that Lord Tarlton could be rid of her, Eliza so that he could keep her for his own. He almost lost her once, I thought. Proud and unmasterable Elspeth had determined to leave him and take her daughter with her when the sea took her instead. The sea had taken another who had balked him, the *Saratoga*—again, just in time. It must seem to him that he were god of the sea.

My mind had been groping for the basic bond between Eliza and Isabel Gazelle. Both had been given grace, elegance, honesty, and the great manner which is natural when it is not consciously ceremonial. Isabel Gazelle was of ancient lineage. Eliza was not so on her mother's side, and a train of thought had set me to doubting whether her father's descent was as high as he believed, but that made little difference if one were raised in a royal environment and had not the least self-doubt. For the rest, she had long, clean lines—in this like Isabel, too—was yare like her, wide and childish of smile, blithe of voice, beautifully muscled and boned, and superbly alive.

Thus endowed, it was almost inevitable that she would spring off her horse and walk beside me down the road.

"The country people still talk about your fete," she was saying. "I think that giving thousands of people such a wonderful day was almost as important as giving forty people a decent home."

"That's an interesting viewpoint."

"You remember how they cheered you!"

"I haven't forgotten it."

She gave me a quick glance. "I wish I could say something——"

"Please say anything you like."

"That last cheer. Lord Bray—I was visiting his daughter—is a kind man and was afraid it would hurt your feelings. I didn't think so—but if it did, you took it wrongly. They were trying to put out their hands to you. It was so beautiful I almost cried."

"I didn't take it wrongly, Eliza, I took it rightly."

"I'm so glad. And I like to have you call me by my first name. You wouldn't if I weren't welcome. Aren't given names the important ones, instead of last names? A whole clan may bear the same last name—all are born with it, and that's that. But those who love you give you a first name for your very own."

"I never thought of it that way."

"I am Eliza. As much as I love Papa, I don't want to be Papa, I want to be me. When anyone calls me Miss Tarlton, I feel more his daughter than I feel myself."

"Kings and queens are of similar mind. They are Charles or Elizabeth, maybe with a numeral, but nothing about Stuart or Tudor. I knew a princess in Africa who had no last name."

"A black princess?"

"A brown one, and you remind me of her."

"What was her first name?"

"Isabel."

"Isn't that strange?"

"I think so."

"I want to hear all about her when we have time. Would you like to have me call you Holgar? I knew you before any of the others—at least, I was your guest. It would sort of break the ice——"

I was afraid she would go into complicated explanations and embarrass herself.

"I'd be greatly pleased."

"I'm so glad. And it will give Dick a jar! Papa, too, may be taken aback—although I never know how the cat will jump, as we say in the West Country." Her brow clouded a little, and she went on in a voice not as glowing as before. "After having that wonderful time at Tavistock, of course I couldn't bear to miss this affair, and there was another reason I wanted to come. I've been a little worried about Papa."

"Is that possible?"

"It doesn't seem possible, does it? He's so—infallible. But in the last few days—specially since Lydia White's rout—he hasn't been himself. He paces the floor at night or sits very still for an hour or more and has even spoken sharply to me, an unheard of thing. I wanted to be with him and see that he doesn't overdo. I do hope he won't be angry——"

"I'm afraid you won't find him in an amiable mood. There was a little accident today that upset him."

"What was it?"

She had spoken quickly and off guard.

"A fowling piece went off by accident."

"Did the charge almost hit him? I pity the poor oaf who did it!"

"No, it would have hit me if I hadn't knocked aside the barrel."

The free swing of her stride was briefly broken. "Whose gun was it?"

"Lord Tarlton's, but Pike was holding it."

"Pike was holding it," she echoed, not knowing she had spoken.

"He was loading for his master and turned to me to borrow a knife. One hand must have touched the trigger."

She stopped and appeared to be looking at the butts, only a hundred yards distant now. The shooters had gathered about the refreshment wagon and had not noticed us yet.

"I can't read your face, but there's something in your voice," she said in great strain. "I'm going to ask you a strange question, and it's necessary you give me a straight answer. Did you suspect he did it on purpose?"

"Why should he?"

"That wasn't what I asked. Oh, please tell me."

"The question rose in my mind, of course."

"Had you done anything to make him angry? I'll tell you the kind of thing I mean—won a great deal of money off Papa or made Papa trouble or even said something to him that Pike might think was insulting. Pike is a terribly dangerous man. He worships Papa like a dog—more like a tamed wolf—and of course Papa has no right to have him around, but won't get rid of him. I know that once he had

355

to keep him from killing someone—a drunken fool who slapped Papa's face. If you're the one who's causing him this trouble—and I just now thought you might be—well, you'd better stop or keep out of Pike's way."

The threat came suddenly, unpremeditated and passionate. As she gave it, she looked full into my face.

"I think you may misjudge Pike—in a curious way."

"What do you mean?"

"I think he may be capable of murder. But he had nothing to do with my being behind him and in easy reach."

"If you happened by and he saw his chance——"

"I didn't happen by. Lord Tarlton said he's been flinching and asked me to sit there, to help him correct it. He said to sit ten feet behind Pike. Happily, I sat only six feet behind him—otherwise I couldn't have knocked aside his gun barrel."

Eliza uttered one little "Oh!" as though I had struck her, then walked rapidly toward her people. When they saw her come into the open field and turned and stared, she waved in well-feigned gaiety.

4

Without hurrying, I was close enough behind her to watch her reception. Dick turned his back on her in open disdain. From Sophia it was warm—I felt sure she loved her—while Harvey looked anxiously from her to Lord Tarlton. The little nobleman gazed from her to me, and it must be that some inner force failed him for a few seconds, for suddenly he looked old. The debility passed, and he spoke to Eliza in an exasperated but not harsh tone.

"What in the devil are you doing here?"

"I was invited, and you practically promised I could come. Holgar said he was glad to have me, didn't you, Holgar?"

"I certainly did, Eliza."

But this frivolous interplay was forced and out of place, as she knew full well. Meanwhile, she could not look at Pike, and instead gazed at Lord Tarlton—small, perfect, delicate but indestructible, his hunting habit handsome as a fop's, but stronger than the thorns; his white hair gracing his pretty face, and his white hand toying with his stick; but the east wind at his call, and the icy blue of winter sky serving his glance. Was she reassured? Although lost and forgotten things sometimes cast their shadows over her ways, she could never doubt his love. Believing in that, how could she doubt him?

Yet I watched her in deepening anxiety and suspense. Meanwhile, the face of nature began to change. Her mood became dark and her voice sorrowful and her signs ominous. The yellow stubble lost its cheerful winter color under cloud-shadows. The rising wind made the boughs of the gaunt trees rattle.

"Blackburn, has my daughter your permission to address you by your given name?"

"My lord, we've both agreed to employ first names, since she's been my guest before."

"Well, miss, I don't think your stay will be very long. There's a change of weather coming, unkind to bones as old as mine. If it turns out as I think, I'll have to forego our host's good cheer and return to London tomorrow."

"I think you should, Papa, since you look worn and nervous, but you'll have Pike and the servants to look after you, so I don't see why we others shouldn't stay on."

She spoke in a clear young voice, without hint of entreaty, her head high, her eyes fixed on his and very bright, and a high flush on her cheekbones. Her little gesture of defiance against the evil and tragedy thickening about her should have cut to the quick even Godwine and his malign son.

He doesn't love you, Eliza. Evil can love nothing but itself. He only covets you and wants to command you as he did your namesake. It is too late for Sophia to escape. Is it too late for you?

What if I should love you, a last hostage-giving to fortune? I could learn to easily, for love of woman is the mother spring of my nature and manhood, and you are woman in her young and declared beauty. You grace the ground on which you tread. I could easily see you as personifying the beauty of woman everywhere, the thrill of life, the joy of youth. And you remind me of Isabel Gazelle.

Such love might be only an ideal which I would cherish in the days to come and smile over by my lonely hearth. Thus it could not harm you, and in the final fury of the storm just now beginning to break, it might save you. But fate is not satisfied with this kindly and due conclusion. You are lovely and touching, but your color is very bright. You have golden hair and snowy skin which flushes crimson and wide red lips and luminous gray eyes. As you stand there, fearing my gaze, you cause a brightness in the lowering gloom.

There are surgings through me of great power. I cannot deny

them. I do not try to master them. Like wild horses I have roped and would ride across the desert, I give them free rein.

5

The wind shrilled, and some kestrels, seeking shelter from a gale breaking on the rugged Kentish coast, cried overhead.

"Why, Eliza, if you and the others wish to stay a few days, I'd have no objection, and would get along well," the nobleman had answered.

"We'll talk it over later." This soon she was penitent.

"Now let's go to the fire," Sophia said with a little shiver.

"Eliza, if you want to walk with your father, I'll have Perkins take your horse to the stable."

"Thank you, I do."

"We can pass the stables without going out of our way, and I'll show you a gray stallion almost as handsome as your bright-bay mare. Lord Tarlton, I've been wondering how he'd run against your magnificent black—in some not too-distant future. Perhaps you'd like to see him, too."

"There are few sights I like better than a good horse."

I had Perkins turn El Stedoro into the paddock and he came whinnying to the gate where I stood. He was in fine fettle, his dappled skin like satin, and the wind made him skittish and tossed his black mane and tail; still he was too big, raw-boned, and ungainly-looking to please these lovers of the classic type of English hunter. As they took in his long, gaunt neck, big feet, block-shaped head, and Roman nose, they did not know what to say.

"Look at those quarters!" Lord Tarlton exclaimed. "He's a 'chaser, or blow me down! But you called him handsome!"

"I think that was Blackburn's little joke," Dick said.

"What is he, if you'll tell me. There's a hint of Arab about the ears and the tail, and those shoulders are pure English."

"An agent of mine got him in Alexandria. His name is El Stedoro, and though he's not much to look at, I've gained a deal of confidence in him when the going's rough. If you're a little cold, maybe you'd like to warm yourself and Donald Dhu, setting him a pace." Donald Dhu, meaning Black Donald, was Tarlton's great 'chaser.

"I'm not cold in the least, but amenable to the suggestion."

"A good course is down this road, across the brook, over the pasture gate, on the grass to the hedge, jump it and return—straight out and back just over a mile. You took all three jumps riding to the duck blinds yesterday afternoon."

"That's not too hard for me, but Dick rides in my place when the course is long and the jumps cruel. Both nags need a sweating, and I a limbering. Shall we put a small premium on coming in first?"

"That would be agreeable."

"Would a hundred guineas suit you?"

I expected him to say ten guineas at the most. He had been over the course, but had never run it.

"It would suit me well."

"Then, Pike, get him out here; and I'm glad you thought of it, Blackburn, to round out the day."

El Stedoro and I had learned to communicate freely concerning my riding and his running. I could give a good show of letting him go while he understood perfectly he must hold back from his most furious bounds to save strength for some trial beyond. I had plotted to let Donald Dhu win, then have the excuse of seeking revenge. Now, although Lord Tarlton's wager was intended to persuade me he hoped and expected to win, I was quite sure he was out to lose, in preparation for a *coup de main*. He was an old turfman who ran no foolish risks. He had a higher opinion of my mount and me than the rash bet would have me believe.

So I decided to come in first provided I could do so without turning the gray brute loose, and if I could not, the game was not worth the candle.

In a few minutes Dick cried, "Go!" I had already known that Donald Dhu was a superhunter, the supreme product of the English and Irish stud farms developing the type, and hence one of the great 'chasers of the age. His pedigree was awesome, a returning again and again of the blood of the Byerly Turk and the Darley Arabian, with the magic name of Eclipse mixed with parvenus of great achievement. He and his few peers took turns at beating one another—the slightest mishap or fault by horse or rider could decide the issue—and only the phenomenal horse could put him in the shade. I owned a phenomenal horse, unless the hard-bitten horsemen of the Beni Kabir missed their guess. Both Donald Dhu and his lordly owner would be surprised to know that the gray fright was the splendid black's cousin on both sides of the family.

In the brisk run of a mile with six easy jumps, I held El Stedoro more than a shade under his top speed, his performance being impressive nonetheless. I was quite sure that Lord Tarlton's hands had

359

been light on the whip, heavy on the rein, despite his manner of surprise and chagrin when the gray won by a length. Eliza appeared relieved, as though this little victory had closed my account with him. Harvey raised his eyebrows to Dick, a piece of stupidity that Dick rebuffed by looking away. For reasons I could not calculate, Sophia looked ill.

6

The flames in the big fireplace of the drawing room crackled and cavorted, charming the eyes with sunset colors alive and leaping, and the cozy warmth of the body lulled the mind; but the windows darkened before their time and sometimes rattled in the wind, and now and then the sitters heard the elm trees cough.

I did not sit with them, having left them to their silences, their sporadic talk, and their secret speculations. Only when the gloom of early night had infiltrated unseen the heavy shadows of late afternoon, and they were dreading going to their chill rooms to dress by a hasty fire, did I come with a welcome proposal. It was to have the evening meal served on small tables set about the hearth, and we to partake in our warm field clothes. Except in battle and during storms at sea, Lord Tarlton had changed for dinner as regularly as a chicken molts, but he was the first to agree.

The many dishes lost no savor, glasses brimmed with cheer. Only Sophia and Eliza remained sharply on guard, ever the woman's part; warmth and insinuant wine lulled the three men. But when brandy glowed in the crystal decanter, a footman brought me a message.

"There's a fellow witin' in the kitchen entry what gives 'is name as Peebles, a woodcutter from Ashdown Wood. 'E says you sent for 'im."

"See that his hands are clean and his clothes brushed and show him in." Then to the others, "This is quite a remarkable man—one of the last of the witch masters, if I can believe my tenants."

An instant later the great ventriloquist, Walt Chalker, entered the room.

I could hardly believe this was the same man. I could not have possibly recognized him if he had taken me by surprise, and I lost all fear of Eliza associating him with the amazing showman she had watched at Tavistock. His clothes were a hard weave of undyed wool with boots of undressed hide, three days' growth of black stubble covered his lips and jowls, and without the dark rings under his eyes that I thought were walnut stain, he could be taken for either a

360

forest hermit or a gypsy. He came shyly toward me, his cap in his hands, without the slightest trace of showmanship.

"Thank 'ee honor, for ye've a'n't forgot ye bade me coom along," he said in perfect and uninscribable imitation of the country speech.

"I'm glad you've come, Matt Peebles. And what can you do to entertain my guests?"

"I can tell fortunes with cards. The ladies like that. I can read palms, too."

"They've seen that before."

"Sometimes, I can prophesy. The spirit won't come on me every time and sometimes an evil spirit speaks through my lips, and I prophesy false. But it takes a deal out o' me, your honor, and shakes me to the marrow of my bones."

Lord Tarlton, playing with his stick, spoke in mock sympathy.

"No doubt you're not up to the morrow's labor, and deserve an extra fee."

"Nay, your lordship. I charge naught for what comes to me from I know not where. But if the yarbs I dig in the wood helps a sick body, or drives off pain from a liddle child, I'll take red money for 'em if the folk be poor, or white if they're well off." And it came to me that Walt Chalker was living his part.

"Is it second sight, that you knew I was a lord?"

"Nay sir, I've seen you pass, in your coach, on the road to Tunbridge Wells. The country folk know well your face, and that of your son."

"Do you think the spirit would come to you tonight?" I asked.

"'Tis a good night for't, your honor, bitter and dark, with the east wind raving. Horses stamp in their stalls on such nights, and the wild things cannot rest, and it must be them we can't see, go abroad. But your honor, these be great folk here tonight. And if ye want me to prophesy, some of 'em will have to clasp hands with me."

"I'll be one, Matt," Sophia said quickly.

"I'll be the other," I told him. "Do we sit in a ring?"

"Aye, with the lamps out, but the fire will give light enough. And ye must sit still a liddle while, and be patient."

When we began to form the ring, Lord Tarlton took Sophia's other hand, with Dick on his other side. Harvey sat next, which left Eliza between him and me. She seemed loath to give me her hand. When she did, it felt chill. But it was a lovely, silken, shapely hand, stronger than I had thought, and reminding me of Isabel's.

I had told the footman not to enter the room, so the fire went unmended. But the light receded so imperceptibly that no one noticed the growing shadow on the performer's face. Reclining his head, he seemed to go straight to sleep; in about five minutes he stirred and moaned as though in a bad dream.

Then he spoke in a strained and halting tone.

"Harvey! Harvey!"

"Yes?"

"There's a soldier here—an officer—he's been wounded in the breast. His name is Edgar—Edmund—Edward. He bids you mind the Indian bow and quiver you found in the old trunk."

"I had an uncle of that name," Harvey said in a trembling voice. "I found the bow and arrows he'd sent from America when I was a babe."

"He wants you to know he wasn't murdered by his captors after the battle at Freedom—Freeman's farm. He was brought in sorely wounded, and cared for kindly, until he died."

This last was the fruit of an easy investigation I had had made in America. Sophia had told me of the bow and quiver a little boy had prized.

"Great God!" Harvey breathed.

"Dicky! Dicky!" the supposed witch master moaned. "There's an old woman—her name is Bertha—she was your nurse."

"I never had a nurse named Bertha," Dick snarled.

"Yes, you did, Dick," Sophia breathed.

Then what seemed a woman's voice rose from the dimness across the room.

"Don't deny me, Dicky."

"There's someone—this fellow's confederate—in this room."

"Look and see, Dick," I said.

"What is it? What does she want?"

"She begs you to have no more dealings with Jules—Julian—Julius. It will cause your death."

"Who's Julius? I never heard of Julius."

"She says you met him—was it last night?—at a wine shop in—Notabile." The performer pronounced this name clearly. "It's on an island. The women wear black drapes on their head. The name of the shop is—Don John of Austria. She says that your brother—your sister's suitor—waited outside. And because you dealt with him, many died."

"Of all the lying——"

"Nay, nay, 'twas not last night. She don't know when it was. And

362

now one who died from that dealing has come here. He wants to speak to Sophia."

"To me?"

"He asks, Have you forgotten the witch's cave?"

"What is his name?"

"Homer—Whitman."

"I've had enough of this trumpery," Lord Tarlton burst out, breaking the circle.

Then a deep voice, with the twang of a New England skipper's, rose just at hand—as though the speaker were standing by the hearth.

"Wait a minute, Captain Sir Godwine Tarlton!"

"That's trumpery, too!"

"Trumpery, is it? I'm Captain Phillips of the *Vindictive,* that you betrayed to Murad Reis. For that you'll die on a gibbet, and go to hell."

It was a remarkable but patent feat of ventriloquism. Godwine, Lord Tarlton, sprang to his feet and seized an iron poker. As he turned on the limp figure in the chair, I caught his little wrist in a grip like iron. All the rest were on their feet, and now every movement was arrested by a sudden writhing of the man's body and his deep, harrowing groan. A fallen ember blazing up showed his eyes wide open in a stare like death's and his face pale and flaccid as in death.

His lips began to move in great travail. Forth came a voice that seemed from a vast distance, speaking words sacred to me that I had never repeated to a human soul.

"Fight on . . . till . . . Cap'n's gone."

Lord Tarlton had raised his free hand to strike me when he saw the pallor of my face. The iron he had held dropped clanging on the stones of the hearth.

CHAPTER 29

Parry and Thrust

1

SHORTLY AFTER my home-coming at Tavistock I had had Alan call upon Lloyd's in London on the matter of buying an American ship. The great association of underwriters had the inside track in the news and gossip of shipping; and one of its agents offered to pursue the inquiry for a reasonable fee. Since autumn I had been told of several vessels being available and had looked at two.

I had hardly returned from Elveshurst after Lord Tarlton's visit there when the agent sent a *commissaire* to my house on Charles Street. I was to meet him at once at Blackwall to see something pretty. Since he himself loved ships, I was sure he would not disappoint me, and on arriving there, I was surprised only by the moderation of his language. No palace in England was more beautiful to my sight than the long, low, sharp brig not long from Boston.

Her master and owner had died two days out from Land's End, and her competent mate, Mr. Blain, had brought her into port. He was of the opinion that his widow, English-born and accompanying her husband for a visit to her old home, would like to sell the ship and remain in her native land and never take to the seas again. So Jim and I surveyed her with great care.

She was of three hundred and ten tons, rather large to come down a New England ways considering she was built to fetch and carry, but small compared to an East Indiaman. The flare of her hull and her clean lines and her deck plan represented the best Yankee shipbuilding unsurpassed, if equaled, in the world; her masts were sweeping, in a style so new that Lloyd's had never seen it; her timbers were hand-picked, and if it came to outriding a hurricane, I would trust her before a great ship of the line five times her tonnage.

Her price was twenty thousand American dollars, which I paid without question. Appointing Mr. Blain to brevet captaincy, I bade him sail her between French and English Channel ports in what was little better than packet running, putting into London whenever handy until further notice. "And de good Lawd make de time pass soon," Jim prayed.

It might pass sooner than we had thought, bequeathing us dire defeat. Before the week was out, Lord Tarlton sent word to me at my house in Charles Street that he had business with me of signal importance, and could he wait upon me, accompanied by two gentlemen, within the hour? The message was brought, not by a respectable servant or *commissaire* but by brutal, murderous Pike, which fact alone heralded his master's mood of arrogance, and whose leer was arrogance's grotesque reflection. I was sitting down to dinner when the tidings came. As Jim carved me a final slice of venison roast, a footman announced my visitors' arrival.

"Since I haven't quite finished and don't want to keep them waiting, invite them in here for a glass of brandy," I replied.

"Cap'n, do you want me to stay and serve 'em?" Jim asked when the footman had left the room. "I don' mind."

"No, old shipmate. I know you wouldn't mind, if it was needed, but I don't want to see it. Besides, if you stay here, they might guard their words. But take a good look at them through the port hole."

This last was Jim's word for an aperture, about three feet square, between the butler's pantry and the dining room, through which dishes and trays could be passed. It afforded a straight view of the table, but since it opened at the end of the immensely long room—actually a banquet hall—the distance was nearly thirty feet from my chair and too far for easy hearing of low-voiced conversation between diners.

Jim set a brandy decanter and glasses on the table and went to his pantry. Lord Tarlton entered first, leaning a little on his cane, walking not like an eagle, as Sophia had once said, but like a phoenix. He was beautifully dressed, his hair silver, his lips pursed thoughtfully, a meditative expression on his small, beautifully molded face. Behind him strode a tall man whom I recognized as Sir Edwin Thatch, an official of considerable elevation in the Foreign Office. In the rear came a gross figure in resplendent dress, boozy and close to sixty, whose coarse, malign face caused me to see ghosts. I did not yet recognize it. It was associated in my mind with the Sepulcher of Wet Bones and those who had died there; but it was not the face of the quarry master or the foreman or any of the guards whom I could recall. I would place it in a moment, though—my memory was moving in great surges—and meanwhile I was grateful for the flint of my own face.

"We meet again, Mr. Blackburn, and I owe you an apology," Lord Tarlton said in his softest voice when I had risen and bowed.

"You needn't apologize for coming at this time. I'm through my meal, and hope all of you will join me in a glass."

"'Tis in regard to another matter, which I'll unfold when I've introduced these gentlemen, but I fear we've not time for tippling. Perhaps you've met Sir Edwin Thatch."

"No, my lord, I've not, but I know of his eminence."

"The other gentleman is Captain Henry Holmes, a former sailor like myself, but now home from the sea, and staying in Lincolnshire. You may be surprised to know you've met him before."

"I can't for the moment recall him to mind."

365

"You will in a minute," the man answered, with a knowing glance at the little lord.

"Meanwhile, will all of you sit?"

"Yes, while I convey my apology."

"And while you're about it, Lord Tarlton, why not accept the glass that Blackburn offers us?" the man introduced as Captain Holmes asked, with a longing glance to the decanter. "The weather's right for it, and we might as well make the business pleasant. If no one will join me, I'll help myself."

"Pray do."

"Wait one instant, Captain Holmes," Lord Tarlton ordered, at which the reaching hand stopped still. "You can positively identify this gentleman, our present host, as Holgar Blackburn?"

"Beyond all question of doubt."

"To be plain with you, Blackburn, there was a time I doubted it. You see, you didn't sound West Country to me, as I mentioned to you, and I was half-persuaded you were a Yankee traitor, taking that guise for purposes I couldn't guess. But Cap'n Holmes spent nigh half his lifetime in North Africa, and he saw you at the town of Nulat, some two hundred miles from Tripoli, about twelve years ago."

I looked once more at this Captain Holmes, and now I remembered our meeting. It was not at Nulat, where I had never been, but on the deck of a Barbary pirate not far from the Aegadian Isles. At Tripoli I had seen the last of him until now. If his name were ever Henry Holmes, it was the one he had borne as an American Loyalist serving under Captain Godwine Tarlton on *Our Eliza* against his native land. I had known him as Murad Reis.

Although I heard grapeshot swish again over the *Vindictive's* deck and saw my shipmates fall again, one by one, my face, my voice, and my least movement gave no sign.

2

"I don't recall the occasion," I answered Lord Tarlton.

"You don't?" Murad Reis broke in, in vicious mockery. "I guess when you got gold fever it fogged your memory."

"It wasn't a very happy occasion, Blackburn," the little lord went on, "but I dare say you'll have to call it to mind, for the Foreign Office of His Majesty's government has taken an interest in it. It came about through a remark I made in all innocence to my former lieutenant. But it's only fair that Sir Edwin should hear your account of it before any steps are taken, so what if we three subjects of the king—Mr. Holmes has sworn allegiance to the Pasha of Tripoli—retire to the drawing room?"

"I'll stay here with the brandy," Murad Reis agreed quickly.

Sir Edwin Thatch looked relieved. Evidently he couldn't stomach the half-drunk renegade. This Lord Godwine had clearly perceived. His own manner toward me was courteous to a fault.

"Mr. Blackburn, I'd like to ask a question which you may answer if you see fit, or decline to answer," Sir Edwin began, when we were seated just outside the great open door of the dining room. "Were you once a member of the elite corps of Mamelukes serving the Pasha of Tripoli?"

I hesitated only long enough to recall what my prisonmate had told me of this matter, and that was no longer than "water could flow out from a broken jar."

"If I did, sir, it was a part of a past I don't wish to disclose, so I respectfully decline to answer."

"Henry Holmes—for many years one of the Pasha's reis—says that you did. He states further that you'd been put in a position of trust and were about to embrace Islam when you made off with the paymaster's chest, containing ten thousand silver rupees. He has it you fled through Nulat, and he saw you there, although he wasn't aware at the time of the alleged crime. After this, if we are to believe him, you made your way to Central Africa with these ill-gotten gains, went into the slave and ivory trade, and made an immense fortune."

"Sir, I take note of what you say," I remarked when the diplomat paused.

Meanwhile my thoughts flew fast. If Murad Reis knew this much, he knew that Holgar Blackburn had been caught at Nulat and sentenced to living death in the Sepulcher of Wet Bones. Why had he not said so, and proclaimed me a fugitive from the prison? I thought that the answer might be twofold. In the first place, the Sepulcher did not officially exist. All men sent there were listed as dead, and the only records kept of them were the day book of the harbor master and the secret lists of the Reis Effendi. In the second place, any story of Holgar's capture and the recovery of the pay chest would spike one of Lord Tarlton's guns—perhaps the heaviest he had any real hope of bringing to bear upon me. If it were believed that my riches began with robbery and had been multiplied by trade in slaves, my own guns would be spiked or silenced.

Murad Reis had stood high in the confidence of the Reis Effendi.

Since he knew the beginning of Holgar's story, likely he knew its end —death on the iron hook. In this case, Lord Tarlton knew it, too, whereby my real identity became an easy—although unprovable— guess. Hence his apology for doubting that I was Holgar—his open- ing lines in today's play—became not merely a fine piece of histrionics but irony worthy of his strange and terrible mind.

But I could hardly give him the credit he deserved this particular moment because of the actions of my own mind. I had heard a soft sound, not readily amenable to common explanation, in the next room.

"Lord Tarlton encountered Captain Holmes in London, and in speaking of you, chanced to mention that you wore a brand on your hand," Sir Edwin Thatch went on. "This caused Holmes to recall the theft of the chest, and charge you with it. Furthermore, since the thief is still wanted by his Pasha, dead or alive—his escape still irking that North African prince—Holmes intended to report to him at once. This he could do by letter or in person. The Pasha's nearest official representative is a minister—I should say an agent—in Lisbon; but this man has access to His Majesty's government through our ambassador there, and it's through him that he would attempt to obtain your extradition into the Pasha's hands."

Sir Edwin spoke in level, courteous tones. At the last he rubbed his hands lightly together in a gesture of distaste.

"But that would be very difficult, wouldn't it, Sir Edwin?" Lord Tarlton asked. "To have a British subject extradited to a pirate king——"

"His Majesty's government has a consulate in Tripoli. Thus we can- not refuse to recognize his sovereignty or to hear his demands. A demand that a British subject be delivered there to answer a charge of theft would greatly distress the Foreign Office and create an awk- ward situation. Hence, although I cannot officially concur with the suggestion you wish to make to Mr. Blackburn, I'll not interfere."

"What was the suggestion, Lord Tarlton?" I asked.

"You ask me, and I'll tell you," the little lord answered, caressing the handle of his cane. "You admit you are Holgar Blackburn—you can't deny it now—and the Pasha wants to hang you on an iron hook. You've recently bought a ship—whether you expected trouble and wished to be able to take French leave, I can't say. What I do say is —the best advice I know, and given to you straight—is this." His voice changed a little and the east wind blew through it. "Get the hell out of England and stay there."

He did not know why I smiled into his eyes; and he would like to know, very much. It was to the diplomat that I spoke.

"Sir Edwin, may I ask if Mr. Holmes has as yet made any depositions to the Foreign Office?"

"No, sir. He's no longer a subject of the king, and must deal through representatives of his Pasha. My visit here today is at the request of my old friend, Lord Tarlton. My hope was, that a situation awkward to the Foreign Office could be forestalled."

"I think perhaps it can. If he'll answer it, I've a question to put to Mr. Holmes. Let's return to the dining room."

But at the door of the dining room, the diplomat stopped. Lord Tarlton took three rapid steps forward, then he stopped, too. Perhaps their first fleeting impression was that Henry Holmes—Murad Reis—had been overcome by brandy. Hard drinkers had been known to slump in their chairs in this way—arms flung down on the table, head resting between. But the liquid staining the cloth and dripping on the floor was more red and more viscid than any spilled brandy they had ever seen.

A second or two later both saw what I had looked for and seen at the first glance. From the neck of Murad Reis there were two curious projections. One, about eight inches long, could be the wooden or bone handle of a carving knife. The other, on the opposite side, looking like shining silver dotted with red drops, was undoubtedly the tip-end of a long blade.

The little nobleman whirled on me, chalk white, and shaking with fury.

"You'll hang for this, God damn you."

I did not need to answer, for Sir Edwin spoke in low, well-modulated tones.

"Don't talk rot, my lord."

Beside himself, Lord Tarlton rushed to the kitchen door and flung it open. Through the doorway I caught a glimpse of Jim, putting glasses into a cabinet, and a footman.

"You did it, you black devil, at your master's orders," rose the rasping, frantic voice.

"Did what, please, suh?"

"You there, you footman—you know when he left this room. You saw him come back and wash his hands. Come out with it. Don't try to shield him or you'll get it too——"

"Your ludship, 'e ain't left the room since you gentlemen was at table, and that's the truest word I ever spoke," the pale footman answered.

"Can you swear to that?" Sir Edwin broke in.

"Aye, I can, your honor, and burn me if I lie, and Tilly there will tell you the same." He pointed to a gasping kitchen maid.

"We've all three been 'ere, your honor, talking of this and that——" the girl stammered.

"Sir Edwin, I was partially to blame for leaving that carving knife where Captain Holmes could get hold of it," I broke in. "They say there's nothing like guilt, abetted by strong drink, to induce self-destruction."

Evil was in my mouth as I spoke: the devil's unction was on my tongue, and I could feel it draw my lips in a barely hidden, mocking smile. But there was no evil in Jim's heart, and by this grace I might yet be saved.

3

One path of thought that my mind had taken had caused me to wonder what kind of man Godwine Tarlton was before he took command of *Our Eliza*. The inkling had come to me that he might have been a puny man in his own eyes—his captaincy obtained by preferment—and not much more than that in other eyes. Was it thereafter that the rattle of sleet came into his voice, that his bearing grew princely, his eyes wintry blue, his smile terrifying? This would require no miracle of the devil. The vision of himself that a man sees in the mirror comes to be his real self, or else he goes mad. Men grow or change or deteriorate according to their self-opinion. Immense and unshakable conceit is only second to great achievement in winning public acclaim.

In these studies, I had Alan make an extensive—and expensive—inquiry. To do so, he had to engage several professional genealogists—some of them former underlings in the College of Heralds, others retired curates who had made a hobby of the strangely unchristian pursuit—who supplied pedigrees for burghers newly rich in trade. They were a pack of genteel liars, on the whole, but in this operation Alan demanded strict truth. Its purpose was to determine whether Lord Tarlton was of the inordinately high descent to which all ascribed him, and which he himself appeared to believe.

Compared to him—so I had often heard—the Hanovers were upstarts. The saying had become a catchword in London society, in the ear and out the mouth, and hence highly suspect in my mind. Still, I was somewhat astonished at the facts brought out in the search. Then a new problem rose—what use, if any, should I make of them? I had no real interest in them now that my curiosity was satisfied; I had taken not a grain of satisfaction in having my suspicions confirmed; the matter seemed to me completely irrelevant to future issues. Even so, they might prove useful as a weapon. In that case I could not afford to let them lie.

So I called at Lord Tarlton's town house, a redoubtable mansion on West Piccadilly. A footman informed me that his lordship was out, but expected to return within the hour. Then could I pay my addresses to either of his daughters, Mrs. Alford or Miss Eliza Tarlton? Leaving me in a sumptuous hall, he went straightway to see.

Presently he returned and showed me into a quite wonderful library, its shelves lined by books in many colored leathers, its chairs deep and luxurious, its oak fire blazing. In only a few minutes Sophia, clad very simply and strikingly in dark brown, came with great quietude into the room.

"What is your will with me, Mr. Blackburn?" she asked, white in the face.

"Isn't that a strange question to put to a visitor—at least a peculiar wording? I presume to ask because I'm unacquainted with the ways of polite society and desire to learn."

"Pray sit down." And when we were both seated, "No, I don't regard it as strange under the circumstances. I'm very anxious about the purpose of your call. What your will is in regard to me, as well as to others in our family, has become a question of great moment to me."

"Do you mean, what I want you to do?"

"Yes, and what will happen to us if we don't obey?"

"That's a surprising remark, too."

"Why should it surprise you, Mr. Blackburn? My father can't make it to you because he's too proud. He would have forbidden me to make it if he'd had any notion I would so humble myself; but women can humble themselves without great agony of soul if the consequences serve those whom they love. Yet my father, too, would give a great deal to know the answers I seek. And, by your pardon, I doubt if you're surprised. I believe you expected me to come out with it."

"How could I expect that?"

"By knowing me very well."

"How could I have known you very well?"

"That I can't answer."

"Do you mean you are unable to answer, or you could if you would?"

"Your using that expression—I could if I would—indicates you know me very well. That 'if' was once a great issue in my life, the most consequential step—or misstep—I've ever taken hinged upon that. But that's aside from the main question."

"You must love your father very much."

"I don't dare refuse to reply to your remarks, no matter how personal. It may be you've already been told—long ago—how I regard my father; but I'll speak again. I love my husband very much. If my father falls, one of its worst effects on me would be my husband falling with him, which I fear would happen."

"You ask what is my will with you and your family, and what will happen if you don't obey it. What would be your opinion?"

"There are two possible answers to the first part—only two. One is that you want something—perhaps a large sum of money. My father wants to believe that's the case. The other is, that you intend to ruin him—perhaps destroy him utterly—because of some evil done to you or to those you love. That's what I believe."

"Blackmail or revenge?"

"It could be reparations instead of blackmail, and retribution instead of revenge."

"Are you interested in whether or not they are deserved?"

"No, sir, I'm not. Not now. I can't interest myself in that. Too much is at stake."

"Are you truly interested in who I am, whether a runaway from a Devon workhouse, or some other?"

She gazed a long time into the fire before she answered.

"I think of you not as a person but as a force. It's what you've become, whether you know it or not—if you can ever be a person again, it will be after all this is over. But you were once a person, although I try not to think who. If I knew for sure, it wouldn't help us—there could be nothing I could do about it—and it might weaken me. Because—if you were a certain person—the one that my heart tells me you were—I, too, did you a great wrong. So even if you tell me you were that person, I won't accept it as fact. It might be only part of your campaign."

"Do you mean Homer Whitman, from whom the little woodman brought you a message?"

"The little woodman was a ventriloquist."

"You haven't answered my question."

"And I must answer your questions—I'm afraid not to. Of course I mean Homer Whitman."

"Does Lord Tarlton believe I was ever he?"

"I've never asked him. I was careful not to. But he gave me his opinion anyway—or what he pretended was his opinion. He said you couldn't possibly be he. The confidential records of the Admiralty showed that the *Vindictive* went down with all hands. But perhaps he changed his mind after Holmes, that awful renegade, came here. It was the first time they had met since May, 1801—I heard him say so— and the ship was sunk in June, and Papa left Malta in July. Captain Holmes may have told him there were survivors. But if so, Papa was so triumphant over some turn of the affair that he didn't care who you were—perhaps he would be glad to have you be Homer whom I had loved—until, of course, you had the man killed. I think he's gone back to believing you're a blackmailer, one of the greatest in history. You can ask him if you like. I've just heard him come in."

"Instead I'll repress my ill-mannered curiosity."

"Before he comes, I'll tell you something. You haven't won yet. Papa hasn't broken—he's a man of wonderful stamina and will power. Losing Holmes was a stunning blow, but he revived. He's also a terrible and cunning fighter. In a last-ditch fight it may be you who'll be destroyed, not he. Think of that before you press too hard. If he'll compromise, meet him halfway."

4

A moment later I heard the tap of his stick. A servant opened the door for him; he came in walking like an Indian. I could detect no deterioration in him. He answered my bow gravely and with grace.

"Your coming here has saved me writing you a note," he remarked when we were seated. "It would be in apology of my rash and improper behavior when poor Holmes was killed. You see, he was the last of my two officers who survived the sea fight off Grindstone Island, and was bound up in the loves and hates of my youth. Although he became a Barbary pirate, he did so honorably. He did not wish to become subject to a king who made peace with traitors, and his great passion was to catch those traitors in his haunts and send them to the bottom or into slavery."

A wintry rattle was in his lordship's voice and his blue eyes looked stone cold.

"I had heard that was his passion," I answered.

"His sudden death was a piece of luck for you," the pretty nobleman went on. "No doubt a demand for your extradition will be made —the Pasha's agent in Lisbon is certain to hear soon that Holgar Blackburn is alive and in England—but it will take months to be acted upon."

"I doubt if it will ever come up, Lord Tarlton. I don't think any accredited representative of the Pasha will care to rake over old coals. Only Holmes, of other loyalties, could have made me any trouble."

"Perhaps you're right. Who knows?"

"I'm here today as a result of a suggestion made by your son Dick. Since the matter might concern your daughter Eliza, perhaps you would care to summon her."

His hesitation was so brief as to almost escape the eye, then he nodded gravely. "Anyway, she will be pleasant to look upon."

A footman answered the bell and ran the errand. Eliza appeared at once, her hair and eyes and flesh tints luminous in the half-bright room, her green dress auguring spring on a wintry day. She gave me a grave bow.

"Now you may go ahead," Lord Tarlton said.

"Dick proposed, as you may recall, that I look into the history of the Blackburn family, to see what honors I could find and wear. But I wanted no rosy myths, and feared for the honesty as well as the competence of the paid genealogists. So I decided to put them to an exacting test."

"Excellent," Eliza remarked when I paused. I did not know what she meant.

"It was simply to have them establish the pedigree of some gentleman of high descent, who would be kind enough to compare their report with his own knowledge. In choosing someone, inevitably I thought of you—you who'd refused to meet Beau Brummell, the son of a clerk and the grandson of a shopkeeper, and who regarded the house of Hanover as your social inferiors."

"How did you come by that last supposition?"

"I was told so, long ago, by someone who knew you well. In any case, I've had their report, and will dispatch it to you. It evidenced that your family has borne arms for five generations."

"Five?" he asked, smiling faintly.

"Yes, my lord. According to this report, your great-great-grandfather adopted the arms when he took the name of his former patron, Godfrey Tarlton, Earl of Ballinderry. His real name was Thomas Snow. It was a time of strife in Ireland, and the son of Thomas, enriched by the wars and settling in England, claimed to be the earl's grandson, on the cadet branch. Meanwhile the title, by no means ancient, had become one of the disused titles of the Marquis of Leath, and the claim was never disputed."

As I spoke, Lord Tarlton toyed with his stick, apparently not listening. When I paused, there fell a deep silence; then he looked up as though startled.

"Pardon me, Mr. Blackburn. Will you please continue?"

"These investigators were unable to establish that your mother was descended from Godwine, earl of the West Saxons in the eleventh century, although the mistake would be a natural one. Her family name was Gorman. When it first appears, in the early sixteenth century, the family were yeomanry. When they became franklins a hundred years later, on what were once Godwine lands in the Severn Valley, it was changed to Godwine. Not long thereafter they were recognized as gentry. In fact, your maternal great-grandfather married the daughter of a baronet."

"Quite a feather in our family cap," Eliza broke in.

"And what is the meat of the coconut?" Lord Tarlton asked. But his voice trembled and his lips were pale.

"Only this. If this report is true, you're an English gentleman beyond all doubt, but both sides of your family have elevated themselves by their own bootstraps in no very ancient time. Therefore, I thought you might like to reconsider some advice that you gave me."

"What was it, please?"

"That I should not marry a lady of name, but attempt only a minor rise in this respect, and leave it to my more remote posterity to obtain honor in the land."

"If I withdraw that advice, what then?"

"I wish to ask your opinion of a possible match. There is a beautiful young woman to whom I'm attracted, considerably my junior, but about the age of my African bride, whom I've lost forever. The latter was of authentic royalty, while this girl is only the daughter of a newly created baron. It's quite possible that if I could win her hand, I'd stay away from London, making a home with her at Elveshurst or Tavistock."

Lord Tarlton half rose from his chair. "What in the devil do you mean?"

"You know exactly what he means," Eliza said quietly. "So please compose yourself."

Instead the little lord lifted his cane and struck at my face. I caught the little stick, broke it in my hands, and tossed it into the fire.

"Will you let me hear from you within a fortnight?" I asked as I rose. "I wish to settle my affairs—some of them pending since June, 1801—as soon as possible."

When Sir Godwine could not speak, Eliza spoke gravely in his place.

"You will hear from my father, without fail."

CHAPTER 30

The Great Question

1

ALTHOUGH HEAVY inroads had been made upon my enemy, as yet I had no real reason to believe that I could destroy him by attrition, or cause him to shatter himself against me by attack.

Toward the latter aim, I turned the screw once more. Summoning Walt Chalker, well-acquainted with the waterfront, I asked if he knew any actor who could pass himself off as an English-speaking sailor from some Mediterranean country for a short and not too difficult engagement. He knew several, he said; better yet, he was acquainted with a genuine Italian sailor, presently in port, who could speak broken English, and was at least a skillful liar. Walt knew him as Alberto and never doubted that he would be up and equal to any reasonable escapade not involving him with the law.

I directed that Alberto should find Pike at the Vintry mughouse where he liked to loaf, and offer to tell him something, greatly to his advantage, for the sum of five pounds. In response to Pike's questions, he was to let fall that the business concerned Lord Tarlton, not Pike himself, but Alberto had not known how to approach the big gun, and had been tipped off that Pike could be trusted to represent his master faithfully and generously. He had found out something that he believed Lord Tarlton would pay Pike ten pounds

—perhaps a great deal more—to know. It concerned two men whom Alberto had met in a Gibraltar stews, who were at present on their way to London to make trouble. He, Alberto, did not know what kind of trouble it was, but one of them had mentioned a Negro, known as Jim, who had paid their passage.

Alberto could continue to lower his price as the talk continued and the glasses passed. In case the deal was made, Alberto's information would be nothing more than the names by which the two men had been known in Malta—Julius and the Dago—and two fictitious names under which they averredly traveled.

Three days later Walt called on me to make his report. Pike had taken the bait, had paid two pounds for it, and appeared to regard the sum as well spent. I sent three pounds more to Alberto—more than this might have wakened dangerous dreams of avarice—and gave Walt five pounds.

If Lord Tarlton was convinced that Julius and the Dago would soon be in London to testify to a deal made in Malta nearly eighteen years before—testifying before the Admiralty at my behest—and he thought that I remained unaware of him finding it out, I believed he would take the risk of positive action without delay.

So it did not surprise me when, on the following afternoon, Dick Tarlton called. On being admitted to my study room, he gave me a somewhat sheepish grin. He was a graceful and, when he chose, an engaging fellow. I seated him where I could grab him, if the need arose; actually, there seemed to me no likelihood of such a development. It was interesting to consider how readily he would take to murder if in his opinion the stakes justified the risk. It seemed probable he had taken to it already, since it has always been the sharpest, surest tool of ambitious men who do not hold by law, human or divine. Those who deny the brotherhood of man have nothing but practical problems between them and the great gains obtainable by murder.

The fact remained that Dick was something of a sportsman. He would not cavil over the odds. A little more or less risk cut no ice with him. If the game was good enough, he'd play it.

"What can I do for you, Dick?" I asked—that usually kindly intentioned but often ill-mannered inquiry people make to dubious visitors.

"First of all, a nip," he answered. "The weather's rotten, and I'm on a damned delicate mission."

I did not doubt this last, and my main hope was he would execute

377

it well. Unless the scheme was brilliant, the trap beautifully screened, and the bait made enticing, Lord Tarlton would doubt my gullibility, and be on guard against a counter-stroke.

"I came here in behalf of my father, my two half sisters, and my half—is that right?—brother-in-law," Dick went on, after the drink. "Does 'behalf' include myself? Anyway, I'm one of the petitioners."

"I doubt if it's the right word," I said when he paused.

"Not far from it, by God! Let me put it this way. When you play chess, your king is never taken—he's merely demobilized and dis-potentiated. Since the renegade Holmes so conveniently turned up his toes, my old gentleman's king is in that fix or very close to it. True, we see the situation in somewhat different lights. And I'd better say first that I don't intend to answer the charges that you've made, directly or indirectly. I won't confess them or deny them either. But I'll take the first steps toward what I hope will be a satisfactory settlement."

It was a good beginning. No fault could be found with it. Dick's face was in repose, his eyes full of thoughts. He glanced at me, I nodded, and he went on.

"One of the stumbling blocks to any settlement has been that face of yours. It never changes—truly it suggests stone—and it was hard for us to see a man behind it. Sophia won't—or can't—see it yet. She thinks of you as some sort of retributive force, like Nemesis. But she's wildly imaginative and I'm not. If there isn't a man behind it, I'm wasting my time and yours, but I believe there is."

"Yes, sir, there certainly is."

"What man? Much hangs on that. Are you Holgar Blackburn or Homer Whitman? Whichever you are, you know the story of the other one. Until he talked to Captain Holmes, my father was convinced you were Whitman, turned into an implacable avenger. There would be no settling with such a being, he thought. Unless you were killed or somehow forced to leave England, our jig was up. When Papa asked you to sit behind him and correct his errors at the butts, was he surprised when Pike's gun went off by accident? I doubt it."

"I appreciate your frankness, Dick, and I'll confess that your father appeared greatly surprised."

"Well, maybe he was. Let it go, please. When Captain Holmes came, he told him three men of the *Vindictive's* crew had been taken alive, one of them Homer Whitman, one a small-sized sailor whose name he'd forgotten, and one an American Negro. You'd think that

378

would have confirmed Papa in his belief—but Captain Holmes also stated that beyond any particle of doubt both white men were dead. The little one died in the Jebel quarries. The other two escaped, but only the Negro got clean away—Homer Whitman died fighting. But for years before he died he had been thrown with a pay-chest thief, Holgar Blackburn, and had told him his story. When some of Holgar's friends among the Mamelukes enabled him to escape— I'm guessing now—he made a pile of money, either in slave and ivory trading, or by blackmail. Then he came to England for purposes not yet quite clear. Perhaps it was to avenge his old friend Homer Whitman. Perhaps he had some more practical aim."

"Such as doubling his fortune—which may not be as great as rumor makes it out—and getting into high society?"

"Both would be completely human and understandable, especially in a runaway from an English workhouse. What poor boy in England, tipping his cap to the squire—bowing and scraping to his lordship—doesn't yearn with passionate yearning to have the shoe on the other foot? Papa found out that Blackburn had been branded on the back of his hand with an X. It was almost unbelievable that Whitman would go to such lengths as to brand himself to maintain an identity of no real use to him. That's not all. Papa's agent hunted up a childhood sweetheart of Blackburn. The old people told him about her—it was quite a rural idyl. This woman saw you in Tavistock. She swears before heaven that you're Holgar Blackburn, returned from the grave."

I was not as composed as before. As I poured Dick another glass, I could hardly keep my hands from trembling. It was impossible to doubt that the woman who had loved Holgar more than anyone in the world and who knew his walk and knew I was not he, had sworn that I *was* he. She had promised me she would not expose my masquerade and had kept that promise: was that such a wonderful thing? It was as wonderful as a star burning in infinite lonely vigil in the heavens.

"If I'm Holgar Blackburn, what then?" I asked.

"I think you'll deal with me."

"What if I'm Homer Whitman?"

"You'd still be a human being with red blood in your veins."

"Yes, and that blood shed on the deck of the *Vindictive* has washed mighty thin by now."

I said it without a shudder. It was easy when I was saying it for Captain Phillips, for Sparrow and Farmer Blood and Ezra Owens

379

and the rest, and for men tricked out of their lives by a little lord-ling's pretty ways after a sea fight by Grindstone Island. It did not beslime my mouth when I spoke for all these, and for Holgar Blackburn who was branded on the hand by brutal arrogance and blasphemy.

At that instant, Dick believed he had won the victory.

2

"What would be your notion of a settlement, if you'd care to say?" Dick ventured.

"I'll leave that to you."

"We're not as rich as report has it. If you could clear a cool hun-dred thousand pounds—on a race or a roll of the dice or by some face-saving device—would you let bygones be bygones?"

"We'll never get anywhere with that, Dick. I've all the money I need."

"I told the old man so. I told him you were a man who meant just what you said."

"In this case, I do."

"You said you wanted Eliza. Papa's tried to punch holes in that perfectly plain statement, trying to believe it some sort of bluff, but the two girls, who heard you make it, and I—we've about brought him to his senses. I'll ask you this. What if Eliza doesn't take to the idea? You're twice her age—not exactly an Adonis—and there are other barriers in a young girl's eyes. What would be your position in that case?"

"The negotiations would be dropped."

"That makes it pretty thick."

"I'd consider a so-called marriage of convenience with your half sister Eliza. I have great wealth, she has position and name. I prob-ably could make several just as good, especially if the families needed money. It would begin as a marriage of convenience. If I was able to make something more of it as time went on, well and good. In any case my position in society would be assured. My children would be among those who inherit the earth. And Eliza is differ-ent from every other unmarried girl in one respect—an appeal I find irresistible."

"I can't imagine what it might be, and that's the truth."

"She's Lord Tarlton's daughter."

His eyes rounded slightly, and I thought he was taken aback.

"Well, I should have seen that. I suppose I did see it—but didn't pin it down. Nothing else could give you such a complete sense of victory."

"But if Eliza is unalterably averse, this is a needless discussion."

"I didn't say she was. The truth is, she took it better than any of us—unless it was I, who am very hard to jar. In the first place, she loves Papa deeply. I don't see why she should—she's been his prisoner more than his daughter—but the fact remains. She's romantic enough to want to save him regardless of his deeds—if only as a kind of *beau geste*. To be married to the Ogre of Elveshurst—that's your current name among the bucks—would be quite novel. Finally, she'll need the money."

"That surprises me."

"There was only one large estate in the family—my father's mother's. Papa enjoys the income, but at his death it goes to Sophia—quite a jar when the will was read, ten years ago. I have nothing except five hundred quid a year from the Countess of Harkness. Papa supplies the rest. Eliza's a demure little thing—butter wouldn't melt in her mouth—but she doesn't intend for her nest to go unfeathered."

"May I take it you're encouraging me to sue?"

"Not exactly. I wouldn't go that far. But come down to Celtburrow to see what develops. She's gone back—Papa went frantic and sent her—but you'll be invited there for a week's sport—I can promise that much—and the surroundings will be much more favorable than here in London. Bring the big gray, if it's not too much trouble. Eliza was greatly taken with him. While you're there, don't hide your light under a bushel when it comes to shooting and riding. You're top flight in both—we were fools not to see it straight off—and she'll champion you against me. You know she hates me like poison."

I did not answer, being almost unable to speak.

"Put me in the shade if you can," Dick went on. "I won't slack the game—it would be against my sporting instincts—and the show would be worth seeing. The woodcock will be moving northeast in great numbers; show her what you can do. Take Papa for some stiff bets. Then when the time's ripe, state your case—not too gingerly—and see what she'll say."

"I'll heed your advice, Mr. Tarlton."

"I'm Dick—and I hope to God this can be the answer. What's that line from Shakespeare about someone having somebody on the hip?"

"I recall it vaguely." Actually I knew it word for word.

"It's not a pleasant position for the latter cove, I do assure you. Mr. Blackburn, you'll be hearing from us soon."

In a few seconds he had gone. I felt as though just waking from an evil dream. But it was not a dream, and the mouse that ran under a curtain was only a little rodent of flesh and blood.

3

Five days before our day of departure, I had Perkins, the good hostler, leave from Elveshurst on horseback, leading El Stedoro for Celtburrow but on no business except to attend to his feeding, watering, currying, and petting. Seven days would do it, but I allowed them eight. Thirty or less miles a day in good, cool, misty riding weather would merely keep Perkins limber and the gray stallion in good fettle.

My bags were packed and the carriage waiting at my door in Charles Street when Alan burst into the little reading room where I waited for Jim.

"You didn't summon me, sir, but I had to come," he said, very white, and with his hands clenched to still their tremor.

"I was going to summon you, to bid you good-by, and to have you witness a document before Jim and I go to the dock."

"There would be others present then, and I couldn't say what I wished. Not what I wished—what I felt I had to say—what I can't keep from saying. I hope you'll excuse the presumption."

"There is none."

"Well, then, I hoped you'd take me with you. The reason I hoped it especially was, I've a feeling you're going into danger. I wanted to be with you in that case. I don't know if I could make the danger any less, but I wanted to try. You've made me a man again. It might pay a little of the debt I owe you."

"You were a man all the time."

"Then you've given me my pride again—that a man can't live without. If you can't take me—and I know you would if you could —will you let me speak out of my place?"

"Every man has the right to speak until he speaks what's unfit for a man—I was taught that, long ago."

"Sir, are you armed?"

"I'll have my fowling pieces."

"You're not carrying a pistol?"

"No."

"Don't you realize you're going to danger?"

"In becoming the guest of Lord Tarlton and his family in the old seat in Cornwall? That doesn't seem to make sense."

"I don't know what sense it makes. I only know it's true. A shotgun went off in the hands of Pike, Tarlton's bully. His daughter Sophia asked him how it happened when they were all standing about the refreshment wagon, so of course I heard about it. You knocked aside the barrel just in time. Tarlton came here with an official from the Foreign Office and a renegade from Africa, and Jim threw a knife through the aperture—no jury would believe it, but that's what happened. Now you're going to their very nest. I think very possibly you'll be killed, and you and Jim think the same. Yet you won't take me with you and you won't even take a pistol."

"No, I can do neither of those things."

"To what are you trusting to save your life from that elegant little monster and his malign son and his bully boy and that precious son-in-law, and that angel-haired witch who may be as bad as the rest? Are you trusting Providence?"

"One thing at a time. Lord Tarlton is not a monster—if he were, he wouldn't be half so frightening. He's merely a man who's renounced God in favor of logic—his own logic, of course. I doubt if Eliza is a witch. She's Lord Tarlton's daughter, but also a daughter of a woman named Elspeth and of nature and the moors. No, I don't trust Providence to save me from being killed. It's not possible for all men to live until tomorrow—some must die today—and I doubt if any man should trust Providence to put him in one of the groups instead of the other. If he tries to kill me, and I shoot him down with a pistol, Jim and I haven't succeeded in our undertaking. We're carrying out some orders that put us into danger, but we're not authorized to kill: we're not accredited officers pursuing criminals; as Jim once told me, unwritten law is not law at all. Am I trusting that goddess—again a personification—to protect our lives? She punished evil, but I never heard of her rewarding good. But we put a good deal of confidence in our ability to survive. We've had long practice at it."

I had talked too long. I had tried too hard to explain. My heart had grown heavy.

"I'd like to ask one question more."

"All right."

"If either one or both of you are killed in this undertaking—put to death in your enemy's den—may it bring victory to your cause?"

"I think very likely it will. If so, we've carried out our orders. If not, we've done all we could and gone off watch for good. We may die, and lose. We may die, and win. What we hope is—a long-enduring, solid hope—we may win and live."

"I think you will." Alan was trembling so he could hardly speak. "It may be a false vision, yet I believe it."

"If that vision would fail, you'll find a signed and notarized communication in the locked drawer of my secretary, to which you have the key. A signed copy is in the hands of the lawyer at Tavistock, another on deposit with Baring's Bank; still another has been posted to Captain Tyler, at Bath, in the Maine District of Massachusetts. All copies contain directions for its use; and a sum of money has been provided for expenses involved. Also, there is a private communication, with an enclosure, addressed to you, in the same drawer."

Alan's eyes slowly filled with tears, and he did not attempt to speak.

"Now ask Jim to step in—I wish to get his consent to the deposition I've asked you to witness—and remain in call."

Jim came in, and on my bidding him seat himself—his manner with me was generally that of a Yankee seaman before the mast with his captain—he did so. I brought out a paper I had written the night before.

"Whether one or both of us are alive or dead in June, 1821, we'll have done all we can to carry out Cap'n Phillips's orders."

"'At's more 'an two years from now, twenty years in all. I reckon 'twill be settled long before 'at."

"If we're alive when that time comes, we'll go aboard the *Dolly Madison*—I think she'll have a different name—and set sail. If I'm dead, you'll go alone. If you're dead, I'll go alone. But I agree with you we may sail much before then—perhaps in a few days—if we're to sail at all."

"Cap'n, I believe it in my bones."

"That being the case, I've made my will. It makes provision for certain things we wanted carried out. It provides you with a home and a job on board the vessel for as long as she stays afloat or as you wish; and a living on any count. It sets up a fund of a hundred thousand American dollars for you to buy and free slaves—your old acquaintances and a few you can help. But there are millions of slaves in the Americas alone, and our money wouldn't be a drop in the bucket in trying to buy their freedom. Still, if used wisely, it can strike a good strong blow at slavery."

"How would 'at be, Cap'n?"

"In America and all over Europe the Quakers are fighting slavery. They're fighting it well, joining hands with other antislavery societies. So the remainder of our gold—the great bulk of it, including what this house and Elveshurst will bring—all except the special bequests and the ship—I've willed to them for that use. Does that suit you, Jim?"

"It couldn't suit me no better."

"The gold was never ours, except to use for Captain Phillips and our mates and what they stood for. If we live, we'll keep the ship for our own—I the master, you the cook—we're entitled to it in lieu of reasonable earning. But when we leave England to go home—in a few days, a few months, a little over two years at most—I want to make the same disposal of all the rest as in this will."

Jim's face grew strained, and I thought he might break down; instead he gave me a great, radiant smile.

"There ain't no harm in 'at, as 'em Arabs useter say."

"Jim, do you remember the morning we rode out after Tembu Emir?"

"When I forgit 'at, I won't be no breathin' man or no ha'nt neither."

"He tried to kill me, as was his right, and death came very close. There was no evil in him, nor in Tui whom I fought in the grass, even though the fires of hell shone in his eyes. In a few days death will come close again, this time at evil's bidding. I won't have a gun to use against him, or even a stone rolled into reach of my hand. The issue will be very close; and you won't be able to save me as you did once—twice—before. But let's go forth in good cheer and high hope. Whatever happens, we won't go back into slavery."

"I'll be of good cheer and high hope, too, like when we went after Tembu. And if 'em mens kill you, wif me still alive—but 'at ain't no business I have wif you, Cap'n Whitman."

"Whom do you have it with?"

"'At business is wif my own soul, de soul of a black man, but a man right on, doin' de best he can."

I started to speak, but found I had nothing to say. Instead I called Alan and bade him collect two freemen employed in the house, to witness my will.

I was not made welcome at Celtburrow; neither was I rebuffed. The amenities were pointedly observed by Lord Tarlton, Dick, and Harvey Alford; we exchanged bows but never touched hands; we talked of dogs and horses, birds and guns, and they answered courteously my questions regarding the manor and the countryside, but no one laughed or spoke a light word. The air was like that of the meeting place of enemy commanders when, after a bitter war of attrition, an armistice had been proposed. Dick and Harvey no longer exchanged knowing glances. Rattling sleet came no more into Lord Tarlton's voice; his usual bluff speech remained stiffly polite. Only now and then the blue of eyes changed in tone and became frightening as he played with his cane.

Sophia's manner toward me was not so correct. More than once she caught her breath and turned color; and when Harvey spoke of walking up woodcock in the woods—a sport I should try soon—a desperate expression came into her face that I feared the rest would see. I was sure she would soon speak to me in private. Her chance came when she found me in the gun room, admiring gold, silver, and brass-mounted pieces of bygone days.

"What shall I call you, sir?" she asked, standing beside me and speaking in low tones.

"What you please."

"May I call you Homer? I can talk plainer if I do."

"That suits me well enough."

"Why have you come here? Is it true you want Eliza? Dick says you do, and if you can have her, you'll let us go."

"Do you believe it?"

"It's possible. She's beautiful and bright as a rainbow, and you've lived in Africa nearly twenty years and your face is like stone. I wouldn't blame you if it's true. It would be a human thing, while the rest you've done to us is inhuman. I hope it's true."

"If it lay in your hands, could I have her?"

"Yes—if then you'd let us go. In that way she would save us, though we're not worth saving—not one of us. She would find great happiness in that—paying all her debts of love—and be rid of us besides. Would she be happy with you? Why not? You'd love her, wouldn't you? How could you help it? And if you didn't—if she was unhappy—she'd leave you."

"Do you believe for one moment she might agree to it?"

"Ask her, not me. It's her right to tell you, not mine. But you see, Homer—that wouldn't settle anything. The decision won't lie with her any more than it lies with me. It lies with Papa—and with you."

"I don't understand that fully."

"You understood one night in a little mission house in Malta."

"I know what you refer to."

"Look at me."

Sophia drew up one corner of her lip in a strange and eerie imitation of Lord Tarlton's malign smile.

"Don't do that."

"I don't know what Papa has told her; whatever it is, she expects to do it. I think it was to accept your proposal. But did he mean it? Is it a trick to put you off guard while Pike rigs the guns?"

I glanced at the door in sudden alarm. It was thick and close-fitting and not amenable to eavesdropping. The window was closed, and I stopped to look at the mists blowing through the naked trees. Sophia stood close to my side. She was a daughter of the moors and of tragic destiny, and there was deathless beauty in her face. The fire crackled and the mystery of destiny came upon me swift and deep.

"Sophia, this is evil—deep, immeasurable evil."

"Don't I know it?"

"How did we get into it?"

"We fell into the pit."

"So did an elephant. He wore a great white brand on his side and had been sent into exile in the thorn to wait for me. I killed him, and he went home."

"Are you mad?"

"Yes, but I'll be made sane if the salt spray is flung into my face."

"I could have gone with you—but I didn't."

"Does Eliza know?"

"Evil? No. But she dreams of it sometimes."

"You won't tell her about the guns?"

"No. What would be the good?"

"You said her going with me lies with him, Godwine, Lord Tarlton, and with me."

"You may not take her. Perhaps you've never even wanted her. How do I know what you've become in these eighteen years? What have I got to judge you by? Not a sailor who walked with me down a long beach—who swam with me to Calypso's cave—who took me to his ship. Your saying you want her may be just a trick, and what you really want is death."

"That doesn't stand to my reason."

"Why should it? It's quite possible you want to die, if you can take Papa with you or have him follow you soon. Many people ache to die, not all of them insane. Do you think I've forgotten the *Eagle of Maine* striking the rock?"

"There's many a day—many a night—that Homer Whitman would have liked to know you remembered it and sometimes thought of it."

"How could you doubt me so? But I know—you needn't tell me."

"His shipmates made up a great part of his loss. A girl he loved at Malta healed the wound."

Saying that, I went back to the time and place. I saw the harbor lights as Sophia and I came down from the town and went out to the ship. From thence we went into my little cabin and found beauty and wonder and healing. The spell of that hour was on me.

"How many shipmates were there on the *Vindictive?*" Sophia asked.

"The marine records give the company as sixteen."

"How many are left alive?"

"There may be two."

"You and one more. Do you long to join the rest? Who else have you loved who went away and left you here? Holgar Blackburn was one. You can hardly bring yourself to admit he's gone. No, that isn't like you, not to face truth—it must be for some other reason you make him live on in you." Suddenly her eyes grew very wide and dark. "Did you kill him?"

"If I did, it's a secret between him and me." But I did not know what I was saying.

"I think you did. You did it to save him from something awful beyond words. Either you loved him beyond the power of ordinary people or you owed him a tremendous debt. It wouldn't be otherwise. Were there any more besides your family, and your shipmates, and Holgar?"

"Among those who died, there could have been one more. His name was Kerry, and he was Homer Whitman's workmate. They shook hands at the brink of the cliff. Kerry's hand was cold and wet with sweat, but his face was wet with tears. The chains rattled loudly as he jumped."

"Did you want to follow him?"

"That was unthinkable, since it was Homer's watch."

"What do you mean by that?"

"He'd been given the duty."

388

"Has the time come for him to go off watch?"

"It may be very near."

"Now let me say something very important. Suppose Pike is rigging the guns, as I said. Papa's the one who told him to, but would Papa pull the trigger? You know he wouldn't. He's never got blood on his little white hand, I doubt if he's had the stain of gunpowder. He remains on the quarter-deck and others do what he tells them. He lost his head when he seized the iron poker the night at Elveshurst—the same when he tried to hit you with his little stick; but he's over all that. He's very calm. He's either resigned to something—it might be to losing Eliza—or has great confidence in something. And the one whom you'd least fear—the most likely to catch you with your guard down—would be Harvey."

"I'll look out for him. For your sake I'll stay out of the way."

"Why not for your own sake? Isn't that the part of wisdom?"

"It might be. I can't tell what's wise or foolish. I know that my staying out of his way can't deliver him from evil—only God can do that—and it can't fight evil. If victory falls to me, I'll spare him all I can. And I think that completes the business you had with me."

She did not go out. Instead she walked to the end of the room and looked through the window. Then she returned to me and gazed out the window by which I stood.

"That's the garden—but how bare it looks," she said.

"It must be beautiful in summertime."

"Summer stays such a little while. Look at the gaunt trees with the mists blowing through them and the dark sky."

"I'd like to see it as a little boy saw it thirty years ago. It was so beautiful he had to break in and steal flowers."

"That little boy's gone, and those years are dead. Now the other window gives a view of the paddock and a glimpse of Bodmin moor. It's a rather bleak view even in summer. But there's someone standing by the paddock gate—there was a minute ago—and that brightens it up."

She led me there by the hand. I saw some dark yew trees lining a driveway and, dimmed by mist, the gray moor beyond. But by the paddock gate, giving sugar to a magnificent black stallion, stood a tall girl dressed in a green riding habit, her hair shining as though the sun were out. It was like a shore light, I thought, in storm.

"If Papa will give her to you, will you take her and go your way?" Sophia's low voice came, charging me to answer.

"I can't go my way until the debt's paid."

389

"Maybe you'll be sent on your way with empty hands into the cold and dark."

"That's quite true."

"If the debt's paid, and she'll still go with you, will you take her in lieu of me?"

"I don't know what you mean."

"I can't tell you what I mean, but I'll tell you this. I love her more than anyone in the world."

"I believe that."

"And next to her, I love you."

After looking long into my face, she turned slowly, drew her hand through her dark hair, opened the heavy door, and went out. For a moment the evil dream that I was living had grown thin, but in the solitude and silence it thickened and ran on.

CHAPTER 31

The Answer

1

COMING UP to Eliza was like walking in the dusk toward a light. The bright green of her costume and the wind-blown gold of her hair and the almost scarlet flush on snow-white skin had an effulgent effect on this dark day. Her first warning of my approach was the stallion's scenting me and dashing off across the paddock. Eliza turned her gray eyes on me, and I thought she tried to smile, but gave up the attempt and faced me gravely. The way she stood, an upspring in her feet and her head high, made me think of Isabel Gazelle.

"I'm sorry I scared off your good friend," I said.

"He's just being skittish. I can hardly claim he's my friend, but he acts more friendly with me than with anyone else in the family. I think he admires Dick—they go together with such dash. All horses are mortally afraid of Papa—there's no harm in telling you—almost everyone knows it. Even Donald Dhu sweats and trembles when he comes near."

Sophia had told me this same remarkable thing. "Yet he ran well that day, with your father up."

"He obeys him, as we all do."

"Even a black proud chieftain has to obey someone."

"How did you know what his name meant?"

"A well-educated Irishman told me. He could speak Gaelic."

"A willful girl has to obey someone, too."

"Is that so?"

"Donald Dhu is much more gentle than when I first began to make up to him. But stallions can hardly ever be gentled like mares and geldings."

"I doubt if that's true, Eliza. It takes more time and effort, though. The Arabs make pets of their mares—a hand-raised mare tags her master about and tries to sleep with him and often will fight for him—while they dislike stallions and the beasts seem to know it. Yet El Stedoro responded to my affection for him and is as gentle as any old plug."

"Do you like horses?" As she waited my reply, she averted her face.

"I admire them, and I like them mostly in their relations with people."

"What kinds of horses and people?"

"I thrill over wild horses, and glory in great runners and jumpers and chargers. I have a brotherly feeling toward El Stedoro. In general, the horses that warm my heart the most are workhorses—who plow men's fields and draw their wagons—and old nags that children can climb under and ride on or behind."

"You don't think a high-bred horse is better than a low-bred person?"

"I wouldn't like to think such an evil thought as that."

"Evil?"

"Terribly evil."

"You won't get on very well in upper-class society, Mr. Blackburn."

"I'm afraid not."

"Are you going to try?"

"No."

"What you said when I saw you last gave the impression that you were."

"I've decided that after winding up some affairs in England, I'll make my home in America."

"Then why do you want to marry a girl—a woman—of high position?"

391

"I've decided that I don't care what her position is if we can be happy together."

"This is the first time I've seen you since you came. Papa led me to believe you'd devote a good deal of time to me. That was to be expected after what you said at our house in London. But perhaps you've changed your mind about that."

"I haven't changed my mind about you—you are most beautiful and desirable—but I don't think you have anything to fear from me."

"I find that I don't fear you. Papa does—and I never knew him to fear anyone before—and so does Harvey. I don't think Dick does—he's almost incapable of fear. Papa wouldn't dream of telling me to be nice to you—to encourage you to pay court to me, you of common birth and more than twice my age—if he didn't fear you terribly." She turned and looked me in the face. "The only possible reason is that you have it in your power to ruin him. That could happen in only two ways—he owes you a great debt, or you owe him a great debt. The first would be money, the second revenge. So I do fear you—but for his sake and for Sophia's. I look at you, and I don't think you are cruel, or wicked, or base. My life has never been like other girls' of my class, and I don't expect it ever will be. So whatever he tells me to do in regard to you—if it can save him and save Sophia's husband—I can stand to do."

"You must love your father very much."

"I don't think I do. I don't think it's possible. I think all the women in his life found that out. But he loves me very much. It's being loved, not loving, that creates the unavoidable obligation. And he's a great captain—a great chieftain."

"I didn't expect you to speak so frankly."

"I have to. There's so much at stake—perhaps more than I have any idea. All of you know more than I do. I'll ask you one thing. You wouldn't want me, would you, if I were unwilling to go?"

"At least I wouldn't take you."

"There's a degree of willingness, or unwillingness. One is more, and the other's less than before."

"I'm glad of that, but I don't think you'll have to concern yourself with either one. I believe there'll be another outcome."

Her eyes drew again to mine, and her bright tints changed.

"I'm relieved in one way, but more frightened."

"Why?"

"What you proposed might have worked out much better than I thought at first. It could be a marriage of convenience, as you said.

I'd begun to think it might be the luckiest outcome possible. There's awful bad luck—something worse than that—in the air."

"I hope it won't strike you, Eliza. Look out, for it's very near."

2

Eliza followed my glance to Lord Tarlton and Dick, making toward us down the driveway. Both were in riding habits, but Lord Tarlton carried a black thornwood cane instead of a crop, and Dick had a racing bat. Eliza turned smiling. Again like Isabel Gazelle, she had good ability to dissemble. I thought that the little lord's delicately molded face became ennobled if not beautified on beholding her, and he walked with princely bearing. There was a sheen on Dick's eyes I had not seen before.

"So here you are," Lord Tarlton said. "Admiring Donald Dhu."

"Who could help it?" I asked.

"But he needs exercise, Blackburn, and Dick and I were just saying that we weren't satisfied with the showing he made against your gray at Elveshurst. Eliza, were you satisfied?"

"It wasn't a conclusive test, if that's what you mean," Eliza answered.

"Donald and I were on a course we'd ridden only once. Well, Blackburn would be in the same fix if he'd care to prove to us 'twas no accident that the gray won before. But as the saying goes, turnabout is fair play."

"I maintain it was no accident, my lord," I answered. "If you want proof of it, El Stedoro will supply it with good cheer. As for the course being new, I'll take him over the ground and the jumps beforehand, let him look at them good and smell them, and then if we lose, we'll have no fault to find."

"Dick, here's a buck!"

"But Papa, the course we spoke of is three times as long as t'other if we go out and back," Dick said. "Maybe that's too long for the gray, considering he's newly walked from London. I dare say we could cut it in half——"

"That's not necessary, sir," I broke in when Dick paused. "That walk from London, taking his time, put him in good fettle."

"Then I know nothing to stop a good race," Lord Tarlton said. "It's too long for my old bones, but Dick will do the honors, and Donald puts his best foot for'ard for him, as you'll see. And now, what of a wager or two, to spice the dish? First, Eliza, I'll lay one with you. You told me the gray was a cleaner jumper than Donald Dhu——"

"I don't remember telling you that——"

"Well, you did, and here's your chance to back it. I'll lay five pounds with you my Donald will win by a length."

"Shall I take him, Holgar?"

"All he'll put down and you can cover."

"Then I'll make it ten."

"Done for ten. But that's in the family—I'd be swindled out of 'em anyhow—and I'll make no such bet with you, Blackburn, my honored guest. Against you, it's not a length I'll undertake to win by, but one hair of the nose. I'll stand on one side of the home gate, with Eliza and your Jim on t'other, and if we disagree who's over first, majority rules. Does that suit you?"

"Perfectly, my lord."

"No doubt you'll like to lay a wager, so kindly name the sum."

"Why, I'd like to make it worth my while to make El Stedoro hustle, so what would you say of five thousand pounds?"

"By God, Blackburn," Lord Tarlton cried, looking at me as though in startled admiration. "You take my breath!"

I paid no attention to that. It was part of a show in which, at this point, I took little interest. What arrested me was Eliza turning white.

"Don't bet that much, Holgar," she told me in low tones.

"Come, Eliza——" That was Tarlton's voice, with a rasp in it.

"It's not sporting, and you know it isn't, when he's your guest. Holgar, it isn't gentlemanly, considering Papa is your host."

"I bow to your better taste. What sum do you suggest?"

"A thousand pounds would be a tremendous bet. That's what our old hostler, Quigley, has earned in—in twenty years. And if you'll make it a hundred, I'll give you my glove to carry."

"Then a hundred it will be."

"A sweet little spoil-sport you are!" Dick burst out, his rage barely controlled.

"I'm proud of her, sink me if I ain't," Tarlton reproved him. "Dick, sometimes you and I let our acquisitiveness get out of hand. Eliza, get your bright bay and show Blackburn the old closed road. Once across Dolmen Brook, turn and come back. Then, Blackburn, you can rest your horse and have a bite of lunch. You and Dick can run about three, when the sun's begun to pitch and the light's soft."

I wondered if Eliza's interference with the betting had increased or reduced my danger. Neither seemed very likely. I would carry her glove to win with and I would remember awhile how she looked, standing snowy-white between her father and me.

I wished I could have her for my own. Instead the dark inkling came to me that except for unknown forces moving in my behalf— fate or luck or hidden law or uncomprehended love—I would take another bride.

3

The road had been closed many years before, and there was no sign of cart tracks on the grassy ground. This was good, firm ground, frostbitten and sere except for patches of low heather, and more open than I had hardly hoped. A few yews and birch stood lonely along the way, but only one narrow strip of woods obscured the view and permitted any meddling with the jumps. This was a dense covert of larches running at right angles to the course; and without apparent rhyme or reason, the roadway through was obstructed by a heavy wooden gate. This was the first jump beyond the starting gate, and less than a hundred yards farther on the road turned sharply, which meant that near the end and in the heat of the run we would come upon it rather suddenly, with no time for a careful survey.

Of the five other jumps, only the last was dangerous—a brook with steep, unstable banks. El Stedoro took them all with composure. Eliza's bay followed in good form except for the water gap; in this case she found an easier jump a furlong up the brook.

I could hardly bring myself to speak to my lovely sunny-haired companion, and we rode in frostbitten silence.

The time passed until two in the afternoon. Then I went into El Stedoro's stall and gave him some bread that might make him recall the bread flaps of his colthood, and some milk not tasting like camel's milk which he drank in its lieu, and then I petted him in ways he liked, especially putting my hand into his mouth and letting him gently press it with his great teeth; and I talked to him in Arabic, the sound of which might recall happier days. Jim had groomed him until he glistened, then saddled and bridled him, using a straight, gentle bit.

"You cay him out and you cay him back, and I'll deckirate your bridle with two silver stars," I heard Jim murmur in his ear.

When Jim led him into the paddock, Eliza was waiting at the gate for me. At once she handed me a riding glove.

"For good luck," she told me.

Long ago it had meant more than that. It would have meant that her hand joined with mine in the endeavor.

"I'll try to win you that ten pounds," I answered.

Her throat worked, and she spoke again in almost inaudible tones. "About that other matter. Is it off?"

"It was mostly sword-rattling to start with."

"You say mostly. For my curiosity, what was the little rest?"

"Some lost dreams."

"It being off won't make it worse for Papa and Sophia?"

"Have no fear of that."

"I never believed it anyway. The Ogre of Elveshurst is not up to scratch."

"I know whom you'll marry," I said, haunted by a dream.

"Yes, tell my fortune."

"A youth with laughter in his mouth and sunlight in his eyes, and a great rider and hunter."

"Someone said that to you. Some girl like me. The one whom you mentioned to me?"

"She was very much like you."

Lord Tarlton came up to instruct Eliza in her duties as judge. Dick, carelessly dressed, dark, graceful, a racing bat in his small, hard hand, took the moment to speak to me.

"You and I don't have to humor Eliza," he said in tones just low enough to escape the others' hearing. "We can make a private bet."

"For how much?"

"Not five thousand pounds but ten thousand."

"That's very handsome, but it's too late——"

"You needn't put it in writing. Your word's good enough. We'll not bother with witnesses. If you lose, it's nothing to you. If I lose, I'm in hock the rest of my life. But if I win—win fair—I'll take my winnings and clear out for the Antipodes. My shadow will no longer darken these pretty scenes. You'll have only Papa to contend with then. Harvey's a reed and you'll probably win, and if you want Eliza along with your revenge, you can get her. What do you say?" His eyes burned into mine.

It was too late in a larger sense than my excuse had meant. Fate spoke through my helpless lips.

"I'll let the other bet stand."

"Just as you say, Squire Blackburn. Well, shall we up and at it?"

I nodded and turned to mount. Lord Tarlton spoke in unfeigned amazement.

"Blackburn, I can't stop wondering at that raw-boned brute. He recalls another gray I've seen—had the same black-ringed dapples—but for the moment——"

"Perhaps it was Ottoman, El Stedoro's paternal grandfather."

"Great guns! Of course it was. I saw Ottoman sweep the field. He was sold to a Barbary prince. Who was El Stedoro's dam?"

"Farishti, a pure-bred Arab."

"Doesn't Farishti mean 'angel'? I picked up a few Oriental words when I served in Malta. What does El Stedoro mean?"

"As near as I could hit it, 'The Vindictive.' "

The little silence falling was almost unnoticeable.

"A name I've heard before. She was a horse-of-tree, I think, sunk by a pirate off the Aegadian Isles." Lord Tarlton glanced at his handsome repeater, carried on a gold chain in the pocket of his buff waistcoat. "It's time for the race."

Dick and I took our places outside the gate of the course. Dick's hand appeared light, yet he kept the high-strung black stallion in remarkably good control. Like most horses hand-raised among the Bedouin, El Stedoro had been taught to stand statuesque as a trooper's charger on review. When Eliza's clear high voice cried, "Go!" I touched him with my boot and he and Donald Dhu cleared the gate side by side.

Hooves drummed and I felt the mighty thrust of El Stedoro's thighs that hurled him up and forward, and the brace of his big shoulders as his forelegs bore the brunt of his descent. But I did not give him leave to bound his greatest, as when he had raced with his dam Farishti on the dun pastures of his native land. That would come much later, if at all.

The road curved, we passed out of sight of the little cluster of people, and drew nigh the wooden gate closing the roadway through the woods. Being easy to approach in stealth by a waylayer in the dense larch growth, it was the jump I most feared. I saw it sharply —low heather spread out and covering the course on the other side, greener than its wont in this damp weather, set off every board— and took a swift, searching glance at Dick's hands and feet. He was not holding back to let me go over first; as though to take it on the fly, he quickened the black's surges by light, rhythmic blows of his bat. Unless all signs failed—his form and balance and the beast's approach—he meant to clear it cleanly, not knock it askew to throw me. The next second he was up and over, El Stedoro hard on Donald's heels.

But this was only the first jump beyond the starting gate, and its first essaying, not its last. Anyway, a treason worthy of my great antagonist, standing so high in his order, almost himself a prince, would not take this simple, uncertain form. Not he, my little lord, his white hand on his walking stick, would stoop to a horse coper's jobbery. Sophia had told me something with bearing on this when I was young. I wish I could remember what it was. . . .

4

Surely the most likely deadfall was the water gap, dangerous to start with, far from the watchers, out on the bleak moor. Yet every jump was suspect of ambuscade; no footroom on the course promised safety; I must not overlook one little adverse sign. My mind on this, my soul was free to stray. I dreamed of other fateful races I had run, always against the same opponent. One, with El Stedero under me, had seemed to be with Farishti, bearing Suliman, Sheik el Beni Kabir. We had sped behind the greyhounds, shouting and laughing, and I had not seen the dread spirit gliding beside us until he smote my chieftain amidst his mirth.

On a silver night under the moon I had raced him again, to see which of us would be the first to find a traveler, loveliest of all on whom the moon looked down, and take her for his own. Isabel Gazelle, do you remember? Wherever you are, will you pause a moment, and think of me, and perhaps know my terrible need, and help me? My babe is hardly old enough to leave your arms. You have taken a husband, of youth and beauty and laughter, but remember our rite on the desert, and how your kisses transfigured my jagged face of stone. Mount Farishti and ride once more with me!

Death, whom I had met while flying from the Sepulcher, later among the mimosa trees, later amid the thorn, glided beside me once more. I could not see him, but now and then his shadow flicked across my path as some warning I could not quite seize plucked at my brain. The two mighty stallions, night-black and ocean-gray, seemed more primordial forces than tamed beasts, and they had become wildly aroused by signs beyond my ken. Their pace was too fast for so long a run, yet I checked El Stedoro only enough to keep him at Donald's heels. If the race was not stopped by some interference, both great hearts might fail.

Yet reach after reach of the course dropped behind us. We came to the water gap, and as the black set foot on the far bank the gray

398

flew in mid-air. "Good jump!" came Dick's voice, blithe, close to exultant as he checked to turn. He looked small as huge Donald Dhu reared up, wheeling, but graceful and gay, and the pair made one centaur of fantastic proportions.

As he took off, boldly back across the jump as when he had gone forth, I was not as afraid as before. Partly this came of an insistent working of my mind. The bet Dick had asked me to make would have been uncollectible unless I survived the race. It seemed incredible that he could either rig or unrig a deadfall between then and the start. The course itself was not very hazardous, possibly but not readily lending itself to ambuscade; and he knew I would be on guard. It seemed far more likely that the race was intended to reassure me until the moment I could be taken by surprise.

Thus the war would go on. My enemies could choose the time and place to strike or, discovering my impotence, brush me from their path. I had dreamed that this wintry race across the dismal moors was the last trick that Jim and I must stand; then we could go off watch. But the gods had not come down. There was no goddess named Nemesis, ever the stars looked down and never cared; today the skies grayed, and the mists drifted in ghostly clouds. The wind had run with me on the outward run. Now it beat into my face, its low wailings in my ears.

As we began the long turn making toward the gap in the woods, Donald Dhu seemed to be near collapse. With a savage look on his face, Dick struck him at every surge. I was watching this in great chaos of mind when El Stedoro took fright at something and went into his fastest pace, thundering down the track in prodigious bounds. It was as though he shared my sudden horror of that drawn, dark face and contorted form and flailing bat, and was striving to escape their malign presence. I had the impression of trying to check him, but knew I had not exerted great strength. His ears laid back as we swept by, then pricked forward as we rounded the bend in sight of the jump.

It looked different than when I had seen it less than four minutes ago. Its top had a crook in it and not as much light came through the gaps in the boards. El Stedoro was driving toward it full force. He meant to take it in a great proud leap. But when we were fifty yards away, rushing through low heather that crackled like fire—when I still had time to force him off the track into rough ground and over a gully beyond—I saw that the only change was a branch of a larch tree fallen or laid across its top board.

Gazing at it in perplexity and dread, I had not seen a brown serpent in the heather. It had lain close to the ground at first—perhaps I would not have seen it anyway. Hardly his length in front of El Stedoro's flying hooves, the deadfall sprang into view. It was a heavy, rusted wire, held rigid a foot off the ground. I did not know then how it was secured, for there was no time to look; but there seemed to be time for a memory from long ago to flash and burn. Would the little lord with his little stick stoop to a horse coper's trick? Sophia had told me by Calypso's cave he would play it without stooping.

El Stedoro struck the wire and appeared to break like a billow against a reef. He pitched head first and somersaulted on, I trying to fall clear. That try, instinct-driven, largely succeeded. Only one leg was caught under the fallen giant, and the saddle left enough space that it was not crushed or broken. And although stunned and half blind and seeing streaks of fire, I did not lose consciousness for one instant. I dared not let the haze in my brain wipe out my sense, and in the first rallying of my inward forces, I clambered to my feet.

Even so, it was a feeble and useless effort. Down upon me rode Dick, a horrid grin on his face and his racing bat upended and winging. He struck at my head with murderous fury. Its leaded knob missed my crown, but grazed my temple and flayed my cheek. The blow knocked me to my knees. I tried to lift my arms to shield my head, but they hung limp at my side. I tried to rise, but my muscles failed. I perceived the flame of my spirit burning very low, foretelling it would soon expire. The smell of my blood had caused the black stallion to shy away, but Dick was wheeling him back with a masterly hand, the bat raised and ready. I saw him take good aim. If one blow was not enough, he would dismount and give me a sufficiency; it was as though he had told me so. My head would look as though it were crushed by a flying hoof. I could almost hear the little lord telling the people . . .

Instead I heard sound terrible and real. It was somewhat like a human scream, but louder and invoked by fury beyond measure. I looked up out of blood-filled eyes in time to see El Stedoro rushing upon Dick. He had gained his feet in one raging bound; his ears were laid back, his eyes white, his great teeth bared and agape.

I saw them close in Dick's arm. Jerking him out of the saddle, he shook him in his jaws as a terrier shakes a rat, then flung him with frightful force to the ground. Up he rose then, high and higher, screaming with fury; down lashed the terrible front hooves.

It was not enough to vent his hate, his only answer to a blow against one he greatly loved, and the smell of the blood it had made flow. Again his teeth closed in the shoulder of the now supine form; whirling, he flung it with a great snatch of his neck clear across the track. Running up, he struck and pawed and trampled it until it was a blood-soaked blob, hardly recognizable as a human form. Only then did my voice cut through his screams and balm his maddened brain.

He ran up to me, whinnying. By clutching first the stirrup and then his mane, I pulled myself to my feet. To quiet him more, I stroked his head and then slipped my hand into his bloodied jaws. When the great teeth closed on it gently, I knew that hate had gone out of his heart and he had forgotten what it was, and all he remembered was love, and it was his law.

5

Although I could not clearly remember seeing him, I had been aware of someone springing up from the bushy gully and running into the woods. It was almost certainly Pike, appointed to the task of raising the wire already bighted about the tree beside which he lay. This part he had done well, with perfect timing, and holding the bighted end in his powerful hands. Beyond doubt his further orders had been to loose the wire from its hitch on a tree trunk across the track and to make away with it. These he had failed to carry out in terror of El Stedoro.

He would certainly report to his master as soon as possible. However, I had little doubt that Lord Tarlton was already started to the scene. The terrible outcries had carried far, unmistakably the screams of a maddened stallion; and although he might still hope for the best, his heart must be cramped in the vise of terror of the worst.

Too weak to stand and shaking with fear, yet I managed to clamber on to El Stedoro's back. I had hardly wiped the blood from my eyes when I saw Lord Tarlton rounding the bend on Eliza's bay. Behind him rode only Harvey. It seemed certain that he had forbidden his daughters to come on the scene, as well as any hostlers or servants. However, there would be one more witness as well as guard over me. Jim had run toward the scene by the shortest cut, which had brought him to the edge of the wood ahead of the rest. He had plunged through and took his post as Lord Tarlton rode up. It was about thirty feet from me. In his belt was the hunting knife he had brought from Africa. I knew now he had carried it concealed throughout our stay at Celtburrow.

The meeting of us four was creepily quiet. Lord Tarlton saw me mounted, Donald Dhu riderless, the wire still on the track, and something else at which he stared with glassy eyes. Then he asked a question in a low, incredulous tone.

"Is that Dick?"

"It's what's left of Dick's body."

"God in heaven."

It was a strange invoking. Deathly white, he got down and walked there and bent over and gazed. He did not reel and fall, but the thorn cane he carried dropped out of his hand. Then he looked at the forelegs of El Stedoro, bloody to the knees, and spoke once more.

"Your horse has the right name."

I shook my head, knowing only that this was not quite true.

"Ride him in and have Jim come with you. Harvey and I will bring in—Dick. Then I'll meet you in the drawing room. I'll give all you ask —accept any terms you impose. Only let me go—to the gallows or where you will—where I won't see your face."

I nodded and signaled to Jim. With him beside me, I rode to the stables; then while he stood guard, I washed the blood from El Stedoro's legs and hooves and muzzle. As I started up the stone steps of the manor house, Jim followed still.

"I want you with me, Jim, but unless Lord Tarlton goes mad, there's nothing more to fear."

"I ain't sho, Cap'n."

In my dressing room I bathed and changed my clothes, Jim standing at the door. Then when I had packed my belongings, I descended to the drawing room, not knowing yet what I would say to Lord Tarlton—aware of nothing I could say of any use, since I could do no more. There, too, I meant to speak to Sophia and Eliza. I would do so because I could not bring myself to leave without doing so, and because I hoped that when I saw them, something would come to my lips that would be worth saying. The great chamber was at present deserted. Jim posted himself at the door and once entered to tell me that a newcomer had just arrived on an almost exhausted horse. Jim had seen him through a window and thought he recognized him as a carriage driver from Lord Tarlton's establishment in London. I was too weary to take much interest in the incident, although surmising that it might have a part in the last play.

Exerting far more sway upon my mind was an object—a curio—indeed a palladium of the house I had seen before. It was the ship model in a glass case that had reposed on a teakwood table in the great chamber of Lepanto Palace, when first I went to dine with Captain Tarlton. Again it had the place of honor in the room. Once more I marked its perfect workmanship. She was a sloop of war under full sail, and a beautiful commemoration of *Our Eliza.*

In a few minutes Sophia and the vessel's namesake came into the room. Both looked white, their eyes big and dark-looking, their contrasted beauty unmistakable and touching. I rose and bowed my head.

"Will you sit, sir?" Sophia asked.

"Thank you."

They took seats, and Sophia tried again to speak, but her throat filled and then her eyes and she could not. Eliza spoke instead.

"We know fairly well what happened—long ago, and today," she said. "There's nothing we can say to express our sorrow and our shame. Sophia and I have had a dreadful shock today, but we're glad, a thousandfold, that Dick was killed instead of you. Papa has taken a wound from which he'll never recover. You may think it's light punishment for what he did, and although he lost his only son, you lost all those you loved and your youth and all you had. Still we ask you to be satisfied with this retribution, and be merciful."

As she said this last, my attention became divided. Facing me, with their backs to the open hallway door where Jim stood on guard, they did not see him turn to me and raise his hand in warning. At the same time I heard quick, light steps.

"We beg you, Holgar——" Eliza went on.

She was interrupted by Lord Tarlton brushing past Jim and making a regal entrance into the room. His skin looked gray and his white hands were empty and unsteady, but his eyes were coldly brilliant and his lips were curled in a malign smile dreadful to see. Behind him, pale with fright, came Harvey.

"You beg him, do you, silly child," said the little lord, in a bleak, biting voice. "My daughter begging a Yankee traitor. That's what he is. The only reason he didn't fight the king—and run with the rest of the pack when we burned their capital—he was a slave in Africa. His name's not Holgar Blackburn. It's Homer Whitman, as Sophia knows full well. Well, Yankee Doodle, what do you say now? Your horse went berserk after his spill and killed my son. Why he didn't pick you, with your Yankee stink, the devil only knows. 'Twas a bad blow to me, but it's the last. The next time you make trouble for me, I'll shoot you down, and the law will uphold me in it. Now, Homer Whitman, what do you say to that?"

"I think you've gone mad."

"Mad, am I? I was mad to believe that Julius was still alive on his way to London, but now I know he's dead, and I call your bluff. Eliza, that's a game the Yankees play. They're good at it, they think, making out that they carry cannon when all they've got is pop guns. What can you do now, Yank? You saw the wire, but who'd believe you and your black man? Do you think Pike would turn king's evidence? Eliza, hark to me and believe me. When I sent word to Lieutenant Holmes—master then of a Barbary frigate—to lay for the *Vindictive*, I was standing for our own kind against a pack of traitors. When a dog I thought was dead came back and tried to ruin us, anything I did was too good for him. I never intended—the devil take me if I did—for you to go with him. I let you think so for fear you'd give the game away—you were the bait to get him down here. My plans went wrong, and I've lost Dick, but I still have you, my joy, my life, my beautiful Eliza! You need never leave me now. We'll sail together to the last."

Lord Tarlton dropped into the chair, breathing hard. Then almost to my surprise I heard my voice rise in the hushed room.

"Eliza?"

The stricken girl half-wakened from her evil dream and looked at me.

"What is it?"

"It's true you never had to go with me, but you can go, if you wish."

"What's that?" Lord Tarlton demanded, gripping the arms of his chair. "Answer him, Eliza, as he deserves. Don't be a lady. It would be wasted on him. Spit in his ugly face!"

"Be still." Then, the glassy stare fading from her eyes, life coming back into her inert form, she spoke to me in a low, wondering voice. "Would you wish it, Holgar?"

"My name is Homer. I wish it very much."

"Why?"

"That I may live again."

"The main reason isn't to crush Papa?"

"That doesn't come into it at all."

"If I went with you, where would we go?"

"To America."

"Would we be very rich?"

"We'd not be rich at all. I've arranged to give back—it was taken from slaves and it will be used to fight slavery—all I have except my ship."

"We would live on board?"

"Except between journeys."

"What will be her name?"

"The *Vindication*."

"You're twice my age."

"Yes."

"People find you fearful to look at."

"Maybe they won't, so much, when I come back to life. Anyway, it's how you look at me that matters."

"I think that's true. Sophia, you had a chance to go with him when he was young."

"When we both were young, Eliza."

"Why didn't you do it?"

"Captain Sir Godwine Tarlton—that was his name then—didn't want me to go."

"Couldn't you have gone anyway?"

"Yes."

"Didn't you know he was a madman—driven mad by hate?"

"No, I didn't know it. I don't know it now. I only know that he has great power to do evil. Only if you leave him will it be broken."

"Are you sure?"

"He'll have lost *Our Eliza* for good. He'll stand on the quarter-deck no more. His flag will be struck."

"Do you want me to go, Sophia?"

"It's my dearest wish. It's your greatest chance for happiness—perhaps your only chance. Go with him, Eliza. What does all the rest matter? Go to the new land, the land of hope. Go where men are free—where soon all will be free. Leave the old, unhappy shores to their shadows of the past. Bear him children who can look all men in the face and know they are brothers in the sight of God. He tried to show me that—I knew it was true—but I lost my chance. Don't lose your chance, Eliza."

"What did he promise you, Sophia, if you would come?"

"He promised me adventure."

"Homer, will you promise me adventure?"

"On land and on the sea."

"There's something I've got to find out before I can answer. I'm a woman, Homer, and can't deny my needs."

405

I remembered a tall young girl, with an equal beauty, who had to find out something by the Wells of the Rising Moon.

"Very well."

Eliza rose, came in hope and dread, put her arms around my neck, and kissed me on the lips.

"Oh, they're warm!" she burst out, then hid her streaming eyes in her hands.

"Now will you go with me and love me?"

"I will love you and I'll go with you."

Lord Tarlton, who had listened with drawn face and indrawn gleaming eyes, rose like a king from his throne.

"Hell and fire!" he cried. "May they take you all! May the ship that carries my turncoat daughter burn to the waterline with every soul aboard. May this house with all of you in it fall down in flame. I'll not set foot in it again. Harvey, will you leave the whore you call your wife and follow me? She lay with the Yankee jack before you wedded her, and his tar is on her, and she loves him still. I'll make you a peer o' the realm!"

"No, sir, I will not," Harvey answered.

"Rats desert a sinking ship, but mine will make port yet. You'll see, God damn you all."

He went to the center table and took the ship model from its glass case and put it under his arm. Then he walked with his toes in front of him to one of the fireside couches where leaned a rattan cane he used indoors, and no doubt had left there when, carrying a stick of thorn, he had gone to the paddock. As he leaned to pick it up, his precious charge started to up-end. In trying to hold it level, it slipped out of his grasp and fell to the floor with a crash. It must be that its glue had weakened in long years, for he looked down, his eyes glazed, to see it in utter ruin.

"Devil and damnation," he muttered. "But it serves her right, for she failed me when I needed her most, that cursed Christmas Day. Why, I knew it all the time. I've worshiped a false god. Down to hell with her, I say! I'm done."

He was done and would die soon. I saw death, my familiar adversary, take his small, white hand. He did not pick up the cane, but still like a phoenix risen from the ashes, he walked with high head and princely mien out of our sight and our lives.

And now the time would pass quickly until Jim and I and my beautiful and redeeming one could set sail with our shipmates. Again I would know the winds of heaven, the rolling waves, the deep blue of ocean that is our mysterious mirror of the holy sky. I would foil the conspiracies of the fog. I would live at risk with the reefs of death. I would follow pilot stars through the seven seas, and they would not deny shipway to my gallant prow. I would feel again the flung spray in my face.

In time the clean and stinging drops would wear away the stone and show human flesh beneath. And in my hand, joined with my hand, I would hold the hand of love.